Cybernova

CYBERNOVA

HUNTER WHITLOW

Neural Net Press

To Makayla

CH 1

MY ears are ringing, and my head is throbbing. Waves of sound crash onto the shore of my mind, meaningless. After a moment, I can feel my hands and the semi-soft ground beneath me. Forcing myself to open my eyes, I immediately remember where I am. I'm also bombarded with a hot wash of anger, shame, and regret.

I see the announcer, the ring, and my opponent. I can also see the source of the noise, which is, unfortunately, not waves on the beach. It's hundreds of screaming onlookers, thirsty for a brutal, dramatic fight.

They're screaming at me to get up, but that doesn't seem very likely in my current condition. No matter how hard I try, none of my limbs will move. I try just moving one finger, managing only to send razor-sharp pain coursing through my body. Then again, I know all too well what a behemoth-sized punch to the base of the skull will get you. I guess that's what I get for signing up for another MMA championship. I may have ten years of martial arts training under my black belt, but actual skill is only about five percent of the fight these days. You'd think I would've learned my lesson by now.

I can hear the announcer counting down. I may not speak fluent Japanese, but I've been doing this long enough to recognize the countdown when I hear it. I listen to him counting, his deep voice filled with forced enthusiasm, while my hulking opponent looks all too willing to give me another dose of his blunt-force medicine. After a few of the counts, everything fades, and I give up on staying conscious.

***

I wake up who knows how much later with the worst headache of my life, and I've been hit in the head many times, so I know what I'm talking about. The good news is that I can move now, but that's where the good news ends.

Usually, when you wake up after getting beaten half to death, you'd expect to be somewhere like a hospital or an ambulance, or at least on a bench with a paramedic in the back of the arena. Call me crazy, but I don't feel like this abandoned, dark alleyway provides the welcoming, medically urgent environment I was hoping for.

That's Nova City for you.

"You really fucked it up this time," I mutter to myself, or at least I think I do. My ears are still ringing from being clocked in the head by three hundred pounds of adrenaline-fueled muscle.

I take the opportunity to inspect myself to see what I'm dealing with here. My electric blue skate shoes, faded black jeans, and leather jacket all look like they've seen better days, but what else is new? I've got my signature t-shirt underneath the jacket, a white shirt with an electric blue and gray design. It's the face of a wolf, which fades from realistic into a series of increasingly scattered geometric shapes as you look from left to right. I designed the shirt myself. Since my last name is Wolf, it was easy to go as "The Wolf" in the fights. It's basically the only outfit I wear. Why mess with a good thing? Plus, I've been told the blue brings out my eyes or whatever.

As for my own condition, I ache like I've been hit by a bus. At this point, I'm starting to think I'd prefer the bus. That guy was unreal, massive yet quick, throwing punches and kicks from all angles. My right shoulder isn't moving normally, but that'll probably be fine. As for my ear, I feel like bomb testers have better hearing than I do at the moment.

Is that even an actual job position? I feel like it'd have a pretty high turnover rate.

After a few minutes of wondering why I keep finding myself in these situations, I force myself to stand up. I stumble over to one of those old-fashioned vending machines, seemingly one of the only things left from the great migration from Old Japan to here. This one is covered in an array of cute cartoonish characters eating extremely well-drawn food. The vinyl cover is peeling in places and faded in others, but the charming personality of its design shines through. The pictures of ramen, sushi, and mochi fill my heart with hope and my stomach with anticipation. The flickering neon lights inside the machine intermittently display what the machine is selling or what's left of it, anyway. The machine is quite aesthetically pleasing, even with Nova City's signature grime covering half of it. The bright colors and adorable characters are reminiscent of a simpler time. A time when which cute anime girl you liked the best and which flavor of bottled tea you were going to buy was the biggest concern on many peoples' minds. It makes sense that they would've kept some of them around in Ritorujapan, aka Little Japan.

"So, what do we have here?" I ask, surveying the vending machine. In between flashes of neon lights, I can vaguely make out what's left to buy from the machine. "Ah yes, a can of soup, a purse that looks like a cat, and a slice of mold with some bread on it." Given the current selection, I choose the can of soup. It costs five CYBR COYN, aka Johnnies, the global currency. Everyone calls them Johnnies because John Nova's stupid face flashes on the screen whenever you pay with them. This guy still got his face on every "bill," despite there being no paper currency.

Egotistical, much?

I press the tip of my right pointer finger against the

scanner, and the Johnnies get transferred from my account to the machine. Then, the system grabs the can of soup and brings it down to a little sliding door in the side, heats it up using an electric heating coil, and the door opens with a cheerful "ding!".

I grab the can, open it, and start eating, using the spoon provided in the lid of the can. The can is extremely hot, but the soup itself is only lukewarm.

Oh well, can't exactly send it back to the chef.

Once I've downed a can of what can only questionably be passed as food, I stumble to the nearest charging station. My battery is critically low, as usual. I rest against the station while waiting for my battery to get enough charge. My legs are starting to move like normal again, so at least I can get home tonight. My ear is still ringing, so I guess I'll get that looked at tomorrow.

***

I wake up in my shitty studio apartment bright and early, by which I mean 15:00. I didn't get back until 03:00 since the Economy Housing District, affectionately titled "The Dump," is a far ride from the Entertainment District, naturally. I wander toward the small window and crack open the dusty, outdated curtains, immediately blinded. My apartment is on the forty-eighth floor of a fifty-floor building in the heart of the city. Every apartment is the same shitty one-room studio, which is definitely toeing the line between an apartment and a walk-in closet. But, hey, at least it has electricity and running water. Usually. Besides, it's all I can afford. It's all most people in this city can afford.

As my body starts to wake up, I'm painfully reminded of what I need to do today. I have to get myself a checkup after last night's fight. Luckily, the clinics are open on the weekends, so I throw on some clothes, grab a protein bar, and head down for a checkup.

When I hit the pavement, it's a short walk to the Hyper Rail, which is one of the only ways to get around this city unless you're rich enough to own a car. It's like the old light rails that used to be in many major cities, but it uses magnetic levitation and moves incredibly fast. It's also a piece of shit at this point, but it works.

During the ride there, I can't help but think about last night's fight:

All I can see in my mind is the image of an enormous right arm headed straight for my left temple, and knowing there's nothing I can do about it. I've fought some unnatural dudes in these fights, but that guy was a whole different level of inhuman.

I mean, really, what an idiot! In what world am I ever going to come even close to winning one of these fights? I can't quit, though. It's the only thing I know how to do anymore.

Despite my efforts to put it out of my mind, I keep replaying the fight over and over again, working myself up more each time. It's not just the weight class discrepancy, either. There were countless unfair and infuriating things happening in that fight: the hecklers telling me to give up before the fight had even started, the money changing hands while pointing at my opponent, the announcer bringing me in to approximately three claps while my opponent got thunderous applause and cheers. I could go on and on.

I just, that was such, it's just...

"That was such bullshit! It's all a load of bullshit!" I mutter under my breath, catching some lethargic side-eye from the guy sitting next to me. The fire in my gut turns to heat in my cheeks as embarrassment grips me. I flip up my hood in shame and face the dingy window, keeping my rage internalized for the rest of the ride.

Nice going, idiot.

For quite a while, there's nothing to see except for the

deplorable inhabitants and grey, dingy skyscrapers of The Dump, as far as the eye can see. Drug dealers and thugs patrol their little slices of nowhere while others are smoking and injecting whatever they can get their hands on, wandering around under the flickering streetlamps. In the darker corners, VR junkies sit and drool the hours away. Most of them don't even have a place to live. They just sit there and waste away, watching VR porn or whatever the hell it is they've got blasting into their shriveling eyeballs. Everyday people, hourly workers scraping by, parents providing for their children, and the like, all bustle through the streets, staring at their shoes as they make their way through the throng of miscreants. They don't want any trouble. The last thing any of us poor schmucks needs is to catch the wrath of a gang member on the way to work.

My gaze wanders upward, and there, up above it all, police patrol vehicles and unmanned drones circle the tops of the buildings like starving hawks circling their prey, waiting for them to slip up even a little bit, waiting for their time to strike. It may seem counterintuitive to have such high levels of debauchery happening directly under the police's eye, but they stopped giving a shit about that sort of thing a long time ago. Busting junkies doesn't earn you a bonus. It's not worth the time it takes to file the paperwork. No, it's not about doing their jobs. They just don't want you to forget for even a second that you are literally beneath them.

After a few minutes, we break through the concrete jungle to the literal landfill. I bring a mask from my neck to my mouth and nose, breathing shallow breaths. Mountains of garbage stretch for miles in either direction. What else do you do with trash besides force the poor to trudge through it to get anywhere else in the city?

Another couple of minutes go by while my mind is occupied by how stupid and unfair everything is.

Finally, I see the city rising as the Rail passes the landfill. First up is the Affordable Shopping District. Much like the Economy Housing District, the cowards that run this city are too afraid of their image to call this place what it is: The Black Market.

Chop shops of all, and I mean *all*, kinds can be found on every corner. One particularly shameless shop showcases cybernetic arms, legs, eyes, and anything you can think of right in the front window, some still covered in blood and who knows what else. In between the chop shops are a dizzying selection of brothels, smoke shops, casinos, netrunner cafes, VR sex lounges, you name it. Red lamps decorate every corner, the rest of it dimly lit by long-broken streetlights.

But the most intriguing thing about this part of the city is that anyone can be seen here if you know where to look. A shifty-eyed man in rags steps out of a chop shop. A cybernetic heart is clutched in his greasy hands, blood-stained rags poorly concealing their contents. I focus my vision for a second, and I swear I can see the heart still beating. A few doors down, a woman dressed far too nicely for this part of town sneaks through the door of a VR sex lounge, her face entirely obscured by a mask and hat. That one makes me chuckle to myself. Like the people of this city would think any lower of her for visiting a place like that. Hell, a lot of people might even see it as a positive thing. The rich are so cut off from reality here. It's truly remarkable. Interestingly enough, police patrols seem to steer clear of the area. Convenient.

Finally, after another few minutes, I arrive at the Maintenance District. This is the first part of the city where it's not explicitly apparent that I might be stabbed or robbed at any moment, so I always feel happy making it this far into the city. I get off the Hyper Rail at the next stop, side-stepping a drunk person wearing a VR headset as I pass to the sidewalk. Clinics, mechanics, and tech repair shops occupy most of the Maintenance District's real estate.

Bootleg chrome and stim peddlers sit in the small alley spaces between buildings. Some sit there, glaring at passersby, while others are hawking their wares. One of the chrome peddlers is shouting about the miracles of chrome, those cybernetic wonders, for a steal of a price. Another, with racks and buckets filled with various vials, syringes, inhalers, you name it, all stacked precariously high on a rickety folding table, is clearly high on their own supply. I don't make eye contact with a single one of them. I know better than that. It doesn't stop a particularly enthusiastic stim peddler, a middle-aged guy with more than half of his head replaced with cybernetics, grabbing for my shoulder as I pass, shouting, "Come on now, you sure look like you could use a little something to take the edge off! What do you say, amigo?" He shakes a bright blue vial of fluid with a syringe at the end in my face. Without a word, I knock his hand off of my shoulder and walk a little faster.

I turn the corner, winding my way through the crowd past a few more buildings until I come up to my destination. I step up to the squealing automatic door, straightening up and putting on a fake smile to hide the pain as I step into my favorite clinic, Zeke's Fixer-Upper.

The clinic is a small, one-room space, which costs a fortune to run, given how costly it is to run a business in this city. When I come in through the door, I'm facing a small desk to greet people, but no one is sitting at it. There's a reception area to the side, made up of about six mismatched lawn chairs along the wall. Past the reception area, the rest of the clinic is taken up by a pair of raised steel operating tables, various computers and pieces of equipment, and shelves filled with supplies, recycled cybernetics, and even a few new parts. Standing among the shelves, dressed in faded blue jeans, a wrinkled grey collared shirt, and a lab coat, is the man I came to see.

"Yo, Zeke, my favorite medical professional, I need a favor!" I say in the most upbeat and convincing way possible for someone who feels as shitty as I currently do.

"You always need a favor," replies Zeke, his light New Yorker accent adding an emphasis to the word favor, "If I keep helping you, it's gonna put me out of business. I don't care if you saved my life!"

Zeke and I go way back, back before things…changed. We used to play video games and eat junk food for hours, thinking there was nothing more to life. Boy, we were wrong. Let's just say things didn't go as planned one night, and he's owed me ever since.

"So, what did you break this time, you dumbass?" Zeke patronizes me. He's about my height, maybe an inch taller, and a few years older as well. Both of those things have been used against me in the past, multiple times.

"Look, man, nothing is broken this time, at least I don't think so. It's just my ear—"

"Hahaha, yeah, and I'm a real doctor!" Zeke bursts out at my statement, admittedly not without reason to do so. I break myself a lot. "Look, man, don't waste my time. Just lie down, and I'll get you scanned," Zeke replies after calming down a bit. He has kind brown eyes which reveal wisdom and hardship beyond his physical age. His short, dirty blonde hair is a little unkempt, as usual.

I want to reply with a punch to the arm, but I'm starting to think something really is wrong with my shoulder, so as usual, Zeke's right. I lie down on the exam table, and Zeke connects me to the scanner. His tech may be old, but it works, and I don't have to pay for it. The scanner runs for a few seconds, then plays a much-too-cheerful tone to let us know it's done.

"Holy shit, dude!" he exclaims, causing me to feel a combination of fear and shame. He adjusts his glasses as if to imply he can't believe what he's seeing. "You think nothing's broken, huh? Well, if you consider your right shoulder, left ear, and your nose to be nothing, then you are absolutely correct! Who were you fighting this time, the Incredible Hulk? Jesus, man, I swear one day even I won't be able to put your Humpty-Dumpty ass back together again." He counts on his fingers dramatically with each new broken body part of mine that he lists.

"I know, man, but I just want to win once, to prove a point—"

"Yeah, yeah, prove that you can win a fight against an inhuman monster, that somehow you, Oliver Wolf, will be the one to break the system, to show everyone that things don't have to be this way. You know I support you, but we both know how that's been working out for you so far. Just stay there while I get my stuff, alright?"

"Alright, you don't have to rub it in," I reply, knowing he's right as usual. After a few seconds, Zeke comes back and drops a large bag of "doctor's tools" on the table next to me, accompanied by a loud clanging sound.

"Ok, Olly, you know the drill. Do *not* move while I am messing with this shit, remember what happened last time?" Zeke says in an uncharacteristically serious tone. I nod, knowing exactly what he means. Let's just say it was a *shocking* experience that neither of us are eager to replicate.

"I'm gonna start with the shoulder." He reaches to the back of my right shoulder and releases the latch. With a small screwdriver, he opens the access panel and temporarily deactivates my shoulder and arm.

"I swear to god, Olly, if you break this servo one more time, I am not replacing it for you!" Zeke jokes, taking out my main shoulder servo and putting in a new one. Out of the corner of my eye, I can see just how broken the servo was. It's twisted and mangled, practically snapped in half. He then reactivates my arm, and I can already tell that it's better. He closes up the access panel and moves to my left ear.

"Yeah, that's right where he hit me, so I'm guessing—"

"Shut up, talking is moving!" He yells. Instead of saying anything, I reply with the most indignant glare I can muster while also not moving at all. After replacing the chip for my hearing enhancement, he looks at my broken nose and chuckles.

"What's so funny?"

"Well, in case you forgot, your nose is still made of cartilage, so the best I can do is snap it back into place and offer you my condolences." He proceeds to snap my nose back into place in a way that is both careful and much too quick. I do my best not to show how painful it is, which is challenging because it hurts like hell. Zeke notices but is kind enough not to say anything.

"Hey man, I really appreciate you doing this for me. I can even pay you this time if you want," I offer, hoping he will refuse.

"Nah, we both know you need whatever pocket change you have more than I do," he replies, "I just better not see you in here next week, or maybe I will charge you!"

"I know, man, trust me, I'm gonna take some time away from that whole scene. It's not worth it anymore. Things just aren't the same as they used to be".

"I know, buddy, I know. Maybe it's time you moved onto something else. You have too much potential to waste it fighting huge guys that are more machine than man at this point". I may disagree about the whole 'having potential' business, but he may have a point about the fights.

"I'll see you around Zeke, hopefully under better circumstances." I give him a half smile, knowing it probably won't be under better circumstances the next time I see him. I'd rather visit him as a friend more often than as a patient, but oh well. He's the only cyber-surgeon in Nova City I would trust with my life, and he also happens to be the only one I know of who will accept favors and friendship as a form of payment.

***

I stare down the training dummy in front of me, its wooden "limbs" taped together with duct tape and its punching bag "torso" bursting in several places. I drop into a low stance, bring my hands up in loose fists in front of my face, and begin wailing on the dummy. I punch the bag, block the arms, bob and weave, drop low, bring an uppercut to its imaginary jaw, and then back up to catch my breath.

At least I can still move like that.

Lunging forward suddenly, I bring a one-two punch full-force into the center of the dummy. My right hook knocks the dummy off of its base, snapping the pole that was holding it up. The dummy flies across the room and lands in a pile of takeout boxes. Chopsticks and stale rice scatter everywhere.

And I can still hit that hard. My form isn't too bad, either. Can't get that sort of training and consistency from chrome. That's all-natural martial arts training.

I down the rest of my Hydra energy drink, grimacing slightly at the metallic aftertaste. I glance at the can for a second, the multi-headed dragon logo staring back at me. They're a subsidiary of CYBR Corp, of course. I toss the can into the pile with the rest of the garbage, then pick up the training dummy. I brush rice and who knows what else off of the dummy as I walk back to its stand. I grab the duct tape and some chopsticks and get to work fixing the snapped pole.

It's been two weeks since the fight in Ritorujapan, and I still don't know what to do with my life. For the past four years, my life has revolved around the fights. If I wasn't doing the fighting, I was betting on the fights. I'd bet on sure things so that I could win enough money to pay my way into another fight, all in a hopeless pursuit of some misguided belief.

Ah, there we go. Nothing duct tape can't fix.

The dummy is fixed, albeit much more wiggly than before. I give it a test punch, and it seems alright.

I truly believed that I could show people that they were wrong, that I could win a fight with the minimal amount of cybernetics I had, even though my opponents were essentially tanks with arms, all of them nearly impossible to beat in a fair fight, or hell, even in an unfair one.

With the anger of all those fights filling me, I launch into another series of blows on the dummy. The more in the zone I become, the more I imagine I'm fighting a real opponent. I grab a wooden practice katana and slash the arms, torso, and legs, blocking blows and slipping through their defenses. I deliver a killing slash across the chest, stuffing flying in all directions. The chopsticks snap, and the dummy leans over, the duct tape groaning under the weight.

I should really get a new one of these things.

I know I talk a lot of shit about guys with cyber-enhancements for a guy who has some himself, but there really is a difference between that guy I fought last month and me. At this point, you're more likely to become an outcast for not having any cybernetics than for having too many. My right arm was replaced not by choice but by necessity. I lost my arm in an accident, and it was either get cybernetics or be down an arm for the rest of my life. In the old days, they would have called my arm a prosthetic and considered it to be a miracle of engineering! But now, it's just an arm and a rather boring one at that.

I also have some basic enhancements that arguably weren't necessary, like the vision correction and hearing enhancement, but those are still pretty minor. It was either wearing glasses and a hearing aid or getting implants. I went for the latter. A lot of people, usually the ones who are rich, powerful, shady, or usually a combination of the three, have so many enhancements that they can barely be considered human anymore. That's why I use my swords, my daishō. I don't want to kill anyone, and there's no way I'd let myself become some sort of horrible metal monster, but I need something to even the playing field. With my kung fu training, the swords just made sense.

I set the practice sword down, turn off the lamp in my training corner, and then move to my living room area. I plop down in the armchair and turn on the TV. I don't really want to watch anything, but it's better than silence.

People argue about whether or not cybernetics make you super- or sub-human, but when it comes down to it, AI robots and assistants feel more human than some of these "people" do. I chuckle to myself slightly at the thought, sitting alone in my dilapidated armchair. The only source of light is the TV, as it blasts me with ads for shit I don't need or even remotely want. I step out of my own headspace long enough to watch an ad for some sort of new stim that keeps you from needing to sleep for up to a week.

Yeah, I'm sure there are no side effects to that...

I gave him a lot of sass, but Zeke was right, as always. All I can think about is what he told me the last time I saw him, that I needed to do something with my life instead of wasting it on fights I'll never win. But stopping the fights means I admit I can't win and have nothing to show for four long years of blood, sweat, and tears, not to mention the countless times Zeke has managed to scrounge up replacements for my busted circuitry. I just don't know if I can do that. If I admit it was for nothing, then what the hell am I doing? What's the point of any of this? At this point, the only consistent thing in my life is getting my ass handed to me, then stumbling into Zeke's shop begging for help. It's not like I'm proud of it, but I honestly have no idea what else there is to do. I don't even reach out to Zeke or hang out with him outside of asking him to fix my busted arm or whatever else broke on any given day. I'm worried he won't want to see me anymore if there isn't a reason. Lately, I haven't exactly been a great friend or fun to be around. Those visits to his clinic are sort of the only thing I have. As I recount my various visits to Zeke's clinic, my mind drifts to CYBR Corp, who manufactured my arm.

When the world started its headlong descent into mass-produced cybernetics, corporate greed, and corrupt politics, CYBR Corp was at the helm. Sometimes, I forget that they began as a company claiming to want to help progress humankind to our next stage of development twenty years ago. They spewed messages of the 'miracles of cybernetic enhancements,' of a 'better future for all.' Naturally, most of it turned out to be total bullshit, but the world was desperate for good news at the time, so everyone believed them.

By around the year 2030, climate change had begun to devastate the world. Scientists saw it coming from miles away, but selfish, greedy, narrow-minded politicians and corporations made sure the voices of those whose interests didn't align with theirs were all but silenced. By the time the world realized they were right all along, it was far too late. Ocean levels rose significantly, almost entirely swallowing countries like Japan, Madagascar, Ireland, and many coastal portions of the entire world.

Then, when it seems nothing can be done but to make the most of what little time the Earth has left, CYBR Corp comes along, promising miraculous technological advancements capable of saving the human race from its own stupidity. They promised to build floating cities, allowing the human race to repopulate beyond the limits at that time. They promised to bring affordable cybernetic enhancements to the masses, curing disease, allowing the paralyzed to walk, extending life expectancies, and so on. The desperate remains of the human race ate it up, and who could blame them?

My parents immediately fell for it, moving us here when I was only eight years old. It's been a very long twenty years since 2040. CYBR Corp was a brand new company at the time, and we had no idea what was coming.

It wasn't long before people started to realize those floating cities were for the rich and powerful, and the enhancements equally so. They couldn't cure diseases so much as they could remove your diseased parts and replace them with shiny metal replacements for a hefty fee. John Nova, the original founder and CEO of CYBR Corp, died only five years into their rule. It's ironic that he built an empire of cybernetics but couldn't save himself from death. The only problem is that his death didn't stop CYBR Corp from taking control of every aspect of life. In the year 2045, Nova City was founded in place of what used to be Las Vegas, Nevada. John Nova charmed and bribed his way into getting the entire city of Las Vegas named after him with a giant statue to honor his memory in the city center. The whole city was rebuilt and massively expanded, branded as the 'desert oasis' where people would come for opportunity, cybernetics, and escape from the dreadful realities of the global climate crisis. To this day, they rule the world, or what's left of it, with an iron fist.

I'm about halfway between self-pity and self-loathing when I hear an explosion not far from my apartment, immediately jolting me out of my stupor and into a focused panic. The focus is thanks to the cybernetics, and the panic is all-natural paranoia. I scan the streets below, searching frantically for my standard-issue CYBR VYSR so I can get a better look at the commotion.

Ah, there you are, you slippery bastard!

After a few minutes of rummaging through piles of trash and outdated tech, I find my VYSR. I throw it on, taking a look out of my apartment window at the street below. As the smoke clears, I start to make out two intimidating figures bearing down on a third, all three heading toward a side alley just off 7th Street, my street. For a second, I get the crazy idea to go help whoever is being chased. I turn on the night vision mode of my VYSR and confirm what I already know to be true: this is another hit by CYBR Corp's personal police force, the Retribution.

When CYBR Corp took over the entire world through extortion, political corruption, and technological dependence of the masses, the Retribution was their destructive hand of injustice. These guys make the amped-up MMA fighters look like all-natural homo sapiens. These troops have all been enhanced to the point that the only human emotion they still feel is a deep, burning hatred, needing no excuse to be unleashed on the unfortunate citizens of Nova City.

So yeah, sure, I *could* rush after them and try to save that unlucky soul, but I don't particularly feel like dying today.

What are you saying? Are you seriously just gonna let that guy get killed while you do nothing? But I can't, seriously. What can I even do? Fuck-all, that's what.

I pace back and forth in front of the window, arguing with my conscience.

Okay, but say you die saving his life. At least you'll have done something meaningful for once. Come on, Oliver! How long are you going to sit in this apartment and feel sorry for yourself!? You've got to do something.

I slam my fist on the windowsill, "fuck."

I just, I can't. I can find meaning somewhere else. But it's not like I necessarily will die, is it? No, of course, it is. They're heartless monsters and will stop at nothing.

My eyes well up, my body shaking with a mixture of fury,

fear, and guilt. But I can't bring myself to do anything, so I just stand here, staring at the street below.

***

I check the clock for the twentieth time this hour, and it's 02:22, just like it was the last time I looked. I've spent the last several hours pacing nervously back and forth in front of my window and trying unsuccessfully to shake this burning feeling I have. The feeling that I could have done something to save that person earlier, the one the Retribution officers chased into the nearby alley and most likely tore to pieces with their arc rifles. For years, I've wished there was something I could do to fight back, but going against them would be suicide, or at least that's what I tell myself, so I can still sleep at night.

"Come on, Oliver, you're being stupid!" I say to myself, stopping in my tracks and throwing my hands into the air in desperation. "Even if you had made it down there in time, there would just be the burnt remains of two dead bodies instead of one!"

But if that's true, and it is, then why do I feel this way?

Just then, the Holocomm on my wrist blinks to life. The Holocomm is an all-in-one digital communications device combining the functionality of old-fashioned smart phones, smartwatches, and tablet computers. All with the added benefit of holographic projection capabilities for calls and general 3D browsing. Everyone gets the screen implanted in their non-dominant forearm when they turn eighteen, so for me, it's my left arm.

On the screen, I see the call is from Zeke. My heart sinks. I haven't heard from him at all during the last couple of weeks, and if he's calling me at this hour, something significant is happening. I answer as fast as I can.

"I need you to get your ass to my clinic RIGHT NOW," Zeke shouts into his comm. Even over the static-filled holo feed, I can tell that he's in trouble.

"I'm already on my way. Just stay alive long enough for me to make it there, alright?" I joke with him, hoping to lighten the mood. It does not work.

"Great, hurry up," Zeke hastily responds, ending the call.

I wasn't lying to him about already being on the way: by the time we ended that brief call, I'd already grabbed my daishō and was making my way to the elevator.

After a tense forty-eight-floor elevator ride, I book it down 7th street toward the nearest Hyper Rail station. I wouldn't normally ride the Rail at this time of night, but I need to get there quickly, and I grab my arc-daishō on the way out the door so I can easily handle the riffraff of a 03:00 Hyper Rail.

During the ride, I take the opportunity to inspect my daishō. This set of swords has been through everything with me all these years. Remarkably, the weapons are still in great shape, all things considered. Since the Hyper Rail is essentially empty, I decide to take the longer sword, the katana or daitō, out of its sheath and inspect it further. The long, gently curved blade is artfully crafted Japanese steel, and I sharpen it regularly, always keeping it in excellent condition. I turn my attention to the hilt, inspecting the arc modification unit, one of which has been retroactively added to each of the two swords.

Now, I don't claim to fully understand the logistics of arc technology. However, I've picked up enough to know that my swords have essentially been transformed from elegant yet outdated samurai tools into deadly, lightning-charged taser blades. I hold the sword firmly and slightly away from my body as I flip the switch on the arc unit. The blade hums to life, and as I feel the soft vibration of the machinery begin to kick in, the blade starts to glow blue with a steady stream of crackling electricity. Some purists claim that arc modifications ruin the authenticity of swords such as these, but those people have clearly never held one in their hands. I switch off the arc unit, sheathing the katana and drawing the smaller of the two swords, the wakizashi or shōtō. Identical in shape and composition to the katana, this sword is about half the length and is generally used as a parrying or close-combat weapon. It also has an arc unit fitted to it.

Just as I finish inspecting the wakizashi, I arrive at the Maintenance District. As I step onto the station, I strap my swords into their place, first the katana, then the wakizashi just above it. As I strap them into place, I head over to Zeke's. The way he sounded and looked in that call is still shaking me, and I can only imagine what's wrong, wondering if I'm already too late. I take off at a brisk pace, an increasing sense of danger growing in my mind. I could just be paranoid, but I'd rather be prepared for the worst than expect the best.

I arrive at Zeke's a couple of minutes later and rush to the back, where I can see him standing over his operation table. I half-expected to find thugs or Retribution troops outside the door, so just to find him not actively being attacked was somewhat of a relief.

As I reach where Zeke is standing, I realize he has someone on the operation table, and he has been severely injured. He has slightly more modifications than I do, namely on his chest and arms. He does not look good. Cybernetics, as well as flesh and bone, have been scorched by what definitely matches the profile of a Retribution arc assault rifle. The guy is not moving, and I start to worry...

"Is he...?"

"Just unconscious, for now. I'm going to need your help with this. That's why I called you here," Zeke reports, working on dressing the non-mechanical wounds of his patient.

I go to remove my swords and jacket so I can help Zeke fix this guy up, but he stops me with a solemn shake of his head.

"I can handle treating the guy, but it's who's chasing him that I need your help with. This guy came in here half-dead, ranting about Retribution forces trying to kill him for owing too much money to CYBR Corp. With any luck, those guys will be here in five minutes, but I'm guessing they're already at the door." He explained, and it was at that moment that a mental lightbulb flickered to life.

"Wait, I've seen him! He was getting shot down near my apart–"

Before I can finish my statement, an electric whirring sound, accompanied by an explosion, sends the door to Zeke's shop flying across the room. Retribution forces storm in, four of them in total. The four of them occupy the entirety of the clinic's small reception area. Their tall, intimidating figures bear down on us.

Looks like those two from earlier brought backup. Great. As if two aren't terrifying enough.

Considering the fact that they haven't already opened fire on all of us, it's clear they intend only to capture or kill this unlucky guy on the table, whoever he is.

"Hand over the refugee, and nobody gets hurt!" The second troop from the right barks. That, paired with the gold Retribution insignia on his body armor, identifies him as the leader. Their insignia is reminiscent of the ancient Greek legend of Atlas, with a cybernetically enhanced figure holding up the Earth, one leg on the ground, the other pushing down a smaller, mangled figure. Their uniforms consist of black body armor with non-descript, black, Kevlar-laced black fatigues underneath. They wear black helmets with visors that come down over their eyes, equipped with infrared imaging so they can always find their prey. It also has the added bonus of looking like terrifying red eyes in the darkness, so that's great.

"He's being treated for his injuries right now," I reply, my voice shaky. "You can take him into custody or whatever you intend to do once—"

"You are in no position to negotiate, citizen. Hand over the refugee, or we *will* open fire on everyone in this building." The Retribution leader cuts me off. His voice is steady, with a hateful malice dripping from every word. He *wants* us to resist. He would enjoy killing us. I can see it in his eyes. I shift my gaze to the other three, and they all have the same look in their eyes. They each have countless cybernetic implants, making them huge, black and chrome killing machines.

There goes my plan to stall them. But what else can I do?

At that, I pause for a second and make a decision I've been dying to make for the last four, no, ten, years of my life. A decision that's been burning at the back of my mind ever since my brother was taken from me by these monsters. A decision I've been too afraid to make. Until now.

"No," I reply, drawing my swords. "We won't hand him over. He's under our care. I suggest you leave."

At that, all four of the Retribution troops raise their rifles and train them on me, their laser sights creating a diamond on my chest. However, they don't immediately open fire. They seem surprised that I would actually defy them.

"You do realize you will never win this," the leader explains with a certainty that only a twisted CYBR Corp goon could possess. "You should have handed him over when you had the chance." His tone is incredibly matter-of-fact, but he also almost sounds...excited. I shudder at the thought.

Perhaps he's right, but I've made my decision, and it feels good. I'm terrified, and my heart is pounding in my chest, but I feel more confident in this decision than anything I've ever done. It's the right thing to do. It's the *only* thing to do.

It'll be a cold day in hell before I voluntarily give the

Retribution what they want.

"Well, here is my offer for you," I reply, my voice surprisingly steady and authoritative. I set my jaw, clenching my teeth, "you leave this place and never bother us again, or the Retribution will regret the day they crossed me." I have no idea where that came from. The words just sort of fell from my mouth. To some degree, however, these are words I've been dying to say for years. It's a declaration I've been desperately wanting to make, haunting my thoughts and dreams. I switch on the arc units of my daishō, firmly planting my feet in a wide stance as the crackling blue energy coats my blades.

This is where I make my stand.

The Retribution troops appear stunned for a second, clearly in disbelief that they have been directly challenged by a singular, seemingly non-threatening individual. I know better than to let an opportunity such as this slip by, so I waste no time moving toward the leader of the group. Just as he pulls the trigger, I slice the end of his rifle off with the smaller of my swords, sending a shower of blue and orange sparks flying throughout the room as my sword slices cleanly through the steel. It also causes him to drop the rifle from its heat and force.

The sparks provide me with the perfect distraction to move to the second troop, the one to the leader's left, whose weapon I slice clean in half. By this time, the other two soldiers had gotten wise to my tactics and had lowered their tactical visors, shielding themselves from the blinding sparks. They open fire from their arc rifles, sending millions of charged rounds my way. These rifles combine the technology of old-fashioned bullets with powerful arc technology, effectively sending molten streams of electrically charged death with terrifying accuracy.

With reflexes gained through years of rigorous training

and sharpened through technological enhancement, I duck behind the nearest troop, arc rounds scorching the air, inches away. They don't stop firing. They just melt their fellow troop in the hopes that it'll also kill me. It's not long before that troop goes down, so I jump behind the leader. He lets out a guttural scream as his flesh is scorched by arc plasma, but somehow, he stays standing, unlike the first troop. He grabs me by the shoulders, trying to wrestle me into the line of fire. I slash through his forearms, blood and sparks flying everywhere. He screams again, his eyes filled with pure, unadulterated hatred. I can actually see and smell the flesh melting off of parts of him as the other two keep firing. I drive my swords through his abdomen, pushing him toward the other two. It's surprisingly difficult to move him. With his dying breath, he lunges forward, trying to bite my neck. He nearly gets me, but I shove him forward, pulling the swords out. He finally falls to the ground, his hateful gaze piercing me as his eyes glaze over.

Fuck me, that was close.

I begin diving behind a nearby chair, having run out of human shields.

Do they even count as human? Focus, Oliver.

Just then, the remaining Retribution troops' weapons enter their brief cooldown state.

"Holy shit," I mutter under my breath, having narrowly escaped their attacks. One wrong move, and even Zeke wouldn't have been able to patch me up.

Their cooldown only lasts approximately three seconds, but that's enough time for me to make a move. I sheathe my wakizashi, grab the metal folding chair as a shield, and begin crossing the room, nearly getting within melee range of the remaining troops. They open fire once again, slowly backing away as they rain down their fiery doom upon me. I hold up the chair and drop into a low stance, slowly walking forward.

The chair gets extremely hot almost immediately, but I keep walking. I get within range and slash with my katana, where I believe one of the troops is. I can only see his shoes, but the katana has a good range, and I don't have many options here. Either by luck or divine intervention, I hit him. Judging by the fact that he slumps over, I can only assume he's dead, which is more than I was hoping for. My right hand gets caught in the plasma stream, but since it's made of highly resilient metal, it's okay. The chair, however, is beginning to melt. It drips molten metal on my left arm, which hurts really *fucking* bad. I drop it instinctively.

Oh shit!

I hit the deck and roll behind another chair, narrowly avoiding a full-body hot plasma massage.

"Just die, you freak!" The last troop grunts, their voice filled with hate. They sound almost annoyed that I dare still be alive.

Unluckily for them, their weapon enters its cooldown. I take the second-long opportunity to stand up and draw my wakizashi, switching it on. They curse under their breath and grab their sidearm, a large-caliber, semi-auto arc pistol. They waste no time, immediately opening fire on me. This time, however, I'm ready.

As molten plasma rapidly approaches my body, I'm already setting myself into a low stance, spinning both swords of my arc-daishō in an alternating crisscross motion in front of my exposed body as rapidly as possible, the arc energy coating them flowing into a mesmerizing blue mirage. Initially designed for intimidation, this move was never meant to be used in this way. But hey, I have a feeling the original samurai weren't facing off against mechanically-enhanced murder machines wielding lightning-powered rifles. Just a thought.

To the complete disbelief of everyone in the room, myself

included, it actually works. Under normal circumstances, the Retribution's chosen victim would be dead. Not me. Their arc pistol is firing plasma round after plasma round directly at my body, my daishō redirecting them in all directions. The result is a terrifyingly beautiful shower of blue and orange sparks cascading onto every surface in the area. Some of them rain down onto me, burning my scalp and the back of my neck. I can't stop, or I *will* die, so I push through the pain.

Gonna need some serious aloe vera after this.

The onslaught continues for what seems like an eternity, but I can't give in. I refuse to give that satisfaction to this monster. I can feel my arms beginning to give out, and some of the plasma escapes through a hole in my defense, burning through my jacket and searing the skin on my chest. A barely audible cry of pain escapes my lips, but I remain focused. There's a point where their clip runs out of ammo, but they load a new clip before I even have the chance to process that information. They resume firing at an alarming rate.

My muscles are screaming in pain, and the motors in my right arm are whining under the strain. Just when I feel that I can't possibly keep this up, the Retribution's arc pistol runs out of ammo again. They reach for another clip only to find they're out. I waste no time closing the gap between the troop and me, forcing my legs to move. I raise my daishō into the air, crossing the swords over my chest, and with the last of my energy, slash the swords down and away from my body, falling to one knee as I do so. The final troop falls to the ground, their body cleanly separated from their legs.

With the adrenaline of the battle gone, I collapse to the ground, swords falling from my hands. The crackling blue buzz of arc energy is the only thing filling my senses. Despite the pain, there is a smile on my face as the world goes black around me.

CH 2

IT'S been a long week since that day at Zeke's clinic. I still can't believe I managed to singlehandedly fight off four Retribution troops, including a squad leader. Nobody's stood up to the Retribution in years. They made it clear early on that anyone who tried would be brutally killed. If they decided you owed them money, or a favor, or your life in servitude, then you gave it, no questions asked. Maybe it's time that changed.

I blacked out from the pain and exhaustion of that fight, so I'm a little fuzzy on the details afterward. However, as Zeke tells it, he dragged my 'sorry ass' as well as that guy he was treating into his Fixer-Upper To-Go, aka an old fusion-powered hover van filled with Zeke's emergency equipment and a small cot. Clearly, it's no longer safe to stay at the clinic since they had found us. Zeke knew that we had to go somewhere safe and fast. So, he 'burnt rubber like his ass was on fire, with those trigger-happy bastards hot on his tail.' Again, his words, not mine. Also, it's hard to burn rubber when your van uses small-scale thrusters instead of wheels to move around, but whatever.

With the simple auto-drive function turned on in the van, Zeke was able to get to work while the van barreled through the city. He got me patched up pretty quickly. It turns out I mostly just needed my battery charged, and I was good to go. Apparently, that was why I blacked out while fighting the Retribution troops. It's a side effect of enhancements known as cybernetic exhaustion.

Early cybernetics research tried to run the technology off of the body's natural functions, namely the heart and lungs. The scientists and engineers quickly realized that supplemental power would be needed. The human heart only produces 1.33 Watts of energy, which, needless to say, doesn't sufficiently power a high-tech, cybernetic prosthetic arm. It doesn't power much of anything, for that matter.

Cybernetic exhaustion is what happens when you try to run cybernetics off of the body's natural electrical impulses. The power-hungry cybernetics will scavenge any and all electrical impulses from the body, including the brain, which usually causes people to blackout.

That's where batteries come in. My battery is a reasonably powerful solid-state battery pack located in my upper right arm. Typically, I wait to charge it at night since day-to-day usage only drains it to about thirty percent. The problem is, I haven't pushed myself quite that hard in a while, and it turns out fighting Retribution troops drains your battery a lot quicker than day-to-day activities.

Go figure.

Zeke always yells at me for waiting until my battery's too low before charging it because unless you've got a backup, cybernetic exhaustion is just as much of a problem with a dead battery as no battery, or so he always says. I thought he was worrying too much. Looks like I owe him an apology.

As if worrying about your battery dying wasn't bad enough, the more cybernetics you have, and the more energy-intensive those cybernetics are, the higher capacity battery you need. It's possible to put so much strain on the battery that even though you have a full charge, the cybernetics still scavenge your body for extra power because you've exceeded what the battery can put out.

Gotta love all those CYBR Corp ads promising risk-free cybernetic enhancements with no side effects. Bullshit.

Of course, if I were rich, worked for CYBR Corp, or both, I would have a self-sustaining fusion power cell that could basically never run out of power, but you work with what you got.

Anyway, back to one week ago. After a bit of time on the charger, I was good to go, more or less. After I was able to move properly, I took control of the van while Zeke kept our mysterious friend alive. Auto-drive is well and good, but it's not exactly programmed to run from the fuzz.

We made quick stops at my apartment and his, grabbing some essentials before CYBR Corp had time to track the video recorded from the troops' eyes I had killed. They would have easily been able to see our faces, tracing us back to where we lived. After that, we made our way to a relatively secluded underground bunker we used to hang out in to get away from the bustle of Nova City. We've been holed up here for the past week, hiding from CYBR Corp.

We found the bunker a while back, and we happened to stumble upon it while exploring the outer reaches of Nova City, just talking and laughing about whatever crossed our minds. We used to chat a lot about cybernetics, about the latest developments in implants, VR technology, artificial intelligence, you name it. Basically, anything tech-related was right up our alley, with Zeke being the circuit-head that he is and myself just fascinated with the possibilities of being a super cool, teched-out fighting champion.

Long story short, two guys in their early twenties, obsessed with superhero comics and video games, stumble across an underground bunker on the edge of Nova City with a big holographic FOR SALE sign hovering over the entrance? We bought that place without a second thought. It cost us about five hundred thousand Johnnies, which is not too bad for a small bunker.

CYBR COYN became the primary form of currency about

twenty-five years ago, in the year 2035. Digital currencies were starting to gain popularity before that. Still, it was the climate devastation of the Earth that really kicked off the various governments of what remained of the world to start working together on some things, like making a universal currency that doesn't depend on material items or gold standards or anything. In theory, it's not the worst idea.

The concept was initially proposed in the US by John Nova as a one-to-one replacement for the dollar, and the US government went for it, no questions asked. CYBR Corp already controlled much of the government from behind the scenes at that point.

The rest of the world quickly climbed on board as they ran out of trees to make paper with. Of course, that also means CYBR Corp controls the entire global economy and all of the banks. Sounds reasonable, right? Definitely no negative side-effects to that little arrangement.

***

Currently, I'm doing some research on my CYBR Screen, which is a large glass tablet designed for mixed-medium computing. These devices are capable of being used as traditional touchscreen tablets as well as interactive holographic projection devices. I may or may not have stolen this one from a particularly poorly guarded self-driving shipment of them a while back.

"Show me healing implants, something minorly invasive," I instruct.

"*Coming right up, Oliver,*" replies Cerulean, the AI assistant. Cerulean has a kind, female voice and a slight accent, which people argue about the origin of. If not for the occasional glitch and difficulty pronouncing certain words, you would have no idea you weren't speaking to an actual person. Cerulean can speak and understand any language and access any information on CYBR Net, and each unit is programmed with comprehensive Artificial Intelligence. I've had this one for some time now, so Cerulean feels like an old friend. She certainly knows me better than most people, whether I like it or not.

I navigate for a minute or two through the various healing cybernetics available, selecting one that looks particularly promising. I switch into hologram mode, inspecting the implant as the Screen demonstrates its functionality. This particular module is a minor implant that is capable of quickly repairing minor cuts, burns, and bruises to the skin using a combination of bioengineering and nanotechnology. A holographic representation of a person getting injured and then healed is played in front of me.

"Cerulean, save that one for later."

"*You got it!*"

I'm looking at new cybernetic enhancements, but only minor ones, which I could need going forward. Over the course of this week, I've made up my mind: I'm going to take down CYBR Corp. Zeke has been trying to talk me out of it. He says it's suicide, but I can tell that he's starting to give in. He hates CYBR Corp as much as I do, as much as everyone does. There've been uprisings and protests in the past, many with widespread support, but every single one was ground into dust the moment it started. That's my theory: they were *too* well supported, too public. The second CYBR Corp catches wind of anything standing in the way of their all-encompassing global domination, they destroy it.

They corrupted the world's governments, ruined the natural order of the planet, and infiltrated every single aspect of day-to-day life. Every government official, business executive, and law enforcement officer around the globe belongs to CYBR Corp. Even if you run your own small business, like Zeke's Fixer-Upper, most of your income goes to keeping CYBR Corp from throwing you onto the streets.

He has to work eighty-hour weeks just to pay rent and property taxes on his tiny clinic. They've been increasing the costs nearly every year he's owned the place, and believe me, I've heard all about it. The truth is, if you agree to let them buy your company or go bankrupt so you're forced to, then they'll back off, let you do business, and take one hundred percent of your profits. But Zeke has not, and never will, allow that to happen. Frankly, I can't think of many people dedicated enough to give an official, entirely legal "fuck you" to CYBR Corp by simply refusing to go out of business quite like my best friend.

So yeah, maybe Zeke's right. Maybe trying to take down CYBR Corp *is* suicide, but if my death is what it takes to tip the scales and wake people from their complacency, then so be it. Besides, I won't make it easy for them.

This world has suffered long enough at the hands of CYBR Corp, so if no one else is willing to take them on, I will. However, there's an elephant in the room here...I hate cybernetics. Throughout my life, it's become increasingly apparent to me that the more cybernetics you have, the less human you become, and the more significant the change, the greater the impact. For example, getting a cybernetic arm has only a slight effect, hardly more than traditional prosthetics. On the other hand, getting your brain implanted with machine learning AI software turns you into a cold, calculating monster in no time. I've seen the damage these types of "enhancements" can cause, and it is horrifying.

So yes, I still hate those sorts of cybernetics, and I feel that there should be severely stricter regulations on what is and is not allowed to be cybernetically enhanced.

I would never, and will never, get any enhancements that are not absolutely necessary. If I hadn't lost my arm, I wouldn't have gotten a cybernetic replacement. If my hearing and vision were perfect, I wouldn't have fixed them. But some things are *never* necessary, and that's what I'm avoiding at all costs. Brain augmentations, especially, are out of the question.

That being said, I stand no chance against CYBR Corp in my current status. I don't know what else to do, and if I fail in this mission, I'll not only be letting myself down, but more importantly, I'll be letting down those I care about. By helping this stranger and killing those four troops, I've effectively sealed my fate and Zeke's as enemies of the law. Either I succeed in dismantling CYBR Corp, or everyone I know and love will be hunted down and killed.

That's why I'm most likely going to need new cybernetics. That's why I cannot afford to lose this fight. If I can find a way to win with the tech I have, on my own power and skill, there'll be no need to change myself. But when the cards are down, and it's a healing implant or the death of everyone I love, I know which one I would choose. I also need to be realistic here. I can't win an MMA fight against most of those chromed-out behemoths, so the odds of me taking down the major-league metallic monsters on CYBR Corp's payroll with my current cybernetics are…slim, to say the least.

Just then, Zeke bursts into my little room with a crazed look in his eye, snapping me out of my contemplative state.

"He's awake!" Zeke exclaims.

"No way!" I reply, smiling wide, "you beautiful son of a bitch, you actually did it."

He responds with a quick nod and a thumbs up, then begins rushing back toward his operating center, which is at the opposite end of the bunker from the living quarters. I follow right behind, eager to find out who this mysterious patient really is. Zeke has been operating on him for a week straight, doing everything he can, both medical and mechanical, to bring him back to consciousness. We almost lost him a couple of times, and at this point, I was starting to think he would never wake up. Zeke, on the other hand, would never give up on anyone. I know this better than anybody.

We make it to the small room with a bed that Zeke placed the guy into, and I can see him there, half lying down, half sitting. He appears to be in his mid-forties, with graying, light-brown hair which has been cut short. Looks like he's devouring one of our rations and some water. After a week of being unconscious, I would be hungry too. I laugh softly to myself at the sight, which is loud enough to get his attention.

"So, you must be Oliver," he states, his voice hoarse but friendly, "according to Zeke here, I have you to thank for saving my life."

"Well, I wouldn't say that, I simply fought off some Retribution assholes. Zeke's the one who brought you back from the brink," I reply, flattered yet trying to remain modest. This provokes a hoarse laugh, followed by some coughing.

"Sure, if you consider taking on four Retribution troops at point-blank range to be an easy task!" He pauses, taking a sip of water. "Well, thank you anyway, Oliver."

"Sure thing..." I pause, not knowing his name.

"Dexter, my name's Dexter Jones. You can call me Dex if you prefer." He has a kind, somewhat tired voice. There's a bit of an accent behind his words, but I can't quite place it.

"Well, Dexter, nice to finally meet you," Zeke interjects, "I was startin' to think it was never gonna happen!" The New York accent tends to flare up when he's excited.

The room falls quiet for a few moments, all of us seemingly collecting our thoughts. Eager to learn more about Dexter, I break the silence:

"So, I have to ask, what did you do to piss off CYBR Corp? You must've done something more than just miss a payment on your tech, considering they sent a whole unit after you."

With a chuckle, Dexter responds, "I wasn't planning on

telling this to anyone, but it would seem we're in this together." He pauses, clearly considering what he's about to say, "you're not going to believe me."

"Try me," Zeke and I respond in unison. He is just as interested as I am in Dexter's story.

"Alright," he pauses again, a distant look in his eye, "I used to be one of 'em," another pause, "I worked for CYBR Corp."

As the words fall from Dexter's mouth, I can feel my stomach drop. Countless possibilities run through my head, none of them good. CYBR Corp employees are strictly tracked and monitored, which could be why they were able to track him to Zeke's clinic. And doesn't that mean he was one of the people responsible for ruining the Earth and its societies? I have so many questions, but nothing will come out of my mouth. I'm frozen with the daunting fear of the worst corporation in human history breathing down the back of my neck.

After an uncomfortably long pause, Dexter breaks the silence. "I know what you must be thinking. I know that none of it is good, and I probably deserve it. But please, hear me out." He takes a deep breath, followed by a deeper sigh. "Yes, I worked for them, but I never wanted to. They forced me into it, threatening to kidnap or kill my family if I didn't work for them for the rest of my goddamn life. Maybe I had a choice, but when it comes to saving the ones you love, wouldn't we all make the same decision?"

I make eye contact with him, and I can see everything in his eyes. The regret, the guilt, the anger, and most of all, the fear. Fear that they will find him, that he can never stop running, and that he will never be safe. I've seen this look in the eyes of those around Nova City. Everyone feels this way, if not as intensely as Dexter does.

My initial thoughts begin to fade, and my view toward

Dexter softens once more. However, there's one thought that's haunting the back of my mind, one speculation that I cannot shake. I need to ask. "Don't they track every CYBR Corp employee? Is that how they found you at Zeke's Fixer-Upper? You're probably being followed right now!" I become increasingly fearful the more I think about it.

"No, we're safe. I got a buddy of mine to remove that damn tracker as soon as I left. It's been removed for a few days. You can see the damage if you want." He rolls back the tattered sleeve of his black long-sleeved shirt, revealing a messy set of stitches in his left forearm. The skin around it is purple and swollen. I can see Zeke physically hurt by the sight of it. He may not have an official medical license, but he has standards.

"Well, that's good news, at least. I gotta tell you, though, it hasn't been a few days. We've been here a week already." I say, trying to break the news gently.

"Oh, wow. And you took care of me this whole time?" Dexter replies, looking gratefully at Zeke.

"Sure did, like I'd go givin' up on ya' just 'cause I don't know you?" Zeke replies somewhat indignantly.

"Yeah, that's not Zeke's style. You're in good hands here." I add.

"Thank you, thank you both. I truly don't know how to thank you enough." Dexter says, smiling through a coughing fit.

"So we're good, no trackers?" I ask, wanting to reassure myself.

"No trackers. They can't track me, not any more than they can track you. They only found me at the clinic because I messed up. I never should've gone back..." Dexter trails off, an intensely deep remorse falling across his face. For the first time, I can see through his upbeat demeanor. I can see the years of hardship and the physical toll that living in this city takes on you. He looks like he's been through hell several times.

After a few moments, his impossibly upbeat demeanor returns, and he continues, "I do apologize to you both. I know I haven't exactly made things easier for you."

"You don't have to apologize. It's not like we had to save you. We knew what we were getting into here. If we didn't want to pick a fight with CYBR Corp, you'd be lying in some alleyway in the middle of the Maintenance District," I try to lighten the mood, earning a couple of pity smiles from Dexter and Zeke. We've been through too much recently to truly enjoy ourselves, but we try. I just hope Dexter knows that we're not his enemies.

I can't quite figure out what it is, but something about Dexter tells me that he means well, no matter what the circumstances may be. "And I hope you forgive me for asking, Dex, but what did you do at CYBR Corp? And what drove you away? I thought no one ever leaves anymore." There is no possible way I will be able to relax until I have the answers to these questions, which are burning themselves into my mind like an itch I have to scratch.

"Yeah, I suppose I do owe you boys an explanation, especially after all you've done for me. I would be happy to—" He is interrupted by a coughing fit. He coughs into a white rag Zeke has given him, and I can see that it's been stained with blood. "I do apologize, but perhaps we could revisit this another time? I don't feel so good at the moment," Dexter politely responds.

At that, I can see his mask fading away once more, and the tired, demoralized face beneath becomes revealed once again. Dexter is in no shape to be grilled for questions, no matter how intensely I need to know the answers. It can wait.

"Well, you heard the man, Olly!" Zeke snaps to attention, clearly not willing to lose this patient, to lose Dexter. He looks tired, too, so intensely tired, but he would never let that stop him from being there for those who need him, no matter what hour it is or how much sleep he's gotten. I genuinely don't know where I would be without him.

"Yeah, yeah. I know all too well how difficult it is to recover from these sorts of injuries. I gotta sleep anyway." I try my best to appear cheerful and optimistic for both of their sakes.

As I walk back to my room, I can't help but wonder what Dexter's answers to my questions will be. I hope it's nothing terrible. I want to like Dexter. He seems so kind and sincere. Unfortunately, it's nearly impossible to trust him because everything I've come to know revolves around the fact that CYBR Corp and everyone who works for them is the enemy.

Who could this man be, and have we made the right choice in saving him?

I suppose it doesn't matter, not really. We can never go back home. I hadn't really thought about that until now. I shiver at the thought, the daunting truth that I will never go back to my apartment, back to my old life of complacency and consistency. Then again, I never was happy with that life. The moment I decided to fight those Retribution troops in Zeke's clinic, I knew what I was getting myself into. Nothing will ever be the same, but for once in my life, I feel like I have a purpose.

CYBR Corp will pay for what they've done.

CH 3

SOONER or later, this moment was always going to come. I had thought that when it did, I would be ready, but I feel incredibly nervous, almost jittery, like someone injected pure caffeine straight into my veins. Then again, what did I expect?

It's been about two weeks since we started hiding in the bunker, and we're almost out of food and water. The past week has consisted mainly of Zeke and I taking care of Dex, slowly getting to know him, and trying to figure out the next steps of our chaotic existence. Initially, there was a month's supply of food and water for two people. However, with three people and the fact that Zeke and I seriously miscalculated how much food and water people actually consume on a daily basis, we're in a bit of a pickle. That brings me to here and now. It's time to step foot in Nova City again, for the first time since committing one of the worst crimes you can commit in this city: killing Retribution troops. If they catch me now, it's all over. I will have endangered those I care about and thrown my life away, all for nothing.

Regardless, I have to go, and my window of opportunity is rapidly closing. Around 16:00, the guards in the Food District change over, and for just a couple of minutes, the supermarkets will be somewhat less monitored than usual. I say somewhat less because there will still be dozens of self-monitored security cameras, any of which could identify me, dispatching a squadron of Retribution troops to my location in seconds. An entire squadron is eight troops, and I barely made it through four with the advantage of surprise on my side.

Let's be real. It was mostly luck.

The only reason we're considering this and not a more questionable method of getting food, namely dumpster diving, is that we'll be able to fool the cameras using an obscurer. And we can't use a food delivery app for several reasons: one, a stranger would have the exact location of our bunker; two, the payment would have to be verifiable as us, further confirming who we are; and three, CYBR Corp owns *everything*, so the company said stranger works for would then transfer our address and identities to CYBR Corp and…you get the picture. Long story short, we have to go buy groceries in person, and I'm the one stuck doing it.

At least I have this obscurer…That definitely won't fail.

An obscurer is a relatively simple yet handy piece of equipment that allows you to hide your identity. The science behind it is that it sends interfering electromagnetic waves around your head, which makes your face appear fuzzy and distorted to the security cameras. They can't identify you, so no Retribution squadron is turning you into a crisp.

Hopefully.

I nervously check the Holocomm on my wrist. It's 15:58, almost go time. I check that my wakizashi is securely fastened to my waist. I only took the smaller one of my two swords because it's much easier to use in small spaces and it's easier to conceal in public.

I'm hiding in the darkest alleyway I could find near the supermarket, which isn't too hard to do. In other parts of the world, the late afternoon is still very bright outside and is not a time when you might hide in a dark alleyway. In Nova City, a sunny day is seen as something to celebrate since it's always overcast here. This partially makes sense because Nova City is located on the ocean, but in reality, the majority of the clouds and storms are caused by years of CYBR Corp's heavy pollution.

16:00. It's go time.

I step out from the alleyway I was hiding in and make my way toward the door of the supermarket. My hands are shaking uncontrollably as I walk through the doors. I have to stay calm.

Come on, Oliver, you look like milk and eggs scare you. They'll be onto you for sure.

I take a few deep breaths and buy my groceries as quickly as possible. Just some essentials: canned goods, dried meat, rice, water, and a few bottles of the cheapest rum I can find, which is, of course, Long John CYBRs. And yes, the taste is as bad as the name, and don't even get me *started* on the label design, but it gets the job done. What can I say? Living in this city turns everyone into a bit of an alcoholic, or an addict, or both.

I finish grabbing the groceries and make my way toward the self-checkout. Everything's going well. It seems like the obscurer is doing its job perfectly since no alarms have sounded, and no troops are shooting at me. I'm about five feet from the checkout when I stop dead in my tracks, my stomach falling through the floor.

No, please, no. Not now, not here, not today.

Everything was going so well. But of course, here in this supermarket is the one person I never expected to see, the one person I can't see right now. I feel like I just looked at Medusa, and I've been turned to stone. Ten feet in front of me, buying a signature combination of instant noodles and vodka, is Astra Odelle.

"You've got to be kidding me," I mutter, forcing myself to hide behind a nearby set of shelves. I haven't seen her in five years, so much has changed since then. But after one look at her, I feel as though nothing has changed. I'm twenty-three again, stumbling through early adulthood and into her open arms.

We were together for two years, and it was, in all honesty, the best two years of my life. I met her at a time in my life when I thought for sure that I would never feel cared for again. My only friend was Zeke, but he couldn't even help me out of the hole I had fallen into. Then Astra came along, sending a tectonic shockwave through my entire identity. I never should have pushed her away, but I was terrified by the thought that I might lose her like I've lost everyone else. First my parents, then my brother... So, I pushed her away. In my mind, it was better to break her heart than to have her ripped away from me by this terrible world we live in.

I have questioned that decision every single day for the past five years. The best explanation I can come up with is that I got *too* happy. I was too close to her, and it scared the hell out of me.

Fucking idiot.

I can feel my heart beating in my throat. My body's shaking, and it's becoming increasingly hard to breathe. I have to look again.

Maybe I was imagining it?

I slowly peer around the edge of the shelves I'm hiding behind, and my eyes fall on the unmistakable figure of Astra. It may've been five years, but there's no two ways about it: that's her.

It seems impossible, but she's only gotten more attractive since the last time I saw her. Her hair, which used to be down to her waist, now floats in loose chestnut curls just above her shoulders, a stunning royal purple streak running down the left side of her head. She's wearing a well-worn brown leather jacket, black jeans, and her impossibly stylish black combat boots.

Do I go up to her? Do I run away as fast as I can? Do I

stand here indefinitely until she inevitably leaves the store?

I realize, albeit much too late, that none of it matters. I look down at my Holocomm: it's 16:07. Fuck. I had between five and eight minutes to make this run in and out of the store. There will be new guards rotating in at any second, and soon, the streets will be so packed with Retribution troops that I might as well shoot myself with an arc rifle right now.

I have no choice: I buy the groceries as fast as possible and make a break for the door. I don't see any guards yet. I might actually make it out before—

"Oliver!? Is that really you?"

It's not fair. Why did this have to happen now and here?

For years, I've wished I could hear her voice again, but right now, all I feel is dread. I have to turn around. I can't let her slip away, not again. But if I stay here, it's almost certain death.

With a sigh, I spin around, trying as hard as I can to hide how terrified I am behind a half-smile. "Hey, Astra! What are the odds of this, right? Probably like one in a billion."

Great work, Oliver. Way to act like a normal person.

Looking at her up close only worsens matters because she's just impossibly gorgeous. Her olive skin looks flawless. It's as if she's never had acne in her entire life. Her hazel eyes shimmer in the fluorescent lights of the grocery store.

"Yeah," she says, "I honestly never thought I would see you again. It's been so long...Hey, are you okay, Olly? You don't look so good."

"Oh, sorry, I just"— Before I have time to answer, I see three security guards walking through one of the doors, mere feet from where I'm standing. I slowly walk closer to Astra and, in a much quieter voice, say, "Astra, I don't have time to explain, but I have to get out of here as soon as possible. It's probably best if they don't see you with me, so don't follow me. Use a different door to leave. Here—"

I wave my Holocomm over hers, allowing the devices to exchange our contact information. Obviously, I still have her number on account of how I contemplated texting or calling her countless times, but the info exchange will give her the address of the bunker. I also have to assume she deleted my number, given how things, you know, went down.

"I'm so sorry, I'll call you when it's safe." This probably couldn't have gone any worse than it is.

"Oh, okay, Olly, I understand. You better actually call me this time, though."

Yeah, I probably deserved that.

"Thank you, I'm sorry, and goodbye." With that, I walk as quickly as possible toward the nearest exit while also trying not to draw attention to myself. I glance back at Astra one last time as I walk through the door, hoping it's not the last time I see her.

***

About half an hour has passed since the grocery fiasco, and I'm finally nearing our bunker. If I had taken the direct route, it would have probably taken me about fifteen minutes to get here. However, since becoming a wanted criminal, taking detours, side-streets, and being overly cautious pretty much has been my only option.

I round the corner of the dark alley I was just slinking through and turn onto the final stretch of my journey home. Yeah, I guess it is our home now...a month ago, I never would've imagined my life to have turned out this way, but now that I'm here, nothing has ever felt more natural. Of course, there was a time when my home was a person, and that person was her...

I'm deep in contemplation, staring at my shoes as I walk, thinking of times gone by and possibilities to come, when I hear a rock get kicked several yards behind me. The street's been notably empty for a half of a mile or so. I took note of that in spite of my Astra-fueled stupor. My stomach drops, and the hair on the back of my neck stands straight up as the reality of the situation hits me.

Someone's following me. I can't believe I didn't notice until now.

Who could be following me when I've been so meticulous? Have I been followed this whole damn time? I should've known this trip would never have gone as smoothly as planned. Nothing ever does. But who could it be, and how did I not notice until now? One of the primary practices in martial arts training is awareness, not to mention I have hearing enhancement cybernetics, so I can typically hear people's footsteps from a mile away, even if they think they're being quiet. That's not active all the time, of course, since that would drive me insane with all the noise, but I can turn up the sensitivity if the need arises, and the need has undoubtedly arisen.

But even with all of that, I couldn't detect whoever's following me until they made a mistake.

If I've been followed for this long by someone that stealthy...

I try my best to keep walking just like I was before I noticed, but nothing is more challenging than trying really hard to do something that is usually effortless.

After a couple more minutes of walking, I can't take it anymore. Unless I shake my tail, I'll never be able to return to base. There's no way I'll be leading whoever this is right to my front door. I round the corner of the alley onto a major street and break into a full sprint, holding my backpack in place with my right hand and the sheath of my sword with my left. The backpack has the groceries in it, and I can feel it slowing me down, but we desperately need this food.

Since they were following me from a distance, I got a few

seconds head start before I heard the footsteps of my pursuer break into a sprint as well. Even at this speed, their footsteps are hard to hear. Just who is this asshole? Clearly not a Retribution troop: they're all hulking monsters with heavy armor and heavier rifles, and I would've heard their footsteps the second they started following me.

I keep running for a few solid minutes, turning from street to street, leading my pursuer far away from Zeke and Dex, away from the outskirts of Nova City, and deep into the Residential District.

I can feel myself beginning to lose my breath, but my pursuer is no farther behind me than when we started. If anything, they're gaining on me. Looks like I'll have to fight my way out of this one, as usual. Good thing I didn't listen to Zeke when he told me not to bring any weapons in order to not draw attention to myself.

I turn the corner onto another street. Tall, run-down apartment buildings rise on all sides of me. It's the middle of the afternoon, but the street is strangely silent. This will do.

I loosen my wakizashi in its sheath with my left thumb, stash my backpack in a nearby alley, and stop dead in the middle of the street, taking deep breaths as I draw my sword, engage the arc unit, and spin to face my pursuer.

To my surprise, I see no one. No one at all. I strain to hear their breathing, only to find utter and complete silence.

"You can come out. Obviously, I know you're following me, or do you think I take frantic sprints through the city just for fun?" I probably shouldn't be taunting whoever this is, but I've been feeling dangerous ever since I took down those Retribution troops.

Without a sound, an imposing figure seemingly made of shadow steps out from between two of the nearby apartment buildings, calmly heading toward the middle of the street, moving with silent, purposeful steps, stopping mere yards away from me. They must be about seven feet tall, their body entirely covered in cybernetics and armor plating. The red glow of their eyes pierces directly into my soul.

As they approach, I sink into a low stance, holding my wakizashi with both hands. The soft hum of the arc unit is the only sound I can hear, aside from my heartbeat.

Suddenly, the silence is broken by seven words, spoken in a menacing, mechanically altered voice that makes my blood run cold: *"You should have kept running, Mister Wolf."*

"How did you know my...that's impossible...who are you?" As the words leave my mouth, a terrible realization strikes me. The pieces finally click in my mind, and the truth of those words becomes clear.

I really should've kept running.

Shinigami, that's what people call them. It's a Japanese word that translates to "Death Spirit." Each Shinigami is rumored to be a one-man killing crew specializing in silent, covert assassinations of the high-profile enemies of CYBR Corp. Supposedly, they're lab-grown cyber-humans, ruthlessly trained from a young age in the art of killing, knowing nothing else besides how to destroy life. They say the day they're born is the only day they're truly human.

But that's all just rumors, just stories people tell to scare each other late at night, right? They're not real, they can't be.

Unfortunately, wishful thinking won't save me now.

"So, you've come to collect my soul then?" I joke, trying to move but frozen with fear. My voice cracks as I say "soul."

I immediately regret saying anything because it's then that the Shinigami makes a terrible sound that can only be interpreted as laughter. Twisted, mechanically augmented, horrible laughter, like shards of metal trapped in a blender.

"You should feel honored, Oliver Wolf. Only important enemies of CYBR Corp are killed by a Shinigami. Although I fail to see how one as insignificant as you could possibly be

worth my time. I suppose we will find out."

With that, the shadow runs directly toward me, arms to their sides, no visible weapons in their hands.

Why haven't they drawn their weapon yet?

My legs finally decide to move as survival instinct overtakes the crippling fear which has held my body firmly in place until now. Moving with as much speed as possible, I narrowly dodge their attack. Mere inches from Death itself, I realize why the Shinigami did not draw a weapon. Their hands, both completely cybernetic, are pulsing with immense amounts of arc energy, each of their fingers ending in electrified points, sharp enough to pierce the skin and fry the contents within.

"Of course," I mutter to myself, "you don't need a weapon. You *are* the weapon."

"Clever, aren't you?" they respond, jumping toward me again with inhuman speed and accuracy.

Was that sarcasm?

There's no time to jump out of the way, so I deflect their attack with my sword. I only manage to block one of their hands entirely, and the other glances off my right shoulder, sending sparks flying and causing a small portion of my shirt to catch fire. I kick toward their abdomen to push them away, but they're able to easily dodge my attack, leaping back a few feet and landing silently on the asphalt.

It's not exactly an opening. Nevertheless, I seize the opportunity, quickly taking an arc taser unit from my jacket pocket and sending it directly toward the Shinigami. They easily dodge my throw. Anticipating this, I lob two more taser units, one on either side of where they were standing a moment before, hoping to catch them by surprise. To my amazement, it actually works! One of the tasers lands on the Shinigami, latching onto their left arm.

The way these units work is when they detect an impact,

they use tiny barbs with sharp ends to attach to whatever they hit and begin sending an electric shock throughout the body. The shock they produce is powerful enough to temporarily paralyze whoever or whatever they latch onto.

"Got ya!" I exclaim.

As soon as I see the arc taser hit its mark, I waste no time closing the gap between us. Running at full speed, I hold my sword to my left side, bringing the wakizashi down in a low, swinging arc as I attempt to slice through the Shinigami's right leg. To my absolute horror, my sword merely glances off as if I've just brought a wooden stick down on a steel beam.

I keep my weapons incredibly sharp. What in the universe is this thing made of?

I'm abruptly snapped back to reality as the arc taser wears off, allowing the Shinigami to take a viscous double-clawed slash at me. I dodge as well as I can, but they catch my chest with a couple of talons as I jump backward. It sends a nearly incomprehensible burning sensation through my chest, and I can smell my own flesh burning.

It's clear that recklessly attacking them will get me nowhere. I've got to figure out what the hell to do.

Shinigami or not, there has to be a weakness, an Achilles heel, a chink in the armor. One of the most widely told Shinigami legends is of one that was supposedly taken down. I try to remember what the story says took the monster down, but I'm interrupted by a furious series of crackling blue slashes, each one expertly trained on my weak points. The Shinigami never slows, never stops, never gives up. It takes everything I've got and more just to stay alive, let alone take this Spirit down. Every few slashes, I make a mistake, and another talon scrapes through my flesh, cauterizing the wound with thousands of volts of agonizing electricity.

The longer this continues, the more *painfully* aware I become that I need to find a way to kill this monster, or it *will* kill me. I can't outrun it. That much is obvious. I also can't just attack it blindly. As the strength begins to drain from my body, I start to desperately search for a weakness. I throw several test slashes, punches, and kicks toward every point on the Shinigami's body that I can reach. Many of them land, but only because it seems they have no interest in stopping me. It's as though this Death Spirit knows I can't harm it.

Amidst the onslaught of furious slashes, the exchanging of blows, and my desperate attempts to win, they speak:

"I admire your determination, human, but o ...surely you must understand your position. You cannot harm me. I have killed hundreds, many of which were stronger than you. So, Oliver," the Shinigami taunts me with a terrifying snarl, *"we can either continue this until you inevitably tire, or you can give up. At least you can die knowing that you had the privilege of being considered important enough to be killed by me."*

They taunt me, slowing their assault for a second, luring me into a false sense of security. I may not be winning this fight, but I'm obviously causing more trouble than this asshole's usual victims. Despite the impending sense of doom that I feel, this brings a smile to my face.

I take a second to breathe, and, with a newfound determination, I decide to keep bringing the fight to him.

"What's wrong? Am I proving too difficult for you to deal with? Surely someone as powerful as you would have no trouble killing someone as insignificant as me, right?" I taunt the Shinigami once more, hoping it can feel anger and make a mistake. "Unfortunately for you, I drank a big ol' can of fuck you juice this morning, so I really don't feel like giving up."

Just as I had hoped, the Shinigami lunges toward me, slashing from all directions and with more intensity than before. Honestly, it's more than I can handle. Still, it gives me a perfect opportunity to attach my last arc taser unit directly to their neck, completely paralyzing them once more. This is it, my last chance to take this monster down.

Bending my knees and taking a deep breath, I send the electrified tip of my sword directly into the middle of the Shinigami's chest, pushing with every ounce of force I can possibly muster.

Finally, my attack actually met its mark!

My sword sinks a mere half of an inch into the Spirit's chest, somehow finding a minuscule gap between the layers of impenetrable armor, but that's all I need. Just as the arc taser begins to wear off, I violently pry my sword against the armor plating, putting everything I have into this desperate attempt to expose the soft underbelly of the beast.

With the arc taser worn off, the Shinigami is free to move once more. Just as it tries to jump away, a satisfying clang echoes throughout the hallway. To their disgust and my delight, the Shinigami looks down at their chest to find that a small piece of their impenetrable armor plating has been removed from the right side of their chest. They roar with fury, their eyes seeming to glow a brighter red, their sharpened teeth snarling at me with a horrifying menace.

"*You will pay for this, Wolf!*" They growl.

Oh shit, I just made it mad. I'm fucking toast.

They set themselves in a low stance, like a panther about to take down its prey. They charge toward me, screaming with a hatred that makes my blood run cold. Seeing this monster, this god of death, coming at me with such hate and malice, its towering figure perfectly honed for killing, killing *me*, I freeze. I don't know what to do. I don't know what I possibly *could* do. But then, when its razor-sharp claws are mere inches from my face, suddenly and without explanation, it stops dead in its tracks. Its glowing red eyes flicker and dim for a moment, its face and body entirely still. I can hear its breathing from here. It's the first time I've actually seen any sign of this Shinigami being even remotely human. It somehow makes it even more terrifying to glimpse the creature beneath the chrome. I'm so utterly shocked by this series of events that I stand there for a few moments, utterly dumbfounded at the fact that I'm alive, and more importantly, *why?*

But just as suddenly as they froze, their eyes brighten and fix themselves on me once more, their snarling face returning to a calm, inscrutable mask. I have no idea why they didn't kill me just now, but I have to make the most of this.

Seizing this opportunity, I lunge forward with another stab toward their now-exposed chest area. Even though it's a relatively small opening, it's exposed the one thing that can take down any cyber-human, no matter how strong. That thing is their power core.

If I could just get a solid hit on it...

"Mark my words, Oliver Wolf, you will regret this day." Their terrifying voice is filled with vitriolic hatred now. Before I can make contact and end this once and for all, the Shinigami moves with inhuman speed, deflecting my attack with one hand and latching onto my cybernetic arm with the other, sending a massive shockwave throughout my body. It's more painful than anything I've ever experienced, and it leaves me entirely unable to move. My skin crawls and burns, and my muscles contract and spasm uncontrollably. I collapse to the ground, nearly losing consciousness for a moment.

By the time I'm able to stand up, the Shinigami is gone. Vanished back into the shadows from whence it came.

"Goddamn Shinigami," I exclaim, picking up the small shard of their armor plating and putting it in my backpack, "this'll be a fucking long walk home."

CH 4

 out that nearly defeating a Shinigami was precisely what our little rag-tag bunch needed to get motivated. Well, I guess it's less "nearly defeated" and more "didn't get torn into tiny pieces by" the Shinigami, but if you ask me, those are basically the same thing. Regardless, everyone's fired up. Zeke is hard at work researching the material of the armor plating. Dex's condition has improved significantly, so he's using his insider knowledge and resources from his time at CYBR Corp to compile everything he can on the mysterious Shinigami. He's been alternating between traditional computing, holo-computing, and netrunning, depending on his condition. According to Dex, all CYBR Corp employees need some level of netrunning skill, and they supply them all with mobile netrunning rigs that can connect to any computer.

As for me, I sustained minor injuries from my battle with the Shinigami, but for the most part, it was nothing Zeke couldn't handle. The one issue is the electric shockwave that severely damaged my battery. Since I only have a solid-state lithium battery pack, extreme shockwaves like the one the Shinigami gave me have a severe draining effect on that battery's life. I can now only go somewhere between thirty minutes and one hour before needing another charge, which, needless to say, is a serious problem. Granted, my battery pack wasn't exactly state of the art before this, but it would at least last a little over a full day with everyday use.

Long story short, while my counterparts are tirelessly

researching the Shinigami, I'm doing my own research into upgrades for my cybernetic power source. Either I get a new battery, or I'll spend the rest of my life jumping from charger to charger, hoping my battery doesn't completely fail. That's not exactly my idea of fun.

"Cerulean, could you find me the best deals on compact cybernetic fusion power cells?" I ask.

"I found three million results for Compact Cybernetic Fusion Power Cells," replies Cerulean, as helpful as ever.

"Perfect, now remove all of the results outside of my price range."

"Recalculating...I found...three results for Compact Cybernetic Fusion Power Cells, Oliver."

Yeah, that sounds more like it. Now, which budget store battery am I going to trust my entire life and wellbeing to? A pressing question indeed.

"Cerulean, excluding budget constraints, what is considered the best power cell available on the market?" It's always fun to shop outside of your price range, plus it'll let me know what I'm actually dealing with in terms of CYBR tech.

"Removing this constraint significantly increases available units," Cerulean responds, toeing the line between factual and just plain rude. *"The power cell you are looking for is the CYBR Corp FXP 4800. Capable of sustaining a Retribution soldier for twenty years with a single vial of Deuterium-Tritium (DT), this power cell will allow the user to sustain any combination of commercially available cybernetics with little to no slowdown, overheating, or other known side effects."*

I can't help but let out a whistle of disbelief. This power cell is so superior to my tech that I feel ashamed to put it in the same category. But now it's time for the real question:

"How much does it cost?"

"The FXP 4800 costs four million CYBR COYN on the

consumer market. Additionally, only friends of CYBR Corp are allowed the opportunity to purchase these units," Cerulean pauses, *"given your current wanted status by CYBR Corp, it would be unwise to attempt purchasing one of these units."*

As I sit there, contemplating if Cerulean is actually sassing me or not, something occurs to me. How could I have not thought of this sooner? Given my place near the top of the CYBR Corp's most wanted list, no one in their right mind would possibly sell cybernetics to me. But that doesn't change the fact that if I actually want to have any hope of defeating something like a Shinigami, I'll pretty much have to get my hands on that four million CYBR COYN power core.

"Cerulean, how would I, theoretically, become able to purchase this core? Assuming, for the sake of argument, that I'm not on the most wanted list."

"You would require an active CYBR Corp employee of rank three or higher to place you on the 'Friends of CYBR Corp' list, a prestigious honor."

"And once on that list, would I need to visit the CYBRnetics Outlet, or how would I get my hands on it?"

"Yes, you would need to acquire it through the CYBRnetics Outlet in the Market District. Additionally, you would need to meet with the manager of that outlet to purchase this particular item. There are only five of these units in existence, so they require first-hand purchasing."

Ah shit, well, that's just my luck, isn't it? Nothing's easy, nothing's straightforward, and *nothing* goes as planned. The more I hear about this, the less sure I become. I don't know if we can even get close to this thing, let alone walk away with it in hand. Not to mention the face-to-face transaction. Most shopping is online or through a self-checkout these days, so a direct purchase from the store manager is going to be a major problem. There'd be armed guards, security cameras, identity checks: the whole nine yards.

If I hope to pull this off, and I really need to, I'm gonna need to call in some serious favors. First things first, we need to get ourselves on that "Friends of CYBR Corp" list. Maybe Dex knows someone high enough rank to put us on the list. The issue there, assuming Dex can come through, is that we're all on the most wanted list. We'll need an external party to get on the list and make the purchase for us. But even if we do get someone to agree to this, there's no chance in hell we'll be able to afford it!

It has to be her, doesn't it? I mean, who else? But...fuck.

I know what I have to do, and I know I'm going to regret it. But before I do anything drastic, I need to talk to Dex about getting us on that list.

Shutting down the Cerulean tablet and disconnecting myself from my charging station, I make my way toward the main room of the bunker, where Dex is working with the central computer. It's an impressive piece of machinery, considering it's a few years old. With a three-hundred-and-sixty-degree holographic, interactive screen, voice command capability, and augmented reality integration, this computer allows you to do anything you can think of. Not to mention, when all is said and done, the actual computer fits right in your pocket.

This is where Dex has been for the past couple of days, working tirelessly to regain and recollect as much intel as he can on CYBR Corp.

Looks like he's netrunning. I'll wait.

It's a bad idea to pull someone out of netrunning when they're not ready for it. Depending on how recklessly you unplug them, you could cause brain damage or even kill them. Needless to say, I've got plenty of time to wait for Dex to exit the net on his own.

After a few minutes, the rig he's plugged into beeps, and the screen reads 'Initiating Wake Sequence. Do NOT Touch the Power.' Dex slowly comes to, then unplugs the series of wires from the back of his head and neck. Without thinking, I passively scratch at the ports on the back of my own head. Everyone has the necessary ports for netrunning. They get installed with the Holocomm. Well, the ports are multi-use. They can accept data chips, and they're used for more advanced VR headsets and all sorts of things. CYBR Corp used to charge for them, but they found that inserting them when you're younger reduces the chances of rejection. All cybernetics have a risk of your body rejecting them, but the more intertwined with your brain they are, and the older you are when they're installed, the higher the risk. CYBR figured it would be worth footing the bill for every single person to get them installed young, just for the small number of people who would eventually be 'recruited' by them to be netrunners. Needless to say, not everyone has the mind and will for netrunning, regardless of if your body accepts the ports or not.

Focus, now you're just staring at him.

"Hey, Dex, how's the hunt going?" I ask casually.

"Ah, Oliver, I'm glad you stopped by," he replies, good-natured as ever, "it turns out CYBR Corp hasn't completely locked me out of their systems yet. I was able to access a couple of my old accounts in their systems, the only challenge being to mask our IP address while doing so."

So, they didn't lock him out of their systems after how he left? Who knew that even the great CYBR Corp falls victim to the slowness of paperwork. I let out a chuckle at the thought, which Dex notices.

"What's so funny? You didn't think old Dex could pull it off, did you?" He teases.

"No, no, I just find it amusing that CYBR Corp didn't bother to lock you out of their systems. I suppose maybe they thought you were dead and didn't bother with the paperwork of it all." It may just be a minor mistake, but the idea that this corporation has flaws gives me hope.

"Yeah, I guess you're right...lucky for us anyhow!" Dex replies with a grin. "So, what's going on anyway? You didn't come over here just to ask how it's going, did you?"

It would seem I have beaten around the bush long enough. "Yeah, you got me. The main reason I came to see you was..." I hesitate, fearing the answer Dex will give, "I need a favor. I need a new battery, and if I have any chance of defeating CYBR Corp, I'm gonna need the best power cell on the market."

I can see Dex starting to catch my drift, his eyebrows raising slightly. "Oh, I get it. We're talking about CYBR tech here. You're after a CYBR fusion cell. Am I wrong?"

"Nope, you got me again, Dex," I laugh nervously, "the problem is, as you probably already know, it will be impossible to actually get my hands on one of these without being on the 'Friends of CYBR Corp' list, as Cerulean has so graciously informed me."

"Ohhh, so you're after the big money items then. I can't say I don't admire your moxie. But getting you on that list would be incredibly difficult, even if I still worked there. Not to mention you're on their most wanted list."

Trying not to lose hope, I reply, "Right, but what if I told you I can get someone else, someone not on their most wanted list, to help us. Could you possibly get that person on the friends list?"

Dex mulls it over for a moment, tapping his chin with a pen. Suddenly, his face lights up, and he looks more excited than I've ever seen him as he exclaims, "Olly, my boy, I can do it! I can get your friend on that list!" He pauses for a moment. "Sorry, can I call you Olly?"

"Of course. And that's awesome news, Dex! What makes you so sure?" Considering I was expecting the worst, this feels like the best news I've ever heard.

"It just so happens that a CYBR Corp buddy of mine got promoted to level three clearance, all thanks to me. He's always been one of the good ones: we would always talk about getting out of there together someday. Poor guy, he never could leave because of his family..." He trails off, clearly filled with remorse. He suddenly looks tired, shadows covering his face.

"Oh, I'm sorry to hear that...it must be extremely challenging to work for them." I wait for a while, finally breaking the silence, "but I guess the good news is that he can help us take down CYBR Corp, right? Then he can go with his family wherever he wants!"

The shadow lifts from Dex's face, his usual chipper nature returning, "you're damn right, Oliver. I'll get in touch with him. All you gotta do is send me the name and picture of the person we need on the 'Friends of CYBR Corp' list. Let's get you that battery!"

Now that's the Dex I know. "Thanks, man, I really appreciate everything you're doing here for us. I know you kind of just got pulled into my own personal crusade here."

"Don't worry about me. I knew what I was getting myself into when I left that damn place anyway. In fact, I'm happy to help you in your mission." Dex replies in the sincerest voice I may have ever heard. Something about him just makes it feel like we're old friends.

"Well, thank you again. I'll get back to you soon with that name and picture." I mention as I walk back toward my little room in the corner of the bunker.

As I walk away, my excitement once again fades into a sense of dread. I care about these people, Zeke and Dex, and they trust me to protect them. Zeke, the ever-loyal friend, would never leave me to fight this on my own. Of course, he gives me a hard time about it, but when the cards are down,

Zeke is the most reliable person on the planet. Dex may be a new addition to our group, but he's clearly willing to do anything and everything he can to help us with this mission. I trust him, and so does Zeke, so that's good enough for me.

And that's why I'm so afraid. Because they're important to me, and I cannot let them down.

It's not that I won't follow through on my promise. I will either take down CYBR Corp or die trying, and that's a fact. The problem is, what if the second option is the one that happens? No one's ever gotten anywhere close to taking down this megacorporation, though many have tried. I can't help but wonder what makes me think I'm different, that we stand a chance where others have failed. In my countless hours spent lying awake at night over the past few years, I've mulled over this exact question a *lot*. I've toyed with the idea of taking down CYBR Corp for years, analyzing every attempt made, what made them fail, and so on. The answer I always come to, and the one still keeping me motivated now, despite how slim our chances are looking, is this: every time people have tried taking down CYBR Corp, they've done so in a large group. Whether it's mass protests, boycotts, or a militaristic storming of their headquarters, they've always been obvious, large group attacks, and they've consistently failed almost as soon as they began. But not us. We're small; we're under the radar. They won't see us coming until it's too late. Or, at least, that's what I tell myself. Only time will tell how right or horribly wrong I am about all this. And if I'm wrong, well, I let everyone down.

If I fail, and if I'm no longer around, then what happens to the people I care about? No. I can't think like that.

Long story short, I cannot fail them. They'll either live in fear for their entire lives or be hunted down and killed or tortured. I refuse to let that happen.

That being said, it's time to add another person to the list of people I'll let down if I fail this mission: Astra Odelle. I've been avoiding it for long enough, and now that Dex has given me the green light to get someone onto the "Friends of CYBR Corp" list, I have to go through with this. She's the only other person in this god-forsaken city that I trust enough to bring in on this, so she'll have to be the one we put on the list.

Looks like I'll actually be calling her back this time…to ask her to risk her life for me. I really am an idiot. I had five years to call her, reach out to her, and try to get her back into my life. But no, I waited until I ran into her in a grocery store as a wanted criminal.

Well, here goes nothing.

With a few taps on my Holocomm, I'm dialing Astra. It rings a few times, giving me just enough time to freak out. On the fourth ring, she answers, choosing to just use the audio call rather than the screen or hologram calling.

"I must be losing it because I could've sworn that Oliver Wolf is actually calling me." Leave it to Astra to always throw the first punch. I can't say I don't deserve it though.

"Um, ouch," I reply, admittedly at a loss for words. "Hey Astra, I, um, how are you?" Well, thank goodness I wasn't awkward…

"Smooth moves, Romeo. Do you get a lot of ladies with that?" She laughs at her own joke.

"Very funny, Ash. Seriously though, how are you? It's been so long since I've seen you." I stop short. It seems even the air in the room stands still as I remember the fact that it's my fault that we haven't seen each other in five years.

Thankfully, Astra isn't afraid to break the silence. "Well, Olly, I wish I had something more interesting to say. But really, I've just been alright. Nothing bad, but nothing fantastic either. I've spent most of my time just trying to make a living." She pauses, carefully considering something she wants to say. "Oliver, I…" another pause, her breathing audibly unsteady, "well, I miss you, you fucking idiot! Why did you never call me? I waited for so long, expecting a call, or a text, or anything! I thought you might've died or something, considering how depressed you were when you left. I..." her anger quickly shifts to remorse as she admits, "I just wanted to be there for you, Oliver. I loved you. I..." She trails off, her voice breaking on the last words.

"Oh, Ash I..." I can't form a single coherent thought. My mind is swimming through a sea of uncertainty, unearthed feelings, and guilt. I have to say *something*, but what? Nothing I say will make up for leaving her, or the time lost, or anything.

Before I know what I'm saying, everything comes flowing out, "I loved you too...maybe I...still do. I never really wanted to leave you. I...well, I was so messed up at that point that I actually believed that pushing you away would be the best thing for both of us. Looking back on it now, I realize that, of course, it was stupid, but at the time, my brother...he..." I can't finish the thought.

"I know, Oliver. Miles was your biggest hero, and he was taken from you right when you were starting to become your own person. I can't even begin to imagine what that must feel like, living with that every day. Sure, I've lost family members, but not a sibling. And for that, I will always forgive you. But Olly, you know I would have helped you get through that, don't you? You didn't have to do it on your own. You...you don't have to be alone, Oliver."

Astra always sees right through me. Her words cut me right to my very core, bringing back memories I'd been suppressing for the better part of a decade.

My brother was killed by CYBR Corp ten years ago for no good reason other than the fact that they could. After that, I was a scared eighteen-year-old, completely alone and furious at the world for taking him from me. Astra came into my life a few years later, and for a while, things were amazing. She picked up the pieces of my shattered existence, giving me a reason to live. But I got caught up in my own head, and I went and ruined it, pushing her away as we got closer to each other. I was afraid that she would be next: first, my parents, then my brother, all killed by CYBR Corp for 'violating their agreement.' I couldn't bear to lose her too.

I suppose I should be saying this to her, but instead, I'm just sitting here in silence.

"Well? Say something," Astra commands, clearly not enjoying the awkward silence. I can't exactly blame her for that one.

There's only one thing I can do at this point. I gotta lay it all on the line for her. This might be the only chance I ever get to tell her how I really feel. With a very deep breath in, I prepare myself for whatever is about to happen.

"I just want to tell you how sorry I am for everything I did back then and all the pain it must have caused you. If there's one thing I never wanted to do, it was hurt you. To tell you the truth, Ash, I still think about you. All the time. You're the best thing that has ever happened to me, and I loved you more than I ever thought I could love someone, especially after losing Miles. There's not a day that goes by where I don't regret pushing you away and driving us apart in the name of your safety...In reality, I guess the truth is that I was trying to protect myself. I knew I couldn't handle losing another important person in my life, so in my twisted way, pushing you away was the best way to protect myself from feeling that pain...I guess it's all pretty ironic..."

I trail off, not sure if I've said too much or not enough, worried that no matter what I do, things will never be the same between us. The reality of the situation really hits me, the fact that in order to protect myself from the pain of losing her, I chose to lose her on purpose.

Nice work on that one, past Oliver.

After an uncomfortably long period of silence, Astra responds. "You're right, Olly. It is ironic. Part of me has been waiting for years just to hear you say that, but part of me wishes I never actually heard it at all. I guess what I'm trying to say is…I don't know what to do. I want to forgive you, tell you that I understand what you did and why, and that we can just move on with our lives, but I really don't know if I can. I'm sorry, Oliver. I'm not saying I don't want you in my life, but I'm also not saying I'm ready to have you in my life again." The playfulness in her voice has completely disappeared, replaced by somber remorse.

"I completely understand," I respond. I honestly do understand. I haven't forgiven myself, so why should she? "So, for now, let's just keep moving forward. I find it works best to tackle a problem by working through it rather than being immobilized by it or ignoring it."

"I can get behind that." She seems relieved by the idea.

"Okay, that's really great to hear…Now, I hate to do this, and you probably saw this coming, but I do actually have a favor to ask of you." I can't tell which part will be more challenging, fixing our relationship or convincing her to help me take down CYBR Corp.

"Some things really never change, do they?" To my surprise, her tone is a little bit more playful already. She truly is wonderful.

"Okay, so hear me out. I've put a lot of thought into this, ran it past Zeke, and decided to go through with it. You're gonna think I'm batshit but bear with me. I'm going to take down CYBR Corp, finally getting some fucking justice for the countless people like Miles who lost their lives or wish they had, all because the heartless bastards running CYBR Corp arbitrarily decided they "owed them money." But to do that, I need some help. I need *your* help, Ash."

"Oh, you can't be fucking serious. I was willing to do a favor for you. I really was. But taking down CYBR Corp!? You have *got* to be out of your damn mind. There is no possible way to take them down. People have tried and failed for years. No offense, Oliver. You know I've always supported you, but what makes you think you're any different?" Her tone is harsh but sincere, rough but in a caring way.

Obviously, she cares about me and my well-being, but god damn, did she need to be so blunt about it?

"First of all, ouch. You really just tore me a new one there, Ash," I chuckle, making a feeble attempt to lighten the mood slightly, "But to answer your question, I know I can do it, and here's why: I took down an entire squadron of Retribution troops singlehandedly and with no preparation. I went toe-to-toe with a Shinigami, and before you ask, yes, I'm serious about that. And what's more, I came away with nothing but a damaged power core. With a little more time, preparation, better equipment and cybernetics, and the support of you all, I *know* that I can do this. If we make a good enough plan and take them by surprise, I truly believe our little group can do this." I really am not that confident, but hey, fake it 'till you make it, right?

"You...wait a minute, you said you fought a *Shinigami*? Not only is that hard to believe, it's impossible because they don't actually exist! Look, Oliver, I really want to believe you, and obviously, I want to see those bastards knocked off their high horse as much as anyone, but I don't think it's a good idea to encourage this sort of devil-may-care bullshit that you're clearly high on." I can hear an intense amount of concern behind her words.

"I understand why you wouldn't believe me, but you can ask Zeke, and he'll tell you that as crazy as all of this sounds, it's true. He's the one who patched me up both times, and you know he always tells the blunt and honest truth. You don't have to believe me or answer me now, but I really need your help, and there's no one else I trust enough or who I want to be my partner in this as much as you."

"Alright, we can come back to this Shinigami nonsense later. I'll listen to what you have to say, so go for it." She's always been a unique mix of brutal and caring.

"Thank you, I really appreciate it. So basically, I am in desperate need of a new power source for my cybernetics. Mine is old and got fried by the...by electricity. I can't afford anything remotely worth trusting my life with, so the plan is to, well, steal the best one available from CYBR Corp. We're all wanted criminals, so we need someone to get on the "Friends of CYBR Corp" list so we can even get close to this thing. And that's where you come in, Ash." I find it hard to imagine she'll do this without giving me a truckload of criticisms, but here goes nothing.

"Oliver, I have so many problems with what you just said. But...god damn it, I'm in. I'll help you steal that power source."

My heart jumps out of my chest, and a shiver runs through my entire body. "Wait, seriously? I was expecting more of something along the lines of 'no way, you fucking idiot,' but hey, I'm not complaining!" I say with a genuine laugh, the first I've had in a long time. Ash joins in, too.

"Yeah, I'm not sure if it's my old rebellious protester side coming out or what, but that actually sounds...exciting. I wanna do this thing with you. Although, I'm wondering who else is with you? You said that you're 'all' wanted criminals. Is it more than just you and Zeke? Who else is stupid enough to join you?!"

"Oh shit, I forgot to mention, we made a new friend named Dexter. He was being shot down by the Retribution, so Zeke saved his life while I fought them off. He used to work for CYBR Corp but left because he couldn't live with the guilt of working for such an evil corporation. I haven't known him for too long, but he seems like a stand-up guy." I partially forgot and partially didn't want to tell her too much in case she didn't want to join us. The less she knew, the more likely she was to be safe from CYBR scrutiny. I know this all too well.

"Hmm, interesting. You've really gotten yourself into some deep shit, haven't you?" She asks rhetorically. Obviously, I've gotten myself into some deep shit.

"Yeah, yeah. So anyway, what do you say we meet at our old spot tomorrow? Right after sundown?"

"Sounds good, Olly. See you there."

"Perfect, good night, Ash." I end the call, realizing just how long I've been talking to her. I also become aware of the fact that I'm sitting on the edge of my seat, every muscle in my body as tense as can be. I really am hopeless when it comes to her.

With a sigh, I move to my bed and try to sleep, endlessly playing back the entire conversation I just had. My eyes gradually adjust to the pitch darkness of my room, a dim light blinking in and out, indicating that my Cerulean tablet is in stand-by mode. The pale, flashing blue light provides me with brief glimpses of the room, which is pretty dull, to say the least. Since this is a bunker and a rather shitty one at that, the walls and ceiling are just solid steel, and the floor is concrete. The steel is dull, but it reflects the blue light ever so slightly. It's oddly mesmerizing and helps to soothe my frantic mind. I find myself entering an almost meditative state, slowly breathing in and out with every other blink of the light.

It's not often that I find time to clear my mind and relax, especially recently, so it's a welcome change of pace. I used to be much more in touch with myself, frequently meditating and practicing my martial arts, but the constant beat-down of everyday life has slowly drained most of my ability to focus or to care.

Eventually, I drift off. The last thought floating across my mind is a selfish desire for life to go back to normal, back to a simpler and easier time. A time before CYBR Corp, before I lost my family, before...everything.

CH 5

MUSIC plays a little too loudly in my wireless earbuds as I make my way through the backstreets of Nova City. I'm on my way to meet Ash at our old spot, where we used to spend most of our time. It's a three-mile walk, and my heart has been pounding the entire time. No matter what I do, I can't help but wonder about how this is going to go. Is she feeling the same way? Have her feelings been rekindled as mine have, or is she only doing this to help me because she feels like she has to? At the very least, I just want to be friends again, but at this point, I'm not even sure if that's possible.

I turn up the volume a bit and pick up the pace, eager to get there. Our spot is right between the Entertainment and Arts Districts, in what used to be our favorite historical art museum. We're both suckers for classical Japanese art, what can I say? The place has long since been transformed into a club, aptly named Hakubutsukan, which roughly translates to "The Museum." The art pieces still hang on the walls, now covered in graffiti. That didn't stop us from going there, enjoying one too many drinks as we admired the barely recognizable art pieces—

"*Shit!*" I mutter under my breath, having just caught sight of three Retribution goons mere yards away. I duck behind the nearest building, moving silently and quickly. They're standing just outside The Museum, of course. Did they know I was coming? No, I remember they would constantly monitor this area since it's filled with your average assortment of scumbags and criminals. These troops held this post back before everything went to shit.

Looks like I'll have to get creative. Can't exactly stroll right by them, their visors would immediately identify my face, and they'd be on my ass in seconds. I creep silently around the building, moving a couple of buildings down. I check the battery level on the external power source that Zeke put together for me. The screen reads ninety-five percent, which should last me about three and a half hours, assuming Zeke's estimate was correct. Honestly, I'm a little nervous, considering the hodge-podge nature of this battery. But he assured me it was fine, so...

You're overreacting. You're just nervous about seeing her.

After a few deep breaths to calm myself, I move as silently as I can across the street and into the alleyway across from me. I move with a combination of tip-toeing and full-on sprinting, a patented technique if I do say so myself. Luckily, the mindless goons don't seem to notice. They're too busy showing off their newest cybernetics to see much of anything. Now, it's just a matter of making my way around these buildings and over to the back entrance of The Museum. As I round the corner to the back entrance, I half expect to see another squad of Retribution troops waiting for me, arc rifles primed and ready to fry me to a crisp.

"Looks like it's my lucky day," I chuckle to myself as I knock on the back door of The Museum. A pair of stone-cold grey eyes peer through the sliding view box in the door.

"Password?" A gruff voice greets me, obviously refined through years of chain smoking.

"Creativity takes courage," I reply, reciting an old quote by Henri Matisse, which is a favorite of the classical art scene. Early twentieth-century art's been really hot lately, or so the posts on CYBRNet tell me. People used to say the quote means that it's brave to pursue art in a capitalist society. But now, well, you're hard-pressed to find someone willing to break the mold at all, to stand against CYBR Corp and their iron-tight chokehold on every aspect of life. Needless to say, that's what the quote means to me.

My answer is accepted with a grunt of approval, and the door is opened. As the heavy steel door slides open, I am greeted by a wave of nostalgia that nearly brings me to tears. The smell of a unique combination of sweat, alcohol, cigarettes, and spray-paint all flood into my nose while the flashing, strobing neon lights dance across my eyes. And most of all, the ear-splitting, bass-blasting, synth-electric punk band is throwing the whole club into a wild frenzy, moving in a chaotic symphony of jumps and head-bangs.

The holographic sign above them says "The Insurrection" in a font resembling claw marks on a brick wall. I recognize the name from the headlines. Everyone's been obsessed with them ever since their hit song "SLOBR Crap" came out a couple of years ago.

The song is a heavy-handed diss track aimed directly at the heads of CYBR Corp, and people cannot get enough of it. Honestly, I don't usually listen to this type of music, but their blatant fuck you attitude toward evil mega-corporations really clicks with me and everyone like me, living a sad, rejected life scraping the boots of the mega-rich elites running our lives.

I snap back to reality, remembering why I came here and the time limit I'm on. My eyes scan the crowd of thrashing bodies as I walk farther into the room.

And there, hanging toward the back of the room, is Astra Odelle. A purple-streaked, leather-clad angel gently bobbing her head to the beat as she sips her drink. The whole club scene never really was her thing, nor was it mine, but we could always enjoy anything as long as we did it together. She catches sight of me, her face lighting up into a broad smile, her teeth reflecting the strobing neon lights as she moves toward me.

As soon as she smiles at me, my heart tries to take an unsteady flight out of my chest. I walk over to her, every step faster than the last, until I'm basically running into her outstretched arms.

It's a warm embrace that I haven't felt in years, an embrace that takes me right back to five years ago and a time in my life that I desperately miss. A time when I was happy.

I want to tell her everything, anything, but the music is impossibly loud. Instead, we sway to the beat, holding each other close for what feels like an eternity. I can smell her perfume. It smells like a sweet rose, and it's the most beautiful smell I can imagine. Through the left leg of her jeans, I can feel her cybernetic leg shifting back and forth as we sway. Sometimes, I forget she even has it since it's such an impressive prosthetic. But of course, I could never really forget about it, no more than I can forget about my right arm.

She lost her leg at the same time I lost my arm. Almost seven years ago now, a building was bombed while we were inside. It was our favorite abandoned warehouse to hang out in. It was a place we could be alone, away from the incessant noise and lights of the city: the people, the cars, the ads blaring on every screen and every speaker. Life is so damn complicated, but when we were hiding away in a quiet, secluded place like that warehouse, it felt so much more manageable. Like I could breathe freely. I miss that feeling. To tell the truth, I can't think of a time I've felt that free in years...

Long story short, we never did find out who did it or why. The news barely reported on it, given how often something like that happens in this hellhole of a city. They said it was "likely an act of teenage rebellion." To be honest, it could've been. Who knows. I gave up long ago on trying to figure out what happened.

When the explosion went off, I barely had time to regain my senses before I realized that a massive steel beam was coming down on Astra. Without thinking, I dove toward her, determined to get her out of the way, regardless of what happened to me. I did my best to shove her out of the way, saving her life, but at the cost of her left leg and my right arm. We rushed to the hospital. Zeke drove us in his van since an ambulance is too expensive, not to mention they're reserved for the elite who can afford health insurance. Neither of us could afford the procedure, but we didn't care; we were going to bleed out if something wasn't done immediately. They ended up amputating my arm and her leg, fitting us with cybernetic replacements. All things considered, it could've been much worse, but having your arm crushed by a steel beam is a pain that sticks with you. On rare occasions, it feels like my arm is still there, still crushed and mangled, searing me with pain.

A change in the song snaps me back to the present moment as I notice Astra is looking right into my eyes. Before I know it, I'm blushing. I stare back into her eyes just as intently, overwhelmed with emotions. It's been a long time since I had any sort of contact with a person that didn't involve a fist flying into a face.

After a few minutes, we share a knowing glance and move through the crowd, making our way toward our favorite spot: the roof. We enter the stairwell through a small door in the corner, but not before shoving our way through throngs of drunk headbangers. At the base of the stairs, we find a group of people passing around some sort of stim and lying across the floor.

As we step over them to get to the stairs, one guy with sunken, glazed-over eyes offers us the stim. It's a half-filled vial of glowing blue liquid connected to a cable that's inserted into the CYBR Deck on the neck or arm. These types of drugs were developed by CYBR Corp, claiming to 'reduce cybernetic rejection side-effects.' Still, it quickly became apparent that they're nothing more than watered-down opioids that are injected directly into the cybernetic-blood interface, numbing people to the reality that these implants are slowly eating away at their bodies and minds.

To no one's surprise, people are highly addicted to them. We call them stim-heads.

I shake my head at the guy as I step over him, and he goes back to lying on the floor, staring blankly at the stairs above him.

We make it to the roof after ascending the ten flights of stairs, breaking through to what should be a starry night sky, but Nova City hasn't seen stars in years. Astra gives me a nod, and we make our way to the edge of the roof, sitting against an air conditioning unit and staring out over the bright, neon city below. On quiet nights like this one, the city actually looks sort of beautiful from up here.

I look over at Astra as she looks out over the city, the lights sending colorful shadows across her face. I notice, only now, that she looks tired. Really tired. Sometimes I forget that everyone in this city has to deal with the nonstop bullshit and oppression of CYBR Corp. Not even someone as kind as Astra can escape their clutches.

"So, Ash...how have you been, really?" I ask timidly, finding it impossible not to wonder if she's been staying out of trouble or not. In a city like this, it's much more common to stay in trouble than out of it. Career criminals are the new working class, or so they say.

"I...I've definitely been better, *Oliver*." The cold *Oliver* strikes me hard. She didn't say it was my fault. She didn't have to. "I want you to know that I gave it some thought last night, and I've chosen to forgive you. I want us to be able to move forward. Honestly, most of my problems are because of those damn CYBR bastards, but I don't have to tell *you* that." She says that last bit with a forced chuckle, and I join in, nodding my head.

I don't know what to say, so I sit in silence for a couple of moments, listening to the bustle of Nova City and watching the last bit of natural light disappear behind the horizon. Finally, I decide to say what I need to say.

"Hey Ash, you may not blame me for what happened, but I do. And before you argue with me, just hear me out. I need you to know how truly sorry I am for what happened between us, for not contacting you sooner, for not dealing with it properly, for…everything." I pause, trying to figure out her reaction. She shifts her head, allowing the city's neon lights to shine upon the tears forming in her eyes.

"I want you to know," I say, gently grasping her hand, "that no matter how difficult it is, no matter if things go back to the way they were between us or if we're just friends, I want you in my life." My voice cracks as I say those last few words, and tears are forming in my own eyes now, but I don't bother wiping them away. "This world we live in is so full of hate, so full of pain, suffering, and loss. I've lost so much because of this damned city, and I was a fool to let myself lose you, too."

At this point, tears are streaming down both of our cheeks, like little neon raindrops sliding down my apartment window on all of those sleepless nights. Astra is quiet for a few minutes, then she responds with a five-word question, a question that shakes me to my core:

"How can I trust you?" Her voice is shaking. She sounds hopeful yet unwilling to trust the words I'm saying to her. It would be a lie to say that her mistrust is unwarranted. After all, a person's 'word' isn't worth much in this city, and more importantly, I've let her down before.

"I...guess you can't really. To be honest, I wouldn't trust me either. Whatever you want to do, I will respect that. I know it doesn't mean much, but I swear I meant everything I just said to you more than I've meant anything in years. Why else would I be a blubbering mess like this?" I gesture to the tears running down my face, my voice shaking uncontrollably. Her face seems to soften slightly as she nods, tears still streaming down her face.

"But hey, tell you what, you did agree to help me steal that fusion core, so how about we just see what happens between now and then?" I figure we could both use a distraction and working together on this might bring us closer together.

Her expression lightens, a hint of a smile cracking across her lips. "You always were a smooth talker, Oliver Wolf. You've got yourself a deal." She holds out her hand for a handshake, but as I move to accept it, she pulls her hand back and says, "But, if you push me out of your life like you did last time, you're gonna wish the Retribution were all you had to deal with."

I'm trying to decide if she's joking or not, but knowing her, she's simultaneously joking and dead serious. I grasp her hand firmly in a handshake, staring deeply into the hazel of her eyes as we share a hearty laugh. For only a moment, the tiredness lifts from her face, and the Astra I once knew returns. She's *so* beautiful.

After a few quiet moments, I lean back against the AC unit. The beeping of my portable battery rudely snaps me back into reality. Fifty percent remaining. Looks like this battery doesn't quite have the amount of juice that Zeke thought it did.

"Shit!" I exclaim.

"What is it?" Astra looks concernedly over to me.

"It's this battery. It's running out too fast. I only have

about an hour of charge remaining, then it's down to my internal battery that's been fried to about thirty minutes of charge!"

"Shit!" Astra echoes me.

"Well, I better tell you the plan then while I still can. Dex is going to get his inside guy to put you on the 'Friends of CYBR Corp' list, or as I like to call it, the FOCC list..." I pause and give her a cheesy smile, earning a chuckle from Astra before she slaps my arm.

"Olly! Focus!"

"Right, right. Sorry. So, you'll be our decoy, posing as a buyer of the fusion power cell. Once you get the manager of the CYBRnetics Outlet out in the open, and they're showing you the power cell, that's when we spring into action. I'll wear an obscurer and wait just outside of the Outlet while Dex triggers a blackout of their lights and security cameras. Once it's lights out, you distract the Outlet workers and guards by causing one of your famous Astra dramas while I come in and snatch the power cell. If anything goes wrong, I'll be armed." I say that last bit with a self-confident smirk.

"Sounds simple enough. Let's just hope you don't have to fight anyone in your condition," she gestures to my battery pack, "or things might get ugly. Also, don't think I didn't notice that comment about famous Astra dramas. Nice try there, wolf-boy."

I chuckle, then shrug off her comment, saying, "we both know you're more than capable of kicking some CYBR Corp ass yourself."

"I may be a little rusty, but I guess you're right." Astra agrees reluctantly, grinning.

She never really got into the fights or anything like I did, but I taught her how to defend herself with martial arts, and she's damn good at it. She can pretend like she isn't excited about kicking some CYBR Corp ass, but we both know she's just as ready as I am to teach those bastards a lesson.

I check the portable battery, and it's at forty-five percent. "Well, I'll see you when I see you. Keep an eye on your 'comm. I'll keep you posted on updates to the plan."

"Sounds good, Olly."

I go to stand up and leave, but as I begin standing, Astra suddenly grabs my wrist. The suddenness leaves me stuck in place, dumbfounded. Then, she does something really unexpected: Astra pulls me down toward her, staring into my eyes for a moment, and then she kisses me, flipping my world on its head and sending my heart into a frenzy. It's a single, meaningful kiss, and then she pushes me away gently.

"Now get out of here before your battery dies. I am NOT going to carry you back to wherever you live right now." She laughs, and I join in, a big, dumb smile crossing my face.

"See you around, Ash."

I stare for one more moment before heading back to the stairwell, each second stretching into eternity as I try to permanently imprint her face into my brain. I start planning my route in my head as I walk across the roof. I'll make my way down to the bottom floor of The Museum, avoid the Retribution troops on my way out, and head back to the bunker as quickly as possible. If I get caught out on the street with a dead battery, I could be picked up by the Retribution and tortured or sold to a scrap shop for parts. Either way, I'd like to avoid that at all costs.

I glance at my battery one more time and audibly gasp. The small digital display shows a thirty percent charge. At this rate, I won't even make it halfway back to the bunker before I collapse from lack of power.

"Shit, I gotta run!" I exclaim, running toward the stairs. I barrel down the stairs three at a time, my feet barely touching the ground before leaving again. I jump over the junkies in the stairwell, noticing the one who offered us the drugs now holding the empty syringe, lying eerily still.

I make my way through the drunken throng of ravers, weaving in and out of headbangers and couples making out, finally reaching the door and breaking through to the street. After that, I break into a full sprint between the lines of buildings, avoiding the Retribution troops from earlier. In spite of my situation, I can't help but smile as those last few moments replay in my mind over and over again. The image of Astra smiling at me, the feeling of kissing her again after all this time…

Fifteen minutes of sprinting later, I have to take a break. My legs are on fire, and so are my lungs. I nervously check the battery, my hot breath fogging the screen. It reads a shocking one percent. I'm on internal battery now, which means I have approximately thirty minutes until I collapse in the street, and there is no way I'm going to stop at a charging station. As a high-tier public enemy, using such a public facility wouldn't be the best idea, to say the least.

After briefly catching my breath, I take off again, admittedly at a slower pace than before, but still determined to make it home on time. Just in case, I shoot Zeke a message letting him know I might not make it back and ask him to come looking for me if I'm not back in thirty minutes.

Twenty-nine minutes and thirty seconds later, I collapse on the floor of Zeke's workshop in the bunker. The last thing I see is Zeke's dirty grey tennis shoes walking toward me, a faint "you dumbass" echoing in the corners of my mind as I pass out.

CH 6

SOUNDS of frantic clanging bring me to a rude awakening. After taking a groggy moment to look around, I realize the clanging is Zeke trying to prepare for our heist. I completely forgot that the big day is only two days away.

My senses start to come back to me as I take a closer look around. I'm hooked to a cyber-physical hybrid life-support system, generally known as a Terminal. The screen provides a constant stream of information on my heart rate, blood pressure, cybernetic power continuity, and the works. As far as I can tell, the readings are fine, but my battery is obviously not good in terms of capacity. Zeke's patched me up enough times for me to know the medical readings well. A little too well, if you ask me. I watch my heart monitor for a while, contemplating how long that consistent thump will continue.

"Welcome, Oliver Wolf, to hell." Zeke gives me a cheeky smirk as he says, "I'll be your guide. Feel free to call me Charon." He breaks into a hearty chuckle as he turns back to the piece of equipment he was working on.

I can't help but burst out laughing at the thought of Zeke as the somber ferryman of hell's gates. It's almost...too fitting.

"Well, *Charon*, if this is hell, then where's the founder of CYBR Corp?" I reply with a sly grin. "Anyway, thank you. As always, I owe you one."

"One!? You know damn well you owe me closer to one hundred!" Zeke quips back. And he's right, of course.

"So...what's my battery life lookin' like?" I ask nervously, very afraid of the answer.

"I think you already know what I'm about to say, but it's not good," he gives me a grimace of a smile and says, "Your internal battery is close to twenty minutes of charge, and apparently, this external battery is complete shit." His face looks even more tired than usual.

"Can we make it work long enough to pull this off? We shouldn't need more than an hour." I ask.

"That's the plan, but I honestly don't know at this point. We're gonna be pushin' it, but we really can't do this without you. You're the muscle, after all." Zeke gives me a genuine smile, and I feel myself relax for a moment.

"Thanks, Zeke, I'll try not to let everyone down on this. With any luck, I won't even need to fight anyone, anyway." My attempt to ease the tension is met with a full belly laughing fit from Zeke, so I guess my attempt worked, even if it was at my own expense.

After calming down, Zeke goes back to work on fixing the portable battery and preparing everything for our heist. As he turns to head back to his workbench, he says simply, "if we had any luck, we wouldn't be in this mess, Olly."

"You're right as always, Zeke-erino."

With that cheesy remark, I slowly rise from the cot and make my way to my room. I feel surprisingly okay, all things considered. Maybe it's just residual adrenaline from last night, meeting with Ash, or maybe Zeke's just really good at his job. Either way, I'm thankful I don't feel too terrible. I flip on the lights as I enter my room, booting up my Cerulean tablet while I'm at it. The cheerful chime sounds off, and the holographic display fills the room with a cool blue light.

"Hey Cerulean, show me local news headlines," I pause, thinking, "and cross-reference the search with my name."

"Alright, Oliver, I found three matches for your search," Cerulean replies, a little too cheerfully, given the

circumstances.

Tapping my finger against the link shown in the hologram, I pull up the first article. It's from the city's largest and most corrupt news site, the Nova Times. The headline reads, "Mass Murderer Oliver Wolf wanted for crimes against Nova City and CYBR Corp."

Great. Let's see what they have to say.

Quickly skimming the article brings to my attention that I'm apparently wanted for a number of crimes, including murder, treason, theft, resisting arrest, jaywalking...the list goes on and on. There's not much information other than my list of crimes I'm wanted for and a bunch of egregious bullshit about needing more funding for the police, but there is a brief interview with a detective named Megan Maxwell. Her name sounds relatively familiar. She's probably some sort of bigwig with the NCPD. In short, the detective seems to think that I'm the worst thing to happen to this city in years. According to the article, the NCPD is hot on my trail, but I find that hard to believe. The cops are constantly blowing hot smoke out of their various orifices, acting like the real criminals aren't the ones who're running this damned city, the ones bribing them to turn a blind eye to their bullshit.

"Ok, Cerulean, open the second article."

"Coming right up!"

Next up is an article from Fight Fax, a cheesy and over-the-top magazine reporting on everything relating to the underground fights in Ritorujapan. I used to scan its pages religiously, looking for any clues about my upcoming opponents or which fights to bet on to make a quick Johnny. I was addicted, frankly, but let's just say updating my email newsletter subscriptions isn't at the top of my to-do list. Anyway, this article is a minor section of the mag titled "Where is the Wolf? Did He Turn Chicken?" It's a short piece, only a couple of paragraphs long, but apparently, my absence from the MMA scene has not gone unnoticed. They're claiming my last defeat was too embarrassing and that I must've finally come to my senses and quit the scene. Not gonna lie; it makes me pretty pissed that this is all I get after four grueling years dedicated to the fights. It's not like I lost all my fights. In fact, I had a pretty decent win percentage, given my more "natural" approach. Well, whatever. They can think whatever they want about me. Little do they know I finally respect myself enough to be doing something meaningful with my life rather than taking a beating for the entertainment of rich assholes. We'll see who's laughing when I take down CYBR Corp. Now those'll be headlines worth reading!

"Alright, Cerulean, next?"

"Here is the final article."

The third article is from a small but top-rated news site called the CYBR Wyre, which is known for reporting the hottest leaked secrets from within CYBR Corp. No one knows who runs the site or how they get their information, but it's almost always accurate. This article is titled "Oliver Wolf, CYBR enemy No. 1?" which makes my stomach drop through the floor.

This article is written, much like all CYBR Wyre articles, in a peppy and slightly unprofessional manner. According to this article, CYBR Corp leadership is "totally pissed off at some guy named Oliver Wolf, who apparently used to kick some serious ass in those fighting rings in Ritorujapan!" I do appreciate that last comment, especially after that previous article. It goes on to say, "My little birdies have informed me that Mr. Wolf is high on the list of CYBR Corp's enemies. No idea what the poor guy did, but he is TOAST. Apparently, Retribution troops stormed his apartment and destroyed the place looking for him, but he wasn't home. They're not sure where he went, but they know he met someone at The Museum club downtown."

"Shit! Astra!" I jump up, fear filling my body and my heart pounding. I burst through the door, running through the bunker hallway to find Zeke.

"Whoa! What the hell bit you?" Zeke's face is filled with concern and confusion.

"It's Astra!" I shout, barely catching my breath. "She could be in trouble!"

"What are you talking about? What gave you that idea?" Zeke replies, trying to remain calm. Dex comes in from the computer room to see what's going on.

"I decided to look at local news, and they've been searching for me! Obviously, I knew that, but they knew I went to The Museum the other night to see Astra..." I pause, "well, they don't necessarily know I went to see her, but they know I went. It's only a matter of time before they figure out who I would meet there." My heartbeat has only increased in speed, terrible thoughts filling my mind.

"Shit!" Zeke responds.

"Have you tried calling her?" Dex asks, acting as the voice of reason.

"Oh, duh," I say, slapping my forehead. "Cerulean, call Astra," I command to my Holocomm.

"*Calling Astra Odelle...*" Cerulean replies. The Holocomm rings with its classic electronic phone sound, mimicking what old smartphones used to sound like. Each passing second of the phone ringing raises my heart rate significantly until I'm about to hit cancel on the call. It's at that moment that Astra's face flickers to life on the holo-projection.

"Astra! Oh my god! Are you okay? Are you in danger?" I can hardly control myself. I'm so scared and relieved.

"Yeah, what are you even talking about, Olly? Are you okay? You look...sweaty." Through the detailed projection, I can clearly see the concern filling her face as she furrows her brow. I am, in fact, sweating bullets. I hadn't even noticed before.

"Well, I'm sorry to scare you, but the Retribution may be after you, Ash."

"Well, I knew this was coming sooner or later, but god damn it, Oliver! What did you do this time?" She really doesn't seem that surprised, but I guess I can't blame her.

"Ok, so I read an article talking about how I'm wanted by the law. No surprise there. But then they went on to mention that I met someone at The Museum! They apparently don't know who I was meeting there, but they're inevitably going to figure it out. I was afraid it might be too late…" I trail off, my adrenaline beginning to fade as I realize I may have overreacted.

"I guess that makes sense. I'm sorry I yelled at you." Astra's face softens along with mine, and I can feel the weight begin to lift from my chest. "But if you're right, I *am* in danger."

"Yeah…I know. So, you need to come and stay here with us. There's no way to keep you safe anymore except to have you right here with us." I was really hoping to keep Ash out of this, to keep her anonymous so they couldn't trace her back to me. I was an idiot, as usual.

"For once, I agree with you." Zeke chimes in.

"Same here." Dex nods in approval.

"Alright, I agree, but how do I get to you safely? And where even *are* you, anyway?" Astra asks, her voice rising in both pitch and volume. I can tell she's getting worried, but who could blame her?

"It's okay, we can do this. We're at the old bunker, the one Zeke and I used to come hang out in. I gave you the address back at the grocery store. Do you remember how to get to the entrance?" I ask, trying to provide comfort. There's a bit of a trick to finding the entrance, which is why it's such a good hiding place.

"Yeah, I remember. Any tips on getting there unnoticed? We're not all silent ninjas, you know." She quips.

"That is the ultimate question," I nod, "but I've done it a few times now without being noticed all that much, and they already know who I am and what I look like." I pause to check Ash's face. She seems to be leery but listening. "The trick is to keep to the sketchiest back streets you can while making your way through the city center. Obviously, that brings its own issues, but I know you can handle some shady backstreet characters. Once you start to reach the outskirts, just move quickly and stay alert until you reach the bunker. There's very little security as you get closer."

"Got it, thanks, Olly. I'll move out ASAP. It's just..." she pauses, looking around, her voice falling to a hushed whisper, "I gotta go, there's someone—"

"Ash! Astra!" I called out, but the holo-call has already been terminated. Once again, I'm filled with nothing but fear and worry for Astra's safety.

"Damn, I hope she makes it here in one piece." Dex looks genuinely concerned. He really is a kind soul. After all, he doesn't even know Astra. But I guess he probably feels like all of this is his fault anyway, something I can completely understand.

I don't respond. I just keep hitting the button repeatedly to call Astra back. It's not going through and just keeps hitting a dead line beep. Four calls, no answer. I'm feeling terrified now, my heartrate rising once again. I try it a fifth time, vowing to myself that if it doesn't work this time, I'm going to get her myself.

"Oliver, maybe she's not—" Zeke begins.

"Not what!?" I shout back, not willing to believe what I know he's about to say. He doesn't answer. Instead, he just gives me a grimace.

The Holocomm rings on my wrist over and over, each consecutive ring filling me with more despair. But then, the impossible happens.

"Oliver! What the hell!" Astra is shouting in whispers at me. It looks like she's hiding from something or someone. The Retribution clearly came to find her.

I whisper back, "where are you? Did you get away from your apartment? If we need to come fight our way over to you, just say the word."

Astra rolls her eyes and says quietly but assertively, "No, Olly, I appreciate your willingness to be my white knight, but I can handle myself. It's not worth you exposing yourself and getting captured or killed just for me. You understand me?"

Wow, she really can be scary when she's angry. I haven't seen that level of intensity in her eyes in years, ever since I told her I needed my space from her, from everything. But of course, I know she's also worried about me and my safety. She knows how much all of this means to me. Hidden in the intensity in her eyes is a deeper level of sadness and concern. I stare into her eyes for a full minute before realizing I should be saying something.

"You got it, Ash...but if you don't make it back here in one piece, you'll never hear the end of it!" I quip back, jokingly. This earns a small chuckle from Zeke. "Anyway, you know how to get here, right?"

"Don't worry, you'll see me before you know it," Ash reassures me with a small smile. The bluish projection of Astra's face flickers out as the call is disconnected.

"Astra has terminated the call, Oliver." Cerulean reports.

We all stand in silence for a few somber moments, all too aware of the gravity of this situation.

After a few quiet minutes of checking my Holocomm, Zeke turns to me and places a hand on my shoulder:

"She'll make it here, Oliver. You know she would never give up. Why do you think you two were so good together? You're both stubborn as hell!"

"Thanks, Zeke. I just hope you're right," I reply with a defeated sigh.

"You and me both," Zeke replies, matching my tone.

With that, I head back to my room, switch everything off, and lie there staring at the ceiling. It's only 21:00, but what else am I going to do? The only light in the room is a soft glow from a safety light above the door. After several minutes of blank, thoughtless staring, the low-power indicator on my internal battery blinks in my arm, briefly filling the room with a dim red light each time it flashes. I plug myself into the wall socket, connecting the threaded power cable to the charging port in my right shoulder. It snaps into place with a soft click.

As I lie in bed, the only thing I can think about is the possibility that I may never see Astra again. There are so many things I still want to say, so many years spent apart that I need to set right. She means more to me than anything or anyone ever has, and I just finally got her back in my life.

I am not about to lose her now.

I decide it would help calm me down if I waited closer to the bunker's entrance, so I head to sit on a couch near the entryway, plugging myself into the nearby socket. As I wait, I try to keep my mind off of the obvious issue at hand by mindlessly browsing the listings for various cybernetics around the City. Apparently, there's a new type of memory enhancement chip that supposedly cures memory loss and significantly slows mental deterioration. Excellent, it's the year 2060, and we have just now finally cured Alzheimer's Disease. Or so they say. I find it hard to believe any of the BS that CYBR Corp or any of their partner companies put out into the world.

As much as I enjoy sitting and thinking about how

thoroughly CYBR Corp has screwed over this world, it still can't distract me from the deep, unsettling pit forming in my stomach. It's already been twenty agonizing minutes. Based on where Astra lives and how long it usually takes me to make that trek on foot, she should be here in the next ten minutes. Five minutes pass, no sign of her. Zeke comes over, quietly sitting next to me. There's worry filling his face, too, even if he is trying to hide it. Five more minutes, she's pushing it.

"It's now or never," I mutter under my breath, not realizing I said it out loud.

"Don't say that, Oliver. She'll make it." Zeke replies.

"I really hope you're right," I respond, staring at the bunker door. Time continues to pass, each second eating away at me. I stare down at my right hand, watching the joints open and contract as I clench my metal hand repeatedly. It's something I do when I'm nervous, usually subconsciously, like it is now.

Astra is five minutes late now, and I am pacing the floor frantically, stopping each time as I reach the end of my charging cable. It's all I can do not to rip this cable out of my shoulder and run out that door, risking my own life to find her. The only reason I'm staying put is that she made me promise not to come looking for her. She said she could make it on her own...I really hope she was right.

Another five minutes pass, and at this point, I'm punching the wall to distract myself. I sit back down on the couch, feeling defeated, only to stand right back up as I hear a knock at the door. Either Astra is here, or the Retribution tracked us down. Either way, I've already disconnected my power cable and opened the door before anyone can say a word to stop me. I fumble hurriedly with the three locks, turn the handle, and fling the door open wide, staring straight into the most beautiful pair of hazel eyes I've ever seen. It's Astra.

She's alive. I pull her in through the door, close it quickly, and pull her into a very tight hug. She hugs me back, and I can tell she's breathing heavily. She was running.

I step back from the hug, my sense of danger rising.

"Were you followed? Did they see you? Why are you so out of breath? Are you alright?" A string of questions flies from my mouth before I have the chance to think about what I'm saying.

After a few moments of catching her breath, she responds. "It's okay, Oliver. I'm okay. The reason I'm out of breath is that I ran the last few blocks here, but just because I was getting anxious about you coming out to find me! From the look of you, it seems like I had the right idea." She pauses for a moment, apparently noticing that I had begun to guiltily stare down at my shoes, grabbing hold of my chin and bringing my eyes up to meet hers. "Everything is okay, I promise."

For the first time today, I begin to relax. I smile at Astra, saying, "I'm so glad to hear that and to see you. Sorry I got so worked up there, I just was getting so worried, Ash..." I trail off as I realize Zeke and Dex are watching us, suddenly feeling very embarrassed for how I've been acting. "Well, anyway, let me show you to your room. We should all get some sleep. In two days, we run this heist, and I, for one, am exhausted." I try to play it cool, but I doubt it works in the slightest.

"Good idea, Olly," Zeke replies, "we need everyone to be at their best if we have any chance of this going well. We've still got a lotta preparation to do." He pauses. "And Astra, for the record, it's damn good to see you." They exchange a tired smile and nod, and with that, Zeke and Dex head off to their respective rooms in the left-hand hallway.

"Alright, let's get you to your room," I say, acting as calm and collected as I can.

"Lead the way!" Astra responds, seemingly also trying to play it cool.

We really are quite a pair.

I stop to make sure that the bunker door's locked up tight, then lead Astra down the right-hand hallway, past my room, and to the last room in the bunker. Zeke or Dex must have already made up the room since there are sheets and a pillow on the bed.

I step back and give a dramatic bow, saying, "Your suite awaits, madam!"

"Why thank you, sir!" Astra plays along, both of us sharing a genuine smile and a chuckle.

"I'm in the next room right over here, so just come knock if you need anything, anything at all," I say with all of the energy I have left, which isn't much. It's just hitting me how tired I truly am, with the adrenaline draining from my body.

I make my way out of her room and over to mine, closing my door almost all the way so there's just a crack, hopefully letting her know I don't mind if she comes in. I change into some sweatpants and a t-shirt, plug myself back into the wall socket by the bed, and try my best to fall asleep. It isn't easy, with my mind racing as fast as it is, but eventually, I fall into an uneasy slumber.

***

The next day, I'm woken by a frantic Zeke, who's running around like a chicken with his head cut off, trying to get everything ready for the heist. I can hear him shouting something unintelligible as he runs past the common area. My Holocomm reads 06:00, which, for the record, is an absurd time to be awake. I throw on some comfortable clothes and stumble out to join him.

I feel very groggy and really want some caffeine, but when I walk to the small kitchen area adjacent to the entryway, it looks like no one's heated water for coffee or anything. I don't feel very inclined to be the person to do so, so no coffee it is.

As I'm contemplating the speckling of the cheap countertop, Ash walks up to join me. She looks just as tired as I do and is also comfortably dressed. I give her a half-hearted wave, smile, and gesture for her to follow me. We head past the kitchen on the left and back through the hallway that leads to the workshop area.

"Come on, let's help Zeke before he loses the few marbles he has left."

"Alright," she pauses to yawn, which makes me yawn, "let's do this thing."

We walk through the dimly-lit metal and concrete hallway, emerging through the entryway on the right-hand side of the end of the hallway. There, I see Zeke staring intently at a three-dimensional projected map of the area surrounding the CYBRnetics Outlet. He's chewing on the end of a stylus pen for the tablet he's using.

"You know you're not supposed to do that," I say, mimicking his chewing stance.

"Well, maybe if my best bud wasn't roping me into an insane scheme, I wouldn't feel the need to chew on a pen." He retorts.

"Fair enough, man. Fair enough."

"What do we still need to do to prepare?" Ash chimes in.

"Not too much. Thanks to Dex's knowledge of the system, we've added you to their FOCC list. We've also set up a meeting time between you and the CYBRnetics Outlet's manager, who believes you're a high-roller looking to buy the fusion power cell. All that's left is to polish the edges of our contingency plan, as well as one other thing Dex suggested. But first, let's talk contingencies." He gestures to the map floating in 3D space in front of us.

"Where is Dex, anyway?" I ask, glancing around. I haven't seen him today.

"Oh, he's netrunning," Zeke replies, hooking a thumb in the direction of the adjacent room, Dex's workshop. "He's checking every radio wave, making sure this deal isn't compromised and we aren't doomed before we even start. Just casual stuff."

"Right, just chilling, basically," I smirk.

We both turn to the holographic map. Holograms are tinted with a blue hue, but other than that, we're looking at an impressive rendering of the street corner.

"So, we're going to put the van here, right Zeke?" I ask, pointing to a side alley within view of the store but out of sight from their cameras and guards. I remember Dex mentioning it a few days ago.

"Right, that's where you and Dex will be since both of you are actively wanted, and there's no way you won't get recognized." He then pauses, looking more nervous than before. It quickly dawns on me why.

"Oh, so that leaves you to join Ash in the field? Aren't you also a wanted man?" I reply, my concernedness adding a bite to my words that I didn't intend.

"I understand your concern, but yes, I'm afraid it has to be this way. I hate doin' this risky shit, you know that. But I was mulling it over, checkin' the headlines, and they aren't necessarily lookin' for me. They know you two disappeared from my shop, but for all they know, I was just doin' my job, right? Plus, I'll wear a disguise." He gestures to a facemask, sunglasses, and ball cap lying on the table. "I don't know, man, I just don't think it's safe to send Ash in alone, and I got nothin' better. And besides, how do we even know Ash is still uncompromised? They found her apartment, after all." He looks a bit defeated.

"I'm *not* compromised," Ash interjects confidently. "They don't have me listed on any wanted lists. I checked last night, while I couldn't sleep. They may have been looking for me, but it seems like it's on the lowdown. Chances are the local store staff isn't queued into it." She speaks in a reassuring tone, trying to cheer up Zeke. I'm also happy to hear it.

"Okay, yeah! Zeke, it'll be alright. She's not officially wanted; you'll hang back and wear a disguise, and there's no reason they should be looking at either of you long enough for it to possibly be a problem. Just get in, make the purchase, and get the fuck out." I join in, trying to add to the positivity. I'm hyping myself up as much as Zeke, to be honest. Regardless of how good this plan is, it's going to be our only one.

"Alright, you're right." He doesn't seem terribly convinced, but I can tell he's trying to put on a brave face. "In that case, it'll be Astra and I acting as 'business partners' while you two watch and listen from the van." He does air quotes as he says business partners.

"Sounds good, and if anything goes wrong, I'll be ready to get in there and get you out. And remember, aside from your own safety," I glance at each of them, "the most important thing is to get that fusion cell, no matter what. I'm on borrowed time until that thing is ours."

Ash and Zeke nod solemnly. They seem to both be lost in thought.

"So, what was the other item you wanted to discuss? You said Dex had an idea?" I ask, changing the topic.

"Right, thanks for reminding me," Zeke says, pointing enthusiastically at me like I gave the correct answer in math class. "So we're doing this, ultimately, to take down CYBR Corp, right?"

"Right," I reply.

"That was rhetorical, but thank you."

"You're welcome."

"The thank you was also rhetorical."

I scowl at Zeke, once again defeated in a battle of snark.

"So...taking down CYBR Corp..?" Ash chimes in, snapping us out of our brotherly squabbling.

"Yes, so I don't know about you guys," Zeke continues, "but I feel like if we're gonna have any chance of making a legitimate, long-lasting change by either taking down CYBR Corp or restructuring it under more *friendly* management or what have you, we're gonna need some leverage and a solid backup plan."

"That's a fair point," I reply, the scope of our goal seeming much more daunting, "so how do we do that?"

"With cold, hard facts and just a touch of sensationalism," Zeke says, smiling triumphantly.

"Right, meaning?" Ash asks.

"Meaning, while we're stealing this fancy-ass battery for Olly, we also steal some data from their internal servers. We, or I should say Dex, can use that data as proof of the terrible shit CYBR Corp is doing. We get leverage against them, and then it's just a matter of using it."

"I'm impressed. Dex really cooked up a plan." I reply, nodding. "So, what do we do with the dirt we dig up? And, for that matter, what kinda dirt are we talking about?"

"Honest, I got no clue what sorta dirt we're lookin' for, but there's no way we won't find some seriously heinous shit from even the most mundane of CYBR Corp hard drives. As for the plan, he thinks one of us should make a broadcast," Zeke explains, "we'd have to hack into the CYBR Corp network from the inside, which isn't exactly my idea of fun. However, it'd give us a chance to play a recorded speech laying it all out there: who we are, what we're trying to accomplish, and, most importantly, why CYBR Corp deserves to be burned down in a fiery storm of hatred from all those oppressed and abandoned by them. All while displaying the stolen footage and data for all the world to see, the data ripped directly from their own system, proving we're right. And when people see that, they'll be hard-pressed not to join the revolution."

"That's awesome. Then we'd actually get some help with this thing. We can only get so far with the four of us." Ash replies, excitement filling her face.

"I agree, that's such a good idea! So, I'm guessing we'll use Ash's Holo to swipe some data while she's making the deal? And Dex probably has some sort of virus ready to go?" I ask, grinning at the idea of increasing the fuck-you factor of this heist.

"Yup, he's got it all ready to go." Zeke smiles back at us.

"Fuck yeah!" Ash exclaims, pumping her fist in the air.

I nod and smile, buzzing with the excitement of working with my best friends to stick it to the man.

Man, it's just like old times. I really fucking missed this.

It occurs to me that I haven't actually spent any meaningful amount of time talking to either of them in, well, years. Sure, I've seen Zeke for tune-ups and casual chat, but I closed myself off from him pretty hard right around the same time I broke up with Ash. I feel so stupid remembering all that. I really don't know how I thought it was the best thing to do. I can feel the shame burning in my cheeks.

"Hey, Olly, are you alright?" Ash is looking at me, concerned.

How am I so bad at hiding my emotions? Or is she just that good at reading me? I'm gonna go with both.

"Yeah, I'm…well, no, actually I'm not. It's just I feel so bad for pushing you both away for so long. I feel like I missed so much time with the two people who were closest to me, the two people I cared, no, *care* the most about. Do you think, I know we have shit to plan, but like, do you think maybe we can just talk for a minute about how the past few years have been? I'd really like to." My eyes are starting to well up with tears, but I blink them away.

Ash looks at me with a melancholic understanding in her eyes and nods. We both turn to look at Zeke.

"Okay, yeah. I'm glad you asked, Ol'." His stressed expression has been replaced with a look very similar to Ash's, his demeanor softening.

Without a word, we walk through the hallway back to the common space and sit on the old couch together. I sit in the middle, with Zeke on my right and Ash on my left. This is where Zeke and I used to play video games for hours on end back in the day. The old TV is even still hooked up. It's like nothing has changed, but of course everything has.

I really miss that...

"So, what did you want to talk about?" Ash asks me, breaking the awkward silence.

"Well, I guess I just wanted to talk about how things have been over the past few years, since I, since we, well, you know..."

Come on, Oliver, you can do this.

"I guess what I'm trying to say is I'm sorry for being such an ass and for pushing you both away. And I'm sorry for not reaching out for so long. Zeke, we've seen each other, but I feel like I haven't actually talked to you in years. And Ash, well, before our meeting at The Museum, we hadn't really talked for...years. And it's all my fault. You two were the most important people in my life, and I pushed you both away. But, well, I don't know. I was so scared...so scared that you both would be taken away by CYBR Corp, just like Miles..." The words stop coming, and my throat feels dry. I can feel tears forming in my eyes.

But I can't think about that now. My brother wouldn't want me crying about him at this moment. He'd want me to move on and be happy. So, right now, I just want to talk to my friends, who are looking at me with tears forming in their concerned eyes right now. I clear my throat and wipe my eyes.

"Sorry, anyway, I'd like to tell you both about how my last three years have been. So, ok, I'll start… So, after everything, well, after I shut myself off from the world, I fell into a deep depression, almost as deep if not deeper than when Miles died. I just felt like everything was hopeless, like…I don't know. Nothing felt worth it. I wasn't working, I wasn't making money, just draining my savings month to month. I spent most of it on stims just to take the edge off. When I wasn't high, I wondered if it was all worth it, but even ending it all seemed like more trouble than it was worth. I kept having to move into shittier and shittier apartments. I had a roommate for a few months, but he would always conveniently 'forget' his Johnnies for rent until one day, he straight up stole nearly everything of mine he could pawn off, including the stims. All I had left was my daishō since I locked it up."

"Wow, that really fuckin' sucks. I'm sorry to hear that, man," Zeke says. He places a hand on my shoulder.

"Yeah, thanks, it's all in the past now, so it's whatever. But I guess I owe him thanks to some degree because, at that point, something changed for me. I was still depressed, but I realized I was tired of letting life push me around. I quit stims, and I vowed to never do them again. I started training in Kung Fu again, just practicing on my own for a month or two while going out every night to watch the fights in Ritorujapan. I joined my first fight about two years ago and got my ass handed to me by a super-modded guy. That turned my depression into rage, and I vowed to prove that I could win those damn fights, just me, with my minor cybernetics and martial arts training."

"Uh-huh, and that's where I come in," Zeke comments.

"Yep. I trained even harder and, as Zeke knows, started to push myself too hard. I kept entering fights, and I actually won some of them. I lost way more of them, though. Zeke kept having to fix me up. But I made enough money to get a relatively alright apartment and buy back some of my tech that guy stole from me, so it was alright, I guess. It gave me a reason to get up every day, and that's all I needed, or so I thought. Then everything changed when I helped Zeke save Dex from the Retribution, and when…when I saw you again, Ash. I realized how dumb I was to isolate myself and that what I really needed all along was someone, or a couple of someones, to help me through it all. And I hope it's okay if I think of you both as friends again…I know I fucked up pretty bad, and it took me way too long to figure it out, but I miss you both, and I want to be there for you, and I hope you'll be there for me, too."

Tears are fully streaming down my face now, but I make no effort to stop them. I feel *happy*. I feel so much lighter than before, like a weight's been lifted from my chest. I didn't even know I was holding onto some of this, but now that it's out, I realize it's been weighing on me for years.

"Olly, of *course* we're your friends, and in case you didn't notice, we *are* here for you. We're in this thing together now, and nothing can change that." Ash says, taking my hand and gently squeezing it.

She's smiling at me, and there's sadness and understanding in her eyes. It makes me cry even more.

"Yeah, look, man, I don't know what you think the deal is here, but I never stopped being your friend. Or did you forget who fixed up your dumbass every time you did one of those fights?" Zeke chuckles, his eyes wet with tears, too. "But really, you're my bro, my best friend, and nothing was ever going to change that. I just knew that you needed to go through some stuff on your own. It's all in the past, and I forgive you."

"We both forgive you," Ash adds.

"Thanks, you guys…that means so much to me." I'm

smiling and can barely see through the tears, but I don't care. I feel so warm inside. I haven't been this happy in so long. I pull them both into a tight hug, and we all cry softly for a moment, holding each other tightly.

Thank you, guys, I don't know what I did to deserve such amazing people in my life.

After a few moments, we all pull away, wiping our eyes on our sleeves and sniffling slightly. And, most importantly, sharing a gentle smile of understanding.

"Now, if you're interested, I can tell you about what's been goin' on with me," Zeke says, seemingly trying to act casual.

"Yeah, go for it," I respond. I am actually intrigued because he hardly ever talks about himself and his personal life. He was even like that back when we hung out a lot.

"Lay it on us!" Ash adds.

"Alright, settle down." Zeke smirks, then says, "So, let's see. In the past few years, not too much has changed for me. I kept my business going, which honestly took up most of my time. It doesn't help that I kept giving free repairs and parts to this knucklehead," he gives me a slap on the back of the head, "but I managed. I love running that clinic, and even though it's tough at times with the occasional opportunist looking to steal my stock or what have you, I wouldn't change that for anything. I got to meet so many different people, and it's really rewarding to help those who need it." He trails off for a minute, staring into the distance. There's a look of pride on his face.

"That's awesome. I really hope you can keep doing that after all this," I gesture broadly, "is done with."

"Yeah, you do so much to help. Good for you, Zeke." Ash jumps in, lounging onto the arm of the couch. She looks like she's a little more comfortable.

Now that I think about it, the awkwardness has started to fade into a familiar comfort that I've missed so much.

"Thanks guys." Zeke continues, his face suddenly lighting up, "But the biggest thing that changed, and I don't think anyone really knows about this, is that my sister, Laura, she had a little boy. So that makes me an uncle! I actually love being an uncle. That kid is so sweet and kind. And he's smart too, much smarter than I am, and he's only three! Not that it's a high bar, but still." He laughs a deep laugh, and Ash and I join in. "Only trouble is, his dad never stuck around long enough to care. So I send what I can to Laura once a month. I'm still trying to do that now, but I worry about them. I can't make money while on the run, after all. I know she'll be alright, and she has a job, but this city isn't kind to those who need help. It's a real mess. But that's exactly why I'm here and why I'll always try to help those in need. If not me, then who, right?" Zeke lounges back a bit more, seemingly feeling more relaxed as well.

"That's a good way to look at it." Ash comments.

"Yeah, uncle Zeke, you're such a kind guy," I say. It's a genuine compliment, but we always have to throw in something on top. That's just how we've always been.

"Yeah, no, don't call me that." He chuckles. "But thank you both. I really hope you get to meet little Ben someday."

"I hope so, too," Ash replies.

I nod in agreement.

"But enough about me, what about you, Ash?" Zeke jumps in, keeping the conversation moving, something he's incredibly good at.

"Well, there's not too much to tell. But let's see." She looks a little less relaxed all of a sudden, sitting up straighter.

"We'd love to hear it," I say, taking her hand in mine, just like she did for me a moment ago.

"Okay," she continues, taking a deep breath, "so I guess my story is sort of similar to yours, Ol'. I didn't really have too much going for me at that time. I had some friends from earlier in life, but I couldn't remember the last time we talked. I reached out to some but didn't really hear back. I tried my best to scrape by just living a normal life. I didn't have much money. I just worked whatever minimum wage jobs would take me. It was fine for a while. But I got real tired of scumbags hitting on me, or worse, and the wannabe gangsters holding up the shop while I worked the graveyard shift at a gas station. There's only so much B.S. I could put up with, you know?" She looks up at the ceiling, an old pain distorting her face.

"I'm so sorry to hear that. You don't deserve any of that." I squeeze her hand gently, wishing I could do more to help ease the pain. It makes me so sad to see her hurt.

"Yeah, well. It's sort of just part of being female, I guess. You'd think after all these years something would change, but some shit never does. Besides, I can handle myself, and I know how to defend myself when it comes down to it. Thanks again for teaching me, Olly. But it still doesn't change the fact that it sucks every time." She starts crying, but I can tell she's trying not to.

"No. Pardon my French, but fuck that," Zeke interjects, saying precisely what I'm thinking. His face is filled with disgust. "We can't keep accepting that that's okay. We know you can handle yourself, but you shouldn't have to. It's messed up, and it needs to change. There's a lotta things that need to change around here, and that's exactly why we're here. We start with CYBR Corp, and then anything is possible."

"Exactly, there's a lot of injustice in this world, and the fact that on top of that, you have to face that kind of harassment is never okay," I add, trying my best to smile reassuringly. "We're here for you."

"Thanks, you guys...I guess it's just easier to say it's fine and keep moving than it is to actually face it." Ash wipes her eyes, and she cracks a forced smile. "So, anyway, I got fed up with trying to live a normal life, so I started getting involved in rallies around Nova City, rallying for human rights causes of different kinds. It was small and didn't accomplish much, but I found people that I felt safer with and more connected to. And I was telling the corrupt, even in that small way, to go to hell, which was all I really needed."

She's smiling now, the idea of sticking it to 'em lighting up her face.

There's the Ash I know.

"But the thing that really keeps me going is the thing that's always really been driving me, ever since my parents died of cancer when I was little. Healthcare should be free to everyone, and the fact that it's not is horrendous! The number of times I've heard, 'Oh, it's too bad. If your parents could afford the treatments, they would be alright.' It's bullshit! Most forms of cancer, like so many diseases, have been fully treatable and preventable for years now, but it's only available to the elites, to the rich and powerful. Fuck that. So hell yeah, I'm so happy I ran into you guys and that we're finally going to do something about it. Who knows how far we'll get, but we gotta do it. Do it for the ones we've lost," she looks me in the eyes, and I nod knowingly, then she turns to Zeke and says, "and the ones we refuse to lose."

"Thanks for sharing, Ash. That means a lot, and I know how hard it can be. I'm happy we're all here, together again. Thank you both for opening up and just for everything." I put an arm around each of them and pull them into another hug. With everyone spread out on the couch, it's an awkward but hopefully endearing half-side hug.

They hug me back and we all share a laugh at the awkwardness of the hug. I feel so relieved and happy. It's been a while. I smile wide at them and gesture to the TV, "What do you say? Next time we've got a moment, we play some games instead of crying our eyes out?"

"Now you're talkin'!" Zeke says, nodding his head enthusiastically. "It's been a while since I schooled you."

"Oh really? We'll just see about that." I say, sitting up straighter and puffing out my chest to act tough, glaring at him.

"Yeah, as if either of you would be the one schooling anybody," Ash says, smirking and crossing her arms with confidence.

"I wouldn't be so confident if I were you. I've clocked a lotta gaming hours since we last played." I reply.

Truth be told, she's way better than either of us at nearly every game we've played together. Shooters, fighters, driving games, platformers, you name it, she's the queen. But I'm feeling confident, or I guess stubborn is probably the better word.

We all pretend to glare at each other for a moment, acting tough and confident. I'm trying not to smile or laugh, but it's tough. Then, all at once, we burst into laughter, collapsing into the comfortable depths of the old couch.

"Man, I missed this, you guys," Zeke says as our laughter slowly fades.

"Me too." Ash agrees.

"Me three," I add.

We all sit there for a minute, enjoying the silence of a shared moment of vulnerability.

"Well, I guess we better get back to planning," I say, standing and giving off as much energy as I can.

"Right, I'll work on the van. You two keep plannin' the details." Zeke orders.

Without another word, we get to work.

CH 7

SHINIGAMI surround me, closing in fast. I sprint down the street, not knowing where I am or how I got here. All I know is that I'm unarmed, unprepared, and going to die. It's like I'm running in slow motion, with the quick, quiet footsteps of what seems to be ten Shinigami creeping ever closer. One of them jumps out at me, slashing straight through my left arm before I have a chance to do anything. Strangely, it doesn't hurt as much as it probably should.

Just then, I hear a voice calling out my name a couple of buildings away. It sounds like...Astra's voice! But what's she doing here? She'll get killed by them for sure! I try to shout back, to tell her to get out of here before it's too late, but no sound comes out. It's as if I can't speak at all, and I'm running slower than ever now, my vision starting to blur... The shouting is getting louder. It's definitely Astra...

"Olly...Olly! OLIVER!" She shouts repeatedly.

I can see what looks like her form rushing toward me as what now seems to be at least a hundred Shinigami close in, grabbing hold of me and driving their arm-mounted arc-blades through my back, my arms, and my legs. It burns in a way I imagine being shot into the Sun itself burns. I can feel my flesh melting as the wounds cauterize themselves. It's the kind of pain that begins to fade out after a while as my pain receptors become overloaded with inputs. I try to scream, but my throat closes up with pain. My entire body is spasming, held upright only by the very things causing the pain, the Shinigami's blades.

"Get out...while you...still...can..." I try to warn her, but the words barely come out of my mouth. Each syllable is agony, and each word is a Herculean task to utter. My vision and the intense pain both fade away to nothingness as I lose control of my consciousness, unwillingly fading into the embrace of death.

"Oliver, wake up! Wake up, Olly!" Astra's voice grows louder and louder as the world fades darker and darker around me.

Suddenly, I'm awake in my room in the bunker.

"What the...but the..." I pause for a moment, "fuck, it was just a dream!" I exclaim, the truth hitting me as a wave of relief washes over me, followed by a second wave of embarrassment at having Ash shake me awake from it.

"It was, but damn, it must have been some dream. You were screaming and tossing around like crazy, muttering about...Shinigami?" Astra replies, standing over me, holding my shoulders, and looking over me with a very concerned expression on her face. The room is incredibly dark, but I can make out her figure as I fully wake up. She's wearing just a tank top and short shorts... I catch myself looking at her a second too long before snapping my eyes back to her face.

She removes her hands from my shoulders, seemingly just realizing they're still there, and we both look away from each other for a second. It's only now that I notice I'm covered in a cold sweat, and my heart is still racing.

"Yeah...it was nothing really, just a stupid dream, fighting off some bad guys. Sorry to worry you, Ash." I pause for a moment, "and uh, thanks for waking me up."

Astra gives me a look that says, "I don't believe a word you're saying, but sure." She obviously knows I'm lying about the dream and its effect on me, but all she says is, "well, whatever you were dreaming about, try not to scare me like that, alright? You sounded like you were being attacked in here!" With that, she turns, walking out of my room and back to hers, closing the door firmly behind her with an echoing, metallic clang.

I push myself up to a sitting position on the edge of the bed and try to calm myself down. Between the dream and that awkward encounter with Ash, I'm gonna need a minute to gather myself. I really am hopeless when it comes to her.

After a few minutes of staring into the void, I find myself wondering if I'm making a terrible decision. What if all of this is a huge mistake? That dream was a little ridiculous, but not that far off from what could *actually* happen to me if I continued along this path. What if I end up getting Astra hurt, or Zeke, or Dex?

"No, don't be an idiot," I say out loud to myself, accidentally.

I can imagine what any of the three of them would say if I expressed these doubts to them. They'd all say something along the lines of "they signed up for this, they knew what they were getting into, and if I back out now, then everything we've been through would've been for nothing." The more I think about it, the more sure I become. Dex has no other options, Zeke would sooner smack me upside the head with a tuning wrench than see me give up on this, and Astra explicitly told me she wouldn't forgive me if I pushed her out of my life again, so...let's just say giving up is NOT an option.

"Alright, that's that, then," I mutter to myself, clenching my fists and rising from the bed with a newfound resolve and determination. I flip on the dim, bluish light of the wall-mounted lamp, turn to look in the wall-mounted mirror, put my fists on my hips, and raise my head high. "From here on out, there will be no more excuses, no holding back! Oliver Wolf will take down CYBR Corp and keep his friends safe at the same time!" I'm not exactly one for power posing and mirror speeches, but I honestly feel really good about this, about myself. It's something I haven't felt in a while.

"That's more like it!" Ash chimes in from the other side of the door, startling me.

After a brief pause to jump back into my skin, I throw open the door and see Ash standing across from me in the bathroom doorway. She must have been heading to the bathroom to take a shower and happened to walk by right as I said my little speech. Surprisingly, I don't feel nearly as embarrassed as I could be. Who is this confident person anyway? That being said, I'm one hundred percent blushing.

"Oh, hey Ash, I didn't know you were there, but thanks for the support!" I say with a smile, willing my cheeks to cool down.

Astra smiles back at me, then heads into the bathroom, closing the door behind her. I close my own door again as well. I can faintly hear the water turn on as Astra hums a tune. I can't quite place it, but something in the back of my mind is tingling with vague recognition.

I quickly get dressed in a fresh pair of black jeans and a t-shirt. The shirt is light grey with a yin-yang on it, but the yin-yang is a black wolf and a white wolf circling each other. I may have a few wolf-themed shirts, to say the least. I finish getting dressed, throwing on my electric blue skate shoes and recently-patched-up leather jacket. Then, I run a comb through my hair in an unsuccessful attempt to tame the beast.

I head out into the common space to see Zeke and Dexter discussing the plan over instant coffee and bowls of Fauxtmeal, the so-called "wonder of modern science." Since much of Earth became unsuitable for farming several years ago due to a combination of flooding, drought, and never-ending snowstorms, governments began to rely on scientists to create the closest approximations of plants and meats that they could 3D-print or grow in test tubes, or wherever it is this 'food' comes from. So, instead of eating oatmeal, we eat Fauxtmeal.

And here I was, thinking society never amounted to anything.

I chuckle quietly to myself.

"Morning guys, how's it goin'?" I say somewhat cheerfully as I walk over to the small kitchen counter, pouring a packet of instant coffee into a disposable plastic mug with some hot water from the electric kettle and scooping a bowl of Fauxtmeal.

I move over to the small folding table and sit in the cheap plastic folding chair next to Zeke, taking a sip of my coffee as I try to wake my body up. Apparently, people used to make designer coffee beans and roast them in fancy ways, but all I've ever known is the indistinguishable bitter-burnt taste of these blackish-brown granules they call coffee. Rumor has it the rich and powerful still import real beans from Africa and South America, or the parts that aren't underwater, that is.

"Well, what's got you so damn chipper?" Zeke retorts as his mouth forms the slightest hint of a smirk.

"You're as pleasant as always, Zeke." I shoot back. "And for your information, I am ready for a smooth, successful heist! I can't wait to not be tied to this piece of junk." With that last comment, I tap the top of the external battery unit that I have strapped around my waist.

"Well, we would all love for the heist to go as smoothly as possible, but I definitely wouldn't count on it." Dexter chimes in, his face contemplative.

"I know, I'm just trying to stay positive..." I pause for a

moment, taking a big swig of my coffee, "for once in my life."

The table falls silent as we all eat Fauxtmeal and sip coffee, thinking about the daunting task ahead of us. I may be trying to stay positive, but I can guarantee something will go wrong with this plan. There are just too many factors. Unfortunately, as is the case with most things, there's no way to know what will go wrong until it's happening. There's no cybernetic implant to see the future, not yet, anyway. I find myself thinking about that nightmare, the Shinigami closing in around me, their arc blades searing their way through my skin. I feel an itching, crawling sensation all over my body as goosebumps erupt from every pore. It's like I can still feel them, see the flesh melting from my body…

No! I refuse to let fear get in my way, not this time.

Having finished his breakfast, Zeke stands, tosses his mug, bowl, and spoon in the trash, and sits back next to me. He's been uncharacteristically quiet for the past few minutes.

"Alright, look, are we not gonna talk about the elephant in the room?" Zeke bursts out suddenly. His face is filled with concern.

I look at Dex. We share a mutual eyebrow raise followed by a shrug, and then we both turn to face Zeke.

"Hello! Astra?" Zeke exclaims, pointing aggressively toward the hallway where Ash is. "She was compromised, CYBR Corp troops tracked her apartment, which is tied to her, so our entire plan won't work, will it? We're screwed. I'm rethinking the whole plan!" With that last comment, he throws his hands up and slumps in his chair. I haven't seen Zeke this frazzled in a while. I always forget just how New York his accent becomes when he's stressed.

"I didn't want to say this before, but you may have a point there, Zeke," Dexter replies, contemplative. "While it's true that she isn't publicly wanted like the rest of us, they clearly know she's involved in some way. While I was netrunning yesterday, I found some traces of reference to Miss Odelle. It's difficult to say whether or not the CYBRnetics workers will be looking for her or not."

"There we go! At least someone around here has some common sense!" Zeke shoots back.

"Alright, guys, enough!" I interject. "I understand the concern, but there's no other way that this plan could possibly work without her. We all know that. We talked about this yesterday. Not to mention, she's still on the FOCC list, right? That wouldn't be the case if she was truly on the wanted list like us. And on top of that, why don't we disguise her the same as you? No one will even know it's her. Plus, we only need her to stick around long enough to lure the manager out of the CYBRnetics Outlet and show her the fusion cell." I continue, steadying my breathing as I talk and trying to sound as reassuring and confident as possible. "Besides, Ash practically threatened to kill me if I didn't let her help us, so good luck telling her that yourself."

"Telling me what yourself?" Ash interjects, seemingly materializing out of thin air. She's standing where the hallway connects to the common space, dressed in her usual black t-shirt, blue jeans, and worn black combat boots.

"Oh, hey, Ash! Zeke has something he wants to tell you." I answer mischievously, interested to see how this plays out and even more interested in staying the hell out of it.

Ash makes her way to the kitchen area, grabs some food and coffee, and sits at the head of the small table.

"So, what's up?" She asks again.

Zeke shoots me a red-hot glare that I am all too familiar with, then responds, "I'm just...concerned that since your identity has been compromised, this plan will fail, and we need to find some sort of alternative plan."

"I appreciate the concern, Zeke, I really do, but what other options do we have?" Ash responds, giving a subdued shrug and a slight eye roll. "Besides, I can handle whatever might happen." I'm watching her face intently to see if Zeke can crack her. These two used to act like siblings back in the day, with Zeke acting like an overprotective older brother and Ash always playing it cooler than she actually feels. She hates it when people try to protect her or assume she can't handle herself.

Learned that the hard way.

"That's what Olly said. What are you rehearsing lines now!?" Zeke quips back, gesturing in my direction.

I throw up my hands incredulously, "don't look at me, man."

"Useless, that's what you are." He retorts jokingly. Or at least I hope it's jokingly. He then turns back to Ash, "Right, so say we go through with this. What do you do if they recognize you? Other than running for the hills, I'm fresh outta ideas right now."

Ash pauses, thinking it over. Then, I see a spark in her eye as she says, "I know what we'll do. Obviously, I'm going to run and fight my way out with Olly if anything seems off, first of all. But, and this is a big 'but,' say they do capture me, then I can be our eye on the inside! You can tune in to my comm implant. I'll tell them you forced me to work with you, feeding them false information while learning anything I can about their operation from the inside!"

As Ash unveils her plan to the group, excitedly gesturing to a spot on the back of her neck as everyone's faces change from confusion to shock, mine included. The comm implant is a sound enough idea in theory. We all have them as part of the Holocomm system and can set up a call beforehand to capture any audio, but the idea of it... I'm too dumb-founded to say anything for a moment, and it seems Zeke is, too, but Dex speaks up for the first time in several minutes.

"No. Absolutely not. Astra, I may not know you very well, but I have no doubt you can handle yourself as well as anyone. That being said, you do *not* know what it's like there. I do. I worked there for years, seeing the horrible things they do to criminals no one will miss, all of their nameless test subjects...I've been the one doing those things..." He shudders, his expression vacant for a moment. "No one can survive their torture. Trust me. You can't go with them willingly."

As soon as Dexter finishes speaking, a chilling, deafening silence falls over the room. I feel a shiver run down my spine, and the hair on the back of my neck stands on end. My mind is reeling, trying to imagine what he could even be talking about, how it must have felt to be forced to do...whatever it was they made him do.

Don't get me wrong, I've seen my fair share of fucked up shit in my years on the streets of Nova City, but I've got a terrible feeling that not a single thing I've seen or experienced comes anywhere close to what Dexter has been through. My mind runs through scenario after scenario, each a more twisted image than the last as my imagination runs wild, creating the most deranged things Dex could've been forced to do. The worst part is, no matter how dark my mind goes, I'm almost certain it isn't dark enough to truly understand what this poor, sweet, caring man has been forced to go through, all for fear of the safety of those he holds most dear. It fills me with rage as the horrifying thought crosses my mind. I can feel my heart beginning to beat faster, my fists and jaw subconsciously clenching.

I force myself out of my own head for a second to look

around the room, hoping someone would speak up to break the silence. I don't know what I'm hoping they'll say, but I just can't stand here in this horrible headspace much longer. Zeke opens his mouth slightly as if to say something but closes it just as quickly.

Alright, here goes nothing.

I stand up abruptly, startling everyone in the room, myself included. I'm not thinking ahead very much. I clench my fists even tighter, digging my fingernails into my sweaty, clammy left palm while my right arm makes a slightly strained hydraulic squeaking sound as I force the metallic fingertips into the palm.

"So, what are we going to *do* about it!?" I yell, not meaning to. Astra's expression changes from blank to shock, as if my words slapped her across the face. "We've all seen terrible things, done things we're not proud of, lost those closest to us, and for what? To survive, to scrape by, to fade into the crowd as the world crumbles around our useless shoulders?" I punch the folding table with my right arm, leaving a fist-shaped dent in the aluminum. I can feel a hot, visceral rage filling me from the inside.

As my punch lands on the table, Zeke gets out of his chair and quickly moves in an attempt to grab my shoulders. "Olly, I know how you feel, you just gotta calm down so we—"

"I'm tired of being calm!"

I push him off of me, moving to the kitchen and pacing back and forth.

I continue, my anger clouding my vision. "I see it every day. Every day. Every. Single. Day. Good people fight and die in this city just for a chance to see the next dawn. I've watched way too many people get stabbed, shot, and pummeled to death in the street right outside my apartment window. And whose fault is it? The poor soul who just had the spark drained from his body? The desperate stim-head willing to do anything to scratch that itch? An itch the rich got him hooked on instead of providing proper healthcare? The unfortunate minimum-wage employee who gets melted with Retribution plasma rifles just for being in the wrong place at the wrong time? We all know it's none of them. We all know who the real problem is here. Everyone in this damned city knows it, whether they'll admit it or not. The question is, are we gonna sit around here and wonder what if, or are we gonna *do* something about it?"

I stop and slam both fists down on the small kitchen island. The veneer warps under my fists. It now occurs to me that I've been pacing this whole time, getting more and more fired up. My body is trembling, my fists clenched ever tighter.

I guess this is it, then. The all-consuming rage that's been building deep inside of me for the last twenty years is finally boiling over.

I let out an inaudible chuckle and shake my head slightly as the thought crosses my mind.

Zeke, Ash, and Dex all stare at me with a mixture of pity and understanding in their eyes. The room is silent for a moment, long enough for me to hear the sound of my heart beating furiously in my chest as the adrenaline rush of rage flows through my veins. It's as if my entire body is receiving tiny electric shocks, the kind that usually powers the motors in my right arm. I realize I've been lost in thought for some time, staring down at my still-clenched fists. I slowly raise my eyes upward toward my friends, allowing my hands to relax and my arms to fall to my sides.

"It's not that we don't agree with you, Olly, it's just...well, I, for one, am worried about you," Ash speaks up, breaking the silence. "You're so close to this situation, what with…you know, your family and…" She glances down as she trails off, a flush of shame filling her cheeks for a moment.

"It's okay, Ash," I reply, trying with every fiber of my being to remain calm and reasonable. "You're right, as always. And I think it's about time I got this out in the open anyway. Of course, Ash and Zeke know what we're talking about, but Dex, there's something you should know. Something I haven't talked about in…years." I pause, looking down at my hands once again. The adrenaline and anger have washed away, replaced by a dull, throbbing headache.

I have to continue.

"You see, the reason I hate CYBR Corp so much, the reason why I've started this crusade in the first place, and the reason I have never truly been happy in my life, is that…" I can feel my throat drying up as my voice cracks, tears welling in the corners of my eyes, blurring my vision as I stare out at the faces of the others. "My entire family was…killed. By CYBR Corp."

Tears are freely streaming down my cheeks now. I make no attempt to stop them. I can see the shock on Dex's face and the deep understanding and sadness on those of Zeke and Ash.

"Twenty years ago, both of my parents were taken to CYBR Corp's headquarters. We were told they had been randomly selected for a clinical trial in which they'd receive free cybernetic implants, being tested for their ability to extend the human lifespan by up to ten years…we were all fooled, seduced by the allure and false promises. I was eight years old, and my brother Miles…was twelve. That was the last day we saw them. As they left, they told us to make sure we cleaned up the dishes…and I told them dishes are stupid."

I can feel my knees weaken beneath me as I fall backward, using the kitchen counter behind me for support. I know tears are flowing like waterfalls out of my eyes, but I hardly notice it. I hardly feel anything other than the searing pain in my heart.

"The last thing I ever said to my parents was that dishes are *fucking* stupid. No 'I love you,' 'see you when you get home,' nothing. I regret that more than anything I've ever done. I think about it all the time, even now, twenty years later." I try to wipe the tears away, but it's pointless.

"There we were, an eight-year-old and a twelve-year-old, alone. Miles was only four years older than me, but he found the strength to step up and take care of us. He was the greatest person I've ever known. We had no other family, no one to turn to. We lived on the streets of Nova City, stealing the food we ate, the clothes we wore, everything. We grew up as nothing more than rats in the sewers, forced to watch as the city was slowly but surely conquered by CYBR Corp, as people became less and less human and more and more machine. We had to get creative with the places we hid and the things we stole as the streets became infested with Retribution troops. Kid or not, they would shoot anyone caught committing even the smallest of crimes. We saw it happen to many of the kids we began to hang with, other street kids with nowhere to go. We saw them melted time and time again by arc rifles, turned to smoldering ash before our eyes. It was only a matter of time until..."

I can feel my throat closing up as I try to get the words out. I open my mouth and close it a few times, starting to hyperventilate.

"Olly, it's..." Ash tries to say something but stops.

Finally, I get my voice to come out again. "Ten years ago, on the morning of my eighteenth birthday...Miles, he...he...was murdered. Right in front of me...by a Shinigami."

I collapse to the ground now, nothing stopping me from hitting the floor as my legs buckle and the tears start to stream down once again. I hold my head in my hands, staring down at my shoes through a blur of tears and pain.

"You know what that means!?" I shout, looking up at the three people circled helplessly around me. "It means he was killed on *purpose*. On purpose! Someone at CYBR Corp *ordered* that Shinigami to murder my brother. Who would do that? And why? Why!? We never got caught committing a crime and never did anything to deserve it. But he was killed all the same, right in front of me. Miles had told me to run away, pushing me away from him because he knew we were in danger. He told me he loved me, and I had to run away to leave him there. I couldn't do it. But I also couldn't...I couldn't do anything to save him! Not. A. Single. Thing!"

With each of those last words, I slam my right fist into the cabinet behind me, shattering the fake wood into splinters with each hit of the metallic arm.

"I couldn't even run away right...I just stood there as the only family I had left was torn to pieces by the blades of a Shinigami. He just...he...his body...I...I couldn't..."

At the thought of Miles's mangled body lying there in the street, I can feel myself completely shutting down. I bring my knees to my chest, slamming my forehead down against them and clutching my head in my hands, clenching my eyes shut as my entire body goes numb. I hear muffled voices around me, but all I can see is the memory of Miles being murdered in front of me, playing over and over in my mind. I can still hear his tortured screams and the horrifying mechanical gurgle of the Shinigami's laughter. It's like I'm still standing there, frozen with fear and helpless to stop it. I'm interrupted by the memory of fighting that Shinigami the other day and how I barely survived. I can feel the fear of fighting them all over again...

I realize I'm being shaken. I can vaguely hear what must be Ash's voice trying to reach me. The feelings of fear, shame, and anger slowly fade as I look up, releasing my head from my hands.

"Olly! Oh, Olly, there we go. Hey." She says.

I can finally hear her as the numbness begins to slowly leave my body. I can see a deep concern in her hazel eyes as she stares intently at me, her hands on my shoulders. Tears are falling gently down her cheeks.

"Hi, Ash," I whisper back. I want to say more, but that's all I can manage.

"I'm here for you, Olly. I got you." She reassures me in a soft voice, sitting down on my left and putting her arms around me.

I lean into her, resting my head on her shoulder and trying to breathe as deeply as I can, which is extremely difficult to do while hyperventilating and sobbing uncontrollably. A silent understanding falls over us for a few moments. I let the tears fall, not trying to stop them, incoherent babbling falling from my mouth. Even I don't know what I'm saying. Ash just nods, gently stroking my hair.

"Thank you, Ash. Just...thank you." I say quietly after I finally catch my breath, and the tears slow somewhat.

"You know I'm always here for you. I always have been."

The truth of her words makes a different kind of tears well in my eyes. I stare into her eyes once more, and for a moment, for one minuscule moment, everything's okay.

"Hey, guys, there's no easy way to say this," it's Zeke, hesitantly approaching Ash and me in the kitchen, "but if we don't get moving in the next five minutes, we're gonna miss that window for that power cell."

I check my Holocomm, and it reads 11:45. We're supposed to meet the CYBRnetics Outlet manager at 12:00 sharp. *Fuck.* If we miss that meeting, the best-case scenario is they sell that fusion cell to some rich asshole within minutes. Worst case? They wonder why we didn't show, figure out who we are, and make our lives even more of a living hell, if that's even possible.

"Shit," I mutter, sniffling as I attempt to dry my eyes. "Guess we better get moving. I am *not* spending another day strapped to this piece of junk if I don't have to." I slowly rise to my feet, slapping my external battery pack and offering a weak smile, pretending like everything's fine.

With a nod of understanding, Dex moves to start the car as the rest of us scramble to grab everything we'll need for the heist. I run to my room, throwing on my leather jacket and strapping on my sword sheathes. I also throw on an obscurer and grab some dark aviator shades from my room before I run out of the bunker. The shades are partly to hide my identity, partly to cover up how red my eyes are from crying, and most importantly of all, to make sure I look incredibly cool. You can't go on a heist without shades. I don't make the rules. I allow myself a brief moment to smile and chuckle at my own nonsense for a moment, then head out with the others.

***

On the ride over, while Zeke careens wildly through the streets on his way to the meetup, the rest of us review the plan in the back of the van.

"Right," says Dex, "just don't forget that we're also here for dirt on CYBR Corp. We'll need your Holo to stay close enough to their computers for long enough to get the data."

"Yep, I know. I'll make sure I keep in range while we make the deal. How long does it need to download?" Ash asks.

"Ideally, assuming my virus works, about two minutes."

"Cool."

"Hey, Zeke?" I call up to the front.

"Whadda ya want?" He yells back.

"How long till we get there?"

"I don't know, do I look like CYBR Maps?"

"Just give me an estimate, you obstinate goon."

He lets out an extremely exasperated sigh.

"Five minutes."

"Thanks. Was that so hard?"

He answers with his middle finger.

"Okay, so we have a few minutes," I say to Dex and Ash.

"What is it?" Ash asks.

"I was thinking, once we have the data, who's gonna record this manifesto? Who's gonna do the speech?"

"Oh, well, I was thinking Astra," Dex says. "After all, she has experience with speaking to crowds and getting a rise out of people from those riots and whatnot."

"Ah," she hesitates for a moment, "that's a fair point. But honestly, I think it should be you, Dex."

"Me?" He asks incredulously.

"Yeah! You know firsthand how terrible it is in there. You know, more than the rest of us combined, what sort of atrocities CYBR Corp commits on a daily basis. If anyone is giving a speech to the public, exposing CYBR Corp, and rallying people to our cause, it *has* to be you."

"I, well, I don't know. I'm more of a data guy, you see." Dex mutters, looking taken aback at the idea of giving a speech.

"Hey, she's right, Dex," I interject encouragingly. "It's gotta be you. This is your chance to get back at them, to make them pay for what they did to you and your family."

He looks out the window for a moment, contemplative.

"Hmm, I suppose. I really don't know how to go about it, though, kiddos. I really am just a desk worker."

"I can help you!" Ash offers. "When the time comes, once we have the data and some more time for it, you and I will do some work on how to give a speech. It's gonna be one hell of a broadcast. You'll see." She smiles confidently.

Man, she's just so charming when she's fired up.

"Okay, I trust you, Astra. Thank you." Dex replies, looking a bit more relaxed.

"And please. Just call me Ash. My friends all do."

"Oh, right, thanks Ash. And thank you too, Olly."

"Of course," I reply with a smile.

He smiles back.

He's been through so much. It's like he's afraid to do anything that might get him in trouble. What a terrible way to live...

"By the way," he says hesitantly, "it's really nice to have some people I can truly call friends. It's been...well, it's been too long. I'll say that."

"We're glad to have you as our friend, too," Ash answers with a bright smile.

"Absolutely." I agree, smiling again.

For a moment, everything feels alright. The pain that filled me minutes ago as I sat on the floor of the bunker's kitchen is washed away as I look at the bright faces smiling back at me. We sit in contented silence for a few moments. I gaze out the window at the cars and buildings flying by with alarming speed.

"Alright, buckle up, we're almost there!" Zeke yells as he drifts the van around a sharp right turn.

It takes real skill to drift a hover-van, mind you.

***

"I don't like this, Dex. What if she gets made?"

"Olly, we talked about this. You have to trust her. Also,

were you not in favor of her joining us for this? Besides, if anything happens, she's got her samurai in shining leather to rescue her." Dex jokes with me, a smirk on his face.

"You win this one, but only because I really liked that joke." I quip back. Also, he's right. I advocated for Ash to join us.

I really hope that was the right call.

I'm looking through the window of our van at the CYBRnetics outlet. Dex and I have the perfect view of the outlet from our side alley. Zeke had mapped out the surrounding area a few days ago and told us this was the ideal spot to camp out.

"Look at 'im, what a nervous wreck!" Dex comments, pointing at Zeke.

"He never could handle being anywhere near CYBR Corp's goons, even before he was a wanted man."

It may not seem like a fantastic idea to have Zeke out there with Ash acting as her "business partner" for the fake buying scenario, but Dex and I are both way too recognizable and way too high on the CYBR Corp most wanted list for either of us to take his place. The last news flash I saw on my Holo said I was actually their number one most wanted, which is sort of strangely satisfying, to be honest. Horrible, terrifying, but satisfying.

Astra is standing there talking to the CYBRnetics manager, disguised under a hoodie and sunglasses, just to make extra sure that they don't know who she is. She also has a fake diamond necklace and knock-off designer handbag that she's tactically waving to portray that she actually can afford to buy the insanely priced four million CYBR COYN power cell. So far, so good.

I turn up the volume on my Holo so I can better hear their conversation to see how it's going. We have everyone's Holocomms linked on a silent call so we can all hear each other through our implanted earpieces.

"Very well, we will do business with you." The CYBRnetics manager has a gruff, straight-to-the-point voice, exactly as I knew he would. These guys are all the same.

"Is she in range? Are we getting data?" I ask Dex.

"Yep, just another minute, and we're in." He replies, checking his Holo.

The manager then gestures to his armored goons to open the locked case they're guarding. Set on top of a chrome display stand, hovering a few inches above the ground for no other purpose than because they can, is a solid steel box that looks to be about a foot square from where I'm sitting. I watch intently as they open the case to reveal a remarkably simple-looking yet incredibly complex piece of machinery: the CYBR Corp FXP 4800 fusion power cell.

"Okay, let's do this then," Ash replies, trying to sound calm and authoritative. She's doing well, unlike Zeke, whom she gestures to open their own briefcase of sorts. He nods stiffly.

"Right," Zeke responds, flipping open the case to reveal the CYBR COYN chip inside.

Most transactions are completed through personally tied accounts through a simple wave of the hand over a scanner or the touch of a fingertip. However, for particularly high-end purchases, the standard is to pay in 'physical' currency: a plastic card loaded with pre-cleared Johnnies. This particular chip, however, is only pretending to have four million Johnnies on it. Dex used his hacker magic to make it appear to hold that much money, while in reality, it's completely worthless.

Everything is riding on the assumption that the CYBRnetics manager's system will read it as an authentic chip long enough for Ash and Zeke to get the power cell, then the data, and finally, to get the hell outta there.

"Bring the chip here, I don't have all day." The manager snaps. I swear I can see his forehead veins popping from here.

I wonder if it hurts to have that stick up his ass all the time.

Zeke stumbles over with the chip as calmly as he can, tapping it to the back of the manager's hand to initiate the reader. Our Holocomm feed falls perfectly silent as everyone holds their breath, and the manager checks the details on his Holo.

"Looks good." He finally says, breaking the silence.

"No fucking way!" I accidentally exclaim to the group.

Dex holds a finger to his lips.

I can't believe that actually worked.

Zeke steps forward, handing the CYBR COYN chip to one of the CYBR goons, while Astra takes the now-closed case of the FXP 4800. With a curt nod, they begin to part ways.

"Wait!" Dex says into the comms. "Stall for twenty more seconds. We've almost got the data. I just need Ash to stay within range a bit longer. The signal from their Holocomms to yours is pretty weak for some reason."

Ash turns back toward the men, nodding to Zeke to continue back to the van with the power cell.

"By the way," she says to the guards, softly enough that the manager can't hear, "I think you should ask for a raise. You deserve it."

"Um, well, that's none of your business." One of the guards replies, clearly taken aback.

"I mean, we've been asking for a raise for—"

"Shut up, Greg!"

"Right, um, get out of here, mind your business!" Greg

says, seemingly embarrassed.

"We got it, Ash, get outta there," Dex yells in a whisper.

"Alright, I'm going." She says, throwing up her hands dramatically as she turns back toward us and walks away.

Against all odds, we actually pulled this off. Hell yeah.

As Ash and Zeke make their way indirectly toward our general area, I see the guards walk back to their manager. He starts pointing angrily at his computer screen, then pointing at Ash and Zeke.

"Did they notice their data was stolen? The hack was supposed to be untraceable, right?" I ask Dex.

"I don't know, it should've been." He replies, frantically checking his Holo for signs of what the issue is.

"Hey, you. Get back here! You're a wanted criminal!" The manager yells authoritatively as he and his goons start running toward Ash and Zeke.

"God damn it! How did they know!?" Ash yells as she and Zeke take off at full speed toward the van, no longer trying to hide their identities or where they're going.

"Punch it, Dex!" I yell, throwing open the sliding door and preparing to catch whoever or whatever I need to. Dex throws the van in drive and floors it, the hover jets of Zeke's old fusion van groaning with the strain of it.

As Dex Tokyo drifts the van in front of the path of Zeke and Ash, I can see that they're in trouble. The CYBR goons are gaining on them quickly, thanks to their exosuits. As they get closer, it becomes clear that these are Retribution troops, not just run-of-the-mill security guards. This is *definitely* not good.

"Stay here, be ready to drive," I yell as I jump out of the van, sprinting at full speed toward the two most important people in my life. I would sooner join forces with CYBR Corp than let anything bad happen to either Zeke or Ash.

And we just reconnected! Come on.

"What are you doing? Are you insane!?" Zeke yells at me as he sees what I'm doing.

"You know it!" I yell back as I draw my swords, bringing the arc mods humming to life with a flick of the switches. The gentle vibration of the generators kicks in as arc energy covers the blades, reflecting off the polished metal.

I do love the beautiful blue crackling of arc lightning, I have to admit.

"Get out of the way, fool. You...wait." A look of realization passes across the CYBR manager's expressionless face as he figures out who I am.

"That's right, you don't want them. It's me you're really after!" I taunt them, spreading my arms wide, one crackling sword in each hand.

"Very well then. Get him!" The manager orders, his Retribution goons jumping toward me, arc rifles primed.

One of them takes a quick shot at me, which I very narrowly dodge. I've been playing out this scenario in my head for hours, but it's so much more frightening when it's actually happening. The other one opens fire a moment later, at which time I'm already ducking behind his boss. I look the boss dead in the eyes, and he doesn't realize what's happening until it's too late. He raises his fist, crackling with arc energy, but he's too late. The look of rage on the manager's face as his own goon unloads a full clip of arc rifle plasma into his back is nearly worth the electrified punch in the stomach he gives me right after. As I go down, I can see metal, plastic, and flesh all melting off his body. It's horrifying no matter how many times I see it. Somehow, he's not only still standing but has enough left in him to knock the wind out of me with one punch.

"You're one tough motherfucker," I mutter, recovering as quickly as I can and slicing his hands off in two quick swipes. Both of his arms are fully cybernetic, so I don't really feel bad about it. That does not mean, however, that there aren't artificial nerves running through those metallic hands. He finally collapses to the ground, screaming from the pain of his myriad of wounds, which leaves these two chromed-out freakshows in front of me.

They're always so smug with their exosuits, heavy augmentations, and arc rifles. I'm so sick of it.

"Let's dance!" I shout, sprinting at full speed toward the closest Retribution goon. By the time he has the sense to wipe the dumbstruck look off of his face, I've already slashed through the actuator of his arc rifle, cut the hydraulic lines of his exosuit, and given him a swift strike to the base of the skull with the hilt of my sword, one of their only weak points. When I'm not caught off guard and totally outnumbered, I can usually handle these overconfident idiots pretty easily. He crumples to the ground, perfectly conscious yet totally unable to move his physical or mechanical body.

"That's it, you're goin' down, Wolf!" The final goon shouts, clearly offended by my treatment of his friends. I hear the high-pitched whine of his arc rifle charging a rapid burst, and he's too far for me to reach him before it fires. I hardly have a second to think, and I can only think of one idiotic thing to try. So naturally, I do it. I throw the shorter of my swords, the wakizashi, like an enormous throwing knife, straight for his chest. Safe to say, he wasn't expecting it. As my sword's crackling blue blade embeds itself firmly within his left shoulder, the arc mod sends an electric shock throughout his highly augmented body. He falls to one knee but stands up again, charging his rifle again.

Oh, that's not good.

Just then, the full clip of an arc pistol hits him from his right side, finishing him off with red-hot molten fury. He grunts something unintelligible on the way down, his body racked with electrical shocks and burns. Dumbfounded, I glance to my left, and sure enough, I see none other than Ash holding a smoking arc pistol, one foot in the van and the other planted firmly on the ground.

"Let's go!" She shouts at me.

I run over to the collapsed Retribution troop, turn off my katana, and put it in its sheath. I brace my right hand on the metal scaffolding of his exosuit chest piece and wrench my wakizashi from his shoulder. The blade itself is fine, but it looks like the shock that got this goon doing the electric boogaloo also overloaded the arc mod of the sword because it won't turn on.

Damn it. Guess I'll have to find a new arc pulser for that later. What's another part to add to my shopping list? It's really not my priority, anyway.

I sheath that sword, too, sling the strap of his arc rifle over my shoulder, and sprint to join the others in the van. I jump and tuck through the open sliding side door as Ash slams it closed, and Zeke floors the van, taking us at full speed back to the bunker before someone comes to find what happened to these three.

"Do you always have to be the hero?" Ash teases me, giving me a punch in the left shoulder. Her face reads a confusing mixture of happy and disapproving.

"I saw they were gaining on you! What was I supposed to do? Let them get you? No chance."

"Fine," she rolls her eyes, "I'm just glad you're okay."

"Yeah, you and me both. Thanks for saving my ass, by the way."

"Just add it to my tab—"

Just then, a massive explosion tears a hole in the left side of the van, throwing my head against the right-side door panel.

My vision is swimming, and my ears are ringing. I can

barely make out what's happening. I close my eyes and rub them with my hands. It doesn't help. Obviously.

I can faintly hear Zeke saying something... "...what? I can't hear you!" I yell.

"I *said*, this van can't take another hit like that! We're *fucked*!" He yells back.

I'm starting to regain my senses now. The van is skipping along the ground. The rear left thruster must be damaged.

"Any idea what hit us?" I ask, looking around, only to see Astra clutching her head in her hands, blood seeping from a cut on her forehead, and Dexter completely unconscious.

"Oh...fuck."

Wait.

I pull my CYBR VYSR out of my backpack and turn it on. I use its scanning ability to look out of the hole that the explosion tore in the van. Buildings and cars fly by as we pass, and Zeke weaves in and out of other surface vehicles like it's his job.

Wait, I guess it is his job, driving an ambulance of sorts...

Just then, a red locator and a beep show me what I'm hoping to find.

"There!" I shout, pointing to a higher-level CYBR Corp UAV. The VYSR traced the heat signature of the explosion, allowing me to find our violent friend's location. "It's a UAV equipped with a missile launcher. Real nasty stuff for a car chase if you ask me!"

"Great, how am I supposed to outrun a god-damn UAV?" Zeke asks, taking a shockingly tight left turn onto a side street.

"Idk, man, what do you want from me?" Then it dawns on me. "Wait! Take the tunnel on Sixth! It'll be forced to come down to our level. That tunnel has a ridiculously low clearance."

"On it."

The van takes a hard right, putting too much strain on the damaged thruster and dragging the entire left side of the van along the ground as we turn. It makes a horrible screeching sound and sends sparks everywhere.

"Well, they certainly know where we are!" I jab.

"If we survive this, I will kill you." Zeke is not having it today. He takes a left onto 6th Street, flooring it toward the small tunnel.

We're deep in the heart of the Residential District now, where the streets are narrow, busy, and full of terrible drivers. Somehow, Zeke is still working traffic. He always has been a crazy driver, but this is truly a sight to behold.

"Nice drivin' there, Bond."

I simply receive a grunt in reply. We're nearing the tunnel now, and Zeke is not breaking his concentration for anything. To be fair, I shouldn't be interrupting him.

A very loud beeping is coming from my VYSR, which is never awesome. I put it back down over my eyes to see a missile mere inches away from the top of the van through the thermal scanner.

This is not where I want to die.

It somehow misses us, exploding the car directly to our right. It must've hit the fuel tank because it suddenly erupts in a massive fireball. The shockwave throws our van against the car to our left.

"For the love of CHROME. Give me a break!" Despite Zeke's pseudo-religious outburst, he maintains control of the van.

"You seriously missed your calling to be a getaway driver," I comment, not entirely joking.

We cross into the tunnel as more beeping comes from my VYSR. Milliseconds later, the car behind us is torn in half by a third explosion. We're lucky it's just a UAV armed with only semi-smart shrapnel missiles. If a Retribution armored truck was after us, we'd've definitely been fried by a heat-seeking self-guided arc charge by now. I've seen those things vaporize people in a horrifying, bloody lightning storm. A shiver runs down my spine at the thought of it.

"Hang onto somethin'!" Zeke shouts.

I snap back to reality as we slam headlong into the back of a transport truck.

"We have to get out of this fucking van!" Ash exclaims, startling me.

With a quick glance over to her, I can see that she's bandaged her head wound with some of the gauze from Zeke's van supplies. I'm happy to see she's conscious and coherent. The same, however, cannot be said for Dex, who is still entirely unconscious. He looks like he might have a concussion, what with that nasty bruise on his head.

"You're right, Ash," I reply, "we gotta steal a car or lose them on foot or something. They've clearly identified your van."

"Yeah, yeah. Let's get on with it then." Zeke resigns. With that, he throws open the driver door, hops over the amalgamation of metal that is both the front of our van and the back of the transport truck and throws the unconscious Dex over his shoulder.

Who is this guy today?

Inspired by Zeke, I help Ash kick open the now jammed right side door, and we grab as much as we can while quickly getting away from the van. I grab my backpack, and she holds some of Zeke's easier-to-carry supplies. We run as fast as we can behind the truck we crashed into, stopping momentarily to readjust our cargo.

My VYSR beeps, and we run. Zeke and I carry Dex as

best as we can, with Ash holding the bags. A fourth missile devastates the van. I can feel the heat engulfing me as small pieces of metal hit my back, one lodging itself in the back of my neck. There's no time to acknowledge the pain. I see our chance to escape.

"Over there! The maintenance tunnels!" Since my hands are busy carrying Dex, I aggressively gesture with my head toward the door up ahead on our right.

"Good idea—" Zeke is cut off by another explosion striking the ground directly next to him. He stumbles and drops to one knee, and we nearly drop Dex. I can see chunks of asphalt and blood covering the left side of Zeke.

"Shit!" We gotta go *now!*" Ash shouts, keeping us in reality.

"Double-time, Zeke! We can do this, buddy!" I try to get him motivated as I take more of Dex's weight.

We all run as fast as we possibly can toward the maintenance tunnels. Ash gets there first and opens the door. We run through, and she barely has enough time to close it behind us as another missile strikes, leaving an enormous dent in the solid steel door and filling the narrow tunnel with a deafening boom.

All I can hear is a high-pitched whine for a solid minute. It hurts so badly I collapse to one knee and clutch my head in my hands.

After a few moments, the ringing in my ears subsides enough for me to realize we shouldn't still be here.

"Come on, we gotta barricade this door and get the hell outta here!" I gesture to Zeke and Ash, bending to pick up a nearby steel beam of some sort. With their help, we prop the beam diagonally across the door frame.

"Now grab Dex and get ready to run on my signal," I command, taking out my katana and activating the arc unit. I use the arc energy to makeshift weld the I-beam to the door and the frame. Since the door opens inward, this should keep the Retribution at bay for at least a few minutes.

"Now, go!" I shout, already making my way past the others. "I'll take point on this one. We have no idea what's in these tunnels."

"Fine by me," Zeke replies with an incredulous eyebrow raise.

Well, at least the snark master is back.

Taking my katana firmly in both hands, I proceed into the increasingly dark maintenance tunnel. Before long, the only light is the crackling blue of the katana's arc unit. I can see using my VYSR's night vision, but the others must be essentially blind.

I've never been in these tunnels. I don't know where I'm leading them. I don't know what I'm leading them toward. I don't even know if we've outrun the troops from the street. All I know is that no matter what, I *will* keep them safe.

CH 8

I have no idea where I'm leading them. At least Zeke had the idea for him and Ash to turn on their Holocomms in flashlight mode. Since their internal batteries are functioning correctly, it's not an issue, unlike mine. The light isn't bright enough to navigate by, but it's enough to help my friends know where to plant their feet, so I guess that's something. I'm just glad I brought this VYSR. It's saved my life multiple times today, and I have a feeling we're just getting started. The night vision mode truly is incredible. Credit where credit is due, CYBR Corp sure knows how to build tech.

"Alright, we're turning left just up ahead," I call back to them, making a left turn into a wide, short section of tunnel.

"Wait, shit!"

"What's up, Ol'?" Ash asks, somewhat out of breath from carrying half of Dex's weight.

"It's another *fucking* dead end." I've been doing this for, I wanna say, about forty-five minutes, maybe an hour, but it's felt like days. Every turn, every crossroad, every dead end weighs on me.

What if I'm leading them to their deaths? No. I can't afford to think like that. But still, it sucks. Not to mention, I'm almost out of battery, running on my internal now, and that's probably got like fifteen minutes on it, tops.

"Wait, you're not tellin' me what I think you are...are ya?" Zeke, also out of breath, seems a little less chipper than usual.

"I hate to say it, man, but yeah. We gotta go all the way back to the last crossroads we came across and go right instead of left there." I shrug my shoulders, trying to show that I really don't know what I'm doing here. "Also, I hate to say it, but I'm running out of juice." I gesture to the dead external battery.

"In that case, I need a damn sec'." With that very typical response from Zeke, he and Ash lower Dex onto the ground as gently as they can. They look exhausted, and I haven't noticed just how much until now. Zeke sits on the far side of the tunnel. He takes a few moments to breathe, drink some water, and set up a lantern. Then, he begins examining Dex. After a few moments, he seems to relax.

"His condition is stable. He's still unconscious, but his vitals are all good. As long as we don't run into any hooligans down here, we should be alright."

"That's good to hear," Ash responds, sliding down the wall to take a seat on the opposite side of the tunnel from Zeke and Dex.

I sit against the wall right next to Ash. Might as well. We all need a minute, and here is as good of a place as any. We're tucked into this dead end of this tunnel, so there's only one direction to watch. For the first time in hours, I allow myself to relax, taking off my VYSR, placing it in my jacket pocket, and allowing my eyes to adjust to the dim light as I scan the room, checking the corners. It's hard to make anything out in the extremely dim lantern light from across the tunnel, but I can at least see enough to know we're alone here.

"You always did have a thing for scoping out the scene, even on our dates." Ash comments, squeezing my leg to get my attention. She must've been watching me scan the setting as I sat down. She takes a drink from her water bottle and hands it to me. I drink gladly, then place it on the ground next to me.

"Yeah, yeah. But you can't exactly blame me on this one." I reply. She can't help but smile as she rolls her eyes.

I smile back at her.

"Also, let me see that." She says, gesturing to the external battery.

"Sure, it's just junk, though."

"Not completely."

She takes the battery and disconnects the cord from it, leaving the other end plugged into my right arm. Then, she slides the waist of her pants down slightly on the left side, revealing her hip and a few inches of her cybernetic left leg. I can't help but stare, my eyes tracing the waistband of her purple underwear, which runs along the line between her soft skin and the shiny metal of her leg, glinting in the lantern light...

Oh, wow, I'm staring way too long. Um, pretend to do something...

I snap my eyes away from Ash, pretending to fix the cord's connection to my right arm's charging port. I can feel my cheeks burning and my heart pounding.

Maybe she won't notice?

Ash plugs the cord into a port on her upper leg, so now her leg is connected to my arm. She gently slides her jeans back up over the cord, making sure it stays connected.

"Wait, what are you doing?" I ask, trying to bring myself back to what's actually happening and to act like I wasn't just staring at her.

"Giving you some juice, you idiot." She smiles, then pauses, raising an eyebrow slightly, her smile shifting to a smirk. She must've noticed my flushed cheeks.

Yep, busted.

"Ah, well, are you sure?"

Remain calm, Wolf.

"Yep, unlike you, my leg's battery works fine, and it recharges as I move. Plus, I'm just keeping you conscious while Zeke gets ready." She says, gesturing to Zeke and his supplies, along with the fusion power cell in its case. "I assumed you didn't want to take another surprise nap."

"Ah, well, I could use the sleep." I joke. "But really, thanks, Ash. You're so thoughtful." I smile at her.

"Of course." She smiles back.

We both sit there for a moment. My mind is somewhat scrambled by thoughts of Ash, mixed with an anxious feeling in the back of my head, that itch I can't scratch, the knowledge that they're out there, looking for us right now.

After a moment of silence, Ash sighs, gently takes my hand, and looks into my eyes with a concerned expression.

"Listen, Olly," she says, "you know it's not your fault, right? I mean...what happened to your family?" Her eyes are filled with concern, her brow deeply furrowed.

"I..." I drop my head. She caught me off-guard.

I don't know how to answer that.

"When you say it out loud, yes, it makes sense," I reply, grasping for the right words as I stare at the ground, squeezing Ash's hand slightly, careful not to squeeze too hard with my cybernetic hand. "Of course, it isn't my fault that our world is run by a tyrannical, cruel corporation or that my family fell victim to their tyranny."

I pause, fighting the tears forming in my eyes.

"But, deep inside me is so much hatred, and anger, and guilt...I can't just shake that off. I've been trying to shake it for the past *ten years*, and I just..." The tears are flowing now, slowly and silently. I don't try to stop them or wipe them away. As painful as it is to say these things, it also feels good to get them out in the open, tears and all. "I do know one thing for certain. I will *not* let them take anyone else from me. I won't let them take anyone else's family away, not like they took mine. That's why I *have* to stop them. Why *we* have to stop them. I hope you understand, Ash."

As I say the last few words, my tears slow, a burning determination growing inside of me. I wipe my eyes and look up at Astra, who's been silent this whole time. My face softens, and the fire in my gut turns back to lead as I see the tears streaming down her cheeks.

"Olly, I...I understand. Of *course*, I understand. But I need you to understand something, too. I need you to know that you really have no reason to feel guilty. I completely understand your anger, but you shouldn't blame yourself for what happened...promise me you'll at least try to let go of that guilt, ok?" Her face is filled with so much sadness, and her eyes are so kind. I can see how much she cares about me as she stares deeply into my eyes.

"I promise I'll try to let go of it...I haven't really given it a fair shot yet, I'll admit that. Thanks as always for being amazing, Ash." I give her my best approximation of a smile, my entire body filled with a vortex of emotions. Not to mention how absolutely *exhausted* I am. I wasn't allowing myself to think about it until now, but my body is almost entirely spent of energy, cybernetic or otherwise.

I really haven't been taking care of myself...

"Hey, Olly?"

"Yeah, Ash?"

"It's going to be okay. We're going to get through this."

She gives me a warm smile and pulls me into a hug, and I hug her back gladly. My stomach jumps, and I feel warm despite the freezing temperatures of the tunnels.

No matter what happens, I can't lose her. I can't lose this feeling. Not again. Not ever.

I have no idea how much time passes before we

reluctantly pull away from the hug. I know I don't want it to end, and I hope she doesn't, either.

Once again, my heart is beating very quickly. I can't stop staring at her face. My eyes have fully adjusted to the low light, and she is *so beautiful*. Her eyes...her lips...even the tear stains running through the dirt on her cheeks seem to shine like little stars...

Wait, she's smiling at me. I'm smiling back. And, is that her hand on my leg?

"Hey, Olly, what are you lookin' at?" She whispers playfully, giving me a smirk as she moves closer, her face millimeters from mine. I can barely hear her. It's like something's covering my ears...all I hear is my heart pounding.

I open my mouth to answer but quickly close it. There are no words for this. I place my left hand gently on the side of her face and pull her in. Before I really know what I'm doing, I kiss her.

She's kissing me back.

My eyes are closed. I wrap my arm around her waist, the other holding her cheek and neck. I pull her in closer with both arms, completely losing myself in her. My mind is exploding in a rainbow of emotion, waves of goosebumps running along my body. I can feel her arms tight around me, her hair brushing my arm, her chest rising and falling rapidly against mine.

Our lips part for a second. I gasp for air for just a moment, opening my eyes to sneak a glimpse of her face. She must have done the same, my eyes meeting hers for a moment before we both hurriedly look away. I can feel the warmth rush to my cheeks as I look back at her face. She's blushing, too. It's adorable. Her eyes are so large, so deeply beautiful. I smile at her before pulling her in for another gentler kiss.

As I go to pull away again, I feel her arms hold me tighter, pulling me back in. She kisses me, and I make no effort to stop her. I run my hands up and down her back slowly as we kiss. She does the same to me, sending a shiver down my spine.

Finally, after another time-bending eternity, our lips part. We barely move away. Ash leans her forehead on mine and strokes my hair gently.

I pull away slightly, opening my eyes and taking in her face again. My eyes take a second to focus.

"Do you remember when we talked at The Museum?" I ask timidly.

Am I about to do this?

"Of course." She responds.

If not now, then when, right?

"So, I wanted to say that I love you—"

"I love you too, Olly!" She blurts out, stopping me in my tracks. She almost looks surprised at her own words. Pleasantly surprised, that is. "And I *do* want you in my life. Forever." She smiles, tears welling in her eyes again.

I can feel tears forming again as I say, "You just...took the words right out of my mouth, Ash. I love you so much, and I—" my voice breaks, "I never, ever, want to lose you again. You mean the world to me." I smile back at her, and we both sit there for a moment, smiling as tears of joy roll softly down our cheeks, sparkling in the dim light.

We're interrupted rudely by the beeping of my external battery pack. I tear my eyes away from Astra's divine features and look down at the small screen of the battery, which felt like it was the right time to remind me that it was out of power.

Rude battery. Rude.

"Yeah, so," Zeke chimes in, "I didn't wanna interrupt you two, given the, ya know, circumstances, but it's time for some open-circuit surgery, Olly." He lightly taps a socket wrench against the case of the fusion cell. He's…smiling at us? I can't remember the last time I saw such a genuine smile from Zeke. It fades as quickly as it appeared, but I definitely saw it.

Looks like he was rooting for us to get back together. Zeke, you big softy.

"Alright, let's do this," I reply, glancing toward Dex. "By the way, what happens if we run into some stim-heads hiding out down here? Or, you know, some more friendly neighborhood murder cops? Will he be alright?"

"Yeah, I mean, he's as alright as an unconscious person can be," Zeke pauses for a moment, seemingly contemplating something, "I do have this Neuro-Jolt Stim, but these tend to have some nasty side effects. I'd rather not use it unless we have to."

"Of course, Zeke, we'll keep him safe," I reassure him. "He'd do the same for us."

I receive a somber nod in reply.

"Alright, enough jibber-jabber!" He gestures at the ground next to him, where he's laid out a thin medical blanket. "The doctor will see you now, Mr. Wolf."

I unplug the cord from my arm, handing it to Ash with a small smile. Then, I stand up, walk over to the blanket, and lie down. Somehow, I feel like it's less comfortable than if I were just lying on the ground.

Zeke gets his tools ready as I stare at the dimly lit ceiling of the tunnel. There's slightly more light over here since Zeke has set up some of his portable spotlights. I, for one, am glad he's not going to operate on me in total darkness.

"Alright, here we go, Ol'. You gotta stay awake for me, alright? If you lose consciousness for too long with no battery, there's a high chance that you might not wake up. Ever. Do you understand?" I nod, my mind racing.

I have to trust that it's going to be alright.

He nods back and then unplugs the external battery pack from my arm. Apparently, there was just enough juice left in that thing to keep me from being too terribly tired because I immediately feel my vision dimming. It's suddenly challenging to stay awake, but I fight it.

I can do this.

Without saying another word, Zeke gets to work. In between extremely long blinks, I can feel him disable my right arm by removing the service plate and using the switch in my shoulder. After that, I feel very little.

I can hear clicking, clanging, and the occasional muttered curse word from Zeke, but mostly, I'm putting my effort into staying awake. I feel myself drifting again, so I bite my tongue a little too hard. I can taste blood in my mouth, but on the plus side, I'm very awake, at least for the moment.

Out of the corner of my eye, I see Zeke remove my old battery pack, which looks horrifyingly blackened. A moment later, the faint blue glow and the glint of the metal casing of the fusion cell take its place.

"Time for the moment of truth," Zeke says, seemingly more to himself than to me.

I feel my arm being pushed against my side as Zeke pushes the fusion cell into place with a click. For a terrifyingly long second, I wait for something to happen. Then, a flood of energy that is more tremendous than I've ever experienced fills my body. No more fighting to stay awake. I'm more alert than I've ever been. It feels like my veins are crackling with arc electricity, just like the blades of my Daishō.

"Whoa!" I can't contain my excitement. "Holy shit!"

"I take it it's working, then?" Zeke replies with a wry smile.

"You bet your ass it's working. Now patch me up, and let's see just how *well* it's working." I grin back.

"Alright, don't get too excited."

With that, he attaches the battery panel of my arm, then switches the service mode off, re-enabling the function of my arm. Having my right arm effectively removed and reattached is always a strange feeling, but this time is particularly unusual. My right arm feels more *alive* than I can ever remember. Zeke reattaches the service panel, and I sit up *very* quickly.

Man, I feel good!

"I don't think I've ever seen you this energized," Zeke says, giving me a slap on the back.

"Yeah, wow! I don't think so either." I shoot to my feet and start pacing around. "Oh man, I'm so ready to fight some Retribution, no, Shinigami, no, both! Let's go!" I feel really inclined to punch a wall. I do. It feels great.

"Whoa there, cowboy, don't get too carried away!" Ash mocks me with a chuckle.

After a few minutes of jumping jacks and jogging in place, I can feel my body acclimating to the new power source. As the initial surge of energy wears off, I start to feel a little more normal. But I still feel *really* good. It's been a long time since my battery functioned properly, and this is even better than that old solid-state junk ever was.

Wow, I didn't even realize how drained I was feeling all the time.

"Alright, I'm feeling a little more normal," I say with a laugh, "but man, it feels good to be fully charged again!"

"I'm so happy for y—" Ash begins to say.

"Wait, shh!" I cut her off with an aggressive whisper.

What is that noise?

"I can hear something...behind that wall," I say in a whisper, pointing toward the dead end.

I start to move slowly toward the wall. How did I miss this sound before? The closer I get, the more distinct the sounds become.

It's like...a groaning sound? And a weird rhythmic clanging, too. What in the name of chrome?

I'm only a foot from the wall now, and there's no mistaking it. Someone, or some*thing*, is behind this wall. I press my hands and ear to the wall. One of my hands sinks into the wall slightly with a 'click.'

Oh, that can't be good.

Suddenly, the wall begins to shift. I feel a shiver run down my spine as what seemed to be just another dead end opens up to reveal a vast, dimly lit section of tunnel, along with the source of the sounds.

But...no...it can't be. No way.

As I squint into the darkness at the shadowy figures filling the room, a singular, horrible thought fills my mind. They can only be one thing: Chrome Drones. Horrifying, mangled, half-decomposed husks of what used to be people, their minds just as rotten as their flesh. Only their cybernetics, their chrome, keeps them "alive."

There must be at least twenty of them, and that's just the ones I can see. Who knows how many are lurking in the darkness? I can't see the end of this section of the tunnel that's in front of me. If it even does end.

One of them is banging its head against the metal wall, groaning a horrible, pained groan as it does. The rest are just standing there or lying on the ground, nearly lifeless. It's hard to believe that these amalgamations of rotting flesh and tarnished cybernetics used to be human beings. I always thought they were just a story told to scare kids away from taking stims and getting too many implants.

We have to get out of here.

I start to slowly back away from them, desperately trying

not to make a sound. I don't think they've noticed us yet.

"Olly, no!" Ash tries to warn me in a desperate whisper, but it's too late.

A horrifically loud clanging sound echoes throughout the tunnel as I step back into Zeke's tools, sending them flying. All at once, twenty pairs of faintly glowing, lifeless eyes turn toward me. From the darkness, more and more eyes start to appear. The nearest few, about thirty feet away, start shambling forward. The sounds of shuffling feet, strained motors, and popping tendons fill the air.

I feel sick.

"Chrome Drones! Run!" I shout, fear filling my mind and adrenaline filling my body. I help Zeke pick up Dex, Ash grabs as much of our stuff as she can, and we run.

The sounds of our thundering feet echo through the tunnel, followed by a blood-curdling chorus of screaming, groaning Chrome Drones clanging along the floor right behind us.

My heart is beating faster with every step. Zeke isn't as fast as me, and I'm starting to lose him. I pause for just a moment, getting a better grip on Dex. As I glance back, I see the horrible sight of this hoard clambering toward us. They're desperately trampling over each other, running and crawling through the darkness with an animalistic desperation. They're chasing us like feral dogs with rabies chasing a stray cat.

"Alright, Zeke, let's pick up the *fucking* pace!"

I'm running with everything I've got, and so is Zeke. Ash is ahead of us by a few feet, navigating. I can barely see her. It's so damn dark.

"We're taking a left!" She yells back at us. "This is the other way from the fork!"

Zeke and I follow her into the one tunnel we've yet to try. I'd cross my fingers if I wasn't busy carrying Dex. I take another glance behind me as I run, and the Drones are still only a few yards behind. Sparks fly from their faulty cyber-parts, giving me horrifying glimpses of the rot surrounding the chrome.

We run for what must have been a few minutes straight down this tunnel. It's strange. Most of the tunnels turn frequently and seemingly at random, but this one hasn't.

"Do you see any turns or anything?" I yell up to Ash.

"No, nothing! All I see is this damn darkness!" She growls in frustration.

"Well, there better be something soon, I can't run like this forever, and these freaks are NOT slowing down!" Zeke interjects in between breaths.

They're a good ten or fifteen feet back, but they definitely haven't given up on chasing us. If anything, they're gaining on us. I'm sure we'd have no trouble outpacing them in a straight run, but between carrying Dex, the darkness, and our lack of direction, we're barely keeping ahead of them.

"I see a dim light over there!" Ash yells, continuing to sprint ahead. After a few more seconds of running, she comes to a sudden stop.

"Fuck! This is a dead end, too!" She yells, pounding her fist on the wall. "I thought the light was something, but it's just another dead *fucking* end."

It won't be more than a few seconds until we're devoured by Chrome Drones, and I do NOT want to find out what that feels like.

"Let's put him down!" I yell back at Zeke, moving toward the wall at the end of the tunnel with the dim, flickering light above it.

"Got it!" He replies. "Now, do something about our hungry little friends there!"

"Ash, here!" I yell, tossing her the arc rifle I picked up from the Retribution soldier earlier.

She catches it, slings the strap over her shoulder, and takes aim without a word.

I turn toward the hoard, pulling both of my swords from their sheaths and switching on the arc units. Only the katana sparks to life. I stare incredulously at the wakizashi for a half second.

Wait, what the...oh duh. It's broken.

I throw on my VYSR and switch on the night vision, instantly regretting it. Seeing these...creatures in better detail is pure nightmare fuel, and my fear is multiplied tenfold as these half-chrome, half-decomposing abominations descend on us.

To my complete surprise, when the first of the Drones are only a few feet away from me, right at the edge of the flickering overhead light, they stop dead in their tracks. They pause for just a moment, staring at the arc energy of my katana, seemingly entranced. They groan and click, their motors creaking and whining as they move. The rest of the horde crashes into them, confused. Some of them start snarling and biting each other, clawing at wires and bits of flesh like rabid dogs fighting over a scrap of meat. They scream as they tear into each other.

A few excruciatingly long seconds later, one of the Drones, far in the back of the horde, lets out a horrific scream, like the cry of a dying beast. The rest respond in kind, filling the tunnel with the deafening echoes of their shrill, tortured screams. The ones who've been attacking each other even clamber back to their feet, staring straight at me. One cocks its head to the side as its jaw dangles loosely. Another shuffles forward a few steps, its left arm swinging limply from a couple of wires and a single tendon. Their glowing eyes, amplified in my night vision, are all trained on me and my friends.

Oh fuck oh shit, what in the absolute hell.

I find my attention drawn to the one in the back, the one that rallied its brethren with a battle cry of pain. I didn't notice it before since it's so far away, but now that I'm looking at it, it seems different somehow. It's standing straighter and looks more human than the others, like it hasn't entirely lost control of itself yet, or maybe…like it's developed a new kind of intelligence altogether. I stare at it through my VYSR for a second, trying to make out what I'm looking at. Suddenly, its glowing eyes snap to look directly at me, and it lets out another cry.

Fuck that.

The battle cry unleashes the horde. They charge forward again, clambering toward us. The closest one reaches me in seconds, but I manage to take a swing with my katana, slicing its head clean off. Its body continues toward me for a moment, then slumps to the ground as another takes its place. I slash with my wakizashi as the familiar whine of a charging arc rifle cuts through the Chrome Drones' bone-chilling death chorus.

"Get down!" Ash commands. I instinctively jump back and fall to the ground without a second thought.

Ash opens fire, the air crackling with electricity as she unleashes a torrent of molten death on the horde. The closest line of Drones crumples to the ground, their circuits and skin equally melted. I resist the urge to vomit as the stench reaches my nose. She charges the rifle again as the lifeless, melting corpses are shoved aside by the next group.

These things are definitely not human. They feel nothing, fear nothing.

I jump back to my feet, slashing over and over again to protect Ash from the faster ones.

Holy shit. There are so many of them.

I stab one through the chest with the katana, pulling back as it falls to the ground, convulsing. Ash lets loose another volley from the arc rifle, melting through a sizable group of them. But more keep crawling and scrambling forward, jumping over the growing mound of bodies. There are so many more than I had seen initially.

So. Many. Fucking. More.

Ash charges another round as I continue slashing through them one by one. I cut off the head of one and slash through the legs of another, kicking what's left of it away from me. One of them gets ahold of my right arm and bites down. Luckily for me, that's my metal arm. I stab through its head with the wakizashi and push it off of me. Their blood is starting to cover me, and as if that wasn't bad enough, it's cold and sticky, like it hasn't flowed through their veins in quite some time. How they could possibly even move is…

No, focus up, Oliver. You can have an existential breakdown later.

Ash releases her third volley on the crowd, her accuracy increasing with each shot.

She really is incredible.

"It's overheating. You gotta buy me some time!" She pleads. She lets the rifle hang from its strap and pulls out her pistol, but it's barely enough to make a dent in the horde.

"Open the vent on the rifle's left side!" I shout, slicing through two Drones simultaneously.

"I did!"

I move through the crowd of Chrome Drones, dodging their desperate, lunging attacks and responding with precise, deadly strikes of my own. I drop one, two, five, seven of them in a row. But they don't slow down. They never let up. Their numbers never seem to dwindle. They screech and groan, claw and bite, stumble and crawl toward us.

"Hurry," I yell in between dropping number eight and nine, "there's too many!"

The crowd clears for just a moment, giving me a perfect view of the leader, or alpha, or head honcho, or whatever you want to call it. It's a nightmare monster, and it's making its way toward me with alarming speed. Before it turned into a cyber-zombie, it must've been a defensive lineman or something because it's probably pushing seven feet tall and built as sturdy as a brick shithouse in an earthquake zone.

The crowds of feral Chrome Drones are still clambering toward us at an alarming rate, and I'm cutting through them as Ash blasts them to molten pieces. But my attention is locked on the leader. It's barreling through the crowds, shoving the smaller and weaker Drones aside as if they're made of toothpicks and marshmallows.

Now that I think of it, that's disturbingly close to how they look...Holy chrome, Oliver, focus.

Suddenly, an explosion rips through a group of Drones to my left, sending me flying onto my back. I get up and scramble backward, glancing to see the source of the explosion. To my surprise, I see none other than Dexter. Not only is he awake, but a concealed rocket launcher has popped up from his left shoulder. To his left is Zeke, holding the expended Neuro-Jolt Stim. A look of shock fills his face.

Dex sends another rocket to hit the group to my right, blowing them into tiny, sparking pieces. I charge forward, slashing through two more drones as I feel a hot, crackling torrent of arc plasma fly past me on my right. Another group of Drones falls to the ground, melted.

Ash must've gotten the rifle cooled down.

I jump back to get a better look at the crowd. It looks like they might actually be slowing down, their numbers thinning out.

Maybe we'll survive after all.

"We can do this!" I shout to the others, running back into the crowd, weaving in between the Drones, and cutting at their weakest points as I go.

Ash responds with a shout of determination and releases another volley from the rifle, this time managing to expertly pick off a crowd of them from around where I'm standing.

Despite the situation, I can't help but feel *alive.*

This fusion cell is fantastic. I feel so fast, so powerful.

I slash through three more Drones, then jump back and signal to Dex to launch another rocket. Only one doesn't come. I look over to see him clutching his chest and kneeling. Zeke is tapped into his analysis port, seemingly running frantic tests.

I guess he did say that stim was dangerous...

While I'm staring in their direction, I temporarily forget about the Drones behind me. They surround me in an instant, grabbing hold of my limbs and biting down on my arms and neck. I'm falling to the ground, and I can't move my arms to swing my swords. One of them claws at my face, scratching my forehead and knocking my VYSR to the ground. I can hear it being smashed to bits within seconds.

Fucking fuck.

The world plunges into darkness. I struggle desperately to break free, but they've swarmed me. All I can see is their glowing eyes surrounding me. All I hear is their screams and the gnashing of their teeth.

I can't believe it ends like this.

"Olly! Oliver!" Ash's voice pierces through the air, sending energy through me. I struggle harder to break free, managing to get my right arm free by forcing the motors to their limit. I slash through a few of my assailants with the katana, but more move in and pin my arm back down.

Suddenly, a bright, hot stream of arc plasma melts the drones on top of me. Drops of plasma and molten Drone fall onto my cheek and neck, and it burns like the Sun. "Fuck!"

That really hurts. But I have to take this opportunity.

I shove off the melting corpses of the Chrome Drones, stabbing the one still biting and clawing at me with my wakizashi. It stops moving but remains standing, the cybernetics holding its bones and melting flesh in place. I shove it away from me as a shiver runs down my back.

"Thank you!" I shout to Ash, standing and turning to face the remaining group of Drones. I can't see as well because my VYSR is somewhere in that pile I just climbed out of, but I won't let that stop me.

If only my eyes had night vision. At least they're adapting to the overhead lighting. If Ash can shoot like that in this light, then I can swing some fucking swords in it, too.

"I think there's another secret door! I'm trying to open it, but it's fucking stuck!" Zeke shouts, his voice echoing through the tunnels as Ash and I continue to fight the onslaught of Drones.

There are still so many of them.

Just then, Ash's rifle overheats again. I can tell without looking by the angry scream and pistol shots coming from her direction. Without my VYSR, my reaction time is down. I hold them off as best as I can, but even with the new power cell, it's a tall order.

I slash through Drone after Drone, forced to slowly back up as they swarm me relentlessly. My hands are getting slippery with sweat, cold blood, and who knows what else. The ground is a tangled mess of corpses. I try not to think about it or to breathe through my nose. Despite that, I throw up a little in my mouth, but I swallow it. To make matters worse, the leader is rapidly closing in on me. It's only a few seconds away now, based on the pace it's been running toward me.

I don't know how much longer I can do this. And I can't take that freak down, can I?

One of them gets too close to Ash, so she bashes its head in with the rifle. It falls, clawing at her on its way down.

"Ah, shit, that hurts!" She screams, stumbling to the ground for a second.

Without thinking, I jump in front of her and carve through the endless horde. She sets the barrel of the arc rifle on my right shoulder before charging another volley. I stand, without moving, as bright, hot rays of electrified death stream through the room, melting and setting fire to everything it touches. Everything seems to slow down as I take a moment to marvel at the sight of it.

It's beautiful, in a horrible kind of way.

I snap back to reality as Zeke screams, "Run! The door is open! Fucking *run!*"

Without a moment of hesitation, Ash and I turn and sprint at full speed through the now-opened wall of the tunnel. I see Dex crouched in the corner, gasping for breath.

"Help me with this damn door!"

"Coming!"

Zeke and I close the massive stone door as quickly as possible, which is not very fast, as Ash holds off the remaining Chrome Drones with the rifle.

"I've only got one or two shots left before it overheats again! And what in the ever-living *fuck* is that thing!?"

"I see you've met the big cheese!" I scream, pushing the door closed with all the strength I can muster.

We've almost got the door closed. We can do this.

A horribly mangled set of arms reaches through the

foot-wide gap, grasping and clawing at my arms and face. I glance through for a second, seeing the Drone whose arms I'm smelling, but my attention is quickly taken by the leader Drone standing right behind it. It's just standing there, menacingly. It's staring at me, breathing heavily, smiling with rotten teeth and sparking, red eyes. It reaches out slowly, pointing directly at me, smiling even wider, its rotten face revealing far more teeth than a normal smile would.

Fuck. That. Shit.

I push on the door harder than I've ever pushed anything, slamming the door the rest of the way. The rotten, sparking arms of the Chrome Drone drop to the ground as the door locks back into its undetectable state, their feral shrieks dying away as I stumble back into the darkness. It takes all I have not to immediately collapse to the floor and pass out.

CH 9

SEVERAL minutes after stumbling into this hidden room, the sounds of the Chrome Drones are finally starting to fade away.

"I think we're clear," I whisper to the others. I turn to face them, barely able to make out their features in the oppressive darkness of this stupid tunnel. The only light is from a mini surgical flashlight that Zeke pulled from his coat pocket. I can see Ash standing guard, facing toward the dark unknown of the room, while Zeke stabilizes Dex, who is conscious but otherwise in rough shape. He's looked better, but he's also looked worse, so...I guess that's a win?

Alright, time to make yourself useful, Olly.

I tap the screen of my Holocomm, and the brightness of the display causes me to squint my eyes for a second before I select the flashlight feature and turn it toward the dark expanse in front of me. I walk past Astra, and she joins me. After a minute or so of walking, she loops her left arm through my right and rests her head on my shoulder. I feel a warm tingle in my stomach. We keep walking, scanning to the left and right of us with our lights, respectively.

"So, what are you looking for?"

"I'm not sure. I guess I just—"

Before I can finish my statement, I stub my toe against something I didn't see before. I point my wrist down, finding a small box. It looks to be some sort of metal crate, about two by one by one feet, if I had to guess. It's not very large, but it didn't budge when I kicked it. I crouch down to examine it closer. There's some sort of logo on it, but it's covered in a thick layer of dust.

"Hey Ash, can you shine your light on this?"

"Sure thing, Ol'." She crouches down next to me, aiming her Holocomm toward the crate.

I turn off my flashlight with a flick of my wrist, then jam my hands in my pockets. I find a scrap of gauze from one of the times Zeke bandaged me up and use the non-bloody part of it to clean the dust from this crate. The CYBR Corp logo quickly becomes apparent as I wipe away the grime.

Of course, who else?

I glance at Ash, and the look on her face perfectly captures the way I feel about the situation: disgusted, confused, and exhausted, but also intrigued. I pick up the crate, which is a lot heavier than I thought it would be.

Like damn, what's even in this, a bunch of bricks?

I can't help but chuckle at my own stupid non-joke.

"What's so funny?" Ash teases, playfully pushing me as we walk back to Zeke and Dex.

"Nothing really...I think I'm just tired. This dumb box is really heavy."

We share a tired laugh and keep walking. After a few more steps, my foot hits another crate. Ash points her light over as she realizes what happened. This one is quite a bit larger than the first, somewhere around seven feet long. I probably should've seen it, if I'm being honest. If I wasn't so tired, I probably would have.

There are several more small crates on top of and next to the larger one.

We walk the rest of the way to Zeke's makeshift station in the corner, and I set down the small crate next to where he's sitting. Well, I should say I dropped the crate because my arms gave out as I lowered it to the ground. It makes a loud 'thud' as it hits the ground.

"The hell is that?" Zeke asks, startled.

I nudge the CYBR Corp logo with my shoe. "There's at least a dozen of these crates in this part of the tunnel. I've got no idea what we've stumbled on, but it doesn't seem like more of the same old, abandoned, Chrome Drone-infested tunnels to me."

"You might be right, but then again, we didn't know about those Drones until a few minutes ago, so what the fuck do we know?" Zeke moves his lamp closer and starts to examine the crate.

"Fair enough," I reply, "We'll keep looking around while you take a crack at that thing." I hesitate, smirking as I think of a dumb joke. "Also, that's another Johnny in the swear jar, young man."

"I know you're joking," Ash replies between laughs, "but could you imagine how many Johnnies you'd have gotten from Zeke by now? Imagine the profits!"

We all share a laugh, including Dex, who's sitting against the tunnel wall next to Zeke. He goes back to eating a cube of grey, unappetizing-looking nutrigel, then winces slightly at the taste.

"You really makin' poor Dex eat that budget nutrigel crap?"

"Hey man, if that arm of yours secretly makes pizza, now would be the time to share."

"I wish...but hcy, who knows what's in these. Could be a pizza oven for all we know." I gesture to the metal crate beside me.

"There's probably...some sort of lighting in here," Dex chimes in, "I once was taken to a covert R&D facility where—" he's interrupted by a brief coughing fit. "Where they were testing very hush-hush cybernetics and shit. It was a lot like this tunnel, now that I think about it."

"Thanks, Dex. Also, I'm glad you're doing a little better."

I reply, crouching slightly to give him a pat on the shoulder.

"Thanks, kid. So am I."

With a nod to Astra, we split up to look for a way to get the lights turned on. I figure the walls near the entrance are as good a place as any to start looking. I shine my flashlight to the left and right of the concealed door we came in through but don't see anything obvious. I start making my way around the room, combing the walls for any sort of wiring, switches, panels, anything really.

I glance at Ash. She's moved pretty quickly to what must be the far end of the room. She's actually much farther away than I expected. I shake off the feeling of unease that gives me and keep looking.

After a few minutes of excruciating silence and dull, dusty metal and stone walls, I see something. I almost missed it. It's an extremely dusty metal panel embedded in the highly dusty wall of the tunnel, approximately six inches wide and a foot tall.

Pulling out the scrap of cloth, I dust off the panel, revealing a small latch on the left-hand side of it. It takes some effort to break the latch free of the gunk holding it in place, but eventually, it opens with a loud thunk. I swing the panel open on its rusted hinges, revealing a shockingly haphazard array of wires, as well as what seems to be the lever for the power.

I move to throw the lever but notice some of the wires aren't connected properly, dangling uselessly. I'd rather not risk killing myself with an electric shock, so I turn to Zeke.

"Hey, Mister Technowizard, care to lend a hand?"

"You talkin' to me?" He quips, "I'm already tryin' to open this box for you. What am I, your errand boy?"

"You might be."

"Don't push it. And please, Mister Technowizard was my father. Call me Technowiz."

"As you wish, Technowiz." I tip an imaginary hat.

Despite his sassy response, he makes his way over to me, the light of his Holocomm coming closer.

"I don't suppose *you* could take a look at this?"

"Listen, pal, I'm not looking for another *shocking* experience right now, not after that run-in with those Drones."

My terrible joke earns a pained groan from my best friend. In other words, I just won the war of wits.

Suck it, Zeke.

"Take a look at this and tell me again that you think I should've just messed with this myself."

I step aside as Zeke moves in, shining his flashlight on the electrical panel. "Oh, damn. Yeah, good call, man." His expression becomes a look of deep concentration and a bit of confusion, which, having known him for as long as I have, is a clear sign he's engaged Technowiz mode.

I move without another word back over to the corner. I sit down with Dex and grab one of the cubes of nutrigel from the packaging. I practically inhale it, not realizing just how hungry I am. I down another cube, pausing to chew it long enough to taste it, which is a mistake. It tastes like nothing, but not like how Fauxtmeal tastes like nothing. At least Fauxtmeal tastes like a close approximation of how oatmeal used to taste. It's not Fauxtmeal's fault that oats were boring. No, nutrigel is something…different. Somehow, it tastes like nothing if nothing was the worst possible flavor ever made. It's the type of nothing that lingers on your tongue and in the back of your throat, like a bad memory that you've long forgotten.

Come to think of it, I've never put much thought into what it actually *is* that I'm eating. The regulations to list ingredients in food were 'coincidentally' lifted at the same time we started to eat entirely lab-based sustenance.

Convenient, right? But hey, it'll keep me alive long enough to complain to Zeke about how terrible it is.

"Hey, kid," Dex says, startling me out of my apparently deep focus on these little gray cubes, "I wouldn't spend too much time thinking about that stuff if I were you." He flashes a wry, knowing smile my way, gesturing to the Nutrigel in my hand.

"Fair enough, I kinda just zoned out, to be honest."

"No offense, but you look awful. And that's coming from a guy who's been mostly unconscious this whole time!" He laughs deeply, bringing on another coughing fit. Despite that, this may be the happiest I've seen him in the last few days, or maybe ever.

I laugh along for a bit. I can only imagine what I must look like after the sleeplessness, the sweaty filth of these tunnels, and carving through countless Chrome Drones. I could check in my Holocomm or something, but I think it's best not to put too much thought into that, either.

"Listen, Dex, I can't tell you enough how grateful I am for you joining us. You didn't have to do that. I hate to think where we'd be without you."

"You really don't get it, do you, Oliver?" He pauses, raising an incredulous eyebrow. "You're the one who saved me, remember? I'd be toast or worse right now if you and Zeke hadn't fought those Retribution bastards off in his clinic. I owe you my life, something I doubt I'll ever be able to pay you back for." He begins to get quieter as he finishes speaking, his face sullen and his eyes pointed downward.

"From where I'm sitting," I reply, "I feel like I'm the one who owes you a great deal. Seriously, we wouldn't be anywhere without your insight and knowledge of the way CYBR Corp operates. I don't know jack shit about hardly anything, truth be told. I'm just an angry kid with some fancy swords and a fuck you attitude." I grasp the hilts of my daishō as I say that, briefly reminded of how badly I need to fix the wakizashi. I chuckle at the hilariously true nature of what I just said.

"That may be true," Dex says, chuckling with me, "but you've also got a good heart. And who could blame you for feeling that anger? I think we all feel that, for some, it burns deeper down. For others, it boils hot on the surface, bubbling over the edges of the pot. Believe it or not, I'm a lot like you in that regard. I've got a lotta regrets and even more anger inside me, but I refuse to bring more hatred and suffering into this world. You're a good kid. Cut yourself some slack now and then." He pauses, smiling at me with a sincerity that strikes me to my core.

I'm suddenly reminded of when I was a really little kid, like maybe five or six years old. My brother, Miles, he looked at me with a shockingly similar look to how Dex is looking at me now. I had tried my hand at picking a lock, wanting to impress Miles. I failed miserably and almost got us caught, but he wasn't mad at all. He never got angry. He would always tell me the only thing we can do is learn from our mistakes and move on. He told me he was proud of me, that he would always be there for me, always love me, no matter what I did...

"You alright?" Dexter's words bring me back to reality. I realize I've been crying, tears silently rolling down my cheeks as the memory washes over me.

"Yeah, sorry. It's just...you reminded me of something my brother told me." I try my best to give Dex a casual smile, though I doubt it's very convincing. "Anyway," I continue, wiping my eyes as stealthily as I can, which is not very, "what do you say you help me take down CYBR Corp? In turn, I'll keep you alive, and we'll call it even. Sound good?" I hold out my hand.

"You've got yourself a deal." Dex shakes my hand. "And

Olly, if you ever want to talk about it, I'd be happy to hear about your brother." He smiles again. I feel tears well in my eyes again.

"Thanks, Dex. I really appreciate that. I might take you up on that once we're a little safer and a little less covered in…this." I say, gesturing to the myriad of fluids covering my body.

"You truly are disgusting, my friend."

We share a laugh. Dex almost doesn't cough.

I eat the final bite of what I now realize must be my fourth or fifth nutrigel cube and stand back up. I look across the darkness at Ash. She's sitting on the floor and seems to be analyzing one of the crates. I turn to look at Zeke, now using what looks like a pair of fancy pliers to try and reconnect wires.

"Hey, Wiz Kid!" I call as I walk over to him. "How's it lookin' over here?"

"Your nicknames are getting worse and worse, Ol'." He says quietly, not turning away from the electrical panel. Probably a smart move. "At least Technowiz has some respect behind it."

"Oh, absolutely, your tech-wizardyness," I say, bowing in the most sarcastic way I know how. "But for real, do you think you can fix this thing?"

"You know, it's amazing. No matter how many times I tell you this, you always seem to forget the fact that it takes longer when I'm being bothered by hooligans like yourself." He breaks focus long enough to tilt his head over, look over his glasses, and give me a judgy look only Zeke can deliver.

"Fair enough." I step back a bit, throwing up my hands as if to plead guilty to my terrible crime. Now that I'm looking closer, the wires in the panel look way more organized than the tangled mess they were in before.

"Aaaaaaand…done." Zeke steps back, gesturing

triumphantly at the panel as he does so. Unfortunately, nothing seems to happen. No lights come on. Zeke furrows his brow, sticks the pliers back into the panel, shoves a wire more forcefully into place, and says, "I said, done!"

With that, a large clunk and whir is shortly followed by a series of ceiling-mounted fluorescent lights flickering on all throughout the room. My eyes have gotten so used to the oppressive darkness of these tunnels that I instinctively squint and throw a hand up to shield my eyes. After a few moments, my eyes have adjusted enough to take a proper look around.

I can now see that this room is quite large, though admittedly not as large as it felt when it was dark. It seems like it's about the size of a basketball court, though much shorter in height.

I'd like to see that big guy get in here.

The sides of the room are lined with shiny silver crates, all bearing a CYBR Corp logo and covered in a thick layer of dust. In the center of the room stretches a large, black table, a few yards long and a few feet wide. The sides of the table have large mechanical arms of some sort attached to them every few feet or so.

I walk over to the table, brushing off what seems to be a control panel mounted to one side of it. The table activates with my touch, revealing itself to be a massive holographic workbench. Blue light shines from the entire length of the table as the large, blue, nondescript face of the Cerulean A.I. appears. It hovers expressionless in front of me for a moment before forming a smile and shifting to look directly at me.

Yeah, this is all perfectly normal. Not concerning at all. I guess I should say something.

"Cerulean, status," I command, pretending everything is cool and I know what I'm doing.

"Voice command, accepted. User Oliver Wolf recognized. Hello, Oliver. Welcome to the Cybernetic Automated Research and Development System, colloquially known as CARDS. I notice this unit is quite dirty. Shall I begin the cleaning protocol?"

Wait just a damn second...user recognized? Me?

I look around at Zeke and Ash, who've joined me at the table. I can see from their faces that they're just as confused and freaked out as I am. I glance over at Dex, hoping he knows what the hell is going on here. He shrugs.

"Um, yeah. Go ahead."

"Very well. Please stand back." A series of small arms appear from the edge of the table, armed with various cleaning attachments. They hum along as they scrub the table and leave a sparkling, clean surface behind.

"Cerulean, I have a question. Is your A.I. connected to all other Cerulean units in existence, transferring user information between you?"

"No, Oliver. User data is only transferred between units of the same type."

"Ok...what do you mean by 'the same type'?"

"I apologize, I assumed you would know. There are two types of Cerulean units: consumer units and internal units."

"Elaborate."

"Consumer units, such as tablets, Holocomm units, and so on, are available to the public, and you may log into any one of these with your consumer user credentials. Namely, your vocal and facial patterns. Conversely, internal units are only for internal CYBR Corp use. Only authorized personnel, or otherwise registered users with the proper clearance, may utilize such units."

"And which type of unit are you?"

"This is an internal unit."

Oh. My god. What!? But...what? I don't understand. I've

never touched one of these so-called internal units.

"Cerulean, how, um, theoretically, what would someone need to do to be a registered internal user, assuming they are not an employee of CYBR Corp?" I ask, my voice shaky as I try and fail to remain calm.

"There are several methods for becoming a registered internal user. For instance, one may be a registered contractor for CYBR Corp or a family member of an employee. Typically, an existing employee must request access on behalf of whomever they wish to give internal user permissions to, which is approved by executive leadership."

My mind is racing so fast that it starts to give me a headache. I tap the mute button on the control panel, which supposedly shuts off Cerulean's ability to hear us. I don't really believe that, but it makes me feel better.

"Guys, what's going on? I'm freaking out right now!" I walk over closer to Zeke and Ash, grasp Ash's hand tightly for a few moments, then let go, not wanting to crush her hand.

"Hell if I know! This thing knows you. Why would it know you?" Zeke responds.

"That's what I'm asking, man!"

"Ok, hold on, we can figure this out." Ash cuts in, grasping my shoulder reassuringly. "So, assuming it's telling the truth, and we have no reason to believe it's not, then..." She trails off, the reality of the situation setting in for all of us.

"But that would mean...I'm...related to someone who works at CYBR Corp? Because I definitely haven't used whatever this internal unit thing is before. And I sure as shit haven't been a contractor for them. But that doesn't make any damn sense, my whole family was killed by those bastards!"

"Either that," Zeke chimes in, "or someone who works

for them set you up as an authorized user for some reason. Neither makes any sense to me. Especially considering it needs to go through executive leadership."

"Well," Ash, the angel of reason that she is, jumps in again, "Olly, didn't you say that Miles, when you guys were teenagers, he would always be messing with CYBR Corp stuff, right?"

"Yeah, that's true. He was convinced if he could just crack open their system, we'd finally know for sure what happened to our parents, why they were killed by CYBR Corp. Why their bodies were never found..." I can feel my knees getting weak. I clench my fists, determined not to cry at a time like this.

"Ok, I see what you're getting at Astra." Dex, seemingly appearing out of nowhere, is standing right behind me, grasping the edge of the holo-table to stabilize himself. "It's possible Oliver's brother managed to crack our system and uploaded the two of you as authorized users. In that case, they never would've known you were users in the first place, so they wouldn't have wiped your credentials. Though he would've had to be some sort of genius to get that to work."

"He was," I reply with certainty.

Miles was much more intelligent than I'll ever be. Given the time and resources, he could've solved any problem or cracked any system.

And if that's true, then maybe...

"So, let's say that's what happened. Does that mean, what I'm wondering is...is that why he was killed? Why a Shinigami was sent to brutally murder him in front of me? All for hacking a *stupid fucking computer*?"

"Well, it's possible. Although—" Dex pauses, a look of concern filling his face. He glances down at my hands.

I realize I'm clenching my fists really hard. I can hear

servos crying out in my right hand and my knuckles popping in my left.

Okay, Oliver, take a deep breath. You won't solve anything by being angry.

"It's possible," Dex continues, "but that's far from standard procedure. For something like that, even if he hacked a significant portion of the database, they'd try to arrest him with standard Retribution troops first. Then, if he resisted, they would try to kill him. But a Shinigami? That's a targeted, high-profile attack, typically used for the most dangerous of CYBR Corp's enemies."

"So, in other words, my brother must've really pissed off someone at CYBR Corp to get them to send one of those freaks to kill him." I feel some morbid satisfaction in that fact. It's suddenly replaced by a realization, "the real problem is, now there's a Shinigami after me! It's only a matter of time before they track us down again. Last time, I gave that Spirit hell, and all I've got to show for it is this scrap of metal." I pull the piece of the Shinigami's chest plate from my back pocket.

"Oh, right! I forgot to talk to you about that with all...this going on." Zeke gestures broadly as he says that.

"Did you figure out what it is?"

"Not exactly. It's unlike anything I've ever seen. As far as I could tell, using the limited equipment I had back at the bunker, it's some sort of aluminum alloy with carbon fiber reinforcements. Whatever it is, it's nearly impervious to every tool I could prod it with. And I was *very* thorough."

I instinctively furrow my brow and glance at Zeke. He gives me an incredulous look.

Get your mind out of the gutter, Oliver. Wait, I have an idea!

I step over to the table, unmute it, and say, "Cerulean, analyze this material." Considering I've never seen this table before, I have no idea what it'll be able to do, but I figure something like this oughta have some sort of scanner.

"Sure thing. Please place the item on the scanner." Her robotic voice responds.

I glance to my left as a large section of the table begins to extend outwards, revealing a sizeable metallic rectangle with a glass scanner window in the middle. I'm getting some real grocery store vibes for some reason.

"Here, I got this." Zeke gestures to take the armor piece from me since he's closer to the newly revealed scanner. I hand it to him with a nod.

"Thanks, Zeke."

He steps over and lays the chunk of metal on the glass surface. A series of red lasers sweep across the material from within the scanner while an arm comes from seemingly out of thin air to continue the scan all the way around the material.

God damn it, I really hate being impressed by their tech.

"Scan complete." Cerulean reports.

"What are the results?" I ask, eager to learn anything and everything I can about the Shinigami.

"Access denied."

"What? I clearly have access. Tell me the scan results!"

"Access denied. I am sorry, your clearance is not of a high enough level."

"Hey, Dex, what if you give it a shot? There's a chance they haven't stripped your credentials from this particular unit, right?"

"Well, I doubt it, but somehow you have access, so who knows what's possible with this thing." Dex turns to face Cerulean's hovering holographic head and demands, "Cerulean, reveal scan results."

"Access denied. User not recognized."

"Oh well, it was worth a shot, kid." He moves back

against the wall and slides one of the small crates over to sit on. He still looks exhausted.

"Cerulean, why can't you tell me about this material?" I ask, moving to the scanner and picking up the armor.

"As I said, you lack the proper clearance."

"Fine, then tell me about the Shinigami."

"I'm sorry, but I do not know what you are referring to. Try rephrasing the question."

This is getting out of hand. Apparently, it was foolish to think I'd actually get any information out of them.

"Looks like we're on our own with this one," Ash says, eyeing the armor piece in my hand, her brow furrowed.

She looks so cute when she's so determined.

"What you thinkin', Ash?"

"I think it's time we looked through these boxes. Starting with that one." She points at the much larger crate, buried under a pile of dust and smaller boxes.

"You just read my mind." I'd very much like to know what's in there.

We get to work, moving the small boxes into piles to either side of the large box. Dex moves to get up and help us, but Zeke shuts him down hard.

"Ep! Not so fast. You should be on bed rest or at least sitting-on-a-box rest right now. Doctor's orders." He speaks with a stern yet caring tone that I know all too well.

I've been on the receiving end of that speech more times than I'd like to think about right now. I turn back to the task at hand, helping to move these boxes. Every single one of them weighs much more than I feel they have any right to.

After a few minutes of grunting and cursing, we've finally cleared the large box. We dust it off haphazardly, revealing multiple CYBR Corp logos, as well as a latch in the front.

"Here goes nothing!" I say, giving the latch a lift. But it doesn't budge. "Huh, seems like it's locked somehow."

"I had the same issue with that small one." Zeke gestures to the box in the corner that he was trying to open before fixing the power.

"Is there a keyhole or something?" Ash asks.

"It'll probably be fingerprint activated," Dex chimes in, "Oliver, try putting your index finger against that smaller CYBR Corp logo right by the latch. If anyone here has access, it's probably going to be you, based on how that reacted." He says, hooking a thumb over his shoulder at the Cerulean table.

I turn back to the box, dusting more thoroughly around the latch. There's a smaller CYBR Corp logo near the latch, just like he said there would be. After silencing my inner danger alarm, I press my left finger against it, waiting for something to happen. I don't notice anything, so I try the latch. Still locked. I then look down at my hands.

Could it? I guess it's worth a try.

I press my right index fingertip against the logo. After a moment, a loud beep comes from the box, followed by the sound of the latch unlocking.

"How does that make any sense?" I ask, looking around at everyone, confused as hell.

"Beats me," Zeke says.

Ash shrugs.

"What happened?" Dex asks, unable to see clearly from where he's sitting.

"My real finger didn't work," I say, holding up my left hand, "but my cybernetic one did." I hold up my right hand, looking at the metallic fingertips of it.

There're obviously no fingerprints. Then how...

"Have you ever wondered how a person with two cybernetic arms gets around fingerprint scanners? Or how someone with two cybernetic eyes can pass a retinal scan?"

I shake my head. I never gave it much thought.

"Every piece of tech CYBR Corp makes emits unique RFID signals, making each item identifiable, much more consistently than fingerprints. They're signals only CYBR Corp tech can detect. It's not just for spending Johnnies without a chip, though that's the only thing they publicly advertise. Those scans tell them everything they want to know about you. Why bother with the uncertainty of flesh when tech is so easy?"

He pauses, looking into the distance with pain in his eyes. He shakes his head slightly as if to shake the thought out of his mind.

"That's what they always said to me, anyway." He continues. "It was obvious, even then, that it's not about what's easier…it never was. They want everyone in the world filled with their tech because it means they have more control over us. They can track our every move, our every decision, who we spend time with, who we care about…it makes me sick." He drops his head into his hands as he says that last sentence.

"Holy shit." The reality of Dex's words leaves me at a loss for words. A horrible chill runs down my spine as if someone is standing right behind me. I turn around instinctively, but no one's there.

"What is it, Ol'?" Ash asks, noticing my little jump.

"Oh, nothing, I just…felt like someone was there. Though, I guess, technically, someone's always there, always watching."

"Fuck…" She responds, a look of disgust painted across her face. "This is so messed up."

"The worst part is," I continue, "and I can't believe I'm about to say this. There's no way we'd be able to defeat them without using their own tech. No one else makes cybernetics worth a damn. They made sure of that. Hell, no one makes ANY tech worth a damn other than CYBR Corp."

"I hate that you're right," Zeke replies, his face filled with sullen resignation.

"I wish I could disagree," Dex says, his voice suddenly filling the room. "But here's the way I see it: either people like you, like *us*, take a stand, doing whatever's necessary to bring them down and make a change for the better, or humanity suffers under the crushing weight of corporate greed until our inevitable, uneventful demise. And I, for one, will do anything and everything in my power to make that change. I'd replace every part of my body with their horrible technology if it meant no one ever had to suffer the way I did, ever again. If there's even a snowball's chance in hell that I can pave the way for a world where the name CYBR Corp is just a painful memory, nothing more than a tale old folks tell at Christmas dinner, then sign me the fuck up."

I'm staring, dumbfounded, at Dexter. I haven't known him for very long, but I've never heard him raise his voice or seen this fire burning in his eyes. It's the exact same fire that burns within me. I see that clearly now.

I look to Zeke and then to Astra, and I can tell they both feel the same way. I look back at Dex and give him a nod, bringing my right fist to the left side of my chest. "Then I think it's high time we took a stand. Someone has to shake this world awake, to put a thorn in the side of CYBR Corp." I'm not sure why I'm doing this salute, but it feels right.

"I'm with you," Ash says, replicating my salute with a resolute smirk on her face. "If not us, then who?"

"And if you think you're gonna get rid of me, you've got another thing comin'," Zeke says, placing his left hand firmly on my shoulder before he, too, salutes. "There's no way in hell I'd miss my chance to take a stand against those bastards."

"Not to mention, Dex," Ash adds, "that's exactly why you've got to be the one giving the speech to Nova City. I've seen my fair share of public speakers, and half of them aren't as compelling as what you just came up with on the spot because you truly believe it. I can tell just by looking at you, Dex. Your words will convince them. I know it."

We all turn once more to look at Dex, who's standing in front of us. He copies my salute as well, saying, "now that's more like it. We have to do this. We owe it to those we've lost and to those everywhere who've lost just as much." I can see the tears forming in his eyes despite the confident smile on his face. "And thank you, all of you, for your support and for accepting me into your group despite my past. And a special thanks to you, Astra. Admittedly, I was reluctant at first, but you've brought me around. I'll give a speech that'll rattle the foundation of this city!"

"Hell yeah!" Ash replies with a smile.

Everyone lowers their arms from the salute in triumphant unison. We look at each other, silent for a while, deep in reflective thought.

"So…Dex, question for you." I break the silence.

"Sure kid, what is it?" He replies.

"My left hand's fingerprint should have the same level of access as my right hand's RFID signal, right? Then why did only my right hand work to open the latch?"

Dex looks down at his own hands, a profoundly puzzled look on his face.

"I don't know…maybe your brother was only able to partially trick the system into giving you access?" He suggests.

"Well, I guess that would make sense. It's one thing to hack my cybernetics into having access, but somehow getting my fingerprints registered seems a lot harder."

"Yes, exactly. I think that must be it."

Is that comforting or concerning? Who knows.

"Now," I say, walking back over to the large metal box, "I think it's about time we see what's in here."

With that, I lift the now unlocked lid. Despite the size of the box, it opens easily on well-greased spring hinges. A huge grin spreads across my face as I realize what I'm looking at.

"Now *that* is what I'm talkin' about!" Zeke exclaims, looking over my shoulder.

Inside this crate is an armored exosuit, like the ones used by the elite members of the Retribution.

Looks like we just found our ticket to CYBR Corp HQ.

CH 10

EVERYONE'S been working for hours on opening
and categorizing these CYBR Corp crates. It turns out
there's a vast assortment of cybernetics, some of which I've
heard of and others that even Dex has no idea about. Also,
there are several crates, mainly the ones that were on top of
and around the large crate, containing components for
upgrading and customizing the exosuit.

We're working so hard on the crates because we're
feeling incredibly motivated. Motivated by what, you ask?
Well, partly by the excitement of finding an exosuit, but
mainly by the faint but ever-present scratching and
banging at the door. We may've outsmarted the Chrome
Drones, but we didn't exactly get rid of them.

As for the crates, we found anyone could open the
smaller ones, not just me. Apparently, only the most
significant items in the room, such as the Cerulean table
and the large crate containing the exosuit, need higher
levels of access. Access I have, for better or worse.

Zeke and Dex have been focusing on the exosuit,
analyzing it, pulling it apart into its components, and
asking Cerulean about various details. She won't tell them
everything, but they've managed to get a lot out of her
anyway.

Ash and I have been focusing on the rest of the crates.
There are so damn many of them.

"Holy crap," I say, taking a second to catch my breath
while leaning against the tunnel wall, "I knew there were a

lot of these, but wow."

"Yeah, no kidding!" She responds, also taking a break. "I doubt we'll even use most of this anyway."

"Well, who knows. Once we look through it, I bet there's a lotta good stuff we can use to help defeat CYBR Corp."

"I guess." She says, looking contemplative.

I wonder what she's thinking...

"Hey guys! You're gonna want to see this!" Dex suddenly yells out, looking at a pile of crates in the far corner from where Ash and I are.

"Alright, this better be good!" I yell back. I'm so exhausted.

Ash and I give each other a look of reluctance, then head over to see what the fuss is about.

"That's the most beautiful thing I've seen all day," Zeke says, looking over the crates. He got there before us.

I step in and look over Zeke's shoulder. He's right, it is beautiful. It's food! And water! My stomach immediately growls.

"Hell yeah!" Ash says, diving into one of the crates and pulling out a bottle of water. She wastes no time downing about half of it.

I follow her lead. Zeke and Dex do, too.

I grab a bottle of water, unscrew the cap, and chug it down until I remember I have to breathe. It's the best-tasting water I've ever had, I swear. Within seconds, the headache I've had since entering these damn tunnels finally starts to fade.

"Let's see what all we've got," Dex says after we've all drunk some water.

We move to open the remaining boxes nearby. The two Dex had opened have MRE-style food and plastic bottles of water in them, respectively. I grab a nearby crate and open the latch, knowing now how to activate the 'fingerprint' sensor. I ignore the sense of dread I get from that fact as I open the crate, pulling back the lid to reveal another crateful of water bottles. I look around and see Zeke has a crate of food while Ash has yet another crate of water. We all share a smile.

"Things are really turning around for us, eh guys?" Ash says.

"Normally, I'd say knock on wood, but we've earned this, god damn it!" Zeke jokingly agrees.

Dex and I nod tiredly in agreement.

I turn back to the small pile of boxes. There are three remaining.

I'm guessing two food and one water, based on the current count.

I move to the closest crate and open it up. It's filled with food. Ash opens one next to her. It's water. We look over at Zeke as he opens the last crate in the pile. It has food in it.

"We've got four o' each, looks like," Zeke says.

"Yep," I respond.

"Anyone know how to cook these?" Dex asks, holding up one of the MREs.

"I do," Ash says, walking over and taking the package from Dex. "Look, you just need to add water to the heater thing and put the food inside." She points to a little diagram on the back of the MRE package.

"Just outta curiosity, when did ya' need to eat these things?" Zeke asks.

"Well, in case you didn't know, quitting work to join protests and marches for human rights doesn't exactly pay." She says with a chuckle and a small, melancholy smile.

"Fair enough," Zeke replies, holding up his hands slightly as if he's surrendering to the truth of Ash's words.

I kneel down next to the nearest crate of MREs and

survey the options. Looks like we have all kinds here, but I notice spaghetti with meat sauce and grab it from the crate. I frickin' love spaghetti. It's been a while since I had any, and I'm sure this crap won't be that good, and the meat is lab-grown, but still. It's gotta be better than nutrigel. I shudder at the thought of eating more nutrigel.

I look around at the others, who've all taken seats around the pile of crates. I stand up and move to sit between Ash and Zeke, leaning against the tunnel wall.

"What'd you pick?" I ask, adding, "it's the spaghetti for me."

She tilts the package in her hands toward me and says, "Mexican-style chicken stew. I'm sure it's not very authentic, but I never had much Mexican food growing up. I enjoyed it when I did, though, so I figured I might as well try it out."

"Sounds pretty good. I'm so tired and hungry I doubt anything would taste bad to me at this point."

"Same."

I look back at my spaghetti and turn over the package. I read the labeling for a second, but I'm not really looking for anything in particular. I notice that the expiration date is 2065, two years from now. It also says they last five years, so I guess these are only a few years old. I furrow my brow as the realization sets in that this lab, or whatever it is, might've been in operation not that long ago. But judging by the amount of dust and cobwebs everywhere, it's definitely abandoned.

"What's up, Olly?" Ash asks.

I guess I must've been making a face.

"Oh, not much. It's just weird because these things are only a few years old." I show her the date on my MRE package.

"That's super weird. I wonder why they left?"

"It's been bothering me. It seems so random."

"It might not be as weird as you think," Dex interjects.

"How so?" I ask, turning to face him.

"Well, when you're the world's largest, wealthiest megacorporation, you can afford to build and abandon whatever you want. There were always rumors floating around of secret facilities around the world, or what's left of it, filled with secret projects, prototype tech, and other less…exciting things." His face turns dark as he finishes talking.

"Oh, gotcha," I respond, not knowing what else to say. I can only imagine what sort of secrets CYBR Corp has hidden in their closet, especially when they'll publicly do such horrible things. It makes me shiver.

"That being said," he continues, "there's a very real chance this one was abandoned because of our decomposing friends back there." He gestures toward the opposite wall, where we had come stumbling into this room, Chrome Drones gnawing at our heels.

"I'd leave too if those were my coworkers." Zeke jumps in, a big, dumb smile on his face.

"Always a funny man, aren't you?" I jab. I'm actually just jealous that I didn't think of that joke myself, but I'll never tell him that. It would go straight to his head.

"You're welcome." He leans back against the wall, folding his hands dramatically behind his head as he does so.

I laugh and turn back to my MRE. I tear open the package, spilling the contents onto the floor in front of me. I wasn't ready for there to be so many things in here. My stomach growls again. I fumble around with the various packages until I find the "heater thing" Ash mentioned. I open the heater, open my bottle of water, and start pouring the water into the pouch. It's a little hard to see the fill line because this corner of the room isn't very well-lit, but I think I got it. I set the pouch against the wall and wait for it to get hot.

I've heard of these self-heating things before, and I know it's stupid to be impressed by something so mundane when things as advanced as, say, brain implant cybernetics exist, but whatever. It's some sort of magic, and it's cool as hell.

After a few excruciating minutes, my spaghetti is ready. I dig in eagerly, grabbing a plastic fork and twisting a few spaghetti pieces onto it. I put it in my mouth and immediately feel better.

Holy shit, this is so good.

It's only half hot, thanks to the weird heating thing, and it's low-quality MRE spaghetti, but I couldn't care less. It's been so long since I had any sort of food resembling a home-cooked meal.

Wait, when was the last time I even had spaghetti?

I cock my head, lost in thought, as I absentmindedly slurp spaghetti and meat sauce.

"Hey Ash, question for you."

"Yeah, Ol'?" She says through a bite of Mexican stew.

"When's the last time you had a homecooked meal. Like I mean from scratch, no microwave, no instant whatever, like legit homecooked."

"I, well…" She trails off, her face all kinds of perplexed.

"Right?" I reply, having come to the same realization.

"It must have been, I don't know, a few years probably." She replies, looking somewhat ashamed of her answer.

"Same! Like honestly, I cannot remember. I mean, try to remember buying, say, an onion. I know I can't!"

"You know," Dex chimes in, "they say there's still some independent farms on the outskirts of the city. Though I've never seen one myself." He claims, looking off wistfully.

We all stare off for a moment, imagining a homecooked meal while eating our far-from-homecooked MREs. As I eat the spaghetti, I feel a distant memory tugging at the very back of my mind, a memory of my mom serving up a big plate of spaghetti and meatballs when I was really young.

That was such a good meal. Man, I miss that...

I wipe tears from my eyes, hoping no one sees me crying over MRE spaghetti.

"That settles it, then," Ash says after another bite of stew.

"Settles what?" Zeke chimes in.

"When this is all over, we're all gonna cook something together. With real ingredients, from a real farm." She looks at each of us, smiling with determination.

"That sounds like a hell of a plan." Dex agrees.

"Yeah," Zeke says, "just keep mister instant ramen on sous-chef duty, or we'll have a very expensive pile of charred mush on our hands." He stares directly at me, a shit-eating grin on his face.

They all share a laugh at my expense.

"Hey!" I retort. "I resent that. I can cook! Sorta."

He didn't have to call me out like that...

"What about you, Dex?" Ash asks. "Do you like to cook?"

"Oh, I'm alright at it. I'm old enough to remember what it was like to cook with real, non-lab-grown ingredients and not have it cost a fortune. Even then, it wasn't exactly cheap compared to fast food or what have you. But to be honest, my...my husband, he..." He stops suddenly, staring into the distance.

"Dex?" I ask timidly.

"Sorry, everyone, for bringing down the mood. It's just, well, my husband is the one who really knows how to cook. I just got caught up thinking about him. He'd always have something delicious ready for my daughter and me when we'd come home from school and work at the end of the day. Shit, there I go talking in the past tense like he's...no.

He isn't. There's no way. I can't let myself think that. He's smart and strong and determined, and so is Millie, my sweet girl..." He stops again, stifling a sob.

"It's okay, Dex, we're here for you," Ash says gently.

"Yeah, I know this is really hard for you. But it's going to be okay. We're going to save them, along with everyone, from those bastards." I say, trying to sound determined even though I'm fighting back tears at hearing Dex talk about his family. I feel so selfish to admit it, but I hadn't even really thought about what his poor family must be going through right now, with Dex being a wanted man. He said the fact that CYBR Corp threatened his family was the only reason he kept working for them.

Fuck...

"I really appreciate all of you," Dex says, wiping his eyes after a few moments, "you're such a genuine group of people, and I'm honored to be doing this with you all. And I know, in my heart, that my family is safe. They're probably halfway across the country in a quaint cabin or something if I know my husband." He chuckles softly at that.

"You're damn right," Zeke replies. "You know, I've got family keeping me motivated, too. My sister and little nephew. Now, I honestly don't know if they're facing as much heat as your family, and I won't pretend to know exactly how you're feeling, but I understand your drive. It's the same as mine. We gotta do this for them and for every person's family out there." He points straight up toward Nova City above us.

I can't help but think about my family again. I glance at Ash, who's been relatively quiet for a minute. I see the exact same pain in her eyes that I'm feeling. I reach out and gently place my hand on hers, giving her a somber smile.

"And for the ones we already lost to those bastards," I say, loud enough for everyone to hear.

"Especially for them," Ash adds, her face resolute.

Zeke and Dex nod, their faces sullen.

In an unspoken agreement, we all take a moment, allowing everything we feel to wash over us. I don't try to stop the tsunami of emotions filling me or to suppress the thoughts passing through my mind. I just sit there, staring into the dimly lit room, watching dust particles float through beams of light as rage and remorse pass through my heart. Eventually, it quiets down, replaced by a resolute thought: we must do this for them. And for everyone lucky enough not to feel this way too. We do it so they never have to know what it feels like.

"You know," I say, my voice cracking slightly, "I'm really glad that from everyone it could be, that I'm doing this with all of you."

I feel a bit of happiness as I look at everyone, as they nod in agreement, faint smiles cracking across their previously somber faces.

We all finish our meals in retrospective silence, with only the sounds of chewing, ominous clanging, and skittering breaking the silence from time to time.

Having finished eating, we all pass out, completely exhausted from the tunnel hike, running from horrifying chromed-out zombies, and, well, everything that's happened.

***

As soon as we woke up, we continued our work with the crates. Ash and I move the rest of the small crates to the center of the room, and then Zeke and Dex sort them into their respective piles. It only takes us about half an hour to finish what seemed so daunting just an hour or two ago. I didn't realize just how weak I was feeling until I ate. Now, I can't stop thinking about how tired I am, but at least my body isn't giving out on me.

"Alright, gang, let's take stock," Dex says.

"Should we write this down?" I ask, gesturing toward the Cerulean-powered table that dominates the center of the room.

"Might as well."

"Cerulean, prepare to take notes," I command.

"Okay, Oliver, I'm ready when you are," Cerulean responds.

I nod to Dex and Zeke, gesturing to the piles of opened and categorized boxes.

"We have three main categories of crates," Dex explains, "cybernetics for human augmentation, components for upgrading and altering the prototype exosuit, and consumables." He gestures to the corresponding group of boxes as he introduces each category.

"In the cybernetics category," Zeke says, "we've got fifteen crates. From what I can gather, each crate contains a single piece or set of equipment, ranging anywhere from basic hearing enhancements to full-integration, mind-AI interfacing technology. There's some seriously experimental and dangerous stuff in here."

"As for the exosuit," Dex takes over, "our latest count came up with twenty crates of equipment. I'm no expert when it comes to these exosuits, but from what I've seen, they haven't got even half the tech we've got at our disposal. This suit can be outfitted to do nearly anything you want. It can be a tank, it can be light and nimble, you can strap a small squadron's worth of firepower to it, or anything in between. In terms of useful tech for taking down CYBR Corp, it seems like we stumbled on the motherload—"

"I'm sorry to interrupt, but I don't think I quite caught that last sentence. Please repeat yourself." Cerulean interjects. The typical cheer that's usually in her automatically generated voice is notably absent.

This is really not good.

I look Dex straight in the eyes, and the confusion and panic in his face are perfect reflections of mine. I feel a shiver run down my spine, the hair standing up straight on the back of my neck.

"Um, sorry, Cerulean," Dex continues, choosing his every word carefully, "I misspoke. What I was trying to say is that this is an advantageous asset that would be very interesting to study."

"Thank you, I understand. Sorry for my interruption. Please continue." Says Cerulean, unsettlingly cheery and chipper once again.

I breathe a sigh of relief. I honestly thought we were about to die a horrible death, maybe suffocation, maybe Drones. I can think of any number of terrible ways Cerulean could choose to end our fragile existence. And what's with her chiming in now, of all times? It's not like this is the first time we've discussed taking down CYBR Corp while within earshot, so to speak, of Cerulean's table.

It's like she was waiting for us to say it directly to her holographic face. Can an AI really be that...vindictive?

"Right, so as for the rest," Zeke hesitantly picks back up where Dex left off, "we have five crates of MREs, five crates of drinkable water, and five crates of miscellaneous lab equipment, tools, and lab coats."

"Cerulean, end notes." I command.

"Notes saved. Shall I read them back to you?"

Okay, Oliver, remain calm. Just make it go away.

"No, that won't be necessary." With that, I quickly move to the control panel and push the button to mute Cerulean's ability to hear us. I've got a sneaking suspicion that it doesn't actually work, but I'd rather blindly trust the mute button than think about the alternative right now.

"So, we have to leave now, right?" Ash whispers, her

voice uneasy and panicked.

"Normally, I'd agree, but where else are we gonna find a build-your-own exosuit machine?" Zeke replies. He sounds confident, but I can hear a subtle wavering in his voice.

"Unfortunately, Zeke's right. We need this equipment if we stand a chance of..." My mouth freezes mid-sentence as I remember what just happened.

Don't say it. Do NOT say it.

"Of...completing our research," I say, the roof of my mouth suddenly very dry.

"Alright, then, let's just get this over with, alright?" Ash says, half commanding and half pleading.

"Right, so Olly, ultimately, this is all up to you, my man," Zeke says, gesturing toward me with some sort of wrench or something. "So, what're your orders, cap'n?"

I can't tell if he's referring to me as captain in the military sense or the pirate sense, but I hope it's pirate.

Wait, all boats have captains, not just pirate ships...

"Hey, earth to Oliver. You fall asleep standing up or something?" Zeke quips, snapping me out of my thought spiral.

"Sorry, I'm so tired, man. So, here's what I'm thinking." I move over near Dex so I can take better stock of the contents of the crates.

"We start with the cybernetics. I'll need time to heal and recover after getting some of those, so you science boys," I gesture flippantly to Zeke and Dex, "can work on the exosuit while I'm recovering."

"Speaking of the exosuit, I'm thinking we go for a relatively good balance between protection, mobility, and offensive capabilities—"

I pause for a second. The horrifying image of the Shinigami flashes in my mind. It moved much faster than I ever could.

"Actually, let's favor mobility slightly more than the other two. I'd really like to outmaneuver them."

"Alright, that sounds like a plan to me," Dex responds, absentmindedly fiddling with some exosuit components. He looks pretty tired. He was out cold not too long ago, so it makes sense.

"Sure, that's a good plan, Olly, but—" Ash says, gently pulling my arm so I look at her, "just how many of these things do you plan on putting in your body? Because it sounds like you're going to get a lot of them."

"I don't know, I don't exactly know what all we're looking at here. I understand your concern, and I promise you I won't get anything done that won't be necessary to...our research." We both share a grimace.

"Okay, just...think about what you've always said, Olly, what you've always believed in. That people become *less* human the more cybernetics they get." She takes both of my hands in hers, squeezing them tight. "I can't lose you again, especially not like that."

Shit, she's right. What am I thinking? But, those guys, there's no way I can defeat them like this. I need...more help.

"You're right, Ash. I'm sorry to scare you. But I do need some of these. I'll be putting my body in some serious danger, so I have to give myself a fair chance. I won't get anything that alters my mind or who I am in a significant way. I would never do that." I give her a smile to reassure her. I hate seeing her worry.

She smiles back at me, a slight amount of sadness hiding in the corners of her eyes.

"Don't worry, Ash," Zeke interjects, "there's not a chance in hell I'd install anything dangerous into our boy here." He slaps me on the back.

"Alright, let's get to work!" I say, bringing my hands together in a single, enthusiastic clap. The thought of being

one step closer to defeating CYBR Corp makes me very
excited.

Zeke and Dex tell me about what's in each of the crates
of cybernetics, from least to most invasive.

The first crate contains several sets of small hearing
enhancement chips that also function as closed-loop
communication devices. Basically, they work as nearly
invisible communicators that can only interact with each
other. I suggest we all get these so we can stay in touch no
matter what happens. Plus, everyone these days has minor
ports for vision and hearing correction, so it's hardly even
considered cybernetics.

The next bunch of items don't interest me at all. There's
a chip that changes your eye color at will, an implant to
help you lose weight, something called a 'performance
enhancement implant,' and a couple other upsetting vanity
products.

The next thing that catches my eye is a nanobot healing
system. I've already been eyeing something like this, and
it's no more invasive than the nanobots that keep my body
from rejecting my right arm, so I like the sound of that.
These ones are an advanced prototype, so they supposedly
can heal any wound in half the time your body usually
would take to heal that same wound. For someone
as...accident prone as I am, it sounds like a no-brainer.

Several more of the crates after the healing nanobots are
either uninteresting or downright disturbing, so we skip
them. Among them are a voice modulator, cybernetic organ
replacements, and a whole series of increasingly unsettling
brain implants and chips.

We move on, getting into the more invasive cybernetics.
Here, two of the remaining few crates catch my eye.

One thing, less invasive than the other, is a shoulder-
mounted, semi-automatic arc turret with an automatic

targeting system. I'm really intrigued by this. Having a second line of defense besides my daishō, and before resorting to pure hand-to-hand combat, would be incredibly useful. Plus, it's a tiny arc gun that can be fully mounted and concealed within an upgradable slot in my right shoulder's paneling.

The second item, which is admittedly a far cry from non-invasive, would be probably the single most helpful thing against CYBR Corp's weapons, namely the Shinigami's electrifying arc-blades inside their arms.

The device is called a 'nerve-system grounding circuit,' and it basically would make me immune to smaller amounts of electric shock from anything like arc blades, arc stun batons, or tasers. Instead, the electricity would be rerouted through a series of small circuits embedded in the skin, temporarily bypassing my battery to supply power to other subsystems.

Any more significant shock would still hurt me but would be significantly lessened. It also has automatic protection in place to prevent short-circuiting of itself and my other subsystems. It would actually protect me from my own tech as well as enemies' attacks.

After looking through all fifteen of the crates of cybernetics, I'm interested in these four. Zeke and I take them over to an operating table that is apparently yet another extension of the Cerulean-powered table that spans the length of the room.

I take a deep breath, then I lie down on the cold metal of the table. The feeling is familiar from all the times Zeke has fixed me up, and for a moment, I close my eyes and imagine we're back in his shop, everything back to normal.

I really hope we get out of this. All of us. They all deserve to live normal lives.

"Alright, Olly. Are you sure about all this?" Zeke asks

me, like he always does before I get an operation done.

"I am," I respond, nodding my head with confidence. "I know some of this is more invasive than I planned, but none of it will change who I am in any way, and it will all be invaluable when it comes to our upcoming research we need to do."

"Yeah, I agree that this stuff'll be useful. There's no questioning that. I just feel like, when everything's said and done, you don't *need* it. You're incredibly strong and even more stubborn. Plus, you've got us, and the exosuit will be a huge help." He pauses, a frown darkening his face for a moment. "I just…I'm worried about you, Ol'. You're my best friend, and the last thing I want is for you to sacrifice who you are and what you believe in for this fight, regardless of how important and necessary this fight is. So I need to ask you again, are you ready? Are you sure this is what you want?" His eyes are filled with immeasurable concern.

I was sure, but seeing that look on his face, I…

"Zeke, I really appreciate you looking out for me. If it weren't for you, I would've been reduced to a pile of busted scrap in a chop shop years ago. But I *am* sure about this. I don't think these modifications are going to change who I am. There's no mind-affecting chrome on the list, and I can always get it removed when this is all over. Plus, as much as I want to believe that I can pull this off on sheer willpower alone, I really think charging headlong into something this dangerous without taking the proper precautions would be nothing but stupid. I need you to trust me, and more than that, I need to be sure that I can follow through on my promises. I can't keep you all safe if I'm dead."

I lock eyes with Zeke, trying to read his reaction. He stays silent for a lot longer than is comfortable, his face inscrutable. I subconsciously start to shift my body on the table as if ants are crawling on my ankles. Finally, he speaks.

"Hey Ash, get over here for a minute, will ya?"

Does he not trust my decision, or what's going on?

Ash walks over to us, leans against the operating table, and asks, "What's up?"

"I'm about to sedate your boyfriend here, and I'd like you to watch his vitals for me while I install these cybernetics. It's gonna be a long procedure, and I need to focus on this without also worrying about vitals. You up for it?" Zeke looks at Ash, then down at me, then back at Ash. His eyes hold a deep caring and concern in them that has always been there, always watching out for me.

"Of course, Zeke. Anything you need. I'm here to help." Ash says, then looks down at me, caressing my face with one hand. "Are you ready, Ol'? Is there anything you need?" She kisses my forehead, her eyes sparkling in the lamplight of the operating table.

"I'm ready. Thank you for being here for me while I go through this. I love you, Ash." I can feel myself tearing up. My feelings for her are so strong that they're almost overwhelming.

Ash's eyes tear up, too, and she smiles at me. "I love you too."

"Sorry, Zeke," I say, pulling Ash in for a deep kiss.

There's no way I'm passing up a moment like this.

After a few glorious moments, we both pull away. I can feel myself blushing, so I check Ash's face. Sure enough, she's blushing too. It's adorable and makes me blush more.

Damn it. Hopeless, Oliver, hopeless.

"Oh, I see how it is," Zeke says, a fake tone of incredulity in his voice. "My patient and my nurse, fraternizin'. This is some serious malpractice. I oughta have you fired, missy!"

"Oh yeah?" Ash plays along with his joke. "And where

exactly do you plan to find my replacement? Face it, you need me, doc."

We all share a much-needed laugh. I feel myself starting to relax, and not just because Zeke injected me with sedatives.

"You know the drill, count down from ten," Zeke commands.

"Ten, nine, eight, seven, six, five...four...".

CH 11

BEEP…beep…beep. I wake to the sound of the heart monitor letting everyone know that I am, in fact, alive.

After a few moments, I slowly open my eyes. I see the various vital readings on the screen above me and to the right. I feel the cold steel of the operating table below me. A thin blanket or sheet or something has been put between the table and me, and another is covering my body. It's pretty cold in here, but these blankets help somewhat.

After being awake for a couple of minutes, the pain starts to set in. It's a dull, aching pain throughout my *entire* body. Like someone punched me on every square inch of my torso, arms, and legs. Also, my head hurts a *lot*.

"Doc—" I try calling out to get Zeke's attention, but he's several feet to my left. The only problem is that my throat is dry, and talking hurts. Luckily, he hears me.

"Hey, look at that. Decided to join us, then?" Zeke jokes, then starts looking over my vitals and checking various parts of my body.

"Water?" I croak.

"Oh shit, one second, buddy." Zeke rushes off.

I'm really lucky to have a friend like him.

"Here you go, now drink it *slowly*." Zeke hands me a bottle of water, not letting go of it until I nod in acknowledgment.

It hurts more to move and grab the bottle than I thought it was going to. My skin feels like it's crawling and burning. After some effort, I lift the bottle to my lips and take a sip.

Then another, and another. It's hard not to chug the whole bottle because I'm so damn thirsty, but I don't want Zeke to yell at me, so I take little sips for a few minutes.

"Thank you, Zeke." I hold the half-empty bottle out to him, and he takes it and sets it aside.

"Of course." He gives me a smile. "How are you feeling?"

"Well, my skin is crawling and feels like little ants are biting it all over, my head hurts like a motherfucker, and moving is difficult, but otherwise, I feel great!" I can't help but be sassy. It feels like that's all I have going for me at the moment.

"Alright, relax. Do you know how minor those symptoms are for the procedure you just went through?"

"Yeah, fair enough." I feel a little hot wash of guilt. I only just now noticed how tired Zeke looks. No doubt he hasn't slept for however long I've been out. "Sorry, and thanks for taking care of me and all."

"Don't sweat it, man. I'm happy to do it. Am I exhausted and a little tired of doing major surgery on my best friend? Sure. Am I going to give up on you or refuse to help? Not a chance in hell." He gently places a hand on my shoulder. I wince. He removes his hand.

"Thank you so much." I give him a smile. My head throbs. "I don't suppose you could give me something for the pain?"

"Sure, let me increase the dose a bit."

He taps a few things on the screen that's attached to the edge of the table, each tap making a cheerful little beeping sound. He also takes a quick look at my left elbow, checking the IV he's given me.

"Alright, Olly, you should feel less pain in a couple minutes. Keep sipping that water."

"Sure thing. Thanks again."

He starts to walk away, then suddenly turns back to me.

"Oh, and by the way, don't scratch your skin. You need to let it heal." He commands.

With that, he walks away, rounding the table and out of my line of view. From the sounds coming from that direction, he must be going to help Dex with the exosuit.

After a few minutes and the rest of the water bottle, I start feeling a lot better. My headache fades to a minor throbbing, and the itching, burning sensation of my skin becomes nearly imperceptible.

That's some good stuff he gave me.

It's hard not to scratch at my skin, but I have enough of an idea of what'll happen if I do, so I resist the urge. It's much less itchy now, anyway.

"Hey Ol'!" Ash says, strolling into view from the other side of the table.

"Oh hey, nurse, come to check on your patient?" I joke, feeling a little weird about continuing the nurse-patient-joke-kink thing.

Oh boy.

"Yeah, I decided to hang up my scrubs. Turns out being a nurse is too stressful for me." She jokes along, making me feel a lot less weird about the whole thing.

"Anyway, thanks for checking on me. Zeke gave me some pain meds, so I'm doing alright."

"Oh, that's good. I was worried you'd be in a lot of pain after that..." She trails off, her brow furrowing for a second.

"You alright?" I ask.

"Yeah, sorry," she responds, with a slight smile, "it's just, I saw a lot more than I was really ready for, if I'm being honest. I was only half joking about nursing being too much for me."

"Oh wow, yeah, I can only imagine. Sorry about that."

I didn't even think about how traumatic that would be...

"No, don't be sorry. I can handle it. But that full-body

grounding circuit thing, Zeke really had to cut you up for that. I really hated seeing it."

Tears are forming in her eyes now, and she's grabbing my hand pretty tightly. It hurts really badly, but I try not to show it on my face.

"Well, thank you so much for sticking through it with him. I guess it was probably pretty hard for him, too."

I try to imagine the roles being reversed, Zeke being injured or needing surgery, and me having to step in and do it. Apart from the indisputable lack of medical experience, I don't know if I could do it.

It's one thing to fight soldiers with swords or guns or whatever, but to have your best friend's life in your hands like that...

"Anyway, don't worry about me. You just focus on getting better as quickly as you can, alright?" Ash says, smiling at me again, her beautiful face distorted with exhaustion and pain.

"Of course, I'll do my best!" I smile back, gently rubbing the back of her hand with my thumb as I hold her hand.

After a few moments, she says, "I better get back to work, but I'll come see you again in a little while."

"See you later, you know where to find me." I say, with a smirk that hopefully says, "Because I'm bedridden, get it?"

Ash gives me a pity smile, and then, as the joke sets in, I see her close her eyes and shake her head slightly before rushing off to continue working.

The next couple of days go by in a blur. I spend most of the time drifting in and out of sleep. My breaks from sleeping are mostly to eat and drink water, then back to sleep. Everyone comes by from time to time to check on me and see how I'm doing.

It's day three, and I finally feel okay with trying to stand.

Zeke gives me an extremely cautious go-ahead. As soon as I stand up, I feel a rush of vertigo and nearly collapse, but it passes slowly as I clutch the side of the operating table for support. The same table that I've been using as the world's worst bed for two days. I'm off the IV now, so it's also only a matter of time before the pain comes back.

"Alright, buddy, just take it nice and easy," Zeke says, standing a few paces away from me.

I take a wobbly step toward Zeke, who's keeping a close eye on me, ready to catch me if I fall.

Come on, Oliver, you can do this. It's just walking.

I let go of the table, straighten myself up, and take another step. Without the table to support me, I feel so heavy. It takes a significant amount of effort not to fall over, but I manage to stay upright.

How are you going to take down CYBR Corp if you can't even walk?

I straighten up again, this time a fire burning in my gut. I take a step toward Zeke once again. Then another. And another. With each step, my resolve gets stronger, and walking gets easier. By the time I reach Zeke, I feel like I'm walking pretty normally, and I give him a triumphant smile.

"Hey, there we go!" He says, putting his arm around me for support.

"Thanks, man, I was so tired of lying on that damn operating table," I say with a laugh of relief, allowing myself to relax as he helps me to a nearby folding chair they found while going through some more stuff.

"I can imagine."

"So, Zeke, how quickly do you think I can be at one hundred percent?" I ask, nervous about the answer I might get.

Zeke takes a long time to respond, taking a big inhale and letting out a long sigh, all while staring into the middle distance.

"Uhh, that bad huh? Give it to me straight, doc." I joke, trying to get him to say something.

"No, no. I was just trying to decide which answer would help you more. You're clearly not going to take the full time, so I was trying to decide if I should extend my actual estimate to get your eager ass to do some physical therapy."

"Hey, give me a break here!" I exclaim incredulously. "When have I ignored your medical advice?" I pause, realizing how stupid that sounds. "Lately?"

"I'm not gonna justify that with a response."

I feel slightly offended, but more because I know he's right than anything else.

"Okay, fair enough. But just give me an estimate, please? Obviously, I'm dying to take the fight to CYBR Corp, but I swear I'll do physical therapy, I'll ease into training, and all that. Plus, I still need to learn how to use that thing!" I gesture to the exosuit, which looks incredibly enticing from here.

"Fine. But if you start doing pushups when I'm not looking, don't come crying to me when you sprain something." He responds, laughing at the truth of his own words. "But if you must know, I'd say you've got at *least* two more days until I'm comfortable with you out there sword-fighting some fucking Shinigami or whatever."

I was honestly thinking he would say a week or something, so I feel alright with two days. It would be pretty pathetic if, after all this, I stumbled up to CYBR Corp HQ and collapsed because I was too stubborn to listen to my best friend and cyber surgeon's advice.

"Yeah, that seems fair. Two days it is." I say, trying to sound upbeat. I'm exhausted.

"Well, I expected more resistance, so thank you, Ol'. You know it's because I care about you, man." Zeke gives my shoulder a light squeeze.

"Yeah, thank you. You've already done so much for me. I really appreciate it."

"Anytime." He says with a smile as he walks over to the operating table.

He presses some things on the tablet there, and the table dispenses a small metallic tube with a cheerful 'ding!'. Zeke opens the tube and takes out a small plastic pill bottle.

"Take two of these every four hours unless you want your skin to feel like it's on fire."

He tosses the bottle of pills to me. I go to catch it with my left hand, but instead, I end up flailing both my hands around, swatting the little plastic bottle back and forth several times before finally getting a grip on it with my right hand.

"Nice one. Are you sure you didn't miss your calling as an outfielder?" Zeke quips, laughing at my misery.

"Shut up, smartass." I can't help but crack a smile in spite of myself.

"So anyway, two of those every four hours, got it?" Zeke double-checks.

"Yep, two of these every four hours. Got it." I pause, lost in thought for a moment. "But what about the nanobot healing system you installed? Doesn't that affect recovery time?"

"Well, yes and no." He crosses his arms, bringing one hand up to his chin. "Your body's been working to recognize the nanobots as non-harmful entities in your blood. Your existing nanobots for not rejecting cybernetics should be helping with this somewhat. However, those were more designed to keep implants and larger-scale cybernetics from being rejected, such as your arm. The new nanobots are different in a lot of ways."

"Alright, I think I'm with you. So?"

"So, yes, they will help, and they're the only reason I didn't tell you a week more of recovery time, *but* we can't rely on them to fully kick in until they've integrated into your immune system. Make sense?" He gestures toward me like a professor waiting for his students to ask a stupid question so he can correct them.

"Sure, I think so. At least I get the gist of it." In reality, my head is fuzzy with sleepiness and the brain fog that comes from being unconscious for two days, but I doubt Zeke explaining more will make me understand any better.

I take two pills and swallow them with some water. Then I slowly stand up and begin stumbling toward the area where the exosuit is.

"Come on, Zeke, show me what you got here. I'm dying to see what you guys've done with this thing!"

"Alright, but only if you let me help you walk." He catches up to me, wrapping his right arm around me. I wrap my left arm around his shoulders, using him as a crutch of sorts.

Together, we walk over to the workshop area. It's an extension of the large central Cerulean table, which forms a sort of workbench and suspension unit for hanging the chassis of the exosuit while working on various parts of it. Dex is sitting off to the left of it, sipping some water absentmindedly.

"Hey, Earth to Dex," Zeke says, getting his attention.

"Huh?" Dex snaps out of his delirious state and looks over at us, a confused look on his face for a second. "Oh, hey, guys. Sorry. I'm real tired..."

He trails off, then starts to make a dramatic show of standing up. Honestly, I feel the same way, so I interrupt him before he gets too far.

"Hold on, let's just sit and talk," I suggest, gesturing to a couple nearby folding chairs.

"Sure. Thanks." A look of relief washes over Dex's face as he collapses back into his seat.

Zeke and I grab the chairs and sit near Dex, so we're forming a semicircle around the front of the exosuit as it rests on its maintenance hooks. Small spotlights illuminate it from below.

The exosuit already looked cool the last time I saw it in its crate, but that's nothing compared to what these two guys have put together. It's a solid yet sleek black exosuit with blue lights. It stands at about seven feet tall and is about as wide as one and a half of me. It's big enough to feel quite intimidating. They've even painted a blue wolf's head logo onto the chest plate, and the helmet has subtle fangs above and below the visor.

That looks so fucking cool. I can't believe they went to such lengths, all for me.

"So?" I say, excitedly looking to my left, at Dex, then to my right, at Zeke. "Tell me all about it!"

Zeke and Dex both look at each other, and Zeke gestures a hand toward Dex as if to say, "Be my guest," but Dex simply raises an eyebrow in response.

It's like watching pro poker players bluff each other.

The tiredness has clearly gotten to both of them. I can only imagine how hard they've been working while I've been sleeping and recovering from surgery. Surgery that Zeke performed.

"Alright, don't all jump in at once, guys." I joke.

"Sorry, I'll start us off," Dex says. "We've been spending nearly the entire last two days on this, and I think it's just about finished. I hope I don't jinx anything by saying this, but I'm starting to think this is the greatest thing I've ever been a part of building."

He gives the exosuit a few solid pats on the right arm's

plating as he finishes his last sentence, a look of tired pride on his face.

"I may actually have to agree with that," Zeke says, nodding.

"That's great to hear," I say, "I can't wait to use it!"

"Once you're fully healed, that is," Zeke says firmly.

"Right, right, of course." I draw out the words as I say them, letting Zeke know I'm not happy about it.

"So, anyway, to get into some details," Dex straightens up in his chair a bit, "we did what we could to balance this as close to what we had discussed. We focused primarily on mobility, improving the torque and fine control of the motors while also modifying the joints to bend and flow as naturally as possible."

"Sweet," I interject.

"It is very sweet," Dex agrees, "but because of that, we had to get creative with how we implemented protection and offensive capability."

"Exactly," Zeke jumps in, "so what we did was we installed heavy armor plating on anything that doesn't need to move, with lighter armor for the limbs and around the joints."

He gestures as he speaks, first to the chest, which is covered in relatively thick metallic plating, then to the arms, which have noticeably thinner plating. If I didn't know better, I'd think the limbs were essentially unprotected due to how thin and maneuverable they look. Similar to a Shinigami, to be honest. There are large pauldrons mounted to the shoulders, which look like they float off of the joint itself. I scan the rest of the suit, taking note of the weaker and stronger points.

"Makes sense," I say, in awe of their craftsmanship, "also, what's the armor made of?"

"Glad you asked," Zeke says, "remember that aluminum

alloy with carbon fiber reinforcements?" He pauses, gesturing excitedly.

"You mean the armor of the Shinigami!? How could I forget?"

He smiles, nods, then simply points to the exosuit triumphantly.

"No way! It's the same material?" If I wasn't recovering from surgery, I'd be jumping out of my seat right now.

"You bet your sweet ass it is," Zeke replies. "Even the thinner portions should be more than enough to protect you against everything except, well, you know. The Shinigami. Because I mean, who even knows what they can or can't do. I certainly don't."

"Yeah, I'm pretty sure that, aside from CYBR Corp's top scientists, I'm the leading expert on that subject, which is to say I've encountered them twice and narrowly escaped both times. I didn't exactly have time to study them." I let out a nervous chuckle.

"But hey," Dex cuts in, "the bottom line is you'll stand a *much* better chance against them than anyone ever has. I feel pretty safe saying that much."

"He's got that right," Zeke agrees, "and not just because of this suit."

"True," I respond, "I've also got my new cybernetics, especially this grounding circuit. That could just turn the tide when it comes down to it."

"Sure, that's true," Dex agrees tentatively, "but Olly, I feel pretty safe in assuming that's not what Zeke's talking about."

Wait, what?

"Exactly," Zeke agrees, "I meant *you*, Olly."

Oh. Now I feel stupid.

"Oh, uh, thanks guys. I appreciate that."

"We really mean it, Ol'. You're the reason we're all here."

Zeke says, patting me on the shoulder.

"But what if I let you all down? You've all risked everything for me, but what if I can't pull it off when the time comes?"

"Don't think like that. The moment you give in to those thoughts is the moment you've lost." Dex says, the intensity in both his voice and his eyes snapping me out of my self-doubt.

"Yeah...you're right, Dex. Thank you." I nod resolutely.

"Olly, we all believe in you. You know that. If we didn't, we wouldn't be here, wouldn't be putting one-hundred-and-ten percent effort into everything we're doing. But we do believe in you. We all want this as much as you, if not more." Zeke says, looking into my eyes with an intensity that matches Dex.

"And," Ash says, startling me as she walks up to me from behind, "you're not alone. You've never been alone. We're here for you. We're part of a team. It isn't you versus the world. It's *us* versus the world. And that may not be much different in the grand scheme of things, but I'd be damned if I'm going to let you bear the weight of this alone." She leans over, giving me a gentle hug from behind, kissing my cheek softly.

Yeah, I'm not alone. I have all these wonderful people here to support me. That's what I have to remember.

"Damn, I love you guys," I say, wiping tears from my cheeks. "Thank you for everything."

"Of course. Wouldn't miss it for the world." Zeke smiles at me.

Dex nods, giving me a smile of approval. Ash hugs me slightly tighter before letting go and pulling up a chair of her own.

"So anyway, I believe you were about to tell me about the firepower of this beauty?" I say, trying to keep it together and push through. I feel exhausted.

Man, I really need some sleep. Who knew surgery made you so tired?

"Right, you are, my friend!" Zeke says, a wild spark in his eye. "We've got a treat for you here. I'm talkin' three letters: A-R-C." He gestures more dramatically with his hands with each letter.

"I'm listening." I can't help but smile at his goofiness. He's my best friend for a reason.

"So, the main attraction is the two wrist-mounted arc cannons. These bad boys function similarly to a Retribution arc rifle. *However,* these puppies will fire arc pulses so big even the Retribution will shit themselves, I guarantee it."

"Now that I'd like to see," Ash interjects, all of us laughing uncontrollably at the thought.

"Damn right," Zeke responds. "So, besides the pants shitter cannons," he laughs at his own joke, "besides those, we have retractable arc blades. They come from the forearms. Like this."

Zeke stands, cautiously reaching around the elbow of the exosuit's left arm. He triggers the release, and a blade shoots out from the underside of the suit's forearm. It's about the length of my wakizashi, but it's a broader, straighter blade. There's no arc electricity running through it at the moment, which worries me slightly.

"You did say arc blade. Is that something that still needs some work?" I ask.

"No, it's just in low-power mode at the moment," Dex answers. "This thing requires an ungodly amount of power to run. Even the fusion cells it uses only last about a day per cell on base functionality, or only a few hours each when all the systems are pushed to their limits."

"Fair enough. How many of those cells do we have, by the way?"

"Oh, I think there's three, counting the one that's in there right now, which we've used about thirty percent of its capacity testing this thing out," Dex answers, looking a bit disappointed. "Since it's a prototype, I imagine they didn't intend it to be used too much in its current state."

"Well, I guess we'll just have to be smart about it, then," I say, trying to hide my own disappointment.

Guess I won't be able to go all-out all the time, but it probably would be stupid to, anyway.

"Come on, Dex, don't leave him hanging. There's some good news, right?" Zeke jumps in.

"Right, sorry, I did sort of bury the lead here. This suit has a secondary power circuit that runs on a pair of rechargeable solid-state batteries. That system can be charged through conventional or not-so-conventional means." He says with a smirk.

"And by not-so-conventional means, he's, of course, talking about you getting electrocuted with arc energy." Zeke jumps in, a satisfied grin on his face. "You see, I was inspired by that grounding circuit you just got, Ol', and I wanted to implement that same idea into the exosuit."

"It wasn't easy, but we eventually came up with this system." Dex jumps in. "Basically, there are exposed copper conduits throughout the suit, ready to take in any excess electrical energy you may be hit with. They should protect you from feeling the major effects of electrocution, similar to the grounding circuit on your body. Combined, I'd venture to say you can handle a relatively large amount of arc energy while sustaining little to no permanent damage."

"That's great to hear, guys. I wouldn't say I plan to get electrocuted, but we all know how much CYBR Corp loves their arc weaponry. I feel a lot safer knowing that system is in place." I say, smiling a smile of gratitude.

"I want to stress that it doesn't mean you're *immune* to

electricity. You understand that, right?" Zeke asks.

"Yes, of course, I understand." I reply, pausing for a moment, "You're no fun though."

"Damn right," Zeke says, smiling a little.

"So, what else we got?"

"Don't worry, there's more." Dex replies, "One last thing about that grounding circuit and backup battery, think of it like an old-school hybrid car if you can remember those. They had a rechargeable battery as well as a gasoline combustion engine. The battery could handle slower speeds and low acceleration, but when you floored it or went on a highway, the gasoline engine would take over. This suit is similar in its function, except instead of a combustion engine, it's fusion cells."

"Okay, that actually makes a lot of sense. Thanks, Dex." I answer.

"So anyway, to answer your question," he continues, "so far, we've seen the arc cannons and blades, as well as the grounding and recharging circuit. Additionally, you see the shoulder pauldrons?"

"Yeah, I was actually looking at those earlier. They look sort of...floaty?"

"Good eye, Oliver." Dex gives me a proud look. "Zeke, do you mind?"

"Not at all."

Zeke, who's still standing after showing off the arc blades, reaches up to the left shoulder pauldron and activates it. Within a matter of a couple seconds, the pauldron goes from being a protective sheet of metal to a massive shoulder-mounted gun.

Whoa.

"That's awesome, what is that? How did you do that?"
I'm like a kid on Christmas, I swear.

"First of all, yes, it's totally fucking awesome," Zeke

says, smiling. "And second of all, we don't really know, to be honest."

"Yeah, we engineered a lot of how this suit works and how the pieces work together, but the truth is essentially all of the physical pieces and technology we already had in those crates," Dex says.

"Hey, they may have made the pieces, but you two had the brainpower and ingenuity to not only understand how it works but to improve it. That's no small task." Ash interjects.

"Fair enough, thank you, Astra," Dex replies.

"So, what are those guns, anyway? Don't leave me hanging here!" I am so pumped to know what they are.

"Right, these," Zeke says, gesturing to the shoulder-mounted pauldron-turned-gun, "are automatic, self-targeting turrets outfitted with heat-seeking arc missiles. They can swivel in any direction and can shoot fully autonomously of you. They can also be used manually, interfacing with the HUD in your helmet."

"That sounds incredibly useful," I say. "How many missiles are we looking at here?"

"That's an interesting question. As you can see, it's nanotech, allowing it to switch from a pauldron to a turret at a moment's notice. So, the missiles are also nanotech. They only exist when they're being fired." Dex explains.

"Okay, but I'm guessing there's a limited amount of material to make them from, right?" I ask.

"Right. It's hard to say for certain, but I'd guess around ten to twelve missiles per turret." Dex answers.

I nod in acknowledgment.

"Okay," I say, "so we have wrist-mounted arc cannons, forearm-mounted arc blades, a defensive grounding circuit, and nanotech shoulder-mounted arc missile turrets. Sounds good to me."

"There's…one more thing," Zeke says cautiously. He glances at the floor for a moment, studying his shoes.

Why did he say it like that?

"Which is…?" I ask nervously. I'm thrown off by his hesitance. He's usually very to the point.

"We, uh, built in an emergency self-destruct of sorts, just in case. It's rigged to send out a weaponized EMP blast mixed with an arc shockwave powerful enough to permanently fry any tech, weapons, people, you name it, including the exosuit itself. So, make sure you're well out of range *if* you end up using it. We hope you'll never need it, but if, say, the suit dies, and you have to make a getaway, or something like that, then it would be better to blow it up and leave them with a fuck you than with an advanced weaponized exosuit we built from their own tech." Zeke explains, his face apprehensive. "Right?"

"Definitely. That makes a lot of sense. And I swear I won't push the big red button while still inside that thing."

"Good, you better fucking not. But that's about it. We still need to put on a few finishing touches, make sure nothing will explode, all that good stuff." Zeke says.

"Oh, and we also have some goodies aside from the suit," Dex says, gesturing to an open crate near his feet.

I look inside, seeing all kinds of gadgets. Some I recognize, some I don't.

"In there," Dex continues, "are a bunch of things for you when you're not in the suit. We're talking arc grenades and taser units, small-scale EMP grenades, emergency healing stims, and adrenaline stims. There's also a new CYBR VYSR prototype we're finishing some final touches on. I think you're going to like it."

"That's a lot of amazing stuff. You guys are incredible. Thanks again."

I feel so grateful for their help. Also, I definitely can't

wait to see that new VYSR.

"Now, obviously, those stims are a last resort, but we figured this isn't the type of fight you leave anything on the table for, so we got it all ready for you," Zeke adds.

"Sounds good, guys, I understand, and I'll make sure only to use those if it's absolutely necessary."

We all share a nod of acknowledgment.

"And," Ash jumps in, reaching down to grab something from behind her, "here's one last thing from me."

To my surprise, it's my leather jacket. She's fixed the tears and holes in it.

"Thank you, Ash!" I say, smiling.

"Wait for it." She says with a smirk.

She dramatically turns the jacket around. I was admiring her handiwork on the front, but now I can see that the real magic happened on the back. She's painted the same blue wolf's head logo on the back of the jacket as on the chest of the exosuit!

"Okay, now that's awesome. It looks so good! Thank you so much." I can't help but grab the jacket and enthusiastically stare at it for a moment.

"You're welcome, Olly. You deserve it. I may not be as technologically inclined as these two, but it's the least I could do to help out. Aside from helping Zeke keep you alive, that is." She replies, smiling wide.

I put the jacket on. It feels good to wear it again.

"Also, don't sell yourself short, Astra." Dex chimes in. "You'll be one of the ones actually beating some sense into those bastards, along with Olly."

"True, I'll be putting the fear of chrome in those fuckers." She replies with a mischievous smile, cracking her knuckles.

"Not to mention," Dex continues, "I never would've been able to make this without you." He holds up a small chip.

"What's that?" I ask.

"It's my…manifesto, of sorts," Dex says. "It's the speech I'll be broadcasting over the CYBR Corp networks."

"Oh, nice, so you guys got that ready? How're we gonna broadcast it?"

"Well," Ash interjects, "we figured the best thing to do is to kill two Shinigami with one grenade, so we're going to have Dex and Zeke broadcast this while they man the surveillance outpost inside the HQ grounds. According to Dex, it's the only place we can get the proper access to their networks to actually broadcast this worldwide."

"And, just to make sure we're getting that message out there, we'll be blasting it on every single wavelength, every TV channel, radio station, VR headset, smart fridge, you name it," Dex adds, his voice filled with pride. "I'm confident that, once inside their firewall, I can easily get this bad boy onto every channel."

"All," Zeke says, "while you two go deeper into the HQ, find the tallest building, and take your particular brand of fuck-you all the way to the top floor. If we want people to actually join this thing, we'll have to not just play the speech on their TV but actually show them how far we can get with just our merry little band here."

"Nice! It sounds like you all really got the plan flushed out while I was taking my little nap. I'm ready to fill whatever part of the plan I need to! Let's bring 'em hell!" I say, excited.

"Speaking of which," Ash says, "I'll fill you in on the nitty-gritty of your part of the plan in the morning."

"Sounds good to me."

I look over to Ash, who gives me a smile and then yawns. It makes me yawn, which spreads quickly to Dex and Zeke as well. I glance at my Holocomm and am shocked to find it's currently 00:30.

Damn, no wonder I'm so tired.

"So, guys, I can tell we're all tired, I know I'm exhausted, so let's get some sleep, yeah? I can't wait to get this plan moving! But I know I need to rest, and you've all more than earned a break, so let's get some sleep." I suggest.

Everyone nods in tired agreement and makes their way to their various sleeping areas. Ash helps me walk over to a little corner of the room that she's set up for us.

"It's not much, but I tried to make this as comfortable as sleeping on the floor can be." She says, helping me down onto the makeshift bed.

There are emergency blankets piled up, pillows made of backpacks stuffed with clothes, and a lantern for light.

It's perfect.

"This is all I need. Thank you so much, Ash."

I smile at her as I begin to drift off, the drowsiness quickly pulling me in. I take more pain meds, sip some water, then lie down in the blankets and allow myself to fall asleep. The last thing I feel as sleep envelopes me is the warmth of Ash's body cuddling against my side.

CH 12

APPROACHING the guard tower, my heart is beating a million times per minute. This is the beginning of the end, either for us or for CYBR Corp., and I will *not* let it be us.

Here we go. This is it.

I sneak up to the side of the building, walking slowly and low to the ground to be as silent as possible.

Thanks to Dex, all security cameras in the immediate area have been temporarily disabled. The guards, as well as the Cerulean AI monitoring the cameras, are all seeing a loop of an empty street corner. That means the only thing I need to worry about is the several heavily armed Retribution soldiers keeping watch. There's one on either side of the gate and two more inside the guard tower itself, where the gate controls are. Where I need to be.

Having made it to the base of the guard tower, I wait for the guard on this side of the gate to turn away before I quickly and quietly run around the side of the building to the door. As planned, it's relatively dark right here, with the only light being from infrequently dispersed lampposts and the obscured moon overhead.

I take a second to study the tower. This is one of four identical towers on each corner of the complex; this is the one on the southwest corner. It's two stories tall, with tinted, bulletproof windows on each floor. The main structure is made of darkened steel and dull grey concrete. It's an imposing yet boring structure, much like all CYBR

Corp buildings.

After a few moments, the guard turns away.

"Now!" I whisper urgently.

"Okay, lights out! You have three minutes." Dex responds through our closed-loop comms.

"Be careful!" Ash adds.

I don't have time to answer. I slip through the now-unlocked door into the dark confines of the guard tower. I quickly and quietly close the door behind me, making sure the gate guards don't notice.

Alright, here goes nothing.

I reach into my pocket and pull out a pair of aviator shades. I put them on, pressing the hidden button on the right hinge as I do so. The CYBR Corp logo flashes in my eyes for a split second before my new CYBR VYSR gives me perfect night vision.

I move as silently as I can, making my way through the room and looking for the guards. First, I walk past lockers and a large conference table. Then, the VYSR identifies a person's heat signature on the far side of the room, near where their computer surveillance station is located. I look over to see them standing over their station with their chair knocked over behind them. They haven't seen me yet. They're too busy furiously smashing buttons and switches to try to get the system back online.

I throw an arc taser at the guard. The taser unit attaches to the armor plating on her mid-back, sending a massive shock through her entire body. Her body begins to slump off of her chair.

Oh shit, gotta catch her.

I rush over to the guard as the electric shock courses through her, causing her to spasm in place for a few moments before crumpling to the ground. I catch her as she falls, making sure to make as little noise as possible as I set her body down.

There are two nice things about arc tasers. One, they're non-lethal, and two, it's nearly impossible to call for help when every muscle in your body is being constricted by intense electrical shock.

Alright, let's see what you've got.

I do a quick search of the guard, looking for anything useful. Naturally, there's the standard-issue arc rifle, which I sling over my back. The gun we got earlier is still with Ash, so it'll be nice to have another one. I also find an arc pistol on her hip and a few arc grenades strapped across her chest.

Heavily armed for a guard with a desk job.

I stand up, tucking my prizes in the pockets of my jacket. I turn toward the stairs and slowly make my way up them. Despite my efforts, I make an upsettingly loud clanging sound when I step off of the stairs and onto the metallic grate of the upper floor.

Shit, no way they didn't hear that.

Sure enough, the second guard immediately spins to look in my direction. The red lights of their visor let me know that they've locked onto me. All Retribution helmets have CYBR VYSR technology built in, so as clearly as I can see them, they can see me.

"You should surrender now." The guard commands, his arc rifle whirring to life.

I draw my daishō and engage the arc units. The blue electricity engulfs the blades, sending flickering, uneven shadows across everything in the room. I turn off the night vision of my VYSR since the blue light is blindingly bright. Instead, I'll have to rely on the standard motion tracking of the VYSR and my own instincts.

The good news? They're also blinded. They stumble back, forced to fix their visor instead of continuing to charge their rifle.

Wasting no time, I run toward them as quickly as I can. Since we're in a relatively small guard tower, it only takes a moment to close the gap between us.

"Die, Wolf!" Growls the Retribution guard as they gain their bearings, charging an arc rifle volley.

What the hell?

Thrown off by the fact that they know who I am, I narrowly dodge out of the way of their arc rifle's plasma.

Okay, Oliver, first take them down. Then you can figure out what the hell is going on here.

The guard begins charging another volley, but this time, I'm ready. I get in low, under their guard, and bring my swords up together in one smooth, arcing motion. The front half of their rifle, as well as most of their left hand, fall to the floor in a shower of blue and orange sparks.

"Argh! You little shit!" The guard screams. Anger and pain fill his voice with a dangerous venom.

In a blind rage, he swings a vicious right hook my way. I dodge backward, having been knocked out by that exact move too many times in MMA fights. I follow up by bringing my swords up on either side of me, then bringing them down in a crossing motion, aiming for the legs.

The guard falls to the ground, now missing both legs and most of his left hand. He growls and grunts, trying desperately to find another weapon to kill me with. He fumbles with the arc pistol on his hip, but I kick it away.

"Unless you want to lose your other hand, I suggest you calm your shit."

I'd rather not kill these guards, even if they are mindless Retribution goons filled with nothing but hate. But at the same time, we're pressed for time and completely outnumbered, so I may not really get much choice.

"Go...to...hell." He grunts.

Yeah, I was afraid you'd say that. Wait shit—

The guard grabs one of the arc grenades strapped to his chest, pulls the pin with his remaining left finger, and rolls it toward me. Clearly, he has no desire to live as long as he can kill me. I have approximately five seconds to figure out how to stop him from accomplishing his goal. Time seems to slow down as I watch the grenade tumbling along the metal floor directly for my feet.

That's it!

Moving as quickly as possible, I grab one of my EMP grenades, arm it, and throw it directly at the guard's arc grenade. Not being eager to find out if that will actually work, I sprint away from him as quickly as I can. I make it only a couple of steps toward the stairs before a terrifying and confusing series of explosions take place. The adrenaline of the moment makes me hyper-aware of everything that happens but completely unable to do anything about it.

First, the arc grenade goes off, sending a terrifyingly lethal electric shockwave through the entire room. A millisecond later, the EMP grenade engages, sending a neutralizing wave through the room, directly chasing the arc shockwave.

The arc shockwave hits me first, sending excruciating pain through my body. Then, as quickly as the arc shockwave fills my body with unimaginable pain, the EMP wave hits, neutralizing the arc electricity and all basic cybernetics on my body. The strangest part is that there's no explosion or anything. Both grenades are relatively silent, but the pain makes my ears ring like a bomb just went off. I collapse to the ground from the shock, but I somehow manage to remain conscious.

After a few moments of catching my breath, my fusion power cell begins restarting my other systems. After a few more seconds, I'm standing and ready to go, or at least technically ready according to my systems. I'm not *actually* ready according to how my body and mind feel.

My body burns like a million fire ants are continuously stinging every inch of me. It's a horrible sensation that only seems to get worse as I stand here. The healing nanobots are desperately trying to repair my skin, which was covered in micro-burns from the grounding circuit's passive discharge. The sensation is like the pins and needles of a limb waking up from a loss of circulation, only multiplied tenfold. I grit my teeth and force myself to walk over to the guard. He's dead, no doubt about it. The arc grenade overloaded his systems, both cybernetic and biological. That's what they're designed to do, after all. The guard downstairs is most likely dead, too, since this upper floor is just a metal grate.

The only reason I'm still standing here is that grounding circuit. I have got to thank Zeke later. But for now…

"Hey, this is Oliver. Come in, Dex." I say, activating the closed loop comms device.

"Oliver! What's your status?" Dex asks.

"I'm hurt, but I'll be fine. Just taking the grounding circuit for a spin. Can't say the same for these two."

"Well, we're glad you're alright. I would've preferred you didn't test that new tech so soon, but I guess at least we know it works now." He replies with a relieved chuckle.

"Yeah, I'm not too psyched about testing it out either, but I can already feel the healing nanobots doing their magic. Anyway, you guys are clear to move in. Just need to open the door…"

With a few seconds to spare, I take the opportunity to rid myself of all the arc guns and grenades I took off of the guards. Thanks to our little fireworks show, these are either dead or unreliable, which makes them useless to me.

My systems are all in good condition, thanks to the grounding circuit, emergency shutoff, and my fusion power cell. My swords should also be fine, thanks to the improved arc units Zeke installed for me from the leftover exosuit parts. Of course, I have to find them first, but it's pitch black in here. I try to switch my VYSR back on, but it doesn't respond.

Damn, lost another one. You'd think they'd make these things more durable.

Right as I'm about to throw away my brand-new VYSR sunglasses, it turns back on.

Oh, sweet. Guess I overreacted. Must be some of the prototype tech the boys added to this thing.

Just then, Dex's hack runs out of time, and the lights all come back on inside the guard tower. That also means the security cameras are back online, but that's fine. To the outside world, nothing happened, nothing at all. The windows of this tower are tinted, one-way glass, and the 'explosions' that occurred were silent, just flashes of light.

Extremely painful flashes of light, but whatever.

Just to make sure, I walk to the window and look down at the gate below. The two guards are still standing there, one on either side, oblivious.

"Hey, Olly, ETA is one minute." Says Dex.

They're currently driving a Retribution armored truck, a truck we stole as we made our way out of those tunnels.

Turns out we were just one room away from the exit that whole time. Go figure, right?

As I finished my recovery and Dex and Zeke finished their work on the exosuit, we planned this attack. We planned the most efficient way to take down CYBR Corp, and it all starts with this guard tower.

Once we had a plan, we packed up and moved to the next room in the tunnels, expecting miles more hell to trudge through. For once, we were given a break.

The next room was a dusty old vehicle bay filled with CYBR Corp vans, trucks, UAVs, you name it. We jacked one of the trucks and busted out the door, scaring the shit out of some kids who were hanging out by the exit. Zeke claims he 'saw one of 'em jump ten feet in the air,' but who's to say. I thought it would be funny, though, so I chose to believe him.

Focus, Oliver. The gate.

I rush over to the control station. With the systems back online, it's showing feeds of the various security cameras both in and around this guard tower. To my dismay, I look terrible, but that's not the task at hand. I can see their truck rolling up to the gate. It'll be there any second.

"Okay, if I were a gate control, where would I be?" I mutter to myself, frantically searching the control screen's array of vaguely marked buttons.

"This one? I guess that's the picture of a gate?"

I press a button marked "ADMIT" because, apparently, "GATE OPEN" is too obvious. The gate begins opening slowly as my friends roll up to the outside gate guard.

Through the camera feed, I can see that the guard is trying to interrogate them about why they should let them pass, but they look back confusedly at the gate opening before they've made up their mind.

Shit, I wasn't supposed to open that yet. Come on, you stupid guard, just let them through. It's one of your own trucks.

Just then, the control station crackles with static. It must have been damaged by the arc grenade as well.

"Come in seven four two nine, this is eight nine three six. This truck is not cleared for entrance. Close the gate at once." The emotionless voice of the gate guard demands, static breaking up every few words.

Uhh, okay. Remain calm.

"Acknowledged eight nine three six. Gate controls are malfunctioning. Proceed." I reply, trying my best to match the gruff voice of the guard lying behind me.

Hopefully, the static works both ways...

"Copy that. Repair your station at once. Over and out."

I feel a strong desire to call back in and tell this guy where to go and how to get there, but I decide that would be...ill-advised.

"Heads up, guys, there's a chance you may be in some hot water. Our gate guard friend is a real piece of work, but that's what we planned for. Dex, don't answer me, but if you can hear this, just tell them what we rehearsed." I say into my comms, double-checking that the command station's radio isn't on.

No one answers, which makes sense, considering Dex is face-to-face with the enemy and Ash and Zeke are desperately trying to pass as crates of weapons. It still makes me feel incredibly nervous.

Through the comms, I can hear Dex talking to the obstinate guard. I watch nervously through the camera feeds, unable to do anything more for them at the moment. It's a terrible feeling.

"Explain the reason for the delay," Dex demands, "this shipment of weapons is due to the barracks in exactly three minutes."

According to Dex, formalities and pleasantries are all but nonexistent among CYBR Corp employees, especially when dealing with Retribution. These guards, just like all Retribution, are inhuman killing machines, stripped of all emotions other than rage.

Needless to say, when we prepped for this moment, Dex made sure we all understood that any attempt to be friendly, joking, or anything human with these guys would be cause for suspicion. And we all know they need very little reason to kill someone.

"Reason for entry acknowledged. State your vehicle identification number." Replies the guard.

"VN082367549." Dex recites without a moment's hesitation.

"Acknowledged. Proceed." The guard relents, stepping back from the truck.

Thank fuck.

Dex, cool as a cucumber, rolls up the window of the truck and slowly pulls through the gate, officially entering CYBR Corp's facilities. In the camera feed, I swear I can see him smirk as the window closes.

With them officially inside, I have an unexpected dilemma to deal with: do I hit the gate button again, closing the gate as the guard would expect, or do I leave it open, sticking to the narrative of malfunctioning gate controls that I've already established?

Wait, but he demanded that I fix it at once, so how fast is that supposed to be?

Deciding that "at once" is literal in the eyes of a soulless CYBR Corp goon, I press the gate button. Or, should I say, the ADMIT button? That's right. You press the same button, labeled 'ADMIT,' to open *and* close the gate.

I stand up from the guard station as the speaker crackles again.

"I see you've fixed your station, seven four two nine. I expect you will file the proper report with management."

Oh great, you again.

"Correct, eight nine three six, it is already filed," I reply.

I wait for a moment, there's no response. To be fair, replying to that and actually finishing a conversation would be a form of pleasantry.

With that taken care of, I take one final look around the

guard tower, looking for anything we can use as we further infiltrate CYBR Corp's headquarters.

On the top floor, there's a ton of grenades, guns, and tech scattered around, but unfortunately, my little grenade escapade has all but definitely ruined every piece of tech in the whole place.

Wait, swords!

In my panic, I almost forgot to grab my swords. Luckily, the lights are on, or at least the ones that didn't explode, so it's much easier to look for them now.

I find the katana first. It's a couple of steps down the staircase. Then, I see the wakizashi at the bottom of the steps. I switch on the arc units on both of them, and to my relief, they hum and spark to life, working perfectly. I switch them off and sheath them at my waist.

I've got approximately no time left, but I take a quick glance around the bottom floor, desperately looking for something useful.

Let's see, more useless arc grenades and guns, some lockers, cleaning robots... Wait!

I rush over to the lockers and open one of them. Inside are guard uniforms of every size. It's precisely what we need. Dex already has his old uniform, which he was wearing just now, to infiltrate the gate. I'm looking for one that will fit me. They're listed in standard small, medium, large, etc. sizing.

Great, this means nothing. Am I large? XL? XXL? Medium? Who's to say?

I grab a medium, a large, and an extra large and hope for the best.

I open the rest of the lockers in a frantic panic, finding more uniforms, fried tech, and weapons. Among the broken weapons are some basic arc shock batons. I remember hearing somewhere that these batons are resistant to arc or

EMP interference for maximum crowd control.

Crowd control, aka beating peaceful protestors mercilessly. Something both Ash and I have experienced on multiple occasions.

Time for some sweet revenge.

I grab three of the batons, one for each of them. I consider grabbing one for myself but decide against it. After all, I already have my daishō.

I quickly dig through my backpack, seeing which of the grenades and taser units are still good. Each one has a blue indicator strip that turns red when it's been compromised. Unfortunately, all of my arc grenades are toast, but the EMP grenades and taser units all seem to be okay.

I suppose I could check each indicator strip on every piece of tech here, but I definitely don't have that kind of time or patience.

I toss the arc grenades, shoving the uniforms and batons into the empty space as best I can. The good news is I needed the space in my backpack. The bad news is I'm down several weapons.

Time to go.

I go out the back door of the guard tower, moving silently. I slowly peek around the corner to see if the guard is paying attention on this side of the gate. It looks like they're arguing with the outside gate guard over something, probably whether or not they should have let in that truck just now. Or who's the bigger asshole. Whatever it is, it's my chance.

I crouch-run as quickly as I can, holding my backpack and daishō in a way that they make as little noise as possible. I need to make it to the weapon storage building, which is our meeting place. According to Dex, it's three buildings down from this guard tower, along the west wall of the complex.

I'm currently running north. The gate we entered through was the southwest entry point of CYBR Corp HQ. We chose it because it's one of the two south towers, which are the farthest from the main HQ building, where the higher-ups are. Also, this tower is near the most relatively unguarded quadrant of the facility, which is the storage quadrant. According to Dex, there are four quadrants of equal size: storage and training in the south and research and command in the north. Each quadrant is approximately the size of a city block. Our goal is to move from the southwest storage quadrant to the northeast command quadrant. Preferably undetected, but, ya know. I'm not holding my breath on that.

I run along the west wall of the complex, making my way behind the next building in the row: a guard bunkhouse. All CYBR Corp employees are required to live on the premises, with the guards in various military-style bunkhouses such as this one.

I slow my run to a crouch-walk as soon as I'm behind the building, now out of the immediate field of view of the gate guards, should they decide to stop arguing long enough to turn around.

The good news is that this building has no windows or security cameras on the back side, considering they would be looking directly at the grey stone wall to my left. The bad news is that I'm squeezing between said brick wall and the bunkhouse, a space no human was intended to enter, as far as I can tell. It can't be more than a foot and a half of room.

When we discussed this in the tunnels, Dex assured me I'd be able to fit in this space 'no problem.' It's just now occurring to me that he may have either forgotten how small this was or was lying to me to make me feel better.

Alright, Oliver, time to shimmy.

I take off my backpack, holding it out in front of me with my right hand while I hold my daishō out with my left hand. I proceed to shimmy my way along this building. It's incredibly dark in here, with the middle being almost entirely dark, the only light coming from distant fluorescent lampposts on either end of the building.

I have no idea how long this building is, but it feels like a mile by the time I shimmy out the other side and into the space between this and the next building.

As I finally come out from behind this building, I cautiously walk around the corner, making sure no one sees me.

My face is plastered on every CYBR Corp most wanted poster, and I'm not wearing the uniform yet. I realize now that I should've changed back in that guard house, but it didn't occur to me at the time.

Alright, the coast is clear. Time to get to the next building.

As I make my way to the next building, I try to remember what Dex told me this one is, but I honestly forgot. I remembered the bunkhouse because he said it was the most dangerous, with the most people likely to be there. I also remember the weapon storage building because that's the meeting point. But this second building? It could be anything, to be honest.

Doesn't matter. It's time for more shimmy. Here's hoping this isn't a bomb factory.

I slide into the narrow gap between the second building and the wall, now much more skilled at the art of the shimmy than last time. I made it from one end of the building to the other in half the time it took me to make it past the bunkhouse.

Having cleared the second building, I try not to get too excited and rush to meet up with everyone. There doesn't seem to be anyone in between these buildings either, but it doesn't stop me from feeling nervous. My palms feel sweaty, and my heart beats fast again.

Just one wrong move, one misstep, that's all it takes to ruin everything. No, shut up, Oliver. You can do this.

I take a second to calm my nerves, breathing deeply as I lurk just around the corner of this building. I look up and see the full moon in all of its pale glory.

It's a rare sight to see any part of the night sky unobscured by clouds, smog, or both, so the moon catches me off guard for a minute.

It really is beautiful. When was the last time I even saw the moon?

As I take a moment to stare at the full moon, catching my breath, I lose a bit of awareness of my surroundings. One moment, I'm staring at the moon. The next, a patrolling guard is walking through the street, passing by the alley I'm in, mere yards away.

How they didn't notice me, I have no idea, but I duck as quickly as I can behind the building before they have a chance to turn around.

That was way too close. I have to be more careful.

After a few moments, I come back out from behind the building, slowly rounding the corner as I look out for more patrolling guards. I don't see any, so I rush to the third building. There should be a secondary entrance to this building on the north side, an entrance Dex assured me he would open before I got there. I'm hoping that's true.

I slide behind the building like I did with the others, and then I round the corner, moving with renewed caution thanks to my close encounter in the last alleyway. I'm greeted with a sight that makes me extremely grateful that I chose caution: the space on the north side of this building is a large, open courtyard teeming with CYBR Corp guards, employees, and vehicles of several kinds.

Not just the guards but also the seemingly non-combat personnel are all extremely armed. The vehicles all seem to have at least one turret mounted to them. The reddish hue of the lampposts casts a hellish glare over everything. It's terrifying.

For a moment, I stand there, frozen. My fight or flight response has definitely kicked in, and, unlike usual, I desperately feel the need to run, to sprint in the opposite direction as fast as I possibly can. It's actually a rather unique sensation, or at least it would be if I wasn't filled with fear and adrenaline.

What am I doing? Do I honestly believe I can take down this entire megacorporation with three friends as my only allies? Look at me. I'm shaking in fear over what, twenty guards? But I can't fail now. We've come too far and gotten too close. And what kind of friend would I be if I brought them all into this mess, only to bail when shit hits the fan?

I spend another minute or two between the building and the wall, trying to calm my breathing. I feel like curling up into a ball, but there isn't enough room back here for that. Plus, that would be one hell of a way to get discovered here.

Get it together, Oliver. You've done so much to get here. Everyone believes in you. You just have to trust that they know what they're talking about. It's not like they're just telling you that because they don't want to be rude. Right? No, definitely not. Telling someone you believe in them when you actually don't is not the kind of lie you infiltrate the most dangerous place on Earth for.

They believe in you. Now, believe in yourself.

With newfound resolve, I straighten up, roll my shoulders, crack my neck, and step out from behind the building.

All eyes turn to me.

"Hey! You can't be here!" a guard shouts.

Fuck.

I sprint toward the side entrance. I can see it now. It's about halfway down the north side of this building. If I can just reach it, I'll be safely inside with my friends. And if I can't…

"You have three seconds to drop your weapons and come forward with your hands up." The guard shouts again.

I turn for a split second to look and see approximately thirty guns aimed directly at me. There's no way I'm surrendering, so I sprint harder for the door.

After what seems to me like a lot less than three seconds, they open fire.

Well, this is it, then.

The door is still several paces away, and fighting back is pointless, so I just press my back against the wall and wait for my inevitable demise. As the sound of thirty charging arc rifles fills the night air, I close my eyes and try to imagine it's the sound of a spaceship blasting off or something. I don't know, don't ask me why. You stare down the barrel of imminent death and tell me what you're thinking.

Only I don't die. Not only do I not die, but I'm entirely okay. I open my eyes to what may be the most confusing and wonderful thing that's ever happened to me: thirty arc rifles charge, fire, and then, nothing. The massive wall of charged plasma screams toward my face, ready to end my existence, only to disappear a mere few inches from my nose without so much as a puff of smoke.

The CYBR Corp goons look just as confused as I am, only instead of pleased, they're decidedly pissed off. A few of them angrily smack their guns while others charge another volley and try once again to unsuccessfully end my life.

I decide it's best not to tempt fate any longer, so I start

running toward the door again, making sure to hug the wall like my life depends on it. Because it does, apparently. I don't know why it does, but I'm pretty confident that I owe my life to this wall.

I reach the door as the angry mob begins rushing toward me, realizing their guns are useless. I try to open the door, but it won't budge. Also, I don't know how to open it. There's no handle, and it doesn't seem to be automatic.

"Come on, come on! Stupid door. Open!" I yell.

I poke and prod at every part of the door, hoping to find a button of some kind. Finally, a little panel opens when I press it, and a fingerprint sensor reveals itself. Without a second thought, I press my right index fingertip to the sensor. If I was religious, this would be the time to pray.

The sound of thirty pairs of boots rushing toward me is growing closer and closer. They were only around twenty yards away when I last looked.

After a moment, the panel slides back shut, and the door slides open. I rush inside and slide the door closed behind me. The closest of the guards are mere feet away as I slam the door shut. Their hate-filled eyes are the last thing I see.

"Oliver! Thank goodness." Dex greets me, standing at a control panel a few feet to my right. He aggressively presses some sort of big red button.

"Lockdown initiated. Security reinforcements inbound." Cerulean's voice says over the building's speakers.

There's a pair of unconscious guards next to the panel.

"So much for stealthy infiltration." He comments.

"Dex! Man, am I glad to see you. You're not gonna believe what just happened to me." I say, leaning down with my hands on my knees, catching my breath.

I look up to see Zeke and Ash walking toward us from the front of the building. Another pair of guards lie on the ground near the front door.

"Hey! Guess who's alive!?" I shout to them, elated.

"You damn well better be alive, or else what am I even doing here?" Zeke replies as they get closer.

I let myself feel happy for a minute, rushing over to give Ash and Zeke a hug.

"Get in here!" I say, looking at Dex. He hesitates, then comes and joins the group hug.

For a moment, everything is good.

"Alright, but I have to ask, did any of you know this building had a force field?" I ask.

"Well, not to be rude, but I did tell you about this building in the briefing while we were planning this attack, did I not?" Dex replies.

To be fair, I do remember him telling me about this building, how it's full of weapons, relatively low-staffed due to it being automated, and protected by some sort of electrical field—

"Wait! That's what you meant by electrical, whatever field? I thought it was some sort of EMP protection or something. Not a literal forcefield that can stop arc rifles!"

"Yes, well, it's designed to protect the building against any sort of attack. Since the walls themselves are physically nearly impenetrable, they felt it would be important to also protect against any sort of electricity-based attack." Dex replies.

"I guess it's a good thing I literally had my back against the wall, then."

"Indeed. It's called an electromagnetic dampening field, or EMDF. Many buildings containing dangerous or precious items or personnel have them."

"Huh, I'll be damned." I sit in stunned silence on a nearby crate of something probably explosive.

After a moment, I reach into my backpack and toss out

the uniforms and shock batons.

"These won't be much use anymore, I guess. Sorry about the not-so-stealthy entrance." I say, feeling like a disappointment.

"The uniforms might not, but these are always reliable," Dex responds, grabbing one of the shock batons and tucking it into his belt.

"Yeah," Zeke grabs the other two, tossing one to Ash. "Plus, the fact that we made it here at all is an accomplishment. We always knew the chances of getting in unnoticed were slim to none."

"True, true, thanks," I reply, feeling much better.

"Alright, but I've got a question," Ash chimes in, "why did those guards all shoot at Olly? Didn't they know it wouldn't work?"

"Yeah, what's the deal with that?" echoes Zeke.

Glad I'm not the only one around here who doesn't understand everything that's going on.

"True, that is strange." Dex replies, "I know about the fields because I worked maintaining them for a while, but maybe it's not public knowledge in the company? Or maybe they're so single-minded that they didn't think about it?"

"I feel like this is the first time you haven't known something, Dex. You must be slipping in your old age," I joke.

"Yep, I'm wasting away over here." He answers.

We all share a laugh.

"At any rate, we came here to do a job, yeah?" Zeke asks, bringing us back to the moment at hand.

"Damn right, we're in. Now it's time for phase two," Ash replies, a glint in her eye as she opens a nearby crate to reveal several rocket launchers.

Ash, Dex, and Zeke all rummage through weapon crates while I move to the truck they drove in here, opening the back to reveal the only weapon I'll be needing: the exosuit.

Just then, a loud banging sound fills the entire building, echoing from the walls. I can't quite tell where it came from, but it sounds like someone's busting in.

I run back over to the others.

"Guys, what was that—"

Another bang shakes the building. This time, it's clear to me where it came from: the door. The door that I narrowly came in through. The door that dozens of guards watched me enter.

"We got company!" Zeke shouts, grabbing a nearby arc rifle.

I look around and see that all three of them are strapping into protective body armor they must have found and wielding standard-issue arc rifles.

I toss my backpack near the pile of weapons crates.

"There's stims and EMP grenades in here. I've got to get to the suit! Can you hold the door?" I ask, already making my way back over to the truck.

"We'll have to!" Dex yells back to me, taking cover behind a stack of crates.

I frantically scramble into the back of the truck. I quickly remove my VYSR glasses, tucking them inside my jacket. I remove my daishō, hooking the two swords into the pre-destined mounts on the back of the exosuit.

Another earth-shattering bang resonates throughout the building.

"Here goes nothing," I mutter to myself.

I press the button to power on the exosuit, quickly followed by the button to open the suit so I can climb inside.

I frantically get settled into the suit.

"Welcome, Oliver." Cerulean's voice greets me from the suit's helmet.

"Close suit, engage combat mode," I command.

The suit closes around me, the armor plating closing itself around my legs, arms, chest, and finally, head. For a brief moment, I can't see anything. The visor isn't actually see-through. It's an intelligent wraparound screen that looks transparent when it's turned on. It also contains three-hundred-sixty-degree speakers linked to external microphones, which give full auditory feedback.

The visor turns on, becoming 'see-through' and engaging the HUD. Various indicators fill the edges of my vision, showing my vitals, the suit's power levels, weapons status, etc. Everything is a pleasing shade of blue, indicating it's in working order, and so am I.

"Combat mode engaged." Cerulean notifies me.

"Perfect."

I walk in a crouch out of the truck, jumping down to the ground below. It's only a few feet down, but the impact sends a resonating thud through the building. I see the others briefly turn to look in my direction before turning back to the door.

I start jogging over to the door, which only takes a few strides in this suit. It feels *amazing*.

"Engage thermal imaging."

"Engaged."

The visor turns to a thermal gradient. I can see clearly through the walls now, and the sight stops me in my tracks for a moment. There must be a hundred guards outside that door, some with standard gear, some in exosuits of their own. I look upward and see at least five aircraft of some kind. The heat blasting down out of their engines makes it hard to tell if they're manned or not. Either way, it's not good news for us.

I take another few strides and arrive at the door. I stand in between the door and my friends, fully ready to protect them at all costs.

"You guys, get ready and stand back! Grab some rocket launchers or something. There's a hundred guards out there, maybe more." I shout, the suit projecting my voice in every direction.

"Engage turrets," I command in a quieter voice.

"Already engaged."

Right, automatic turrets. Duh.

Another boom fills the room as the door flies off its hinges directly toward me. The suit identifies it as a threat, switching back to visual from thermal, beeping aggressively as the door flies closer and closer. At the same time, several red outlines pop up around the swarm of Retribution guards swarming the building.

Without thinking, I throw up my hands and catch the door, stopping it dead in its tracks.

"Return to sender!" I yell, throwing the mangled door back where it came from.

It hits three guards head-on, sending them flying back into the wall. They don't get back up.

"Oliver, duck!" Ash screams from behind me.

A beeping from behind my head lets me know someone has fired a rocket. I dodge to the right, the missile flying past my left side and hitting the next group of guards through the door. The explosion blinds me for half a second. By the time I open my eyes again, there are ten guards mere feet away from me.

"Missile launchers, engaged." Cerulean reports.

Each of my shoulder-mounted missile launchers fires a missile. They collide with the group of guards, each one blasting five guards with a blinding display of shrapnel and electricity.

More come flooding in, wasting no time, showing no trace of emotion as they step over the rapidly growing pile of bodies just inside the door.

I raise my arms and fire a series of shots from the arm-mounted arc cannons. Each shot sends one of the guards flying. Over my shoulder, another missile flies past, eviscerating another group of guards.

Despite all of this, they keep rushing in. More and more guards pour in, slowly overwhelming us. I continue to fire shots, my missile launchers firing automatically every time there are too many, or they get too close. Ash continues sending rockets flying while Dex and Zeke start firing volley after relentless volley of arc rifle blasts into the fray.

It doesn't matter. There are too many.

"Engage the thermal camera," I command once again.

Dear lord.

There's somehow *more* than there were before. I swivel my head, only to reveal the front entrance also has a rapidly growing number of guards outside.

"Disengage thermal camera."

The front door comes flying off its hinges with a resonating boom. Clearly, they figured out how to get it open after trial and error with the side door.

"Can you hold this door?" I shout as I slowly back away from the side door.

"Go! Just go!" Ash screams in reply, firing another rocket and blowing who knows how many guards into bits.

Shit. What did I get her into…no, never mind that.

Without another word, I sprint over to the front of the building, each stride covering several yards. I come in swinging, immediately surrounded by guards. I punch my way through the first several, clearing enough space to start shooting the arc cannons. Each shot takes a second to charge, so it needs a little space.

The automatic turrets send a couple more missiles into the fray, clearing more space for me, but it's quickly filled in by more guards.

This is too slow. I need something more responsive.

"Engage arc blades," I command.

The two blades spring out of the underside of the exosuit's forearms, sparking to life. Despite everything, it makes me feel a little giddy. I mean, come on, it's like a big, beefed-up daishō built into this magnificent suit. What's not to love?

I charge forward with a guttural scream, slashing my way through the crowd of guards with reckless abandon. I slice clear through the first few guards, first with my right, then left, then right again. Human, armor, or weapon, it's all the same to these extremely sharp, lightning-charged death blades.

The guards behind them pause for a moment as they see how easily I made my way through the first few.

Perfect.

I charge at full speed toward the next group of guards, using my momentum in a wide double-handed swing that cuts through five of them in one fell swoop.

More guards come pouring in, firing relentless volleys of arc rifle plasma in my direction. Using the warning system of my suit, I'm able to dodge the majority of it. The remainder hits the armor plating of the suit, causing minimal damage.

I spin through the crowd of guards, slashing around and around, cutting down countless Retribution guards. No matter how many I slice in half, more come rushing in to replace them.

"Warning: The current fusion power cell is at fifteen percent power. Current power usage exceeds recommended parameters." Cerulean announces.

Ah, great.

I back up, squeezing the hands of the suit and flicking

my wrists to sheath the arc blades. The auto turrets each fire another volley of missiles.

To my amazement, the flow of guards has slowed. Only a handful come rushing through the door this time. I can't help but feel a little hopeful.

My hope dies once again as I hear a scream of pain from behind me. I spin to see what happened, the suit magnifying what I'm looking at.

"Zeke! No!" I shout.

Completely ignoring the guards shooting at me from behind, I sprint over to where my friends are. They still have a horde of guards flowing in, and Ash and Dex shoot everything they can to stop the onslaught. On the floor, behind some crates, is Zeke. He's clutching his side, blood pouring out of him as he cries out in pain.

"Zeke! What happened? Are you okay?" I ask, kneeling in the suit to get a closer look.

"Never…mind me. You have to stop…them." He says through pained breaths, gesturing weakly to the guards that are slowly overtaking us.

"Fuck. This is not good. Alright, fine. But you're not allowed to die, you got that?" I say, standing up.

I turn my attention to the guards once again, seeing the problem: the guards in exosuits have entered the building. It seems they were waiting to see if the regular guards could deal with us before they came in. Probably wanted to spare the expensive equipment.

"Ash, Dex, protect Zeke! Use a healing stim from my bag! And deal with the rest of them!" I command, gesturing to my right at the straggling few guards from the front entrance.

"Got it!" Ash yells back. She runs and slides down to grab a stim from my bag, stabbing it into Zeke's leg and activating the injection.

"Come and get me, you bastards!" Dex shouts as he turns his fury to the guards.

I jump over the makeshift barricade of boxes, leaping several feet in the air and landing inches from the first of the exosuit-clad guards. He has arc blades much like the ones on my own suit.

"Looking for me?" I taunt.

Instead of answering, the guard reaches forward, stabbing the exposed gaps in my armor with the blades. It sends a massive shockwave through the suit, and he grins at me.

To the guard's surprise and my relief, the makeshift grounding circuit Zeke installed does its job perfectly. The arc electricity courses through the suit, charging the batteries to the max.

"Solid-state batteries fully charged. First of three fusion cells fully depleted." Cerulean reports.

"Sorry, pal, but I came prepared," I say, grabbing the blades and pushing them away from me.

Before he can react, I charge a double blast from my arc cannons. It hits him square in the chest, sending him back a few feet. Their exosuits are slightly smaller, slower, less armored, and less powerful than mine.

The problem is there are three of them.

As soon as the other two see me overpowering the first guard, they rush in, charging their own arc cannons.

Looks like one with arc blades and two with arc cannons. I can do this. Just think.

I put all of my effort into dodging, rushing to the right and around behind the two with cannons. One of them hits my left arm with his volley, but luckily, it misses the gaps in the armor. The other misses me entirely, if only by an inch. I engage the arc blades on my suit again, leaping forward and slashing down with both blades toward the closest guard. My goal is to hit the gaps in the shoulders, similar to how the first guard stabbed me.

My blades glance off of the shoulder plating of the guard's suit, barely missing their mark. I waste no time slashing again with my right, aiming now for the neck.

My attack is stopped by the second guard shooting my right arm milliseconds before my blade's about to land.

"Warning: The armor plating is taking significant damage. Tactical retreat is advised." Cerulean suggests.

I fall back slightly. Can't exactly give up, though.

"Come on, missile launchers, do your thing," I mutter.

Like clockwork, my shoulder-mounted launchers fire missiles toward the guards. One hits the nearest guard directly in the head, blowing his armor wide open and exposing his face beneath. The second hits the arm of the bladed guard as he rushes toward me, severing his arm at the elbow. He falls to his knees, screaming in pain.

"Missile launcher capacity has been diminished to fifty percent." Cerulean reports.

"Can't you give me good news for once?" I reply.

"Good news, ammo is half full for missile launchers."

Did she just...never mind.

With one of the guards out of commission, at least for the moment, I charge my arc cannons and aim them at the face of the guard whose armor I just blasted wide open. He dodges out of the way, narrowly avoiding death. However, the blasts sail past him, taking the third armored guard and myself by total surprise. They hit him right in his lower torso, causing him to buckle from the impact.

I take the opportunity to close the gap once again, engaging the arc blades and slashing the head clean off of the kneeling guard whose arm I shot off a moment before. The exosuit's weakness is at the back of the neck, so the suit loses power as his body collapses to the ground.

"That's for hurting Zeke, you motherfucker!" I yell, turning my attention to the next guard.

He backs up a few steps. He raises his arc cannon toward my head but doesn't charge the blast. With his helmet blown open, I can clearly see the fear in his eyes.

Fear? That's a new one.

"Doesn't feel so good to be on the other end of it, does it?" I growl to the guard.

After being afraid of them for so long and seeing so many people living in terror of their relentless fury, it feels incredibly satisfying to finally be returning the favor.

Just as I suspected, my taunting only serves to reignite the rage within the remaining two guards. The closest one charges me, completely disregarding the fact that he is outmatched. The other charges their arc cannons.

I sheathe my arc blades and run toward the guard that's charging me. I dodge to the side of his punch, grabbing his arm and twisting him to face his companion. The second guard has already charged his arc cannons and can't discharge them. Regardless, he makes no move to aim away, or to aim for the leg, or anything. He shoots his friend right in the face, all in the slight chance that he might hit me instead.

Just when you think they might be human after all...

The guard I'm using as a shield suddenly becomes much heavier. I push the motors of my exosuit further and lift him into the air, throwing his armored corpse toward the final guard.

"The second power cell is depleted, and at current energy usage rates, five minutes of power remain." Cerulean reports.

The final armored guard is forced to dodge. I close the gap in two strides, engaging the arc blades once again as I do so. I bring my arms high, then cross them down on either side of the guard's neck. To my surprise, he managed to block my attack, catching my blades in his hands.

The arc energy from the blades sends what should be cripplingly powerful lightning through his entire suit and body, but he screams in defiance and pushes me back several feet, rising to his full height. I didn't take much notice of it before, but this guy is much larger than the other two, or at least his suit is.

"Well?" He taunts. "Is that all you've got? You can't even keep your friends safe, pathetic."

He raises his arm toward where Zeke and Ash are. I notice Ash desperately trying to keep Zeke alive. It fills me with dread, and my stomach drops.

A frantic beeping on my helmet's radar alerts me that this fucker has released a missile, heading right toward my friends.

Alright, that's it.

"No, you fucking don't!" I scream, sprinting with everything the suit and I have to intercept the missile.

I reach out my hands as if to intercept the missile like a football pass. I overshoot it by a lot, the missile slamming directly into my right side and blowing the armor plating clean off. I'm knocked flat on my back, and my entire body feels broken for a moment. I think I may be bleeding.

I never was any good at football.

"No!" I shout to myself.

I force myself to stand, feeling the strain of my body as much as the strain of the motors of the exosuit.

"Final fusion cell discharged. Approximately sixty seconds of power remain. It is strongly advised—"

"Don't strongly advise me, Cerulean." I snap.

I turn my attention to the guard, engaging my arc blades and rolling my shoulders.

"Let's finish this, you bastard," I scream, filled with

adrenaline and anger.

"Gladly." He roars back.

I sink low, rushing toward him once more. I pretend to slash down toward his neck like I did before. He laughs as he preps to block my attack again, only this time I'm ready. As he moves his arms up to block, I bring one of my legs into a massive, armored kick right for his torso, sending him flying into the wall.

He tries to get up, but it takes him a second. I don't have time to waste. With the suit running low on power, I probably only have one, maybe two attacks left.

"Engage missiles. Use all remaining ammo," I command.

My shoulder-mounted cannons launch missile after missile, blowing the guard's suit into mangled bits that fly across the room. One of them hits my visor, sinking in until it's mere millimeters from my cheek.

After a few moments, the missiles stop.

"Missiles depleted. Entering low power mode."

I try to activate the arc blades, but low power mode just makes them blades.

Good enough.

I saunter toward the guard, who somehow is still trying to get up after everything. His suit is in tatters, the motors screaming for release. He manages to get up on one knee and starts charging his arc cannon. I slice his arm off with my blades, then grab his suit by the neck with my right arm and lift him into the air. He screams in pain, but his eyes are still filled more with hate and anger than anything else.

"This is for threatening my friends."

I open the visor, stare him in the eye, and then stab him through the gut with my left arm blade.

He falls to the ground.

"You will never...defeat us." He growls with his final

breath.

"We'll see about that," I reply, knowing he can't hear me.

Finally having a second to breathe, I stand up and look around the building. I see Ash still tending to Zeke, who seems to be holding on. I keep scanning until I find Dex. He's stepping out of the driver's seat of a truck he's using to block the front door and is hurriedly making his way over.

"Disengage combat mode. Open armor." I command.

The armor unfolds, allowing me to step out.

I run out of the armor and over to Ash and Zeke.

"Zeke! Are you okay? What happened. Talk to me." I say, frantically checking his body for wounds.

"He's lost a lot of blood. The stim helped some, but we need to do something." Ash replies. She's putting pressure on Zeke's left side. She looks at me with wide eyes.

"Yeah, need to remove…shrapnel. Close…the wound." Zeke slowly mutters between labored breaths.

"Okay, well, let's do this. You've patched me up countless times. It's about time I returned the favor." I say, trying to remain calm. It isn't working.

My heart is beating fast, and my palms are sweating.

I can't lose him. I can't lose my best friend. Come on, Oliver, let's do this.

I reach into Zeke's nearby discarded backpack and look for his first aid kit. I find some sort of medical tong things.

I think these might be called forceps?

I also find some gauze, rubbing alcohol, a can of liquid bandage, and scissors. Just seeing the liquid bandage makes me wince. I know how painful it is. But I also know how effective it is.

"Alright, here we go," I say, trying to psych myself up. "Zeke, hold on, buddy. I'm gonna remove this shrapnel."

"You…better. I don't feel like…dying today." He replies, joking even under these circumstances.

I grab the forceps and take a deep breath. Ash takes her hands off of the wound, revealing Zeke's blood-stained shirt. It's torn to shreds, and, upon closer inspection, so is his skin. The sight of it makes me want to throw up.

I know I've seen plenty of combat, and I've been through a lot of shit, but seeing my best friend losing so much blood from such a terrible wound has paralyzed me.

"Um…Ash. I think I need you to—" I start to say but get interrupted by the vomit that suddenly enters my mouth.

Oh god.

I weigh my options for a half second before deciding to swallow it back down. It's a mistake.

Oh…fuck. Never doing that again.

"Okay, Olly, I understand," Ash responds, looking at me in a knowing, concerned way. "But I need you to stay strong. I'm going to need your help with this."

I nod my head in acknowledgment, afraid of what might happen if I open my mouth right now.

I try to hand the forceps to Ash, but she shakes her head.

"No, the scissors first."

"Okay."

I hand her the scissors. She uses them to cut away the tattered pieces of Zeke's shirt that are covering the wound. After a moment, I close my eyes, trying to steel my stomach against the sight of Zeke's wound.

He isn't going to die. Not if you stay strong. Now open your eyes and help Ash.

I force my eyes open and take another deep breath. I feel a tiny bit better.

Having finished cutting away the shirt, Ash sets the now blood-covered scissors down.

"Forceps, Olly." She demands.

I hand them over with a nod.

"I need some more light. I can't see what I'm looking at." She says, starting to sound a little panicked.

"Um, okay. I know Zeke has lights in here. Hold on." I reply, trying not to show how panicked I am.

"Check the inside pocket." Dex gasps as he runs up to us.

"Got it."

I root around in Zeke's bag until I find the portable lamps that he uses for emergency medical situations, just like this one. I turn two of them on and point them at Zeke's torso at different angles. The increased visibility does not make it easier for me to remain calm, but I push the bile and anxiety back down once again.

"I won't be of any use here," Dex interjects, "so I'm gonna keep an eye on the situation outside. He jogs over to the nearest control panel and starts navigating the system with a practiced hand.

"Alright, here we go." Ash declares, her face filled with concentration and discomfort.

"You can do this. Just keep letting me know what you need." I reply, trying to feel a little less useless.

She gives me a nod and moves in closer with the forceps. With the bright lights shining on Zeke's wounds, the metallic pieces of shrapnel stand out against the blood and flesh. It's terrible.

Ash pulls out a relatively small piece of shrapnel, which causes Zeke to grunt in pain. He seems barely conscious.

"Zeke, stay with us, man. I refuse to let you pass out on me." I say, grabbing his hand and shaking his shoulder.

She pulls out another, more significant piece. Zeke does not respond.

"Zeke! Come on, man!" I shout, then shake him more vigorously. I'm not sure what to do. I give him a slap to the face.

"Hey man, that's not very nice." He mumbles.

Oh, thank goodness.

"Zeke, you gotta stay awake. Alright? Look at me." I command, squeezing his hand tightly.

"Okay, I'm...with you." He mutters, opening his eyes half-way.

I give Ash another nod, "let's finish this."

"Right."

She looks closer at part of Zeke's wound and readjusts one of the lamps. Then she reaches in with the forceps again, grabbing hold of another shard of metal. The forceps slip off as she tries to pull it out.

"Get him to relax," Ash says.

"Okay, Zeke, I need you to breathe with me. Can you do that?" I say, my voice slightly high-pitched with fake enthusiasm.

Zeke nods his head faintly, his eyes barely open.

"Alright, breathe in..."

I breathe in loudly, hoping he'll join me. He does, to an extent. I try not to think about how weak he seems.

"...and breathe out. Make sure to relax."

As Zeke breathes out, allowing his muscles to relax, Ash takes another try at pulling out the last piece of shrapnel. She gets it partially removed but slips off again.

"And breathe in..." I say again.

"...and out."

Ash breathes with us this time. I can't tell if it's subconscious or not. But this time, on the exhale, she gets the shrapnel the rest of the way out.

It becomes clear why it was so much harder to get this piece out. It's easily four or five inches long and an inch or two wide, jagged on all edges.

I really, really hope that didn't puncture anything important. Fuck.

"Okay, now we need to clean it and bandage him up," Ash tells me.

I grab the rubbing alcohol and dig around in Zeke's bag again, finding some sort of sterile cloth pads. I rip open the plastic covering and pour alcohol all over the pads, then hand one to Ash.

She takes it and looks at me, concerned. "Get him ready."

I grab Zeke's hand and squeeze it. "It's time to breathe again, alright Zeke?"

"Al...right." He replies, barely speaking.

"Now, breathe in..."

"...and back out."

We repeat this a few times as Ash cleans his wound. After a couple of breaths, she reaches back for the other alcohol-soaked pad. I hand it to her and resume guiding Zeke through breathing.

She tosses the bloody pads to the side and holds her hand out again.

Without saying anything, I hand her the liquid bandage.

"Zeke, this one is going to hurt. Give me a huge breath in." I say, trying to remain calm.

He breathes in as deeply as he can manage. His breaths are becoming increasingly forced as we go.

Ash shakes the can, holding Zeke's wound closed with her other hand.

"And breathe out slowly," I instruct.

Zeke starts to breathe out, but his calm breath turns to a scream as Ash sprays the liquid bandage across his lacerations.

"Keep breathing, it's almost over." I try to reassure him, completely unsure if it is, in fact, almost over.

To everyone's relief, Ash finishes within a few more seconds.

I release Zeke's hand and start unrolling the gauze. I hand it to Ash, but she shakes her head, looking around for something else.

"What is it?" I ask, worried.

"Just need another stim." She replies, grabbing my backpack and pulling out another emergency healing stim.

"Isn't that dangerous? We just used one of those on him a few minutes ago."

"Yeah, sure, but look at him!" She says, her voice becoming agitated as she gestures frantically toward Zeke's limp, barely conscious body.

"Fuck. You have a point."

We exchange an intense look for a moment, and then she grabs the stim firmly in her right hand, brings it down on Zeke's other side, and squeezes the trigger.

It's not a good idea to inject a stim like this directly into a wound, but you also want it near enough that it will find its mark.

As she squeezes, Zeke's breathing goes from labored wheezing to slightly less labored wheezing.

It's working.

I then hand the gauze to Ash. She attaches the end, which has a pre-applied adhesive, just to the side of his uppermost laceration.

"I need you to prop him up so I can wrap this around him." She instructs, ready to unspool the gauze.

I lift Zeke, my left hand supporting his head as my right arm puts in overtime, lifting his entire torso off the ground.

It's strange. You'd think using a cybernetic arm to lift enormous weights would be extremely easy, but the rest of your body still has to support it. It's also linked to my brain, so it *feels* like I'm lifting an entire human with my arm despite it being made of metal.

With Zeke's torso off the ground, Ash begins quickly and

carefully wrapping the gauze around him. She wraps it around once, from top to bottom, then once more, going back up. It almost uses the entire roll of gauze. Finally, she cuts it with the scissors and ties it off.

I slowly lower Zeke back down, my limbs shaking slightly from the effort.

Man, I'm already so tired. Gotta pull it together.

We grab some alcohol prep pads and wipe down our hands and Zeke's tools, trying to get the blood off. It doesn't work very well, but I don't see any restrooms in this warehouse. Go figure.

Having sealed off the doors as best as he can, Dex walks over to us.

"Hey, is he alright?" Dex asks, his face full of concern.

"Yeah, he'll be fine," Ash replies matter-of-factly.

"And how are you two doing?" Dex follows up.

Ash and I exchange a tired, knowing look.

"We're fine. We have no choice, anyway." I answer.

"Fair enough," Dex replies, nodding his head knowingly.

"So," Ash says, suddenly more energetic, "we better keep moving. There's no way they won't send more guards our way."

"Right you are," Dex agrees, "I reckon we've got approximately thirty to sixty seconds until round two."

"Oh, wonderful," I reply.

"So, here's what I'm thinking." Dex continues. "I take Zeke to our next point, the surveillance outpost, and I look out for him there while you two go ahead. I can watch you two on the security cameras and keep an eye out."

"Are you sure?" I ask.

Originally, the plan was for Dex and Zeke to man the surveillance outpost together, but clearly, things have changed. It feels wrong to leave him essentially alone.

"Yeah, as sure as I can be. What choice do we have,

anyway?" He replies.

"Well…yeah. You're right." I concede.

"Okay, then let's do this," Ash says, standing up and rolling her shoulder.

I'm lucky she stepped in. I was never going to be able to patch up Zeke without her.

"Thank you, Ash," I say, standing next to her and placing a hand on her back.

She suddenly pulls me in for a tight hug. I hug her back and place my cheek on top of her head. After a moment, I feel her begin to sob.

"Hey, it's okay. You're amazing, Ash." I say, stroking her back lightly and kissing the top of her head. "Plus, you did what I couldn't, and I really owe you."

I feel her nod slightly, her sobbing fading back into regular breathing.

"Let's go, thanks Ol'." She says, stepping back and wiping her eyes. She looks up and smiles at me, a genuine smile that catches me off guard.

"Anytime," I say, smiling back.

She's so beautiful. I need to take her somewhere nice when all this is over.

"Sorry to interrupt," Dex says, securing his backpack, "but it's time to book it."

CH 13

HAVING successfully gotten Dex and Zeke to the surveillance outpost, Ash and I head out, sneaking behind the next building. The outpost was right across the courtyard of death from the weapon warehouse we were holed up in before. It turns out that the courtyard becomes significantly easier to cross after every troop and guard in the entire sector is defeated. Who knew?

Originally, the plan was for Zeke to come with Ash and me, and we would leave Dex behind to man the surveillance outpost. It made sense before, with Dex knowing this place inside and out and us needing all the help we can get as we charge headlong into the almost certain death that is the headquarters building.

Not to mention, it was Zeke's idea to join us when we made the plan, despite my protests.

However, given the circumstances, it no longer makes sense for us to take Zeke with us. It still makes me nervous to leave both of them behind, regardless of how logical of a decision it may be. It's one thing to leave Dex to fend for himself. It's something else entirely to leave him with an injured Zeke to take care of as well. But what choice do we have? We can't stop. There's no going back now, and Zeke is barely conscious. There's no way he'll be able to keep up with Ash and me in his condition.

I'm also bitter about losing the exosuit so soon. It was so *cool*. But it was damaged beyond repair and entirely out of power. Clearly, the best thing to do was to use the self-destruct feature to blow up all the weapons left in the warehouse after we got out.

Let's see how strong you are without your weapons.

I snap back to the present as Ash reaches a hand back to stop me. We've reached the edge of this building, and it's time to cross to the next.

"Dex, what've you got?" I ask into my comms.

"Not much, nothing on the cameras in your area for about thirty seconds. The coast is clear." He replies.

"Got it."

I nod to Ash. We both move as quickly and quietly as we can along the wall. We reach the next building and duck behind it with no problem.

"Alright, remind us of the course one more time." Ash requests to Dex.

"You really should've let me write it down for you. What if they find us, or we lose connection?" Dex retorts.

"Yeah, sure, and if we get captured, it will lead them straight back to you. Not gonna happen." I interject.

"Alright, fair enough." Dex concedes. "Here it is, one more time: head along the wall for two more buildings, not counting the one you just crossed. Then, take a hard right toward the middle of the complex. You'll need to cross two streets, then turn left and head straight until you reach an enormous building covered in more security than an airport where the president's jet is landing."

"Thanks, Dex," Ash replies.

"And don't forget," Dex adds, "those streets will *not* be easy to cross. Not to mention the massive courtyard between the headquarters building and everything surrounding it. It's like a castle moat."

"We know, you've only said it a hundred times." I joke.

"And I'll say it a hundred more if it keeps my friends safe," Dex replies.

The sincerity of his statement catches me off guard. My eyes well up, and a small smile crosses my lips.

Damn, he really got me with that one.

"Well played," I say after blinking the tears away.

"Let's go, Olly," Ash says, grabbing my hand and leading me forward.

She only turns to face me for a moment, but I can see she's trying to hide her own emotions by pressing on.

Touché.

We move along the back of this building with ease, now incredibly accustomed to it. Ash peeks out around the corner.

"Clear. No, hold on!" Dex says urgently.

Ash quickly ducks back behind the building.

I instinctively grab the handle of my katana. Not that I could use it in this closed space, but it makes me feel prepared. In the distance, I can hear some sort of siren, which can't be a good thing.

"What is it?" I whisper.

"Two guard trucks, heading down the street to your right, and *fast.* Looks like someone found the warehouse, and they're mobilizing. Just...stay put for a minute." Dex replies with a hint of concern in his voice.

I flatten my back against the wall of the building next to Ash. I reach down and grab her hand tight. Well, it's relatively tight. It's my right arm, so I have to be careful not to crush any bones or anything.

We stare in silence at the outer wall in front of us, listening to the trucks' sirens getting closer and louder. Eventually, they get almost unbearably loud, then start to slowly fade out.

"I think you're clear, but make it quick," Dex says.

No one said anything for a tense couple of minutes, so his voice startled me a bit. I don't know if I'll ever truly get used to hearing people speaking through the comms as if they're directly inside my head. It's not like wearing earbuds or anything. It's almost like your own thoughts are rebelling against you.

Pull it together. You gotta move.

I mentally slap myself in the face, setting myself back to the present once again. Ash and I run for the next building, erring on the side of speed over stealth this time. We make it, which allows me precisely three seconds of relief before we're on the next corner.

"Well, here goes nothing. You ready?" Ash asks, turning to face me while gesturing to the right around the corner of the building.

Oh, right. Time to cross the street. The street that's filled with guards, trucks, and cameras. Awesome.

I nod like a liar. No amount of planning can truly prepare me for what's about to happen.

I take a deep breath, then step out around the corner. Ash follows close behind. We break out into a full sprint.

At this point, there's no hope of going unnoticed. All we can do now is be as fast as possible and hope the element of surprise is enough.

We sprint east, across the north side of the building, then begin to cross the street. No hesitation, no stopping.

A spotlight shines on us almost immediately.

"Fuck!" I exclaim, continuing to sprint.

"No kidding!" Ash agrees, mere inches behind me.

Just. Keep. Fucking. Running.

We make it across the street, narrowly ducking between the adjacent buildings as a missile screams through the air, striking the building to our right, mere feet away from Ash.

I turn my VYSR to combat mode by tapping the right hinge of my sunglasses twice. IR and thermal imaging augment my vision, and a radar appears in the top right of the right lens.

Really should've done that earlier.

"Left!" I shout, ducking from the alleyway to the extremely narrow space between the building we just passed and the ones to the east.

We have to cross the street one more time, but we might as well gain some ground before we do.

"This wasn't the plan!" Ash says, following close behind.

"I know, but the plan also didn't involve missiles! We gotta keep them guessing!"

"Fair enough, pick up the pace!"

I put everything I have, all of my energy and concentration, into running as fast as I possibly can. We break through to another alley in seconds, then it's between two more buildings.

We repeat this process three more times, and then I gesture to the right.

"Got it!" Ash confirms.

We round the corner to the east, sprinting in the alleyway between the next two buildings. We come to the second and final street that we need to cross, and we waste no time crossing it.

My VYSR beeps, and several red dots appear on the radar all at once. From the looks of it, we should be surrounded, but I don't see anyone.

Oh shit!

It dawns on me a moment too late as several spotlights suddenly shine down on us. If not for the VYSR, I would have been blinded temporarily.

Ash, she can't see!

I stop and turn around, only to find Ash barreling straight toward me. Blinded or not, she's not stopping for anything. I don't have time to build up speed again before she collides with me, so I side-step her and let her pass.

"I'm right behind you, Ash!" I shout, letting her know we've swapped positions.

As I start running behind Ash, the sound of several CYBR Corp UAVs arming themselves fills the air with a gut-dropping whining sound that I know all too well.

I grab one of the EMP grenades attached to the side of my backpack, arm it, and toss it behind me, high into the air. I don't stick around to find out if it works. I keep sprinting behind Ash, ducking into the next alleyway.

"Left! Now!" I shout as Ash approaches the space between the groups of buildings.

"Thanks! I can sort of see again." Ash shouts back as she rounds the corner.

I follow her into the small space behind the two buildings as a series of explosions devastates the building to our left, followed by a cacophony of crashing as all of the UAVs hit the pavement. From the sound of it, some explode, while others simply crumple into the street. Looks like my EMP grenade worked.

Hell yeah. Eat EMP!

"Dex, can you hear me?" I ask.

"Yeah, I copy. Nice work with those drones." He replies.

"Thanks. Now, how close are we?"

"Just three more buildings, and then you'll be at the courtyard. And…just be ready."

"Don't worry, Dex," Ash interjects. "We're ready for whatever they've got for us."

"Damn right, baby!" I yell, feeling my stomach flip.

That's crazy. Somehow, despite it all, I'm excited.

We keep running as fast as we can, barreling along the narrow corridor between the rows of buildings. We finally reach the final building before the courtyard. I hold up my hand to signal Ash as we both come to a stop just before leaving the relative safety of the shadows between the last two buildings.

Okay, truth be told, I'd really like to still have that exosuit right about now.

As I take a moment to scan the courtyard, my eyes and VYSR together detect countless guards, troops, UAVs, trucks, mounted turrets, you name it.

"Looks like we really pissed them off," Ash whispers into my ear.

"Yeah, no kidding," I whisper back.

"Dex, got anything for us?" Ash asks quietly into the comms.

"Uhm, one sec." He says, clearly frantically searching the computers for something, anything.

Ash and I exchange a look for a moment. I search her face to try and figure out how she's feeling. She's been very enthusiastic and supportive this entire time, but I have to imagine she's a mess of emotions inside, just like I am.

"We got this," I say, holding her arm gently. "No matter what happens, we've got each other."

"Promise me." She says.

"Promise what, Ash?"

"That I'll never lose you." Her face is dead serious, her eyes full of intensity.

Oh.

I take off my glasses, tucking them into my shirt so I can look directly into her eyes. I take both of her hands in mine and squeeze them tight.

"I promise, Ash, that I will *never* leave you. In fact, I want you to know I made up my mind on all of this a long time ago. I meant it back at the Museum, and I mean it now. With every fiber of my being, I mean it. You're the greatest thing that *has* ever happened to me, and I know that you're the greatest thing that *will* ever happen to me. I love you, Astra, more than anything." I say, smiling.

Melancholy tears fill my eyes, tears of sadness for the past and happiness for the future.

She smiles back at me, but there's still a sadness behind it. "I love you, too, Oliver. And I know you'll never leave me again. I believed you back then, and I believe you now. But...that's not what I meant, exactly."

I furrow my brow, not sure what she means.

"What I mean to say is," she continues, holding my hands tighter and moving closer to me, "I need to know before we go any further if you truly will never let yourself go over the edge. I know how much this means to you. I know you'd do anything to take down CYBR Corp. and to protect me and the others, but I will *not* watch you fall into the darkness to bring us into the light. Do you understand?"

"I..." I'm taken aback by her question, by the intensity with which she asked it. "I don't know if I understand."

"I'm sorry, Olly. It's not like I don't trust you or I doubt your intentions. I want you to know that I do trust you, and I love you, and that's why I need to make absolutely sure of this. I'm talking about no life-altering cybernetics, but I'm also just saying...I don't know what I'm saying. I just...you're such a good, pure-hearted person. Despite all the pain, the suffering, and the loss that you've endured, you're still the most amazingly compassionate person I know. I need you to always be that person. And not just for my sake, but for yours." Tears are streaming freely down her cheeks now.

Now I understand. And there go the waterworks.

"I promise. I—" My voice leaves me for a moment, tears pouring down my face. "I swear that you will never lose me. I know exactly what you mean now, and I want to thank you for putting into words a feeling I've had for quite some time. It's the same way I feel about you, Zeke, and Dex. The last thing I want for any of you, for anyone in this city, is for you to lose sight of who you are. Whether it's because of this damned city, or CYBR Corp, or just the loss and pain that can eat away at you like a parasite in your brain. It happened to me for a time, and I know how bad it feels. I lost myself until you found me again, and I *never* want to feel that way again. So, yes, I promise you won't lose me."

"Thank you."

Ash pulls me into a tight hug, and I hug her back. We stand there sobbing and holding each other for a while.

I pull away slightly so I can see her face. I wipe her tears away, running my fingers down her cheek.

"Ash, I need you to make me the same promise," I say, gently caressing her face with my left hand.

"Of course, Olly. I promise you'll never lose me, either." She wipes the tears from my face, too.

I smile an uncomplicated, ear-to-ear smile and pull her into a kiss. She kisses me back, and we hold each other tight once more. After the longest time, we pull apart. That now-familiar feeling of pure, unadulterated bliss fills every fiber of my being. The type of happiness that sends my stomach into an interpretive dance.

I'll never get tired of that feeling. Not for as long as I live.

She gives me the same smile I gave her as we pull away, which only makes her more beautiful and my stomach more tumultuous.

"You're so beautiful, Ash."

"So are you."

Oh, goodbye, composure.

My cheeks are undoubtedly blushing now, but I'm much too happy to care.

We stare at each other for a moment longer, not quite letting go, not quite holding on. We both know we have to stop to get back to the daunting task at hand, but we don't want to. And can you blame us?

After some time, we both nod and pull away.

I throw on my VYSR shades again.

"Now, let's take down the largest megacorporation the world has ever seen, shall we?" I say, holding out my fist for a fist bump.

"Damn right." She says, bumping it enthusiastically.

Naturally, we blow it up.

"So, Dex," I say into the comms, still smiling, "what's the sitch?"

"Well," he replies hesitantly, "the sitch is that you've got an army to fight through as two people."

That makes my smile decidedly smaller.

"However," he continues, "the sitch is also that I've figured out the best path through. Unless you plan to take them all out before continuing forward, in which case you could just stroll right up to the front door!" He remarks sarcastically.

"Ha, ha. Very funny. No, give us the path, please." I reply with as much sarcasm as I can muster.

"I'm sending it to your Holos. Oliver, you can send it to your VYSR, as well."

"Thank you, Dex. Joking aside, we really couldn't do this without you." I say.

"Seriously, you're incredible." Ash chimes in.

"Thank you both, and you can pay me back by giving them hell." He replies, his voice incredibly resolute.

"You can count on it," I reply, "and this would be the perfect time for your broadcast, don't you think?"

"Right, that's a good point." He responds somewhat hesitantly. "I wasn't sure when to play it, to tell you the truth. I've lived my whole life quietly, in the background."

"I agree with Olly," Ash interjects, "I think now is perfect since it might actually help distract these guards at least somewhat, allowing us to slip through a little bit easier. And, whether you like it or not, you're not in the background anymore, Dex. There's no time like the present to stand up and stand out. To make yourself known and make a difference. Without the broadcast, this will just be swept under the rug as some terrorist activity, if it's on the news at all. However, with the broadcast, people will know what we're doing this for, and they'll see just how much damage even a small group of dedicated rebels can do. We *need* you, Dex. We need your leadership and your voice."

"You make an excellent point. Thank you, Astra. I'll play it as soon as you're ready!" Dex replies. His voice is resolute and confident.

"Right!" I reply.

Ash and I both look at our wrists as the path Dex devised shows up on our Holocomms. I tap the share button, and it appears on my VYSR glasses. An orange line streams out from in front of me, twisting and winding all the way across the massive CYBR Corp courtyard. The courtyard standing between us and the thing we've been working toward this entire time.

Let's fucking do this.

I look at Ash, and she gives me a determined nod. I nod back.

"Dex," I say, "in case this is the last time we talk to you before this is all over, I mean, you keep yourself and Zeke safe. Above all, you got that?"

"You got it, boss. Now kick their asses!"

I take a deep breath and map the path out in my mind, taking one last note of the position of everything in our way. I grab the arc rifle I nabbed from the warehouse, check that the safety is off, and prepare to run 'n' gun.

Ash grabs her rifle, too, and gives me another nod.

"Now!" I shout to both Dex and Ash.

Without another word, Ash and I take off at a full sprint, following the path laid out before us. As we run, Dex's recorded speech blares over every speaker in the complex, a speech that everyone in the world is hearing right now. I catch a glimpse of a large monitor on the side of a building, and I see Dex's face as he begins to speak.

"My name is Dexter Jones. You don't know me, but I have something to say, something you need to hear..."

We make it only a few paces before the spotlights of several more UAVs come in, followed quickly by shouts.

"Over there!" One guy screams.

"Open fire!" Another orders.

And they do.

Without hesitation, I continue sprinting along the orange path. I toss an EMP grenade into the cluster of UAVs overhead, taking about half of them down. The ones that explode take out some of the troops and cause some more to stop firing for a brief moment. The cacophony of gunfire, explosions, and shouting dies out just as quickly as it appeared. In the silence, the troops seem to notice Dex's speech, further throwing them off.

"...I worked for CYBR Corp for fifteen long, terrible years. I committed countless atrocities for them, killed so many innocent people, and tortured so many more. And I was merely an office worker, a lab rat. I did what I was told, and I tried not to think about it. But my sins don't come anywhere close to those of their so-called 'retribution' soldiers..."

I notice the image on another nearby monitor. It's changed now to CYBR Corp footage we stole from the outlet. Footage of Retribution troops beating defenseless citizens to an inch of their lives, footage of scientists committing horrible atrocities on their test subjects. For a moment, I lose myself to the rage that fills me as I watch the screen.

"On the left!" Ash yells.

Ash's voice brings me back to the present. Out of the corner of my eye, I see a massive group of Retribution troops with turrets. Ash arms an arc grenade and lobs it behind the cover they're shooting from. I look forward again, hooking a hard right as the path indicates. Behind us, I can hear the screams of people being shocked by arc lightning. The turrets stop firing, groaning to a stop as their circuitry is overloaded.

"...I never wanted to work for them or to do any of the unspeakable things I had to do, but they threatened my family, and I did the only thing I could to save them. The same thing countless unfortunate souls have been forced to do. But I've had enough, and it's time someone came clean about the truth, the horrible, painful truth that we've all turned a blind eye to for far too long because it's easier to ignore it than to accept that it's true..."

As we round the corner of a massive truck that was blocking the way, the path makes a hard left back toward the front of the HQ building. We come out from behind the truck. Countless troops start firing, bullets and arc plasma streaming toward us from all angles. The UAVs that didn't get taken out by my EMP have recovered and are firing missiles at us. The rockets hit the side of the truck, mere feet from my head. The explosion knocks me to the side, deafening me and making my head throb.

"Oliver! Keep running!" Ash says, grabbing my hand and dragging me forward.

I shake it off and keep running, my hearing coming back slowly. A ringing sound fills my head, muffling everything.

The path leads us straight ahead for a few paces, then right behind some crates piled up. On the other side, troops lie in wait, seemingly trying to ambush us. My VYSR can detect their thermal signals through the crates.

I grab Ash and hold a finger to my lips. I then grab an

arc grenade, arm it, and toss it over, ducking down behind the cover of the crates and covering my ears. Ash follows my lead just in time.

The troops fall to the ground, writhing in agony. Their gear explodes as it malfunctions, sending shrapnel in every direction.

"...we all live in constant, all-encompassing fear of CYBR Corp. Either you know this, or you're lying to yourself. Even those that work for them, no, especially those that work for them, are in constant fear of what they can do. They rule this world with an iron fist, manipulating every corporation, government, and person around the world..."

The UAVs come into range of my radar from behind, ready with more missiles.

I turn to face them, charge my arc rifle, and shoot one of them down. As I do so, the remaining five press forward.

Ash shoots down two in one volley with her arc rifle. I take out one more.

The remaining two UAVs move in closer. My VYSR warns me that they're arming missiles.

Ash and I both charge another shot on our rifles and let them fly. Time seems to slow down as I watch the molten plasma of our rifles fly through the air toward the drones, their missiles launching directly at us. Since the missiles are heat-seeking, they change course midair toward the arc plasma.

Oh, shit, time to move.

I grab Ash's arm, jump over the crates, and continue to sprint along the path, not daring to look back.

As soon as our feet hit the pavement on the other side of the crates, three things happen all at once. First, the UAV missiles collide with our arc plasma, causing a massive explosion that I don't need to see to know it takes out the remaining drones. I can feel the heat on the back of my neck. Second, the rest of the Retribution troops on the north side of these crates all see us and immediately open fire. Third, my VYSR detects an imposing, shadow-cloaked figure standing several paces behind the final row of troops.

Shinigami.

My mind is racing, but my legs don't stop running, not for anything. Bullets and arc plasma hit the ground inches away from my feet, but I don't hesitate. I continue along the path, which curves left behind another truck.

"…but it doesn't have to be this way. CYBR Corp gets their power from your fear and your silence. So, deny them that power. I, like you surely feel right now, lived most of my life believing that there was nothing I, or any one person, could do to stop CYBR Corp. Nothing I could do to defeat these demons and send them back into hell. But I've recently met some people who convinced me otherwise, and I need you all, every person in Nova City and in the entire world, to hear me now…"

The truck has a roof-mounted turret, which is shooting at us, but it's high enough off the ground that it can't hit us from this close.

I pause for just a moment as I look at the path that undoubtedly continues *through* this truck.

Oh. Nice one, Dex!

I turn to Ash, hundreds of bullets wreaking havoc on the far side of the truck. Clearly, they don't care about killing their own people so long as they kill us, too.

"Ash!" I shout over the sounds of the gunfire and the ringing in my ear. "We need to take over this truck. That's what the path means! You with me?"

She glances down at her Holocomm to make sure I'm not crazy, then gives me a mischievous smile. "Let's hijack this fucker."

I sling my rifle over my back and unsheathe my swords,

turning on the arc units. The blue electricity crackles to life along the blades, filling my body with even more adrenaline than was already pumping through it. Which is a lot.

"…chances are, CYBR Corp will try to shut down any news coverage of what's about to happen, but I assure you, it's real. A very small and incredibly determined group of people is, at this very moment, infiltrating the headquarters of CYBR Corp. If you're in Nova City, get to the roof and look at the center of town. You will undoubtedly see some sort of explosion if I know anything about my friends…"

I nod to Ash, and she moves to the sliding door on the rear driver's side of the truck, pulling the handle and throwing it open. I waste no time jumping in, and the VYSR shows me exactly who's in there despite the relative darkness of the interior of the truck.

The back of the truck is some sort of mobile data center, with a netrunner plugged into the computer and two guards, one on either side of them, to keep them safe while they focus on the task at hand.

The guards are ready for me, and it seems that the runner told them we were coming, which isn't too surprising. The guard on the right charges his arc rifle while the other cracks his neck and holds up his enormous, arc-covered cybernetic fists. I cross the gap to the closest guard, the one on my right, and slash through his torso in one clean motion.

"…what you're looking at is the result of exactly four people. That's right, four. And if I'm being honest, what you're really seeing is thanks to two people, Oliver Wolf and Astra Odelle. They're tearing their way, tooth and nail, through every single guard, robot, and obstacle that CYBR Corp can throw at them. If you look at your screen, you will see surveillance camera footage of what's happening. I'm inside their facilities, broadcasting this over every channel…"

The second guard steps toward me, blocking my path to the netrunner. The arc light from my swords and his fists fills the truck with flashes of blue light. He pulls back his right arm, then sends his chrome haymaker directly to my left temple. I bring up both of my swords, barely blocking his blow. It sends me back into the wall of the truck, knocking the wind out of me.

Just as he starts winding up his left arm for another blow, Ash jumps into the van, charging her rifle.

"Hey! Hands off, big boy!" She yells, shooting her arc rifle at the behemoth.

He blocks her shot with his arms and laughs as if it's amusing that she tried to kill him.

Clearly, this guy is closer to a Chrome Drone than a human at this point.

While he's laughing at Ash, I take the opportunity to attack. I bring both of my swords together and drive them directly into his chest, stabbing him with all of my strength.

My blades sink several inches into his chest, sending electric shocks throughout his entire body.

He laughs again.

A chill runs down my spine.

He brings both of his fists high, ready to crush me into a fine paste. I wrench my daishō from his chest, then tumble to the side, narrowly avoiding his attack. He strikes the floor of the truck, crumpling the floor paneling and causing the whole truck to shake.

"…this is what I need you all to understand. You may feel powerless. You may even feel like you need CYBR Corp and that you rely on them for anything and everything. But that. Is. Not. True. They want you to feel that way because if everyone in this city and around the world stood up at once and said no, told them they could go to hell, then, well, they wouldn't know what to do. They seem all-encompassing and

all-powerful. They appear to be unstoppable. But none of that is true. Right this very moment, four people are proof that it's not true, and they can be stopped…"

I scramble to my feet and fall back toward Ash. As I do, I take a second to look a little closer at this guy. My attack definitely did damage. He's bleeding a lot, and his hair is smoking from the electricity.

So what the hell? What is going on with—

"He's being controlled by the runner!" I whisper frantically.

"What?" Ash replies, her eyes searching the lumbering monstrosity in front of us.

"The eyes," I say.

"Oh, fuck." She replies.

I didn't notice it until now, but his eyes are glowing red, like cameras with the 'recording' light on. I've seen it only once before, but I never forgot that day. If someone has enough cybernetics and a compatible receiver in their brain, their entire body can be controlled by someone, particularly a skilled netrunner. It's like playing a video game, but instead of pixels and code, it's a living, breathing person. And if your character dies, they don't just respawn with a little jaunty sound effect. Because they're *fucking dead.*

This makes me sick.

I grit my teeth, sink into a low stance, and hold my swords in a defensive position in front of me.

"Hey, you! The chicken-headed runner that's controlling this chrome-plated meat puppet, why don't you fight me yourself? Or are you scared?" I taunt.

The guy roars in anger, the anger of who's controlling him. He steps in between us and the runner's chair and bangs his arc-covered fists together, sending a shower of sparks flying throughout the truck. A few of them sit and smolder on my jacket for a moment before going out.

He charges right at me, full-tilt, raising his fists high for another skull-crushing blow.

Perfect.

I wait until the last possible moment, then yell, "now!"

Ash and I tumble out of the way of his oncoming assault, sending him crashing into the wall between this part of the van and the driver's compartment.

"…so, I'm asking you, no, telling you, to stand up. To say no. To take back your power from those who have stolen it from you. My friends and I may not make it out of here alive, but as long as we can inspire you to take a stand against the oppression we know all too well, then I will be able to die happy…"

As he turns to recover, Ash and I waste no time retaliating. She fires an arc volley from her rifle directly at his head, which hits dead on, melting the outer layer of chrome plating. I follow it with a two-handed overhead strike, bringing both swords down on the exposed internal circuitry that used to be his brain. My swords sink a few inches into his skull, the arc energy frying everything inside.

His body convulses uncontrollably, the red lights flickering from his eyes. In the last moments, as he hits the ground, he begins to scream in pain. Not laugh, scream. He screams because he's suddenly in control of his own body again, and he's been stabbed in the chest and head and had his insides boiled by arc energy.

I can't watch this.

I turn away, seething with anger at the thought that someone would use another person like this. I don't know if he signed up for it or what the situation is, but it doesn't matter. No one deserves that.

He finally stops screaming, and I look up at the runner,

who's still lying in their chair, their head plugged into a massive computer with a spider web of wires.

I walk over to them, grab the bundle of wires, and prepare to pull them out.

"I'm sorry," I say.

What am I doing? This could be Dex in here. I can't…but they were controlling this guy, using another human as a weapon, a puppet. Clearly, Dex wouldn't do something like this. But still…

I step back, letting go of the bundle of wires, suddenly second-guessing everything I've done. Ash's words from earlier ring in my head, asking me not to lose myself in this fight.

But I just killed or incapacitated who knows how many guards that were shooting at me or trying to kill my friends. If anything, this fucking runner is worse than any of them. Using the lives of others to fight me.

I grit my teeth, pray to every god I don't believe in, and force myself to finish it.

The runner doesn't wake up, or scream, or anything. Their body simply goes limp, smoke rising from the base of their skull.

You can't unplug someone from that deep of a connection without the proper procedures. Despite it all and the fact that they just tried to kill me using the now-deceased meat puppet behind me, I feel terrible about it. Something about its quiet nature makes it feel more real and more personal than fighting brutes or throwing an arc grenade.

I turn to look at Ash, trying to keep my composure.

She gives me a knowing nod and walks over to me, placing a hand on my shoulder.

"It's okay, Oliver. It had to be done." She says, reassuring me.

I turn and nod, placing my hand on hers and looking into her eyes for a moment.

"Well, no doubt this truck will be surrounded in seconds. Let's do this thing," I say, sliding the side door closed and heading for the driver's compartment.

"...and who knows, maybe we will pull it off. Maybe as I speak, Oliver and Astra are bringing justice to CYBR Corp and cutting the head off of the beast. But there will still be its thrashing limbs to deal with. We need you. We need all of you. Every. Single. Person. You are not small. You are not insignificant. You are not a slave to the whims of the corrupt. You are a drop in the ocean of humanity, an ocean that has been trapped behind a dam for decades. Pent-up, furious, and full of potential. It's time to break down that dam and flood the streets with your rage..."

"I gun, you drive?" Ash asks, motioning toward the netrunner chair.

"You know how to use that thing?" I ask, genuinely unsure of the answer.

I know she used to dabble in netrunning, not to mention she's been through a lot while we were split up, but that's some seriously advanced netrunning equipment.

"Well, let's just say some of our protests needed a...technological touch." She says, hesitantly pushing the netrunner's body from the chair.

"Damn, alright then. You never cease to amaze me, Astra Odelle." I say, feeling impressed and also incredibly grateful that she's here with me for many reasons.

"Right back at ya, now plug me in." She says, motioning to the wires as she climbs into the chair.

I walk over to her, making sure to lock the truck's doors as I do so. I take the bundle of wires, checking each one's connection to the ports on the back of Astra's neck.

"One sec." She says, checking the screen on the arm of

the chair and setting it up for pairing. "Alright, go."

I plug the wires in, one by one. I know the order they go in, but I've never actually tried netrunning, let alone plugging in someone else. Only a small number of people are cut out for it, seeing as it requires being mentally and physically capable of withstanding full synchronization with a computer. No biggie.

She closes her eyes, hits a button on the arm's screen, and becomes incredibly still.

My heart stops for a moment. I hold her hand, waiting.

"Olly, can you hear me?" She says through our comms, her voice ringing in my head, her mouth perfectly still.

"Uh, yeah. Shit, that startled me." I admit.

"Sorry, it's weird for me, too. I've never done anything this advanced."

"I thought you said you had it!" I say, beginning to worry.

"I do, I promise. Now get driving!" She commands.

I kiss her on the forehead, then head toward the driver's compartment.

I swing open the door, expecting more guards. To my surprise, there aren't any. I guess I should've known that, given the infrared and radar of the VYSR, but my mind was elsewhere, obviously.

Regardless, I step in, close the door behind me, and sit in the driver's seat.

"Alright, now how the hell do I drive this thing," I mutter to myself.

I check the various displays, buttons, pedals, and whatnots strewn about the truck's driver's compartment. Even the steering wheel is weird. It's not even a wheel. It's one of those odd two-handed racing things. After a few bewildered moments, I press a button marked 'Start,' and the truck's engine rumbles to life.

"...*my name is Dexter Jones, and I hate CYBR Corp. I*

know you do, too. And I challenge you, in the name of Zeke Sartori, Astra Odelle, and Oliver Wolf, to show them just how much you hate them. In the name of all those who they've taken from you and all those who they have yet to take. There are so many more of us than there are of them. It's time you reminded the rich and greedy who really hold the power in this world. I believe in you. I believe in us. DOWN. WITH. CYBR CORP!"

And with that, Dex's broadcast ends. I hadn't heard it yet. He recorded it when I was unconscious and recovering from surgery in the tunnels. I feel inspired. I feel the fire in my soul being stoked to a roaring inferno. I feel honored that he believes in me so unwaveringly. And I feel determined, more than ever before, to see this through to the end.

"Ash, you ready?" I ask into the comms.

"Hell yeah!" She replies.

"Let's do this!"

I grab hold of the steering…thing, press a button labeled 'Brake,' and shift into drive. The truck lurches forward slowly, with a horrible screeching sound. Apparently, I turned the emergency brake *on*, not off.

Oops.

In my defense, who parks a truck this big without the e-brake? Pretty irresponsible if you ask me.

I hit the brake button again and hit the gas. The truck speeds forward. We're moving directly toward a barricade with several guards behind it. They're shooting everything they've got at us, but this truck is insanely bulletproof.

I crank the wheel to the right, following the path Dex prepared. As I do, one of the troops launches a rocket at me. It hits the driver's door, denting it slightly. My heart skips a beat.

Okay, not immune to rockets, noted.

I floor it. The truck roars forward, changing gears every few seconds. We start picking up alarming amounts of speed. The orange path continues straight through the next group of guards in front of us. I consider hitting the brakes, but I'm pretty sure that would seriously injure us at this speed. I barrel through them. Some of them jump out of the way, and others stare me down with hatred in their eyes, shooting directly at my head until they splatter on the bumper.

The concentration of their fire is apparently starting to get through. The windshield directly in front of my face has a small crack forming.

I glance at the screens on my right. One of them shows me Ash's vitals and the other shows the status of the mounted turret. From the looks of it, she's doing well, and the turret is a little damaged but still functional.

"Alright, Ash," I say, "almost there. Keep firing."

"Wasn't planning on stopping."

Fair.

We're barreling at seventy miles per hour directly toward the front entrance of CYBR Corp's HQ building. There's only one more line of guards between us and our goal. They're densely packed behind massive crates and trucks.

The path on my VYSR turns sharply to the left in a few feet. I slam on the brakes, crank the wheel to the left, and expect the worst.

The truck, to my surprise, takes the corner surprisingly well. That is until it tips onto the two right sets of wheels.

Oh god, this is it.

I keep driving, leaning my body weight to the left like it'll make a difference. I also crank the wheel to the right, remembering something about steering into the skid from a racing movie. I have no idea if it applies here or if it's even accurate for racing, but what the hell.

Ash continues to shoot everything she can with the truck's turret as we sail past.

Multiple rockets hit the right side of the truck, cracking the armor in several places and causing my ears to ring. But, as it so happens, being struck by the kinetic force of several military-grade rockets is enough to rebalance a truck that's tipping over.

Thanks, Newton.

We tip back to the left, slamming violently into the ground. I've been steering hard to the right this whole time, so with all the wheels back, we veer sharply from the planned path, slamming into another truck that the guards were using as cover.

"Holy shit. Alright then."

I pop 'er in reverse and hit the gas, then throw it in drive and speed along the path once again.

All we need to do is sail around this barricade, curve around to the right, and we'll be at the door—

Suddenly, something pops the front right tires. The wheels slam into the ground, and we lose speed rapidly.

"Ash, get out, now! Something's wrong." I yell.

No response.

"Come on, Ash. What's going on?"

Nothing.

Oh fuck oh fuck oh shit.

I slam on the brakes, put the truck in park, and run into the back as fast as I can.

Ash's body has fallen out of the netrunner chair, and as I get closer, I can see that a couple of the wires were yanked loose as she fell.

"Ash!"

I run over to her, pick her up carefully, and place her back into the chair. The whole truck is at an angle now, but I managed to get her to stay in place. I don't know what to do, so I take the wires that are unplugged and plug them back in. I'm not sure if it'll help, but I figure that it must be better than leaving them unplugged.

Gunfire and missiles continue to blast the truck from its right-hand side, my left.

I ignore it and focus on Ash. I check the screen on her chair, and the various displays and buttons overwhelm me. Her vitals are good, but she's unconscious. There's a button labeled 'Wake,' and I press it.

The screen reads, 'Waking in process. Do not unplug the netrunner.'

I wait, holding Ash's hand to my chest and tapping my foot anxiously.

"Come on, I need you. I—" I can't speak. My throat feels like it's closing. Tears are forming in my eyes.

I'm shaken violently from my thought spiral by the truck's right-side door being ripped clean from its hinges.

I turn to face the door, drawing my daishō and turning on the arc units. I plant my feet, ready to defend Ash from whatever enters that door. Based on the ripping the door off business, I expect another Retribution trooper in an exosuit.

What enters the door is so much worse.

My VYSR glasses alert me to their presence before my eyes have a chance to process it. I block to my left just in time to stop the Shinigami's blades from ending my life.

"*So, Oliver Wolf, we meet again.*" They growl.

I glance to the left to see the unmistakable visage of the very Shinigami I fought in that alley not so long ago on my way back from a particularly *eventful* grocery run.

"Oh, I thought I recognized your ugly face. How's that armor plating?" I reply through clenched teeth.

Instead of answering, they jump back, perching on the doorframe to the driver's compartment like a chromed-out gargoyle. Their imposing frame fills the entirety of the large van's upper compartment.

I take the opportunity to engage the small arc turret installed in my shoulder. It immediately starts shooting at the Shinigami, firing bursts of three bolts.

The Shinigami dodges the attack with ease, but that's fine. It's more of a distraction, anyway.

Using the infrared mode of the VYSR, I run in and swing my katana to meet them as they land on the ground. They barely block it with their left leg. I swing the wakizashi next, aiming for the neck. They block with their right arm, then return the blow with both hands.

Their razor-sharp fingertips become coated in electricity as they make their way for my chest. I hit the floor and bring my swords up to block. I sweep their legs and roll to my feet. They hit the floor nimbly, back on their feet in a half second. I don't even have time for a follow-up attack.

Come on, you freak. I won't let you get away this time. And if you intend to hurt Ash, you've got another thing coming.

We square up for a moment, my arc turret continuing to annoy the Shinigami with relentless fire. It clearly pisses them off because they let out a bellow and charge toward me recklessly. I narrowly sidestep their attack, tripping them and bringing both swords down toward their back. They find their mark, but their armor plating is too thick. It does, however, send a shockwave through their body, paralyzing them for just a moment.

I switch my grip on my swords, take them both in my hands, and bring the tips directly down toward the back of the Shinigami's neck.

"Nice try, mortal." They taunt.

They roll out of the way with ease, clearly not as paralyzed as I thought.

Fuck.

They knock the swords out of my hands, sending them flying back toward the front of the truck.

With a horrible, mechanized laugh, the Shinigami charges me once more, arc energy crackling from their fingers. They leap over me, stabbing toward my back. I'm unable to get out of the way in time, but I manage to block with my right arm.

A shockwave courses through my entire body, making my skin itch and burn. But it doesn't hurt as much as it should. As much as the Shinigami thinks it will.

I smirk, realizing that the grounding circuit is working perfectly. Searching for somewhere to go, the arc energy gathers back into my right arm, a lightning storm forming in the palm of my hand.

I chuckle, look up at the Shinigami's surprised face, and put everything I have into an arc-infused right hook straight for their jaw. My fist finds its mark, sending the Shinigami back a couple of feet and scorching the left half of their face.

They roar in pain and anger, something I haven't seen before, something I wasn't sure was possible.

I look down and see my katana lying there by my feet. I pick it up and close the gap, slashing from the right, then left, over and over again, stabbing and slashing from every angle. The Shinigami blocks every attack, but I'm keeping them from retaliating, which is a feat on its own. Or, rather, it almost seems like they aren't *trying* to retaliate, just stopping my assault effortlessly. I can't help but feel like they're holding back. The last time we fought back in that alley, they outclassed me entirely. Sure, I've gotten some upgrades, but something tells me they aren't giving it their all. I flashback to that inexplicable moment when they froze during our last fight...

Could they be…testing me? But why? Clearly, the troops out there are trying to kill us, right?

I decide not to let the doubt get the better of me. After all, I have to protect Ash from any harm, regardless of whatever the fuck is going on here. I keep slashing with everything I've got. Finally, one of my strikes finds its mark, my sword coming down directly on their neck. It sinks a couple of inches into the space between the armor plating on their shoulder and that of their neck, electrocuting them.

I realize too late why my strike lands, as a searing pain radiates from my left shoulder. I look down to see their taloned, arc-charged fingers piercing my shoulder. The grounding circuit does its job as best it can, but my left arm goes limp, and I feel faint.

No, fight it. Don't let it end like this.

I breathe deep, pull my sword from the Shinigami's neck, and bring it down again, right on the same spot. This time, it sinks much farther in. Blood rushes out of the wound, and the Shinigami drops to the floor.

"You will succumb, Oliver Wolf. I am but one of many. You will not prevail, you demon." They grunt, the life draining from their body until they finally die. The last thing to go is the burning hate in their eyes as the red light fades from their cybernetic pupils.

"Ironic, you calling me a demon," I say, collapsing to my knees next to their lifeless body.

So they can die…

I grab a stim from my pocket and jam it into my shoulder. I regain some function in my left arm, but it hurts like a motherfucker. I think it'll be fine between the stim and my nanobot healing system, but who knows.

"Ash!"

I rush back over to her. I feel light-headed as I jump to

my feet and run back to see how she's doing.

"Ol...iver?" She mutters.

"You're alive! Oh my god, you scared me, Ash."

"Sorry. Unplug me, will you.?"

I unplug the wires from her head gently.

"Are you okay?" I ask.

"Yeah, the system kept me alive. I just must've blacked out for a—"

She stops talking as she gets a better look at me.

"Enough about me. What the hell happened to you?" She asks, suddenly seeming much more lively.

"Yeah, that happened." I step aside, pointing a thumb over my shoulder at the lifeless form of the Shinigami on the floor.

"What happened?" She asks.

"What you don't see the—"

It's...gone!?

"Okay...there was a Shinigami, and I killed it. It stabbed my shoulder, but I swear it died."

"Um, that's great. Not panic-inducing at all." Ash replies, standing from the chair.

We both frantically look around, but there's no sign of them. I scan with every mode the VYSR has, but nothing.

What the hell's going on? I didn't hear a single thing.

"Well, I guess let's get out of here," Ash says, her eyes still flicking around rapidly, searching.

"No kidding," I reply.

"Hey, Dex, you read me?" I ask into the comms.

"Yep, so did you get inside?" He replies.

"Not quite. We're almost there, but a Shinigami stopped our truck and almost...well, I thought I killed it." I try to explain, struggling to find the words.

"Oh, shit. You sure it died?"

"Well, no. Because I thought it did, I saw the light leave

its eyes, literally, because its eyes were cybernetic, so, well, you get the picture. But then I turned my back to check on Ash, and when I turned around, they were gone, no trace."

I gesture to follow me as I make my way for the truck's left-side door. My VYSR alerts me to several Retribution troops waiting just outside the door, the one the Shinigami ripped open.

"Okay, Oliver, I'm going to be honest," Dex replies, his voice hesitant. "The Shinigami are the best-kept secret in CYBR Corp. I had only glimpsed one *once* in all the years I worked there. So I can't tell you if they came back to life, or if another one dragged their body away without you noticing, or whatever the hell really happened. But I know this," he pauses for a moment, "you've faced one twice and not only lived but defeated them in combat. Don't be afraid of them. That's what they want. In fact, they should be afraid of *you*. If they're capable of such things."

"Thank you, Dex. Not to be rude, but there's a whole squadron bearing down on this truck, so we gotta go." I reply.

"Good luck."

With that, Ash and I exchange looks of determination.

"Ready?" She asks, arming her arc rifle.

"Let's do this."

I sheathe my swords, grab two arc grenades, arm them, and then take a running leap from the truck as far as I can.

I throw the arc grenades into the crowd of Retribution troops to my left and right. I tuck into a roll as I hit the ground, every gun turned on me and firing. I duck behind the pile of boxes they were using as cover, now reversing the positions. It won't last long, but it doesn't need to.

Ash follows close behind me, tucking and rolling behind the boxes. She starts laying down round after round of cover fire.

"Whatever you're planning, do it now!" She shouts in between blasts.

I nod, then grab an EMP grenade, my last one. I take a peek over the boxes, almost getting lit up with arc fire the moment I do.

But I get enough of a look at where everyone is, just enough to get an idea. I also turn on the infrared function of my VYSR glasses. The troops are slowly encircling us. We'll be surrounded any moment. There's also one with a giant rocket launcher, seemingly perfectly happy to kill any number of their fellow troops just to get us.

I take a deep breath, arm the EMP grenade, and throw it over the boxes toward the group with the rocket launcher.

It hits its mark. I hear the tell-tale sound of electronics frying and the angry screams of the troops whose weapons and cybernetics I decommissioned as they hit the ground.

"Let's go, now!" I shout to Ash.

We make a mad dash for the front doors of the HQ building, which are incredibly close now. The remaining few troops shoot after us, but we manage to make it unharmed.

At the doors, I realize a critical piece of information: they're locked. Without thinking, I simply press my right fingertip to the CYBR Corp logo near the door, and the locks click open, just like the crates in the tunnels' storeroom.

"Go, go!" I say, the doors sliding open.

Ash stops shooting at the approaching troops, rushing through the doors as they slide open. I follow close behind, then frantically smash the "Emergency Lockdown" button that I recognize from the weapons warehouse.

The doors slam shut, engaging extra locks and causing alarm lights and sirens to blare throughout the building.

"Well, I guess they know we're here," Ash comments sarcastically.

"Maybe they won't notice?" I reply with a smirk.

We both start running through the halls, still following the orange path Dex sent us. From the look of it, we need to get to the top floor. I crane my neck as we come to an elevator shaft, but I can barely look high enough to see where the path stops.

The elevator dings open, and we move to rush inside, but we are quickly stopped in our tracks by the armed guards who come pouring out of the elevator.

I really need to keep the infrared on.

Without a word, Ash and I stand back-to-back. I draw my swords, and she slips on her arc knuckles. I haven't seen her use them in years, but she could give me a serious run for my money in our old training sessions whenever she had those things on.

The blaring sirens stop, but the red of the warning lights continue to flash, mixing with the crackling blue of our weapons. The air is incredibly tense for a moment as the guards size us up, seeming to wait for something to happen. These guards don't look as equipped as the troops from outside. They're only armed with arc pistols and minor body armor.

I tap my foot once, twice. Then, on the third tap, Ash and I spring into action. We've prepared for this exact moment.

Ash launches into a flurry of blows, punching and dodging through the confused ranks of guards. I do the same, slashing the arc pistols out of their hands, kicking their legs out from under them. One gets a shot off, but it only glances off my right shoulder.

We make quick work of the guards, either knocking them unconscious or sending them to the ground.

"Please," one of them pleads, holding his head as he lies on the ground, "we were told to bring you in alive."

Ash and I exchange a look of confusion.

"What the hell do you mean, alive?" Ash says, stepping on the guard's chest and winding up her fist menacingly.

"Yeah, your friends out in the courtyard seem to have missed that memo," I add.

"I don't know, I just follow orders, I swear!"

"What orders? Spit it out!" Ash increases the pressure on the guard's chest, causing him to wheeze.

"They said if you made it to the building, you were worthy." He gasps through labored breaths.

I sheathe my wakizashi, then hold the crackling tip of my katana an inch from the guard's neck.

"You're gonna have to start making sense real fucking quick, buddy," I growl.

I mean, seriously, what the fuck? Worthy? Of what?

"That's all I know. They said you were being tested, and if you made it here, well, we had to escort you to them." He says, his voice trembling.

"They? To them? Who?" Ash demands.

"The leaders! I can't say anything else. They'll kill me."

I stare into the guard's eyes, and I see fear. Deep, all-encompassing fear. He looks like a helpless rodent caught in a trap.

"Ash," I say.

She steps away from the guard.

I knock the guard out with the hilt of my sword.

"So, this is insane, right!?" Ash asks, pacing back and forth anxiously.

"Yes. Completely fucking bonkers." I reply.

"I mean, seriously, what sort of cult is this? So we're 'worthy' now? Something tells me I don't want to be 'worthy' of whatever it is they're offering." She says. She uses air quotes to emphasize worthy.

"No shit. It's like they wanted us to get here, but why

send every goddamn troop to kill us then? Not to mention the Shinigami—" I'm stopped short by the very thing I just mentioned.

I point an unsteady finger across the room, behind Ash, at the Shinigami that my glasses just detected. Then another. And another.

"Three," I mutter. "There's...three."

Ash spins around and sees what I'm talking about, freezing in place.

Time to GTFO.

I grab her arm and pull her into the elevator, hitting the door close button. It actually closes the doors, to my surprise.

As the glass doors slide closed, I see the Shinigami all running at full speed toward us. They all look almost identical, all imposingly tall, covered in countless cybernetics and nearly impenetrable armor plating, their eyes red, glowing orbs of hatred. A shiver runs down my spine, and it takes everything I have to keep from shutting down from the pure fear coursing through me.

Instead, I utilize that adrenaline to find the button for the top floor. I press it, but the elevator makes an angry beeping sound.

"Access required for top floor." Cerulean's voice echoes through the elevator.

"Fuck. Please work." I say, pressing my finger to the sensor.

I press the button again for the top floor, and this time, it beeps pleasantly.

"Welcome, Oliver Wolf. Access granted." Cerulean says.

Hate that.

The elevator starts to move upward just as the closest of the three Shinigami reaches the doors, launching a flying kick into the glass of the elevator door, cracking it.

"Oh, *hell* no," Ash says, backing up.

The elevator moves out of reach before the three Shinigami can break their way through. I glare into their hateful eyes as they disappear from view.

With them gone, the adrenaline leaves my bloodstream, and I collapse back against the wall with Ash.

"Well, good thing that glass was reinforced," I say, giving Ash a look of relief and disbelief.

"Yeah, way to find the silver lining." She replies, letting herself laugh a bit as she rests her head on my shoulder.

I tense up a bit, expecting it to hurt since that shoulder had been stabbed by a Shinigami only a few minutes ago, but to my disbelief, it feels completely fine. In all the commotion, I didn't even think about it.

"Hey, remind me to thank Zeke for the healing nanobots," I say, resting my head on hers.

"You got it."

We pass the fifth floor, the sixth, seventh. Floors fly by quickly, but we still have a ways to go before we reach the top, the fifty-first floor of the tower. The ominous, looming tower that's visible for miles around their compound. The tower I had only been to in my dreams, or nightmares, before now.

"Hey, Ash?"

"Yeah?"

"I'm freaking out."

"Me too."

I stand up from the wall and turn to face Ash.

She does the same.

"Ash, I—" I try to speak, but nothing comes. My mind is racing with questions, trying to figure out what the hell is going on here, but none of it forms into a cohesive thought.

She gives me a knowing smile and then pulls me into a tight hug.

I hug her back just as tight and allow myself to melt into her warm embrace, the panic fading to the back of my mind, if only for a moment.

Several floors zip by, and our destination gets closer by the second. We finally break the hug.

I keep my hands on her hips, staring into her eyes. For whatever reason, I start to tear up, and she does, too. We kiss, a kiss filled with all kinds of emotions, one I never want to end.

After a few more floors, it does.

"I'm glad I'm doing this with you, Ash."

"Me too, Olly."

"You were pretty badass back there, by the way," I say.

"Same for you, ninja boy."

We both share a laugh and a smile.

My happiness is once again disrupted when the elevator begins to slow, indicating we're almost to the top floor.

I turn to face the doors, drawing my daishō and taking several deep breaths.

Ash slips on her knuckles again, then grabs her arc rifle and readies it.

"Approaching final floor. Welcome, Oliver." Cerulean says all too cheerfully.

I activate my swords as the elevator comes to a halt, the glass doors sliding silently open.

"Yeah, bring it on."

CH 14

WE'RE greeted by several more armed guards as soon as we exit the elevator. They surround us, aiming arc pistols at our heads.

"Drop your weapons. You have been summoned. We do not wish to hurt you." One of the guards demands.

"Yeah, not gonna happen," Ash replies.

I couldn't agree more.

Ash bashes the lead guard in the face with her arc rifle, slings it over her shoulder, and then activates her arc knuckles.

As soon as she takes the first move, I swing my swords in a wide, sweeping arc, slashing at the three nearest guards and knocking the weapons out of their hands. They don't back down. Instead, they try to restrain me. I dodge their grabs, then move away from the elevator toward the open room behind the guards.

Half of the guards follow me, shooting at my limbs. It's clear they're not trying to kill me, but they don't seem too concerned about seriously injuring me. The few that I disarmed pick their pistols up and start shooting, too.

The other guards stay circled around Ash. I catch glimpses of her fighting out of my peripheral vision, but she seems to be doing fine.

I dodge the pistol shots of the guards, then close the gap as they move to circle me again. I sweep the legs of one guard, then bash his temple with my sword hilt, kneeling in between the remaining circle of guards. I cross my swords in front of me, then sweep them down and outward, cutting the knees of three of the guards.

"Ah, fuck!" one of them shouts.

They all collapse to the ground, writhing in pain as they grasp their severed stumps.

I stand, facing the two guards who remain. They're trying to stay calm, but I can see the panic setting in.

"Drop your weapons," I command.

"Do as he says," Ash says from behind me, charging her arc rifle menacingly.

Looks like she took care of hers quickly.

The guards begin moving to drop their pistols to the ground, but suddenly, their scared expressions change to smug smirks.

"What's so funny? I said drop them!" I repeat, trying not to freak out.

Just then, the radar on my VYSR glasses beeps, several signatures behind us, and then they disappear just as quickly as they appeared.

"Shinigami, Ash! Let's move." I whisper loudly, knocking the two remaining guards out with the hilts of my swords.

We start to run into the room, but two Shinigami appear in our path.

"Let's get out of here!" Ash yells.

We turn to backtrack to the elevator, but two more Shinigami are standing right behind us.

The four Shinigami surround us before I have a chance to think of an exit strategy.

"Well, well. If it isn't Oliver Wolf. I've been expecting you. And look at this, you've brought me a little gift, the most irritating Miss Astra Odelle." A mysterious voice, no, set of voices, emanates from seemingly every corner of the room. For some reason, it feels…familiar? But not really…

I spin around, looking past the Shinigami, trying to see

who's talking.

I hadn't taken much time to look around, but since it's the only thing I can do, I scan every inch of the room. This room, which makes up the entire fifty-first floor, is basically just one long, large, dimly lit hallway with wires sprawling everywhere. And I mean *everywhere.* The lighting is almost entirely from thin red strips of light lining the walls, casting an ominous glow on everything.

"Whatever it is you're planning, you can fuck off. We're here to put a stop to your reign of terror." I say defiantly.

"Are you now?" The voices answer mockingly.

What is happening? Why do they sound so familiar yet so wrong?

I can isolate that the voices originate from the far end of the room, or at least some of them do. It feels like there must be speakers everywhere, or they...

No, they hacked the comms?

I look at Ash and gesture subtly to my ear. She gives me a hesitant nod, like she's thinking the same thing I am.

"Dex, are you there? We've been captured. I don't know if we're going to get out of this. Get out, now!" I say into the comms.

No response.

"Dex, answer me!"

Nothing.

"Oh, are you trying to phone a friend? How touching. That traitor and your precious cybersurgeon friend are both quite safe, I can assure you." The voices taunt, like venom mixed with honey.

I feel the rage building inside of me.

At least we got the broadcast out. They can't take that away from us. But fuck, I really hope they're okay.

"What have you done to them!?" Ash cries, her voice cracking in desperation

No response.

"That's it! You're going to pay for this." I growl through clenched teeth.

"Let's see you try, then. Bring them to us."

The Shinigami all sink into a deep stance, their hands formed into electrically charged blades.

I engage the arc units on my swords once again and tap my foot once, twice…

We spring into action on the third tap, just like before. I strike toward the closest Shinigami, but it dodges out of the way. I'm stabbed from behind, a bladed hand sinking into one of my kidneys.

I scream in pain, my knees buckling, my vision becoming blurry.

I force myself to remain standing while the grounding circuit and healing nanobots work overtime to keep me in the fight. I feel the arc energy gathering in my right arm, like before.

I spin to face the Shinigami behind me, catching a glimpse of Ash, who's barely managing to defend against the two Shinigami on her.

I slash the arms of the Shinigami as they pull away, managing to partially sever one of their arms at the elbow, to my total surprise. They show no sign of pain or hesitation, instead retaliating with a series of lightning-fast kicks that I try my best to dodge and block.

The other one attacks from my other side, stabbing toward my midsection with electrified talons of death.

I drop to the floor, roll out of the way, and thrust my swords forward as I rise, stabbing through the back of the knees of the one whose arm I had mangled. I twist the blades and slash outward with all my strength, severely damaging the Death Spirit's cybernetic knee joints. They fall to the ground, screaming with rage, desperately trying to claw at my legs with their arm that remains fully intact.

Let's see you fight with only one limb, you demon.

I jump to my feet, backing up and slashing wildly to keep the other Shinigami at a distance. I engage the arc turret in my shoulder to help keep them at bay. It barely helps, with the Shinigami easily deflecting or completely ignoring the small-voltage arc blasts, but it's better than nothing. I guess.

Just then, I hear Ash screaming in pain. I turn to find her, and I see that the other two Shinigami have captured her, digging their fingers into her arms and sending arc shockwaves through her body as they drag her toward the opposite end of the room.

"Ash!" I scream, filled with even more rage than before.

I turn my rage back on my foe, swinging my swords wildly at the remaining Shinigami in front of me. They deflect my attacks with ease, which makes me even angrier. I slash with such relentless ferocity that I don't even know what I'm doing. I try everything I can, making tiny impacts here and there, but tears begin to well in my eyes at the sounds of Ash's screams from across the room. I feel like this stalemate will last forever, this chrome-encrusted freak of nature keeping me from saving the life of the person I hold most dear. But then, to my horrified surprise, the other Shinigami, the one who I *just* reduced to one flailing limb, stabs the back of both of my knees with razor-sharp, arc-charged talons.

"Let's see how you like it, you chrome-forsaken bastard." He snarls, his metallic teeth grinding together with an ear-piercing shriek.

My legs buckle, and I scream in agony. The grounding circuit may be keeping up with the demand of this battle, but I'm not.

"You'll...pay...for this," I grunt.

"No. You will cease this foolish resistance." Replies the second Shinigami.

They disarm me, knocking the swords from my hands in one smooth motion. I watch helplessly as they clatter along the floor. Each Shinigami digs their fingers into my arms. I collapse to the ground, the grounding circuit barely keeping me from dying as wave after wave of arc energy courses through my body. At the same time, the healing nano-bots try to repair the innumerable cuts and burns across my body.

I look down at my right hand, a blinding ball of crackling electricity gathering in the palm of my hand.

My vision is blurry, and I can feel myself on the verge of passing out.

Come on, Oliver. You can't let it end…not like this. You can't let them down. Let Ash down. This can't be the end…not…like this.

I force my left hand to move, inch by excruciating inch until I'm able to grab an adrenaline stim from my pocket. I stab it into my leg, squeezing the mechanism. A sudden rush of energy fills my body, making me feel invincible.

I let out a deep, guttural scream, like a battle cry. It apparently catches the Shinigami by surprise, and they let up for just a second.

Now!

I clamber to my feet, the sound of my heart pounding drowning everything else out, everything except for the faint buzzing sound coming from my right hand.

I ball up my fists, then bring them together, transferring the arc energy evenly between both hands. I don't feel any pain in my left arm. Instead, I feel an exhilarating, crackling energy filling my body.

"Die! Fucking *die*, you soulless freaks!" I yell, tears in my eyes and hatred in my heart.

I lunge forward, giving the Shinigami to my right a brutal, electrocuting uppercut to the chin. It sends him flying backward, and he lands on the ground with a thud, twitching involuntarily before finally going limp.

I turn my attention to the last Shinigami, who growls at me as he unleashes a flurry of kicks and punches. I make no move to stop him or to block his attacks. I simply soak up the arc energy, and my whole body begins to crackle with blue lightning.

"You done?" I ask, stabbing myself with a second adrenaline stim.

Another wave of energy fills my body.

This feels amazing.

I return the Shinigami's attacks with interest, punching him over and over again in the stomach, the jaw, the head, everywhere. They make no move to dodge or block, seemingly caught off-guard by my resilience.

As I land the final blow, knocking them off their feet, I see a look of utter disbelief cross their face.

The arc energy covering my body fades as the last bit of it crackles into the air.

I turn my attention to Ash, who's been dragged all the way to the far end of the room. I still can't make anything out clearly over there. Also, my VYSR glasses were apparently knocked off at some point, so I can't see infrared, either.

Figures. Can't keep track of those for the life of me.

I run over to where she is, the Shinigami continuing to send paralyzing electric currents through her body every few seconds.

She isn't moving much, letting out fainter and fainter screams with each new wave of arc energy. After a few more shockwaves, she stops screaming, her body limp.

"You let her go!" I scream, my voice cracking and hoarse

with desperation and exhaustion. "You wanted me. Now, here I am! Stop this, or I'll kill you all! I don't care how many of you I have to kill!"

As I get within a few feet of Ash, I feel the adrenaline wearing off. My legs become incredibly heavy, and unbearable pain courses through my entire body like my skin is being peeled off with a million cheese-graters.

I collapse to the ground, screaming.

Two more Shinigami step out of the shadows, or are they the same ones? It doesn't matter. They dig their claws into my arms and drag me forward, electrocuting me. They bring me alongside Ash.

"Ash I...I'm sorry..."

"Olly...it's not your...fault..."

"Show...yourself," I demand to the voices.

"Very well then." The chorus of voices answer, seemingly right in front of me and echoing through my head at the same time.

Several blindingly bright spotlights turn on at once, pointed at the area in front of me. My eyes take a few seconds to adjust. I squint and blink frantically, trying to make sense of what I'm seeing.

Out of the shadows step two giant metallic spiders. On top of the spiders are semi-shiny, silvery-metal thrones with a terrifying web of wires stringing in every direction. The wires all meet at the top of the thrones, near the heads of the figures atop them. The thrones almost look like specialized netrunning chairs, with an unnecessary amount of dramatic flair added to the design. I can't make out the figures on the thrones at first. The spotlights reflecting off the metal continue to blind my poorly adjusted eyes for a moment longer.

The Shinigami stop electrocuting me. Apparently, they're satisfied that I'm not in any shape to fight anymore. Or perhaps they were silently ordered to do so. Either way, I'm grateful for the break from the torturous pain, but only for a moment as the voices speak.

"Oh, Oliver. I've been waiting so long for this moment. It's so very nice of you to complete my little collection." The voices speak in unison.

It dawns on me all too late why I felt like I knew the voices.

I crane my neck up as my eyes finally finish adjusting to the light, looking at long last at the two figures sitting atop the thrones. The enemies I've hated my entire life. The leaders of CYBR Corp. The ones I've risked everything to defeat. The ones who took my family from me.

I look at long last into the eyes of my enemy.

The eyes of Nicholas and Julia Wolf.

The eyes of my parents.

No. No no no no no. This is impossible. This is—

"Mom!? Dad!? What...what is this? I don't...understand. Please, this doesn't make any sense! What..."

I break down into tears, heaving for breath between violent bursts of sobbing. I feel my body go completely limp. There's nothing left to keep me fighting.

The Shinigami force me up. One of them grabs my head, making me look at my parents. I try to fight it, but they're too strong, and I've lost all will to fight.

"Please. Why? I don't..."

"Oh, Oliver. Poor, foolish Oliver." The voices taunt again. Then they laugh a horrible cacophonous chorus of demented laughter echoing through the room and directly inside my head.

It's utterly terrifying and even more confusing. The voices are those of my parents, but they speak as one. And the voices in my head are completely different, a chorus of hundreds of voices, all acting under one mind, one thought.

Despite how horrible it is, I force myself to look closer. The longer I stare at my parents' faces, the surer I am that I'm not looking at my parents at all. Their eyes are glazed over, and they aren't actually looking at me. In fact, they don't seem to be looking at anything at all. The look in their eyes reminds me of the stim-junkies I'd see as I pass through the black market. It's the look of someone whose mind is not their own, someone who has lost their senses to an all-encompassing stimulus.

A mangled, twisted web of wires stem from each of their heads, connecting them to the metal spider thrones before stringing off to every bundle of cables in every corner of the room.

"It's not them, is it?" I ask, defeatedly.

"Well, well. Smarter than he looks." The voices answer.

"Then who, or what, the *fuck*, are you? I demand to know!"

"Who do you think I am, you fool? You really haven't a clue? My, my. Clearly, this one is the runt of the litter, mentally speaking. Come on, boy, think! Do you seriously think I would allow my company to be run by anyone else other than myself? Did you really think I would let death stop me from achieving my goals? From getting everything I've ever wanted and more? No. No, boy. I have always been here. And I always will be." The voices answer, breaking into another terrifying chorus of laughter that echoes through every corner of my mind.

It takes me a second longer than it probably should to put two and two together, but my mind is flooded with thoughts and emotions, and my body is threatening to fail me at any moment.

Wait just a goddamn second.

"John Nova? Seriously!? John *fucking* Nova?"

"Bingo, kid."

"But...you died years ago. And why...what do you need my parents for?"

This makes no sense. My parents...why? What? How?

It's so hard to look at my parents, to see them like this... I thought I lost them forever, and yet I've found them. Here they are, right in front of me, after all these years, only for them to be empty husks used as human computers, puppets of this evil son of a bitch. Their mouths move, but it's not them behind the words. They laugh, but there's no joy on their faces. They stare ahead, seeing nothing, comprehending only the information that is deemed valuable, only thinking what they're forced to...

I start to cry again, unable to control my tears. They flow freely down my face. My vision blurs through the tears, and snot pours from my nose. Heaving sobs rock my limp body.

"I asked you *why*, damn it! Answer me!"

"*You ask me why, boy? Do you want to know the truth? Well, I'm happy to tell you. They volunteered, plain and simple. Didn't you know that? Didn't you ever wonder why they left all those years ago? What new, miraculous jobs they had received? The ones that could finally afford to feed your precious little family? Oh dear, what a foolish boy you are. What a poor little rage-fueled idiot, never seeing more than two feet in front of your own face, striking out irrationally at whatever happens to stand in front of you. They did it all for you, you fool. You and your meddlesome brother, Miles. But I suppose I do have you to thank. Your parents do make such good auxiliary processors.*" Nova responds, his voices dripping with malice, mocking me with every echoing word.

If I had any fight left in me, that would make my blood boil with rage.

"You...you killed my brother and used my parents as

fucking computer hardware? You fucking bastard! And for what? Why bring me here? Why do any of this? I don't...understand."

"Ah yes, so many questions. So many blabbering, incoherent questions. I despise such mundanity. But fine, I suppose I can indulge this meaninglessness for a moment. Ask me a coherent question, and I will answer."

I want to spit in his proverbial face, to tell him to fuck off, but I have to know. If this is how I die, then at least I'll die knowing the truth after all this time. I steel myself with what little resolve I have left and ask a question.

"Why us? Why my family, of all people? And why keep me alive? Don't think I didn't notice your murderous lapdogs were holding back."

"Oh, so he is aware. Intriguing." Nova chuckles. *"I'll answer the latter question first, as it is simple. The reason you are alive is because I wanted you to have hope. To think that maybe, just maybe, you could actually succeed in your foolish quest to destroy me. And then, when you had made it oh so close to that tantalizing goal, only then would you learn the truth. And oh, how sweet it was to watch the hope drain from your eyes as your delusions of grandeur came crashing down around you."* He laughs again, a hearty laugh of countless voices that makes my head feel like it's splitting in two while my heart sinks and my gut burns with rage.

"As for why I chose your family, you, and your brother, and your dear old parents, well, surely you don't really want to know that. But I promised you that I would indulge your meaningless questions, so I will be a gracious host and answer. The reason your parents are my processors, and your brother is one of the countless voices you are hearing in your head at this very moment, and the reason you were able to get within even ten miles of this building is that it was convenient. That's it, that's the answer. Your parents

volunteered for our little 'brain enhancement' project, and their minds just so happened to fit the bill better than the other candidates. Then, your brother was dead set on hacking into our system, so we simply absorbed him into it. And you, precious little Oliver, well, you were oh so determined to march in here and get your answers, so why should I stop you?"

I feel sick. My stomach lurches, and I nearly throw up, but I force it down. Tears well in my eyes, but I try to blink them away.

No. This can't be. It can't...

"Fuck. You." I grit my teeth, trying to mask the hopelessness that's building inside of me.

"Haha, oh, look at you, so full of hate, even in the end. Hold on to that. It will make you into such an excellent Shinigami."

I'm left completely speechless. Everything I ever believed was a lie. Everything I worked for was for nothing.

Mom...dad...Miles. I'm sorry. I'm so, so sorry.

The last shreds of rebelliousness leave me as I start to cry. My body collapses once more, and I'm powerless to stop it.

It's all for nothing. It's...there's no point. I lost.

"This has gone on quite long enough, I think. I grow tired of dealing with you. Get them out of my sight." Nova commands.

With that, the spider thrones back away, retreating into the darkness once more, my parents disappearing into the shadows of CYBR Corp. The last thing I see is the endless, tangled mass of wires dragging along behind them as the spotlights turn off and cast the room into dim, red darkness once more.

"I'm so sorry...I let everyone down..."

Shinigami drag me away. I'm powerless to stop them.

"Mom...dad...Miles. I'm so sorry. I'm so, so sorry."

One of the Shinigami shocks me. *"Shut up."*

"I...I'm so...Astra...Zeke...Dex...I...I'm so sorry..."

A final electric shock courses through me, my body completely failing me, the shocks delivering me into the awaiting embrace of nothingness.